08/2022

Y

rd
)6-4198

Should
I Fall

Scott Shepherd

THE MYSTERIOUS PRESS
NEW YORK

SHOULD I FALL

The Mysterious Press
An Imprint of Penzler Publishers
58 Warren Street
New York, N.Y. 10007

Copyright © 2022 by Scott Shepherd

First Mysterious Press edition

Interior design by Maria Fernandez

Library of Congress Control Number: 2022902588

ISBN: 978-1-61316-312-2
eBook ISBN: 978-1-61316-313-9

10 9 8 7 6 5 4 3 2 1

Printed in the United States of America
Distributed by W. W. Norton & Company

For Holly,
As always—For You

PROLOGUE

With This Ring

J ILY XO R
R ILY XO J

It didn't become a reality for Rachel until she saw the inscriptions inside the matching gold wedding bands.

John. I Love You. Hugs and Kisses. Rachel.

Rachel. I Love You. Hugs and Kisses. John.

"Do they meet with your approval, ma'am?" asked the Tiffany's clerk. Everything about the woman was perfect. Her tailored jacket and skirt. The half smile. The slightest trace of an accent.

But it wasn't British. Rachel Grant should know. She had lost a good part of hers since moving to the States a few years back, but she could spot a fellow Brit the moment they opened their mouth. One thing was for sure—Rachel would never act or look that picture-perfect, nor would she ever want to.

"Totally," Rachel replied with a smile of her own, amused at her increasing ease with using the American idiom.

The clerk reached behind her to pick up a tiny box sitting beside the register. "I believe you ordered these as well?"

Spanish, thought Rachel. *More specifically—Catalan.* She'd been lousy at math and science but always had an ear for languages, having taken a slew of courses during her Oxford years.

"I did." Rachel took the box from the woman. Her mother might not have been the poshest person back in Maida Vale, but early on she'd taught Rachel that good things were always to be found in tiny, bright-turquoise boxes that came from Tiffany's. It was one of the reasons Rachel loved that Audrey Hepburn movie so much.

She opened the box and peered inside. The gold oval cuff links glistened up at her, the reflection of the store lights bouncing off the *JF* monogram on each one.

"They're perfect," Rachel said softly.

They summed up John Frankel to a tee. Solid and strong. Simple but elegant. The man she loved with all her heart.

"I presume these are a gift?" asked the clerk.

"You presume correctly."

"Perhaps you'd like to write a card while I have it wrapped?"

Rachel said that would be great and the clerk produced a note card that could have been mistaken for a thimble. Rachel thought to ask for something bigger, then realized she could say what she wanted in the space allotted. She picked up a pen from the counter and scribbled seven words.

I can't wait to be your wife.

Something that would become a reality in less than two weeks.

Across the Atlantic, atop the Heath in London on a sunny (a girl could always dream, right?) July day.

In the exact same spot that her parents had wed over three decades earlier.

Moments later, Rachel was out on Fifth Avenue, making an immediate turn to head downtown. John's apartment was about twenty blocks south in Murray Hill. And being one of those pretty-as-a-postcard Manhattan afternoons, a casual Monday summer stroll seemed like the perfect opportunity to soak in what was lying directly in front of her.

She was marrying Detective First Grade John Frankel of the New York Police Department.

A man she hadn't even known six months before.

Back then, she hadn't been talking to her father—the soon-to-be-retired Scotland Yard Commander Austin Grant. And now she was about to have him walk her down a rose-petaled aisle, just steps away from where her mother Allison had been laid to rest.

As Bob Dylan had occasion to sing—*things have changed.*

No question about it, her romance with John had been a whirlwind. Make that a tornado.

They'd met on a case that had drawn her father and the NYPD detective together and taken them across three countries, encountering a slew of dead bodies and unraveling family secrets that still rocked Rachel when she thought about them. If it hadn't been for John, Rachel was pretty sure she wouldn't have survived it.

Still, her closest friends told her not to get her hopes up once she and John resumed their normal lives back in Manhattan. Rachel could see their point. Common sense said that she and John had been caught up in the moment, with every synapse and emotion taken to the nth degree due to the extraordinary circumstances that had thrown them together.

Life back home turned out to be even better, despite their crazy work schedules. It wasn't like crime was going to take a permanent sabbatical in New York City and give John nothing to do, or not provide fodder for the feature articles she'd penned for various outlets, like "The Last Commandment" piece for *Vanity Fair*—but Rachel and John had somehow managed to spend every other waking hour together.

And both only wished there were more of them in a day.

Yet Rachel had been caught off guard early one morning, a month after their return, when she'd laid half-awake in John's secure arms and he suggested they get an apartment together. She smiled and told him, based on a couple of previous missteps in that direction, that she had vowed not to live with someone again and go through the heartbreak that came when one of them had to move out, so thank-you-very-much-but-no-thank-you. But she did punctuate the declination with a kiss on the tip of his nose.

"So, maybe we should make it a permanent thing."

That woke her up.

"Wait. Did you just ask me to marry you?"

John took a beat as Rachel realized that he might have even surprised himself.

"Yes. Yes, I suppose I did." Then he gave her a grin—the grin she could never get enough of. "So?"

She immediately said yes.

At least a dozen times.

And that was from a girl who usually looked at a situation every which way, top and bottom, right and left, inside and out, and then all over again before making a decision. And then she would spend the next day or two wondering if she'd made a huge mistake.

But not in this case.

There had not been a single regret that day. Or the next one. Or since.

And now here she was, rings in hand along with a wedding gift she wanted John to wear on the blessed day.

Seeing as how she was catching a flight out of JFK to England the next morning to begin preparations for the wedding, this was her last chance to pull off her surprise with the Tiffany box. It was why she had offered to pick up the rings and told John that she would bring them to dinner that night. That way, she could get the cuff links as well, and she figured he would be touched finding them and the note hidden in his suitcase when a week later he'd pack to join her in London.

John's studio apartment was on Lexington between East Thirty-Seventh and Thirty-Eighth Streets, on the second floor of a walk-up. They hardly ever spent a night there as it was more than a tight squeeze—when the Murphy bed was dropped from the wall, there was barely a place to stand. But for those rare occasions, John had bestowed a spare key upon Rachel, tethered to the end of a small chain, with a white teddy bear wearing a little red I-Heart-NYC sweater. It was dopey but so lovely that Rachel kept the chain attached and tucked inside her bag. She pulled it out to let herself inside the lobby.

She climbed one set of stairs, entered the second-floor hallway, and moved down the corridor toward John's apartment. Even though she was ninety-nine percent sure that John was out making the Manhattan streets safe for one and all, she knocked on the door and called out his name.

When no one answered, she couldn't help smiling. Her plan was going off without a hitch.

She unlocked the door and slipped inside, closing it behind her, and then flicked on the light.

She dropped the Tiffany's bag on the floor.

It turned out she wasn't alone.

She stared at the other person in the apartment.

Julia.

Though they had never met, Rachel knew all about Julia Molinari and certainly recognized her.

It wasn't like John kept pictures of his ex-wife on the mantle or his desk. But it was only natural for Rachel to be interested in what the woman looked like.

But never had Rachel expected that the first time she saw Julia in person, Julia would be lying on her betrothed's floor in a pool of blood.

With a bullet wound in the center of her chest.

Dead as could be.

PART ONE

To Have and To Hold

Chapter 1

If it had been the previous year, the British Airways 777 would have been the last place on (or more specifically, *off*) Earth that Austin Grant would have expected to find himself. Before the events of his final case, he had done everything possible to avoid getting on a flight of any kind, especially of the transatlantic variety, where there was nothing to break what he was certain would be the jumbo jet's inevitable free fall, resulting in the plane and passengers lying on the ocean floor in a zillion pieces.

Now, he was making the trip so often, he had a frequent flyer number.

Grant chalked it up to the two Rs.

Retirement and Rachel.

Working at the Yard had become a chore following the death of his beloved Allison. He had found that his heart was no longer in the cases he was investigating, and it didn't really matter what the crimes were. A series of house burglaries or financial improprieties proved mundane at best—there wasn't enough of a puzzle to keep his mind focused and he had handed them off to his colleagues whenever possible. Even a few of the murder investigations he'd been brought into didn't keep his mind from wandering back to those days when he knew that no matter how badly things went at the Yard, at least he'd had Allison to come home to.

And then there was his last case—the one that had brought him and his only child together in the most unexpected manner. Grant and Rachel had been estranged for reasons that both wanted to put behind them and were now truly happy to be back in each other's lives.

When he'd decided to retire, he had been counting down the days like a prisoner in solitary awaiting the sunlight. He couldn't wait to do all the things he'd never had time to do, to live a life filled with everything he'd been missing over thirty years of service to queen and country.

Suddenly, the final day had arrived—and Grant hadn't a clue what to do with himself.

He'd slept in (or at least tried to). Started and discarded half a dozen books. He'd found that he didn't particularly love eating by himself in restaurants he had never frequented, and the idea of going to some distant beach on holiday where he didn't know a bloody soul held no appeal.

Okay. Retirement wasn't what it was cracked up to be.

He was bored, that's what he was.

"I'm worried that you're going to be lonely," Allison had said to him on more than one occasion when discussing who would go before whom.

"Nonsense," Grant would say. "You'll outlive me by decades and make some other fellow think he hit the lottery."

Allison would playfully wave him off and say that she was his and only his for the rest of her life.

It broke Grant's heart to realize she had been right about that.

Thank goodness for Rachel.

After he left the Yard, they had started talking numerous times a week and Grant had taken great pleasure in hearing how her relationship with John Frankel had progressed. He'd been extraordinarily impressed with the young NYPD detective—and not just from a professional standpoint. Though Grant couldn't have imagined solving his last case without John's skill and bravado, what gave him the greatest satisfaction was the love and respect he had shown for his daughter.

It was true that their courtship had been brief and that they had tried to keep it secret from Grant at the beginning—but he couldn't find fault

with that. Though Rachel and John had gone from meeting to marriage in just over six months, Grant had wooed and wed Allison in one
third of that time. As for not telling Grant that he was sleeping with
his daughter—put in the same position, the former Scotland Yard man
would have used his clandestine police skills to maintain the impression of a church and state (professional and personal) separation. Grant
had to hand it to John though; when he'd confronted the man with his
suspicions that Rachel and he had gone past the just-friends stage, the
detective hadn't denied it and had promised to do right by her.

Not only had John Frankel saved her life (and Grant's for that matter),
he'd also flown across the Pond to ask him for his daughter's hand. Grant
had considered torturing the lovestruck Frankel by asking if he could
sleep on the matter, but the man had traveled thousands of miles to do
the proper thing.

Grant smiled to himself now, realizing things had come a long way in
his own relationship with Rachel—they'd gone from being incommuni-
cado to him literally being her father confessor. With Allison gone, father
and daughter were determined not to blow this second chance they'd been
given, so Rachel was forthcoming with nearly everything that happened
in her life—sometimes to the point of making Grant slightly uncomfortable, something he suspected his daughter took great delight in doing.

But not with this latest news.

John's ex-wife, Julia, had been found shot dead in his locked Murray
Hill apartment.

Grant couldn't help thinking that this was supposed to be the day
that he picked up Rachel at Heathrow to begin final preparations for her
nuptials in less than a fortnight. He couldn't have been more touched that
Rachel and John had decided to get married on the same spot where he
had taken Allison as his bride decades ago.

Instead, Grant was winging across the Atlantic in the opposite direction, now wondering if that event would ever take place.

He had never met Julia Molinari. It wasn't like John had talked about
her that much. Grant knew she was from a family of questionable repute;

in other words, some sources of income in their franchises of electronics stores supposedly came from suspicious and unidentified places. As far as he knew, she hadn't gotten caught up in the family business, but had made a few unsuccessful forays into the fashion world. The last thing Grant knew was that she had run off with the super in John's building to the Big Island of Hawaii and was working at some sort of beach bar.

How she'd ended up lying in a pool of her own blood on his future son-in-law's carpet was beyond Grant—he couldn't fathom a single explanation that could be framed in a good light.

When he'd been awakened by Rachel's phone call in the middle of the night, it had taken him less than two minutes to tell her he would be on a flight that morning to the States.

"That's not necessary, Dad," she had told him. "I don't even know exactly what's happening yet—"

"What does John have to say?"

"Well, that's the thing—"

And in that moment of his daughter's hesitation, Grant had started to scroll the internet for available flights to the New York area, regardless of cost.

Because he sensed what was coming next.

"I haven't been able to reach him," she admitted.

"Surely someone at NYPD must know where he is."

"They tell me they have no idea. As they say over here, he's gone off the grid."

Grant clicked the computer icon that read BOOK FLIGHT.

"British Air 173 gets into JFK at 2:05 p.m. your time," Grant informed her. "With any luck, I'll miss rush hour traffic and be to you by four o'clock."

———

Grant realized he should have known better.

Every time he'd had the misfortune to be on the "world's biggest parking lot," aka the Long Island Expressway, he'd been stuck in bumper-to-bumper traffic. When he couldn't get Rachel on her mobile, he texted his new estimate of a five o'clock arrival at her apartment—and knew that was being optimistic.

But it did give him time to evaluate the situation.

Rachel had chosen not to argue against Grant's decision to hop on the first BA flight out of London, knowing that once her father had made up his mind, it would be a Herculean task to change it. They'd talked briefly while Grant had waited at the Heathrow gate and she'd told him to come directly to her Upper West Side apartment once he arrived in the city.

But that had been the last time that she'd been in touch with him.

He knew he couldn't expect any sort of contact with Rachel as internet wasn't an option when flying over water on this particular flight. The disgruntled businessman sitting beside him had complained that man could put astronauts on the moon and labs on Mars but couldn't get "frikkin' Wi-Fi over the Atlantic"—which Grant thought was a blessing, in that the signal was one less thing that could interfere with whatever electronics were keeping the 777 up in the air, a place something that big had no business being in the first place.

Still, when his texts and calls went unanswered upon landing, he had to admit his daughter's silence was, to say the least, disconcerting.

Just for the hell of it, he thought he'd try John, though he figured it would be a worthless endeavor, seeing how his fiancée and the entire NYPD couldn't find a trace of him. His suspicions were confirmed when his call went directly to voice mail and there was no response to his text: *John, it's Austin. I'm here in NYC if you need me.*

After a jammed eighty minutes that should have taken twenty on a fifteen-mile stretch of highway, the cab was finally lumbering into the Midtown Tunnel when Grant got a text from Rachel.

Will be there soon as I can. Let yourself in.

Short and succinct.

Grant knew his daughter well enough to realize that if she could have called him, she would have.

Naturally, his mind went to wondering what could have prevented her from doing just that.

Maybe they've finally located John, he thought. *If so, where? And what did he have to say for himself?*

Rachel had told Grant that she had called NYPD directly after finding Julia's body and not being able to locate John. The detectives had arrived within minutes to the apartment and questioned her for over an hour before sending her home, which was when she had reached out to her father. It wouldn't have surprised Grant if they'd brought her in to the precinct again, especially if they'd been unable to locate John Frankel.

Though no longer possessing the title or credentials that placed him on the other side of an investigation, he hadn't gotten used to ceding control. All Grant could do was provide a shoulder that he knew his daughter was going to want to lean on in the days to come. He didn't need thirty years of service at Scotland Yard to know that when a murder victim is found in the home of their ex, it isn't going to be the smoothest ride for the former husband.

By the time the cabbie dropped him at Rachel's apartment, Grant had a lot fewer answers than questions—and no daughter in sight to pose them to. He gave the driver a handsome tip, then lugged his two equally weighted small bags (knowing there was a fifth-story walk-up in his near future) toward the entrance.

He had visited Rachel a couple of times since the holidays, staying once in her place and the other time at John's studio apartment. But in this case, the latter already had an occupant, albeit a dead one, and happened to be doubling as a crime scene.

So, it was a copy of Rachel's key that he used this time to gain access to his temporary lodging. Trudging up the four flights of stairs that were another reason he preferred to stay at the detective's place ("the cardio does you good, Dad," Rachel would chide), he plopped his bags outside her door, caught his breath, and knocked, hoping that Rachel had returned.

No such luck.

A few minutes later, he had let himself in, deposited his bags in the tiny closet, gotten the kettle going for a cup of English breakfast, and sat down on the small couch in what tripled as a living room, kitchen, and dining area. It was nicely furnished and neat (*a bit too much*, thought Grant, figuring Rachel had primped a little knowing her old dad was arriving, despite the gravity of his visit); he was sadly and sweetly reminded that Rachel was a chip off Allison's tasteful block, as the apartment shared many of the same qualities with the Maida Vale house. Homey and comfy for sure.

He was just starting his second cup of tea and flipping telly channels, having landed on a newscast giving scant details about Julia's murder, when the door to the apartment unclicked and a harried version of his daughter burst in.

"I'm sorry, I'm sorry, Dad—I couldn't get here sooner—"

Grant put the teacup on the table and got up in a flash. He crossed the room and opened his arms to put them around Rachel.

Whatever else she said got lost in a series of sobs and blubbering, so much so that he only made out the end of it.

"—I'm so glad you're here."

And that's all that matters, thought Grant.

She eased enough away from him to catch the tail end of the news story. There was a chyron that read MURDER IN MURRAY HILL and an anchor saying they would "report more as it came in."

"Still no sign of John?"

"Actually, I just was with him—"

"What? You didn't tell me."

Rachel nodded. "He showed up early this morning—your plane had already taken off and there was no way to get in touch with you. And after that, well, it just got even crazier."

"Why isn't he with you?" asked Grant. "He couldn't have gone back to his place—"

"Dad."

"—because I'd like to see him."

Rachel shook her head, on the brink of waterworks again.

"You can't, Dad. That's what I'm trying to tell you."

Grant stood still, fearing the worst. And suddenly he knew what was coming.

"I just left John at the Seventeenth precinct. They're holding him on suspicion of first-degree murder."

Chapter 2

Rachel had stared down incredulously at the body of her fiancé's ex-wife and had no idea what to do first.

She'd seen less than a handful of murder victims in her life and zero before she had hooked up with John Frankel. An unnerving thought ran through her head—was she looking at a life of piled-up corpses in the matrimonial days and years ahead? That was when she realized she needed to get a clear head and do the right thing here.

Call the cops.

She'd fumbled through her bag for her cell and dialed the one she desperately needed to hear from.

But John's number had gone directly to voice mail.

Rachel had found herself tongue-tied. What was she supposed to say? *Hi darling, I'm standing in your apartment with your dead ex-wife at my feet and was wondering when you were going to be home and what we should have for dinner?*

His voice had sounded on the message. "You've reached Detective John Frankel. Leave a message as long as you like and I'll call back as soon as I can."

Beep.

Rachel had disconnected.

It was at that point that Rachel had realized she hadn't seen John that day. The last time had been at breakfast in her apartment the previous morning, as he'd told her he was going to be working late and didn't want to lumber in and wake her in the middle of the night.

"I'll just crash at my place," he had said. "Might as well get a little use out of it while I still have it."

They'd planned to let go of the Murray Hill studio after the wedding—stay at her one-bedroom and think about looking for a bigger space.

A little use out of it?

As what? A shooting gallery? Rachel couldn't stop staring at Julia—trying to wish it away, hoping it would just disappear like a bad dream.

She'd taken a deep breath.

Maybe he's in the middle of an interrogation. It had to be something like that. He *always* picked up the phone whenever she called.

She'd hit redial—and had gotten the voice mail message again.

This time she had managed to get something out, short and to the point. "Hey, it's me. Call me. I need to talk to you—as soon as you can." She hesitated, her eyes still on the carnage at her feet. "Love you," she had murmured and ended the call.

Now what?

Her options had been limited. She could turn and walk out of the apartment, leaving the scene of a crime unreported. But what if someone saw her leave? The soon-to-be wife of the police detective on the second floor fleeing the apartment where her predecessor had been brutally shot. That didn't bode well.

Rachel had known she had no choice but to call the police.

So, she had dialed Taryn Meadows.

———

Back at the start of the year, when John had been recuperating from a gunshot wound, he had been persuaded by his superiors to take on a partner when he returned to regular duty. As John was used to working solo and pulling colleagues into his cases only when needed, he hadn't been thrilled, but he also wasn't given a choice in the matter by Lieutenant Desmond Harris. John had told Rachel that he wasn't so sure that Harris was doing this out of concern for his well-being so much as punishing him for "going rogue and gallivanting all over Europe" with her father on the case that had brought them together.

And that was how Taryn Meadows came into the picture.

Having joined the NYPD fresh out of college, Taryn had risen through the ranks quickly, and she had teamed up with John back in February, a few months shy of her thirty-fourth birthday. From what Rachel could see, John had adapted to the partnership surprisingly well. Not that he was forthcoming about how things were at work. When asked how it was going with Taryn, he'd given clipped responses like "Better than expected" and "She knows what she's doing."

Rachel had met her maybe a half-dozen times, usually when getting together with John after his shift, and had found her to be pleasant enough and totally dedicated to the job and Rachel's soon-to-be hus-band. Perhaps it was her imagination, but Rachel couldn't help but wonder if Taryn had a bit of a crush on John, or at least placed him on a pedestal.

Well, let's see what you think of this, thought Rachel as she had scrolled through her contacts for Taryn's cell.

"This is a surprise," the female detective had said, picking up after just one ring.

Rachel had tried to remain casual. "Is John with you?"

"No, he was taking the day off," Taryn replied. "I thought to do some last-minute wedding stuff with you. Aren't you leaving for London tomorrow?"

Hmmm. Either Taryn had pulled that out of John or he was much more of a sharer than she'd given him credit for.

They'd had no such plans.

Rachel could only hope that John had been out on the hunt for some wedding surprise, like the cuff links she'd tucked back in her bag.

But looking back down at Julia and the pool of blood made that seem far-fetched.

"What's going on, Rachel? Is everything all right?"

Rachel knew she had wavered too long.

"No, it isn't."

She'd told Taryn Meadows where she was standing and then the rest of it.

———

Julia Molinari stared up at them through lifeless eyes.

"His ex-wife?" asked Taryn. The black NYPD detective was wearing a form-fitting conservative gray suit that was no-nonsense enough to command the authority that went with the job, but did nothing to deny the fact that Taryn Meadows was a very attractive woman. Rachel couldn't help but notice the first time she'd met John's new partner, and she had kidded him about it.

"They couldn't team you up with some old codger?" she had asked.

"I think I'm the old codger in this case."

"Uh-huh."

He had put an arm around her at that point and pulled her close. "You've got nothing to worry about."

That had been then. This was now.

"We'd never met, but I'd seen enough pictures," Rachel said. "As far as I knew she was living in Hawaii."

"That's what John told me." Taryn nodded. "Did you have any idea she was back in New York?"

"None. I don't think John's mentioned her in a few months."

"Speaking of John—do you know where he is?"

Rachel was tempted to make something up, wanting to get ahold of him before she committed to anything. But she knew from years of watching her father investigate cases, her own crime reporting, and living with John—people got themselves in hot water saying one thing and then changing their story further down the line.

"I don't." Rachel shrugged her shoulders, trying to dampen down the exasperation that was beginning to swarm over her. "Maybe doing something for the wedding, like he told you."

"When's the last time you saw him?"

"Yesterday morning. At breakfast. Then he was off to meet up with you."

"Did you talk after that?"

"A couple of times during the day. Quick—on his cell."

"I remember." Taryn nodded. "So he didn't meet you yesterday afternoon when we knocked off around four o'clock?"

Taryn had a pad in her hand and was starting to take notes. This action alone was almost enough to make Rachel start hyperventilating—realizing that every word she said was being recorded and could possibly be used down the line against the man she loved.

"No. Like I said, the last time was breakfast at my place."

When he'd distinctly told her that he was going to be working late, presumably with Taryn.

Rachel felt her heart do a deep dive.

She jumped when there was a series of raps on the door.

Rachel never thought the arrival of crime scene techs could be such a blessed relief. Taryn had called for them within seconds after arriving and it had taken the three-man crew just under a half hour to fight Midtown traffic and get there.

Taryn told Rachel she'd need to move out to the hallway to allow the crew to do their job. The apartment was so small that just standing there the six of them (counting the dead Julia) gave the stateroom scene from *A Night at the Opera* a good run for the money. Before Rachel stepped out, the head tech, a wizened-looking man in his fifties, asked her a few questions, practically by rote, as he had clearly done often over the years—where she had been in the apartment, what she had touched, and whether she had moved or disturbed the body.

Rachel asked Taryn if it was okay for her to step outside the building to get some fresh air. Taryn said that was fine—but that they were by no means done. She still had a lot of questions.

Rachel nodded, thankful for the opportunity to catch her breath. And to see if she could somehow get the hell in touch with John.

—··—

Perched on the edge of the planter boxes outside the apartment building, Rachel had stared at her phone, helpless. Once again John's cell had gone directly to voice mail and she hadn't gotten a return message from her previous text.

She'd realized she didn't have a clue as to who she should call. John was a solitary soul; when thinking about who he might be in touch with, the only people that came to mind were herself and his partner. Sure, there were fellow NYPD officers, but if Taryn hadn't heard from him, Rachel doubted that anyone else on the force was talking to John.

More than anything, she'd been troubled that they'd been out of touch for nearly a day and a half, the longest time they'd gone without speaking since they'd returned to Manhattan from Europe after New Year's.

Well, save a silly argument she had started about what he could move into her apartment after they got married and what he couldn't. In the end, they both came over to the other's point of view and couldn't even remember what they'd been arguing about and ended up spending the entire Sunday in bed together with the two *Times*—from London and New York.

What she wouldn't have given in that moment to hear his voice or see that half grin. As much as she'd tried, she couldn't separate the circumstances of his being off the grid, as they say, and Julia ending up dead in his apartment. There was coincidence and logic. The first only occurred in books and films; the latter would lead one to believe that John was somehow connected to Julia's death, if not responsible for it.

Could she be that wrong about the man she was about to commit the rest of her life to?

She'd noticed that the sun was just starting to set, realizing it was pushing toward eight on a warm night. She had watched New Yorkers making their way home, heading out to dinner, or just out for a summer evening stroll, most unaware of the foul play in their midst, though more than a few had slowed down to look at the gathering of squad cars in front of the apartment building.

Rachel had looked at her watch and done a mini-calculation, figuring it was already way past midnight in the small Maida Vale house where she had grown up in London and that her father was more than likely asleep. But with no one else to turn to, she'd taken a deep breath and dialed a phone number that hadn't changed since she'd been a little girl.

"Hello?" The sleepy voice had floated over the cell waves across the Atlantic and Rachel knew that she had indeed woken her father.

"It's me, Daddy," Rachel said, and with those few words, the flood of emotion she had been holding on to since she unlocked John's apartment door came bursting forth and tears began to run down her cheeks.

"What's wrong, Rach?" Grant had asked, clearly more awake. Rachel figured he didn't need his former Scotland Yard skills to ascertain that his daughter wasn't just checking in with a "How's it going" call.

"It's John—" she blubbered. "I think he's in a lot of trouble."

"Take your time and tell me about it," her father had said, with the reassuring voice that had calmed her down for much of her life.

No sooner had Rachel told him about Julia, and that John was nowhere to be found, than Grant was making reservations to fly to the States. When she'd mentioned upending the wedding plans, so many of which her father had insisted on paying for, Grant told her to never mind any of that.

"The important thing is finding John and getting to the bottom of this."

"John's not a killer," Rachel had blurted, finally saying out loud what had been bouncing around her head for the past couple of hours.

"We both know that. Let me get my stuff together and I'll see you tomorrow afternoon."

It was at that point that she'd noticed Taryn Meadows coming out the front door. Rachel wrapped up the call—telling her father she loved him, that she'd try to talk to him before he took off, and thanking him profusely.

"Nonsense. What else are fathers for?"

She'd managed a small smile as she had disconnected, then turned to face Taryn.

"Was that John?"

Rachel shook her head. "My father. I figured he'd want to know what was going on."

"Any chance he's heard from John?"

"Why would you think that?" asked Rachel quickly, finding herself suddenly on the defensive.

"I don't know. Cop to cop maybe?" Taryn had shrugged. "I'll admit, I'm pulling at straws here." She'd turned around to take in the apartment building. "I have to say this doesn't seem like John."

"He didn't kill that woman."

"I'm not saying he did. But the circumstances don't look very good—you can't deny that." She'd swung back to face Rachel. "No, I meant him dropping off the face of the Earth like this. What was the last time you two have been out of touch this long?"

"We haven't," Rachel had been forced to admit. "But I'm sure he has his reasons."

"Hopefully it has nothing to do with what's going on in there."

"The timing isn't lost on me, Taryn." Rachel motioned up toward the second floor. "Just what is happening in there right now?"

"The usual. Lots of fingerprinting, checking for trace material, establishing patterns of movement—"

"What about time of death?"

"A bit too early for that," Taryn had replied.

"But they must have an idea, right?" The last thing Rachel had seen before exiting the apartment was a lanky Latino man in a white coat and gloves starting to examine Julia's body.

"Let's say within the past twenty-four hours and leave it at that for now." Taryn's gaze had focused on Rachel. "But I'm not the one who should be answering questions."

"Sorry. The journalist instinct kicking in."

"And concern for your fiancé."

"Of course."

Taryn had proceeded with a host of questions, many similar to those asked upstairs. She tried to get a better line on John's movements the previous day ("I told you, we haven't been in touch"), what Rachel knew about Julia Molinari ("We'd never met and frankly, I wasn't interested in hearing about her") and if she'd noticed anything different about the apartment once she had entered.

"Besides the dead body lying on the floor?"

"Obviously."

"Can't say that I did," replied Rachel. "I was sort of preoccupied with Julia at that point."

"Understandable." Taryn flipped her pad back a few pages. "Let's talk keys."

"Keys?"

"To the apartment. How many copies are there?"

"As far as I know, just the two for us," Rachel had answered. Then her eyes flickered, as she remembered. "Oh, we made a set for my father as well. One for each of our places when he comes to town to visit."

"But I presume his are with him in London?"

"Actually, I think they're headed here." Rachel had gone on to explain how Grant was in the process of getting ready to fly out of Heathrow.

Taryn scribbled something on the pad, then looked back up at Rachel. Her eyes were filled with genuine concern.

"And the door was locked when you got here?"

"Yes, definitely." Rachel had nodded. "And I know what this looks like. Your prime suspect at this point has to be either John or me."

"It's certainly a place to start."

"If I was dumb enough to call you and report a murder I just committed."

"You could be that clever."

"Do you honestly believe that?" asked Rachel.

"Not really. But we will want to examine your hands for GSR before we send you home—unless there's an objection."

Rachel had made a production of holding her palms up in the air. "Test away."

"Believe me, we will." Taryn motioned for Rachel to lower her hands. Then she shut her notepad. "Right now, we're just gathering information. I will want you to come down to the precinct in the morning to make a formal statement."

"Of course."

"And after we run the tests, get your fingerprints and such, I'd suggest you go back home in case John decides to get in touch with you there." The detective had glanced back up at the apartment one final time. "We've got this place covered."

"Obviously."

<hr />

By the time Rachel got home, it was close to nine and she realized she hadn't eaten anything. She fixed herself some eggs and toast, but after two bites realized she wasn't the slightest bit hungry. She'd tried settling down in front of the television but found herself besieged with stories about the murder in Murray Hill, so she started channel flipping. But she couldn't find a show or film that engaged her attention enough to keep her mind off what she'd found in John's apartment.

She'd taken to straightening up, since her father would end up staying with her. Grant had insisted on checking into a hotel the first time he'd visited but she and John told him it was too expensive, especially now that he was retired and collecting a pension (a healthy one after three decades of service at the Yard, but still). By crashing at one of their apartments it would allow him to remain in New York for as long as he wanted without overtaxing his pocketbook.

Later, she'd double-checked her stock of English breakfast tea, vacuumed, and made up the bed on the convertible couch. She crossed to the closet to grab the pillows that were stored inside it and threw open the door.

Julia Molinari's corpse tumbled out of it. Rachel fell to the ground under its crushing weight. She struggled and screamed in the clutches of the dead woman, the blood from her chest wound dripping all over Rachel's face.

Rachel woke up screaming.

And realized there was another pair of arms wrapped around her midsection, holding her tight. One hand moved to cover her mouth. She almost bit down on it until she heard the intruder urge her to calm down.

"Ssssh, ssssh. It's just me."

Rachel had settled and slowly extracted herself from John, who'd slipped into the bed while she was in the throes of the nightmare.

She resisted the urge to throttle him, then the desire to hold him close and never let go. Finally, she blurted out what she'd been wondering for hours. "Where the hell have you been?"

"I can't tell you that," John had whispered. "I wish I could."

"What do you mean you can't tell me? Do you have any idea what has happened since I saw you yesterday morning?"

"I'm starting to—"

She straightened up in bed, now fully awake. Rachel thought John might have been wearing the same clothes she'd seen him put on the previous morning; everything certainly looked rumpled and lived-in enough.

"You know about Julia, then?" she'd asked.

"Yes—"

Her eyes widened and she saw the expression on his face go from concerned to being on the verge of panic.

"No, no, sweetheart. I didn't do it." He shook his head. "I couldn't do that."

Rachel had slowly calmed, wanting to believe him. "I-I was the one who found her."

John gave her a solemn nod. "I heard it on the news. It must have been awful."

"You can't imagine."

"This couldn't have been meant for you to discover," John said. "I'm pretty certain whoever did this wanted me to be the one to find her."

Rachel shook her head, trying to make sense of everything she was hearing.

"Wherever you were, whatever you've been doing that you can't tell me about—does this have to do with her?" Rachel asked.

John had nodded. "It does. But it's a long story."

"A long story you can't tell me."

"Right now?" He'd shaken his head. "No, I can't."

"Why the hell not?"

"Because I need time to sort it all out. Someone's trying to set me up for this and I have to find out who."

"Are you going to tell Taryn? The police? You know you have to go talk to them."

"I know."

"And you'll tell them what you've been up to?"

John shook his head. "Not until I know more about what's going on."

"I don't understand."

"You're not supposed to. You have to stop asking me about it, Rach."

"John—"

"I didn't kill her, Rachel. You have to believe me."

"Of course I believe you."

He'd moved closer to Rachel and held her.

And in that singular moment, all had felt right. She was in their perfect place—alone in the world, safe, wrapped up in each other's arms.

But it had only been a matter of seconds before reality had taken over and Rachel asked the question that was hovering ominously over them both.

"But will the police?" she asked.

"We'll just have to see, won't we?"

Chapter 3

"Apparently, the police didn't believe him," Grant observed.

"Apparently," replied his daughter, sitting across from him in her apartment.

Rachel proceeded to fill in her father on the rest. She had accompanied Frankel to the precinct. Once they'd arrived, they had lingered on the sidewalk while Rachel hopped on her cell and called Taryn Meadows—figuring a friendly face might be the best way to start.

That had been the first supposition to go sideways.

Rachel said that upon seeing John, Taryn went into full detective mode—treating him as a suspect first, not a fellow officer, never mind the man she'd worked with side by side for six months. Taryn had ushered Frankel inside the precinct where supposition number two went awry, Rachel having figured she could stick with Frankel while they had a civil conversation with Taryn.

The detective had escorted Frankel directly to an interrogation room and locked him inside, right after giving Rachel two choices: she could head home or wait in the reception area. Rachel chose the latter, figuring sooner than later John would emerge and they could go home together, after the detective had offered up an explanation that cleared him from any wrongdoing.

Supposition number three gone bad.

Rachel had worn out a good patch of the tiled floor because she was too antsy to sit and had a cup of lousy, what had to be instant coffee from a vending machine. It was four hours later when Taryn appeared from somewhere in the bowels of the precinct.

"You might as well go back to your place, Rachel."

"I'm fine waiting."

"It's not going to be tonight."

Rachel had thought she'd heard Taryn wrong. None of this could be happening.

"But he's been in there with you for hours already."

"And we can hold him for up to seventy-two."

"Three days?" Rachel had stared at her, incredulous. "Wait. You're arresting him?"

"Let's say we're holding him for more questioning."

"You are. You're arresting him."

"Go on home, Rachel."

"He didn't do this. *You* know John, Taryn. He *couldn't* have done this." A totally exasperated Rachel had taken a deep breath. "What has he told you?"

"You know I can't say anything. This is a full-blown murder investigation and John's a suspect. I don't know why that surprises you, given who the victim is and where she was found."

"I can't believe this—"

It was only at that point that Taryn had let down her officious police guard and resembled the woman Rachel had come to know, the one that she had sat outside with at the Murray Hill apartment.

"I don't want to believe it either, Rachel. It's hard for any of us—everyone here holds the utmost respect for John. But that doesn't mean we know everything about him," Taryn said. "You might not either."

"I know him," Rachel had immediately countered. "I'm marrying him a week from Sunday."

"I hope that happens." The ominous tone to those words had sent a chill running through Rachel. "If I were you, I'd be looking at getting someone here for John."

"Someone? You mean a lawyer?"

"You didn't hear it from me," Taryn had said. "If something changes, you'll be the first to know. I promise."

Taryn had turned and headed back down the long hallway, leaving Rachel in a brand-new world of total uncertainty.

―――

"That sounds like a good idea," Grant told his daughter, having been brought up to speed. "Do you have a good lawyer?"

"A criminal attorney? I don't keep one on hand. I suppose my editor at *Vanity Fair* might have an idea—they're always having to protect themselves on the exposés they do."

"You should call that person right now."

Rachel picked up her cell and scrolled through her contacts. She located the one she was searching for and punched it in.

"Larry?" Rachel said into her cell. "I hope I didn't interrupt your dinner but I couldn't wait till business hours." She trailed off as she stepped into the bedroom to continue the call, leaving Grant alone in the living room with his many thoughts.

He tried to recall what else he knew about Frankel's marriage to Julia Molinari besides her affair with the super and her subsequently leaving him. He remembered their courtship had been brief and that the two of them had met when Frankel had arrested her for scalping tickets outside Madison Square Garden. How things had gone from a cop-perpetrator relationship to husband and wife had been pretty much lost on Grant, but he was fairly certain that Frankel was being grilled down at the Seventeenth Precinct about that and anything else having to do with his ex-wife.

Grant wondered when Frankel had last been in touch with Julia. He found it hard to believe that the woman had just showed up out of the blue and Frankel's immediate response had been to turn around and shoot her. As far as Grant knew, the detective held no hatred for Julia—if anything, Grant remembered John Frankel feeling a good deal of remorse for not doing enough in their marriage and blaming himself for the demise of their relationship.

All of which made Grant think they must have been talking but Frankel hadn't mentioned it to Rachel. And if that were the case, what else was his prospective son-in-law hiding from his daughter?

Rachel returned from the bedroom with a grim but satisfied look on her face. "It's good to feel like I could do *something*."

"Your editor gave you a name?"

Rachel nodded. "Better yet, I already talked to the woman. Eileen Crowe. We've actually met a couple of times when I needed a resource for a few articles. She's no nonsense, Harvard law, the real deal."

"Sounds like exactly what John needs."

"She said she'd meet me down at the precinct in an hour and a half."

"I'd like to accompany you, if you don't mind."

"Of course," said Rachel. "I'm sure I'm going to need to lean on someone."

"As much as you need, Rach. That's what I'm here for."

She gave her father a hug and hung on to him for a few seconds, knowing that even more stressful hours lay ahead of them.

When they broke apart, Grant cleared his throat. "Had John been in touch with Julia recently?"

Rachel shook her head. "If he had, he didn't tell me about it."

"Does that seem like John?"

"None of this seems like John."

"I understand," said Grant. "How's he been the past few days?"

"I don't know—a little distracted maybe? We both have been going in a thousand directions with the wedding plans and me trying to get myself ready to head over to London."

"When did he start to seem 'distracted,' as you say?"

"Maybe I'm just imagining things, but I'd say he's been a little off ever since he got back from Wisconsin last weekend."

"Wisconsin? What was he doing there?"

"A bachelor party," Rachel explained. "Well, at least that's what he called it."

"John doesn't strike me as the bachelor party type."

"Exactly, right? It was just him and a high school buddy of his, Tim Francis. They went to Kohler, a golf resort there. He said it was pretty boring actually. They played a couple of rounds, kicked back in the lodge for dinner and a few beers, and were in bed before ten each night."

"And how was he different when he got back?"

"Nothing I can put my finger on. In fact, I'm not sure I'd even be thinking about it, if you hadn't asked." He watched Rachel trying to recall the events. "He got home later than he'd planned a couple of times after that. One night, Saturday, I think it was, he ended up staying at his place, which was unusual because I don't think we'd spent a night apart, besides his Kohler trip, in three months."

"What else?"

"Nothing really," Rachel answered. She indicated the couch that Grant was sitting on. "I'd find him every so often sitting there staring out the window, lost in thought. I asked him what was up and he just said he was thinking about next weekend and how he wanted everything to be perfect."

"*That* sounds like John," Grant said with a sad smile.

"Doesn't it?" Rachel's eyes welled up. "But there's something more, isn't there, Dad?"

More than anything, Grant wished he could tell his daughter she had nothing to worry about. But over three decades at the Yard had led him to an innate sense when there was more to something than met the eye.

And in this case, Austin Grant wasn't thrilled with what he'd been looking at.

He stood and motioned toward the door. "Let's go meet this Eileen Crowe and see what we can find out."

—~~~—

Silence reigned throughout most of the cab ride to the precinct. Grant was still amazed that here it was almost nine in the evening and the streets were packed like everyone was out on their lunch hour. He supposed it was getting that way in the heart of London, but he pretty much stuck to his quiet lane in Maida Vale, a sanctuary he'd cherished, especially for the thirty years plus he'd shared it with Allison. But now, being there round the clock without the Yard to venture to and truly alone, he'd begun to yearn for some sort of activity. And he had to admit, as dreadful as the current circumstances were with John Frankel, it had at least gotten his brain working and wiped off the sleuthing instincts that had defined the better part of his adult life.

And then there was Rachel.

It was hard to believe that a year ago they hadn't been talking. He hadn't felt this close to his daughter since she was in her early teens and still thought it was cool to hang with her father and listen to the oldie records that used to drive her mother crazy. Now, glancing over at her staring forlornly out at the Manhattan night, Grant was filled with equal parts love and protectiveness—knowing that he would do anything to avoid her getting hurt.

And if John Frankel, despite Grant's belief that he was indeed a good man, had done anything to destroy the trust that Rachel had put in him after committing herself to a life together, the United States justice system wouldn't have to punish the man. Grant would make sure he suffered for the remainder of his days.

The cab dropped them in front of the Seventeenth Precinct and they made their way into the antiseptic reception area where Rachel had spent most of the afternoon pacing. She indicated a place for them to sit but Grant shook his head.

"You wait here for Ms. Crowe. I'm going to see if I can get a better idea of what's going on with John."

Before Rachel could ask how he was planning on doing that, Grant strode to the front desk where a uniformed officer was working the night shift.

"Is Lieutenant Harris here?" asked Grant.

The officer, whose age and girth (at least nineteen stone, thought Grant) had clearly relegated him to desk work, looked up, as if surprised by the British accent. "I didn't see him leave, so I presume he's still working," said the officer. "Who should I say is looking for him?"

"Tell him Austin Grant, formerly of Scotland Yard."

"Formerly?"

"Recently retired, start of the year."

The officer started to ask another question, then did a double take. "I remember you. You helped out on that case the end of last year—that maniac you brought over from London."

"I didn't exactly bring the fellow over, but yes, that was me." Grant gave a slight nod toward the phone.

The officer picked up the receiver, punched a few buttons, and, two minutes later, Grant was brought into the office of Desmond Harris.

The thin black lieutenant in charge of the precinct's detective division rose from his desk with an extended hand. "I'd say I was surprised to see you, but given the reason I'm working this late on a Tuesday night, I'd say you must be here about Detective Frankel."

"And that brilliant piece of deduction is only one of the many reasons you hold the coveted position you do."

Harris cracked a smile. "Still blessed with that sweet British tongue."

The two men briefly exchanged pleasantries, Harris asking how retirement was, some reminiscing about the case that had brought them together at the end of the previous year, but fairly quickly the talk turned to the reason that Grant had sought out the lieutenant.

"It's a terrible situation all the way around," said Harris.

"How long are you planning on holding him?"

"I can't tell you that—"

"Because you won't or because you don't know?"

"Both actually," admitted Harris. "He's basically refusing to tell us anything."

"He told my daughter he didn't kill that girl."

"That much he did say," revealed Harris. "But he pretty much clammed up right after that."

"What about the boyfriend? Pablo—"

"Suarez. Pablo Suarez."

"That's it. Have you talked to him?"

Harris shook his head.

"Why not?" wondered Grant. "I understand why you're looking at Julia's ex-husband, but isn't it normal protocol to consider the man she's been living with the past couple of years?"

"Of course," replied Harris. "But Julia Molinari wasn't found dead in their home in Hawaii."

"Still."

"We haven't been able to locate Mr. Suarez," Harris told Grant. "At least the authorities on the Big Island haven't."

"Did you check to see if he's on the mainland?"

"We're looking into that. Things move a little slower over there than here."

"I'm glad you've widened your scope of inquiry," said Grant.

"That hasn't taken the focus off of Detective Frankel, though."

"How long have you known John?"

"Over a decade. He was already here when I moved over from the Thirty-Fifth to take over the division."

"And I know you respect his skill as an investigator—"

"There's no questioning that, Commander."

"Austin. I'm retired. Remember?"

"Old habits," said Harris, forcing a smile. "But John being an excellent detective has very little to do with what might be going on in his private life."

"But would a detective of John's caliber really be careless enough to murder his ex-wife and leave her in his apartment?"

"Of course we've considered that. But remember that the door was locked. He might have just been keeping Julia Molinari's body secure until he could figure out what to do with it. Especially if it was a sudden crime of passion." Harris gave him a pointed look. "He hardly could've expected your daughter to pop by unexpected in the middle of the day to discover it."

"And the gun? I presume you're checking Detective Frankel's service revolver?"

"You know as well as I do that's the first thing we did. It's been taken into evidence but I can tell you that it looks like it hasn't been fired recently—even though the caliber of the bullets is the same. But that doesn't account for the backup he told us about."

"Backup?"

Harris gave Grant a solemn nod. "John told us where he kept it in his apartment—in an old video game box at the top of his closet. We checked and his backup gun is missing."

"The killer could have found it and taken it with them," Grant suggested.

"Or John could have disposed of it."

"Sounds to me more and more like a setup," Grant remarked. "Same caliber, someone trying to tighten the noose around John's neck."

"You should leave the theorizing to us, Austin."

"Like you say: old habits."

"So, why are you here besides offering your support for John? It's not like you have any official standing, like last time."

"I'm here to look after my daughter, Lieutenant. And that means offering to help her any way possible."

Harris asked how Rachel was holding up. Grant said as well as could be expected and she was waiting downstairs for John's attorney. When Harris asked who the lawyer was, he raised an eyebrow when Grant mentioned Eileen Crowe.

"She's one of the best in the city," Harris informed Grant. "And I think John is going to need that."

"You're entitled to your opinion. But until proved differently, I'm going to stick with my daughter and believe John when he says he didn't kill her."

"I presume that means you believe he's had nothing to do with Julia Molinari all these months?"

Grant felt a familiar tingle at the base of his spine. The one that usually went with something about to turn his world upside down.

"That's what I've been told."

"Well, there's something else you should know," said Harris. "You're going to find out soon enough."

Eileen Crowe hardly looked the part of an elite criminal defense lawyer. She wore her hair long and a bit mussed, and was dressed in a colorful flowery blouse and skirt as opposed to the normal business suit. Her voice had a bit of an Annie Hall "la-di-dah" quality. In her early fifties now, it wouldn't have surprised Grant to learn she'd led a Haight-Ashbury, Flower-Powered adolescence, and somehow stumbled onto the law.

But within seconds of speaking with her, the former Scotland Yard man realized that this was a front meant to disarm; Eileen Crowe clearly possessed acute legal skills and would be a force to be reckoned with, in or out of a courtroom.

Having arrived shortly after Grant had gone in search of Desmond Harris, Rachel had brought Eileen up to date. Grant told them about his conversation with the lieutenant—and how John was sticking to his guns, only saying he hadn't killed Julia and nothing else.

"Let's see what happens outside of cameras and microphones under client-attorney privilege," said Eileen.

"Before you do that, there's one more thing," Grant told them. He turned to Rachel. "When did you say John went on his trip to that golf resort in Wisconsin?"

"Last weekend," replied Rachel. She gave her father the dates.

Grant's lips tightened. "Harris ran John's name through the system and found a round-trip airline ticket, bought and used for those exact dates."

"No reason he shouldn't have," said Rachel. "It wasn't like they were going to drive a thousand miles for the weekend."

"But the tickets weren't for Wisconsin," Grant gravely added. "They were to Hawaii, the Big Island specifically. John left on Friday night and returned from there late on that Sunday evening."

Chapter 4

Eileen Crowe knew the first impression she gave off was that of being a flake—and she took full advantage of it.

With her wispy voice, flowery wardrobe, and poufy coif, she understood that prospective clients didn't initially take her seriously, finding it hard to believe she was a top-notch criminal defense lawyer. But that opinion did a full 180 when she sprang into action, seizing opportunities with prosecutors who had taken her for granted, figuring they'd won their cases before they started.

That didn't seem the case upon meeting Rachel Grant and her father, the former Scotland Yard commander. Maybe it was because Rachel had already dealt with Eileen peripherally on a few *Vanity Fair* stories, but that didn't explain the graciousness and immediate acceptance on Austin Grant's part. Normally, Eileen would have chalked it up to the desperate nature of the situation, with John Frankel looking at a possible first-degree murder charge, but she didn't think that was the case. She suspected that Grant had spent a good part of his life reading others and seeing through their facades—the man seemed to sense that he and Rachel were in capable hands, so Eileen was happy to forgo the usual are-you-sure-we're-hiring-the right-person-here looks.

By the time Grant joined them in the reception area, Eileen had already done a quick check of the internet and media outlets. But the news about Frankel's Hawaii trip upped the ante considerably and she could tell Rachel was shaken.

"Did you talk to him while he was away that weekend?" Eileen asked.

"A couple of times each day. Before he headed out on the golf course and when he was going to bed." Rachel's face tightened. "Supposedly."

"But in retrospect, he could have easily been somewhere else?"

"I guess he could've been calling from anywhere."

Eileen did some quick calculations. "Ten hours from here to Hawaii and given the time change—that would have gotten him in late Friday and he would have had to leave by the crack of dawn on Sunday. Whatever he went there for, presumably his ex-wife, was accomplished in one day: Saturday."

Grant turned toward his daughter. "Have you talked to John's friend?"

"Tim Francis?" Rachel shook her head. "No, I had no reason to. I don't know him very well." Eileen watched her consider those last words. "The truth is, I don't know any of John's friends very well."

"It'd be interesting to see what Tim would say if you asked about the trip."

"Believe me, I'm going to."

"Good," said Grant. He looked at Eileen. "We can see how that lines up with what you get from John when you see him."

"That's presuming John wants me around," Eileen pointed out.

—⁂—

The first thing John Frankel said was that he hadn't asked for a lawyer and didn't need one. But he seemed to waver when Eileen told him that she was there at the behest of Rachel and her father.

"How's she doing?" asked Frankel.

"Just how you'd expect. Frightened out of her mind and wondering what's going on with you."

"Tell her I'm doing okay. And I'll hopefully see her soon."

"Is that my client asking or just you asking me to pass along a message?"

Frankel didn't answer. Eileen turned to glance at Taryn Meadows and a senior detective named Murphy, who had been questioning their colleague. "Perhaps I can have a few moments alone with Detective Frankel?" asked Eileen.

"Only if you're representing him," replied Murphy, a hardened man in his fifties sporting something just short of a crew cut, looking like he'd emerged from a NYPD pamphlet on interrogation.

Eileen threw a look back at Frankel. The embattled detective finally nodded. "If that's what Rachel wants."

Taryn and Murphy exchanged glances. Taryn slowly rose from her chair and Murphy sighed as he followed suit.

"Thank you, Detectives," said Eileen. "Please make sure to disable the cameras on your way out."

"We know the drill," grumbled Murphy. He reached the door first and Taryn was almost out of it when Eileen called out to her.

"Detective Meadows? Perhaps we could have a word when I'm done with my client?" asked Eileen, with a little more emphasis on the final word.

"I'm not going anywhere."

Taryn exited the interrogation room, leaving Eileen alone with Frankel. She held up a finger, motioning for him to remain silent. She let a minute go by, then lowered her hand. "That's more than enough time for them to shut everything down."

Frankel nodded. "I've spent a bunch of times in rooms like this."

"But not on that side of the table, I imagine."

"No. This is definitely a first." He leaned forward. "I didn't kill Julia."

"So you shouldn't have any trouble telling me why you went all the way to Hawaii to see her last weekend and neglected to tell your fiancée about it."

Eileen had hoped for some sort of reaction from Frankel, but he sat there looking nonplussed. She was fairly certain the detectives had asked the same question.

"It doesn't matter anymore," Frankel finally replied.

"Because she's dead?"

Frankel shook his head. "Because it's no longer an issue."

"That's not what those detectives are thinking, I'll tell you that. Were you and Julia seeing each other again?"

"I hadn't seen Julia Molinari since she walked out on me three years ago."

"Then what could possibly possess you to go and see her the week before you were getting married?"

Frankel avoided her gaze for the first time. Clearly she'd hit on something.

"This can't be a coincidence, Detective. Did it have something to do with the wedding?" She leaned forward. "What? Did you need to ask her permission?"

"In a matter of speaking," Frankel answered.

"Don't stop there, Detective," urged Eileen. "Your colleagues already know where you went. It's only a matter of time before they figure out the rest."

Frankel sighed, then lowered his voice as if he were afraid the entire world could hear. "We weren't divorced."

That wasn't what Eileen had been expecting to hear. "How's that?"

"Rachel and I had to apply to the wedding bureau in London to get a license in order to get married there next week," Frankel explained. "I got a message from them about ten days ago that they were rejecting our application because I was still legally married to Julia."

"But hadn't you filed for divorce?"

"I certainly thought so. Julia had actually been the one to start the process. I got served papers two months after she split and sent them back—I only assumed she'd completed her paperwork too." The NYPD detective shrugged. "Looking back, I realized I never actually heard it was all wrapped up, but I also didn't hear it wasn't. I just presumed as much—believe me, this caught me totally by surprise."

"So what did you do?"

"I tracked her down to the Big Island and gave her a call. I asked what the deal was and if she'd finally sign the papers. She refused to do so and when I asked why, she said she had her reasons. So, I figured I'd fly on over there to find out what they were and see if I could talk some sense into her."

"And meanwhile you didn't tell Rachel."

"What can I say?" For the first time, exasperation showed on Frankel's face. "Rachel had so much going on; she was on deadline for an article and with all the wedding planning, I didn't want to add to the stress. I'd just take care of it and only dump it on her if absolutely necessary."

"Did Julia end up signing the papers?"

Frankel paused before answering. "She said she'd think about it."

"I don't understand. What was there to think about?"

Frankel shook his head. "I can't say."

"You won't say or you don't know?" asked Eileen, starting to feel somewhat exasperated herself.

"Like I told you, none of that matters anymore. It's not like Rachel and I can't get married now."

"Some might say that would be a reason for you to kill Julia."

"Well, it wasn't."

Frankel's jaw tightened. Eileen could see she wasn't going to get an answer. She decided to pursue a different track.

"Why was Julia in New York all of a sudden?"

"I can't speak for her," Frankel said.

"And your whereabouts the twenty-four hours prior to her body being discovered?"

"I can't tell you that either."

"Detective—"

"As long as I wasn't in or near my apartment during that time, which I wasn't, it shouldn't make a difference. Right?"

"Can you prove you weren't?"

"I can't account for every single moment of that day, but I don't feel like I have to. I can tell you for a fact that the ballistics on my service revolver will come up totally clean."

"What about your backup? The one that's missing from your apartment."

"I know nothing about it."

"I just have your word for that."

"That'll have to do right now."

Eileen studied the NYPD detective, knowing there was a whole lot more here than met the eye.

"Who or what are you covering for, Detective?"

"Who says that I am?"

"Because I've got a pretty good idea who I'm talking to," responded Eileen. She patted her briefcase. "I did some quick checking up on you. Your record is impeccable—even though you've been known to go to extraordinary lengths to get the result you want. All within the law, it seems. I'm beginning to suspect that this is one of those cases, except you're the one walking the tightrope this time."

"Then you need to trust I know what I'm doing."

"I trust you *think* you know what you're doing."

"Do you think you can get me out of here soon?"

"I think so. For the time being at least."

"Meaning?"

Eileen stared directly into his eyes, her gaze never wavering. "It all depends on if what you're holding back comes back to bite us both in the ass."

"I'll take my chances," Frankel assured her.

"So be it," Eileen said. "Just know that if it does, it's going to take a whole lot bigger chunk out of yours than mine."

—⁓—

"What do you really have?" asked Eileen.

Taryn Meadows stared her down. "Besides his ex-wife lying dead on the floor of this apartment and him refusing to tell us where he was?"

"Yes. Besides that."

46

They were sitting on opposite sides of Taryn's desk. Eileen could easily see the toll this was taking on the woman. She knew that Taryn had to feel she was being pulled in opposite directions—she'd been the first detective on the scene and as such could lay claim to the investigation, yet the prime suspect was her partner. But Eileen knew that every detective in the division had some sort of relationship with Frankel, so Taryn was able to argue she was entitled to stay on the case in some capacity.

"Unless Detective Frankel's mistaken, the ballistics came up clean, didn't they?" asked Eileen.

Taryn gave her a slight nod. "We're running them again, just to make sure. And there's also the matter of his missing backup."

Eileen knew she had no answer for that and her best bet was to blow right on by it. "What about the GSR test? My client told me that was the first thing you administered upon him coming in. That would have shown indications of gunpowder residue if he'd fired any sort of handgun."

"No traces," said Taryn. "But quite an amount of time had passed since Julia Molinari was shot and when John made his way down here."

"Even so, both you and I know it's going to be hard to remove all traces, no matter how much someone cleaned up after themselves."

"That doesn't mean he wasn't wearing gloves. Easy enough to dispose of those along with the weapon—"

"—that you have been unable to find or track back to Detective Frankel," finished Eileen.

"Not at this point," Taryn admitted. "Look. No one more than me would like to see John cleared of this whole mess. But it doesn't help him clamming up when he clearly knows more about what's going on here. I didn't work side by side with the man to not know when he's holding something back."

"So, how long are you planning on keeping him locked up?"

"First of all, he's not incarcerated. We're holding him for questioning and you know we still have two more days before we have to charge him—"

"—or cut him loose," observed Eileen. "That clock is ticking, Detective. I'd certainly hope that while you're waiting for this mystery gun to pop out of thin air, you're considering other suspects."

"Such as?"

"What about the boyfriend?" Eileen checked her notes. "Pablo Suarez? Last heard to be missing from their home in Hawaii?"

"We still haven't been able to locate him."

"And you don't find that the least bit odd?"

"We're able to work more than one front."

"I certainly will be. Has the family been notified?" Eileen referenced her notepad again. "Rachel told me they're just across the Hudson in Jersey and that they have a number of electronics stores here in the city and tristate area."

"Molinari's," said Taryn. "Those gadget type of places all over Times Square and Broadway. Cater to tourists and bargain hunters. They're owned by Julia's father, Leo, and run by a son, Tony."

"And you've been in touch with them?"

Taryn nodded. "Both. But the father was too upset to talk long on the phone, so I ended up calling the brother."

"What did he say?"

"Tony told me his dad hadn't talked to or seen his daughter since she took off for Hawaii three years ago. Seems like there had been quite the family falling out. It was a fairly short conversation, actually."

"How so?"

"After I expressed my condolences, I asked if he'd come into town to formally ID his sister. He said he couldn't be bothered and proceeded to hang up on me."

Huh, thought Eileen. *Some falling out indeed.*

Chapter 5

"It's such a shame about Detective Frankel," lamented Phyllis. The septuagenarian heart and soul of the Astro Diner on Fifty-Fifth Street in Midtown Manhattan shook her head, notepad in hand, ready to take their orders.

"I don't believe it for one second," she continued.

Grant gave the waitress a nod of agreement and motioned toward the other two occupants of the Naugahyde booth: Rachel and Eileen Crowe.

"Thank you, Phyllis. We're having a hard time believing it as well."

"Whatever the circumstances, it's nice to see you as always, Commander. You too, sweetheart," said Phyllis, focusing on Rachel. "Aren't you and the detective walking down the aisle any minute now?"

"A week from Sunday in London," answered Rachel. "At least, that was the plan. But given the circumstances—" Rachel trailed off, noticeably upset.

"Don't you go worrying your pretty head about that," Phyllis told her. "Detective Frankel's got his mind set on making an honest woman out of you—it's all he talked about when I saw him a couple of weeks back. He didn't even order a chocolate milkshake; said he wanted to fit into his wedding suit. I don't remember seeing him so happy about anything, and that boy's been coming here ever since he was able to reach over the counter and grab an extra spoon."

Grant watched his daughter drum up a smile for Phyllis. "I hope you're right."

Phyllis proceeded to tell them she usually was and talked for a few more minutes, as was her wont, and finally took their orders. It was close to midnight, so no one was particularly hungry. Rachel and Eileen ordered coffee and pie while Grant settled for his usual cup of English breakfast and stealing a bite or two off his daughter's plate.

Eileen summarized her conversation with Frankel. She had asked her client point-blank if she could share anything he said with Rachel and her father, or did he want everything to remain privileged between the two of them. The detective had said that anything he told Eileen, she was free to relay to them—but it was the things that he *didn't* talk about that were most concerning to the trio.

"This business about the wedding license was complete news to you?" Eileen asked Rachel.

"Totally. I knew we had to apply for one and I signed the application. But that was the last I heard of it."

"So you don't have any idea if it's gone through or not?"

"No, but I'm bloody well going to check first thing in the morning." Grant couldn't help but notice that her British accent, which had been fading the more time she spent in the States, was more pronounced when she was agitated.

"Speaking of checking on things, we might want to hire an investigator or two to look into not just what John was doing but also to provide alternative theories," suggested Eileen.

"You mean other suspects besides John," Grant said.

"Exactly."

Phyllis chose that moment to reappear with hot beverages and slabs of apple pie. Grant immediately regretted not ordering a piece of his own and started to tell this to Phyllis when Rachel said he should just take hers.

"I really don't have much of an appetite," she told him.

Grant didn't need to be asked twice. He slid the plate across the table.

Eileen took a sip of coffee and picked up the conversation once Phyllis toddled off. "But I warn you, investigator's time gets expensive really fast."

"That shouldn't be necessary," said Grant.

"How's that?"

"You've got the two of us," Grant replied. "Rachel spends her life making inquiries for her stories, mostly exposés, and I've been known to take on an investigation or two during my time."

"And what about bias?" wondered Eileen. "You can't just be looking for ways to clear John. Considering there seems to be a slew of things he's not telling us, it's possible you're not going to like what you come across."

"I think it's a good idea," said Rachel. "No one has better reason to get to the bottom of this than me and my father."

"And what happens when you get there and don't like what you find?"

"I'd rather know the truth than just sit here helpless, wondering in the dark."

Eileen looked over at Grant.

"I learned a long time ago not to disagree with my daughter."

It was past two in the morning when Rachel and Grant returned to her apartment, but neither was ready to turn in. Particularly Rachel, who was pacing back and forth, amped up on coffee and nerves.

"Maybe I ought to give you some room and stay in a hotel," offered Grant.

Rachel shook her head and crossed over to sit down beside her father on the edge of the converted sofa bed. "No, Dad. I want you here. You're the only thing keeping me from going insane right now."

"Well, you'll do John no good if you're too worn out. You need to sleep."

"I know, I know." Rachel ran a hand across her face. "I also know the moment I close my eyes, I'm going to be back in that apartment with Julia. Or worse yet, I'll be imagining John standing over her with a smoking gun."

"Smoking gun? Sounds like someone's been watching too many old movies."

Rachel nudged him with a shoulder. "You know what I mean." She uttered a deep sigh. "What if I'm totally wrong about him?"

"I'm going with the theory that my daughter's a good enough judge of character that she didn't choose to spend the rest of her life with a murderer. Especially when he told you flat-out that he didn't do it."

"Then where was he all that time? What was Julia doing in New York? Did he even know that she was here—"

"Rachel—"

She cut him off, continuing to spin. "But really, Dad—how well do I know John? You know how quickly we got together. It's not like I know much about his life before that. I had to practically drag any information about Julia from him."

Grant reached over to take her hand—trying to allay her fears. "From everything I've seen, John's a decent and caring man. I think he takes things too much to heart sometimes, and like he told Eileen, he didn't mention this divorce business because he didn't want to burden you and tried to handle it himself."

"The same way he's handling an impending arrest by refusing to say where he was when Julia was being murdered in his apartment?" asked Rachel.

He couldn't argue that point. "Before this, has John ever told you anything that turned out not to be true?"

Rachel thought about it for a moment. Finally, she shook her head. "No. Not that I remember."

"So, when he tells you he didn't kill Julia, I think you need to take that as the God-given truth."

"And what about what he's not telling us?"

"He must have his reasons. More than likely he's protecting someone or something."

"The person who actually did it?"

"Not a chance. John Frankel's a policeman. He would never protect a killer."

"Who then?"

Grant let go of Rachel's hand and looked into her eyes. He watched them widen in sudden comprehension.

"Me? What could he possibly be protecting me from?"

"You said it yourself. John doesn't have many friends, certainly no one as close as you. It's not likely to be this partner of his, Taryn—she's been in there interviewing him and if it were something involving her, I suspect she's a good enough detective to sense that."

He took Rachel's hand again. "I've seen the way he looks at you. I listened to him when he came to London and asked if he could marry you. There's no question that he adores you. The fact that he wouldn't tell you about the divorce papers because he didn't want to burden you and wanted to fix things himself? I imagine whatever he's holding back is for similar reasons."

"What could be more worrisome than the possibility of being arrested for the murder of his ex-wife?"

"That's what we're going to try and figure out."

Grant's night turned out to be a restless one. He wasn't plagued by nightmares like those Rachel feared, but he'd gotten up every hour wondering if his daughter had been getting any sleep. Each time he listened for any sound coming from the bedroom—pacing, the television playing—but heard nothing. He was just wider awake and had to force himself to go back to sleep. By the time dawn poured through the curtain cracks, Grant finally gave up thoughts of deep slumber and knew he was going to have to get by that day on maybe four hours of intermittent sleep.

Rachel emerged not much after that, and Grant noticed that she looked a hell of a lot better than he felt. It turned out that she had passed out the moment her head hit the pillow and she dreamt of absolutely nothing.

"I think I worked myself into such a state that I just ended up comatose," Rachel told him.

"You must teach me how to do that."

Rachel fixed them bacon and eggs as they discussed a plan of attack. Focusing on Julia, Grant thought they had a few courses they could pursue. There was the Hawaii angle—not only what had transpired between John and Julia on that Saturday he'd been there, but what her state of mind had been then.

"It would be good to get a better handle on what her life was like over there. The obvious person to talk to would be this fellow Pablo, if we could somehow get in touch with him," said Grant.

"I wonder if he came to New York with Julia."

"If he did, and subsequently disappeared, that would make him even more a person of interest."

"I could check with Taryn and see if she'd let me know what they've come up with."

"I suspect she won't be too forthcoming. But if you trade on her friendship with John, and of course your relationship, you should have better luck making headway than me."

"What about Julia's family?" asked Rachel.

"That's certainly the other track worth pursuing."

"What Eileen said, about how her brother couldn't be bothered identifying her body. What could that possibly be about?"

"That's precisely what I intend to spend my morning figuring out." He pointed at the laptop perched on the edge of the dining table that also served as Rachel's office. "Let's see if we can get a line on Tony Molinari."

From what they were able to glean through web searches and a few phone calls, the Molinari family had a dozen stores in the tristate area. Rachel knew that the family lived across the Hudson, but it turned out that Tony spent most days at the flagship store near Times Square.

After promising each other to check in every couple of hours, Grant got dressed, left the apartment, and headed toward the subway.

The first couple times he'd been in Manhattan in the past year, Grant had stuck mostly to taxis and Ubers to get around. He'd consequently spent too much time in endless traffic jams; if it hadn't been so cold during those visits, he would have walked to reach his destination on time. Rachel had therefore educated him about the subway lines, which turned out to be quite the efficient system once one got the hang of it—if, and make that a Big If, it was operating without glitches.

He'd lived a good part of his life on the Tube in London, and thought that transportation system was the best imaginable, but the one that circulated under the island of Manhattan and the other four boroughs could usually get him within three or four blocks of his destination. So he'd taken to using the MTA trains whenever possible, having a card that he kept adding money to for fares when necessary.

The only drawbacks were how cramped it got during rush hour—bodies pressed against one another; he tried to avoid taking it at that time—and then there were the ones he'd come to think of as the permanent travelers, the homeless who rode the trains back and forth all night long. According to Rachel, it depended on who was running City Hall to decide if they were ushered off the trains at all—as opposed to London, where the cars were policed religiously and freeloading wasn't abided. Then again, England had had more than its share of Tube bombings and terrorist attacks, so he presumed there was something more to the underground policing than a beautification project.

When he emerged in Times Square, it was a completely different world.

For as long as he could remember, Grant had watched a million people pile into the ten-block space every New Year's Eve and throw the biggest party on Earth. But he realized there was *always* a party going on in Times Square. There were at least two or three street performers on every corner, some doing the latest dance craze, others working their magic act for wide-eyed onlookers, and every Disney character, superhero, or movie icon you could imagine doing impressions and extending hats.

Grant knew it hadn't always been like this. For a few decades (the '70s and '80s came to mind), Times Square had been occupied by the dregs of New York. If you weren't a hooker, stripper, drug dealer, or addict, you were putting your life (or at least pocketbook) in danger should you stroll those streets in the after-hours. Even daylight left something to be desired as there was a three-card monte game being played on most corners, where you were certain to lose your hard-earned money in the blink of an eye unless you were fortunate to win a few bucks. Of course then you'd get beat up on the next block by a shill working for the con man who was trying to fleece you. You couldn't walk ten feet without encountering a strip joint, adult bookshop, or theater showing movies with titles like *On Golden Blonde* or *Spank Me Babysitter.*

But then came a regime at Gracie Mansion that made it their top priority to clean up Times Square and turn it into the present-day tourist destination. No one knew exactly where the previous denizens went—many thought they were hanging out by the various bridges and tunnels leading on and off the island, but Grant felt a good many were riding the aforementioned subway trains. Whatever the case, Times Square was now a place where the Disney Store ruled and you could go to a mega M&M's store and get the multicolored candies to spell out anything that your heart and sweet tooth desired.

Through all of this, there had been two constants.

The first were the kiosks and shops where a visitor to New York City could pick up a piece of Manhattan memorabilia like a postcard, snow globe, or *Sesame Street* doll with an I ♥ NY T-shirt on it.

The other had been the electronics stores that carried every type of radio, phone, or handheld device you could think of. They were usually run by Arab and Israeli immigrants and the prices were never fixed, so you always walked away thinking you'd gotten a great deal. It was only when you got home that you realized you'd actually been fleeced.

Molinari's was one of those places on a much grander scale.

Grant's research on Rachel's laptop had told him the store occupying a half block on West Fifty-Third Street had been the family's first, parlaying the profits from their used furniture shops. Leo Molinari, unlike many of his competitors, had kept up with the tech boom and loaded up on computers. Knowing better than to chase Apple or Microsoft, he'd stayed clear of the top-of-the-line products, catering to a crowd who couldn't just walk in and plop down a couple of grand for a state-of-the-art desktop. Leo also knew his customer base thought knockoff brands were the next best thing.

Molinari's had quickly expanded into New Jersey and Connecticut. Math wasn't Grant's strong suit, but he realized that by buying these items in bulk and flipping them for a 250 percent markup in more than a dozen store franchises owned outright by the family, Leo Molinari wasn't going to threaten Bill Gates on the *Forbes* 400 list, but no one needed to throw him a fundraiser either.

The store wasn't quite packed with customers, but there were folks browsing in every aisle. Grant quickly located the phone charger display and picked up a new one, so that he could stand in the cashier line looking like he was going to buy something.

Some five minutes later, it was his turn at the register. He paid for the charger while asking the gum-snapping young woman ringing him up if Tony Molinari were around.

"He's in the stockroom, but should be back out here in a few," said the clerk. "Can I help you with something?"

"It's of a personal nature," Grant told her.

Her ears perked up hearing his accent. "You're not from around here, are you?"

"Not quite."

"I've always wanted to go to Australia. Hug myself a koala bear."

"Me too," said Grant.

The clerk realized her mistake. "England?"

"There you go."

This resulted in a bubble burst and a smile.

"Let me get Tony out here for you." She swiveled a closed sign over her register and told Grant to hang out.

A couple of minutes later, she came through the stockroom door with a muscled, dark-haired man in his thirties. She beckoned Grant over with a waggle of a long fingernail.

As Grant approached them, he sized up Julia Molinari's brother. From the pictures he'd seen of John's ex-wife, there was no question that this was her sibling. He had the same deep-set brown eyes and similar coloring.

Once Grant joined them, the clerk flashed him another smile, burst another bubble, and headed back to her register—leaving the two men alone.

Grant extended a hand toward Tony. "Mr. Molinari? I'm Austin Grant—"

"Doesn't ring a bell."

"My daughter is Rachel Grant. She was the one who found your sister the other afternoon. You have my condolences."

"Shit," exclaimed Tony, cutting him off. "I know who *she* is. She's marrying my ex-brother-in-law. That prick who killed my sister."

"That hasn't been established."

"Haven't you read the papers? She was found in his apartment, for fuck's sake."

"Rather convenient, wouldn't you say?"

"Hey, I never would've expected something like that from the guy. When they were married, I never had a bone to pick with him. But who knows what flips the switch on a guy? She leaves him for that Suarez bastard and maybe Frankel just wigs out when she shows up back here. Hell, the guy's a cop. He's carrying, tempers get out of hand—there you go, *bang*."

Grant nodded. "Sounds like you've got the whole thing figured out."

"Facts are facts, man. She's dead in her ex's apartment. Case closed." He slapped the counter for emphasis and the glass rattled. "What's all this to you anyway?"

"Like you say, my daughter is about to marry Detective Frankel. So you might say I have a vested interest. What you just said about her being 'back here.' Did you actually see your sister?"

"I'll tell you the same thing I told that woman cop on the phone yesterday. My long-lost sis, who I hadn't seen in close to three years, popped by the house a few days ago wanting to see my dad."

"And did she?"

"He wasn't home," Tony told him. "She chickened out after talkin' to Sophia and ended up splitting before he got back."

"Who is Sophia?"

"My stepmom—who Julia never got along with in the first place," Tony said. "Besides which, I'm not sure my pop would've even talked to her. After the way she went and broke his heart, runnin' off like that to Hawaii without saying a fucking word?"

Tony shook his head.

"Next thing any of us hear is that she's dead. And that's that."

Chapter 6

Taryn Meadows had never planned on being a cop. Unlike many of her fellow officers, it hadn't been a dream of hers since she was a little girl or some destiny she was supposed to fulfill because she'd come from a long line of law enforcement. She had been on a completely different track—the kind that goes around in circles, and if one is good and lucky enough, ends up participating in a medal ceremony in a massive stadium watched by a worldwide television audience.

Taryn had been that good.

And for more than a little while, lucky as well.

Finding delight in running and the pursuit to be the quickest girl in all five boroughs, she'd run out of Bed-Stuy all the way to Philadelphia on a track-and-field scholarship to Temple. There she'd risen to the top ranks of collegiate milers and reached the Olympic qualifiers to secure a spot on the team heading to Beijing.

All it had taken was a little pop to derail her.

She'd just won her first heat by a couple of seconds and seemed a sure bet to make the US team, when she took an ill-fated step turning to take a victory lap. Taryn hadn't been sure if she'd actually heard or just felt the pop—all she knew was that one second she was headed for the fulfillment of a dream she'd literally been running toward since she was a schoolgirl, and the next moment she was writhing on the ground knowing that her life had been irrevocably changed with a torn ACL.

She didn't need her coach, a doctor, or a map to tell her that the road ahead was fraught with near impossibilities. With the Olympiad in London four years away, there were no guarantees that she could regain the speed and strength she'd worked her entire life to attain, and with a host of upcoming track stars who would literally pass her by, Taryn knew when to hang up her Nikes.

The question had become what to do next.

Luckily, she'd taken a basic criminology course at Temple on a whim and was immediately taken with it, so she'd decided if she couldn't achieve the dream of running down an Olympic medal, she could chase bad guys instead.

Two days after graduation, she'd entered the New York Police Academy.

She aced the police officer's entrance exam and excelled at the academy, making it clear from the start that she wanted to pursue the detective track. She spent the first year working as a uniformed officer, taking extra shifts whenever she could and compiling an impressive string of arrests in the process. She'd gotten glowing recommendations from her commanding officers and taken additional criminology courses at the CUNY John Jay College of Criminal Justice at night, along with the department's Criminal Investigative Course, where she'd achieved the highest marks possible.

It wasn't like she had much of a personal life. There had been a boyfriend or two here and there, but most of the guys she met couldn't handle the cop concept or that she was simply tougher than them. And it wasn't like Taryn kept up with those she'd grown up with in Brooklyn—except when she'd arrested one of them and they tried to trade in on being from the old hood to get the charges dropped or lessened, to no avail.

As a result, she'd made third-grade detective before she hit thirty and worked her way up to first grade shortly after her thirty-second birthday, about as quickly as any detective, male or female, ever had.

She'd served most of her time in the Bronx, which had been convenient as she was living in a walk-up one Aaron Judge homer south of Yankee

Stadium. But after her partner called it quits, she'd finally moved in to the city, found a place in the Flatiron District and transferred to a nearby precinct, knocking an hour off her commute and promoting a change of scenery.

It just so happened that the transfer occurred about the same time that John Frankel was coming back to active duty after recovering from a near-fatal gunshot.

From the moment she had met John, Taryn knew she could fall hard for this man. Not only was he a great cop, but she could tell after one day of partnering that he was kind, considerate, caring, and intelligent—hardly the makeup of ninety percent of men she met on and off the job. The fact that he was really good-looking didn't hurt.

But as they say, timing is everything—and on that same case that he'd taken a bullet, Rachel Grant had taken his heart, dashing Taryn's hopes before they even started.

Not that there was anything wrong with Rachel. She was lovely; it was easy to see why John was crazy about her. The three of them had shared a few lunches where Taryn found Rachel to be personable and smart, while possessing that slightly wicked bite that seemed particular to Brits.

Taryn also found herself to be a little bit jealous.

But she'd also subscribed to the adage of Partner First—so she had quickly become John Frankel's trusted right hand while he became her left. They'd fallen into a rhythm, working cases with a solve rate that was the envy of every other detective team in the precinct. She watched as John and Rachel grew closer by the day and Taryn was the first to congratulate him when he told her about his engagement, though she couldn't help wondering what would have happened if she'd transferred just a month or two earlier.

So Taryn had been stunned when Rachel phoned that day to tell her what she'd found in John's apartment.

Not that her partner had been acting normal prior to Julia Molinari's murder. He'd definitely seemed preoccupied in the days before it, but

Taryn had just presumed it to be the nervousness that came with an upcoming trip down the aisle.

But looking back on his so-called bachelor party weekend in Wisconsin that turned out to be a quick hop to paradise to confront his ex-wife, Taryn was kicking herself for not realizing something had been off. The trip had come out of nowhere, John informing her just two days before it. Taryn had said it seemed a bit last-minute, but John had waved it off, claiming it was just a couple of guys hitting the links for a weekend. No big deal. Even the inclusion of Tim Francis, a friend she'd heard John mention maybe once in their six months together, should have set off warning bells, but Taryn was just so used to taking him at his word.

Not so much anymore.

There'd been no question something was up with John when she saw him the following Monday. He had been fairly silent most of the morning and hadn't even ordered a milkshake at the Astro for lunch. She'd asked him point blank if something was wrong, but John said he was just recovering from the trip.

That made sense now. Two ten-hour flights in less than three days will wreak havoc with a person's system.

He had mentioned his ex on occasion, but Taryn had no reason to believe they'd been in touch. The story about the divorce papers made sense, as did John not telling the truth (okay, lying) about his trip. But it couldn't be a coincidence that after flying to Hawaii to see Julia Molinari for the first time in three years, she suddenly turned up dead in his apartment six thousand miles away days later.

What had John Frankel been up to during that time, and why was he refusing to talk about it?

Maybe John hadn't pulled the trigger that ended Julia's life—Taryn found it hard to believe he would have been careless enough to leave her body in his apartment, but something he wasn't saying must have contributed to her ending up there.

It didn't help that Hawaii was six time zones away and the Big Island wasn't Honolulu, which was at least a metropolitan city with a sizeable police force. Things were definitely more laid-back there, and it was hard to get a line on Pablo Suarez. She'd managed to grab a cell number for him off Julia's phone and had seen at least a half-dozen calls placed back and forth between them on the two days preceding the murder, but when Taryn tried to call the number, it had gone unanswered. She had run a trace on it that yielded nothing, leading her to believe it had been discarded—and there was certainly enough ocean over there to dump it in.

She'd also run a check on possible flights for Suarez and, so far, he hadn't appeared on any manifests. But when she checked out the Papaya Seed, a bar Pablo owned with Julia next to a resort on Waikoloa Beach, she'd learned that it had been closed since the week before, right after John Frankel had paid a visit.

To say that Pablo Suarez was a person of interest was an understatement. To further add that he seemed to have disappeared—well, that was quickly becoming a statement of fact.

Turning her attention to the Molinari clan had proved equally fruitless.

It seemed that Julia had been estranged from her family for some time. Taryn hadn't really gotten much in a brief phone chat with the patriarch, Leo; he sounded like he was in shock and so full of regret that he couldn't reconcile with the daughter he'd never see again. Realizing that a trip to the Molinari home in Jersey might be an intrusion on grief at this point, Taryn had called the family's flagship store to interview Julia's sole sibling, Tony, who had been only a little more forthcoming.

It seemed that Julia and her father had been on rocky ground ever since the widowed Leo had taken up with Sophia, who happened to be the same age as Julia. When Leo and Sophia married, that had been the beginning of the end for Julia and her father, culminating in the fracture of their relationship when Julia took off with Pablo. Since that time, Sophia and Leo had had a young boy of their own and a second child was on the way, which Taryn figured couldn't have helped any chance of a reconciliation on Julia's part.

At least that had been what everyone thought.

It had been Tony who had given Taryn her first glimmer that something had been up with Julia. His sister had suddenly appeared at the house looking for Leo and then seemed to think better of it, subsequently taking off as quickly as she'd arrived. Tony had expressed no sympathy, simply saying that "Family doesn't leave family," that they stuck together through thick and thin, and he had nothing more to say.

From her short and frustrating interactions with father and son, Taryn thought John should consider himself lucky to be rid of the Molinari family.

Whether it had meant killing his ex-wife to accomplish this was still up for debate.

The ballistics report on her desk did nothing to point the finger at John. There was no indication that his service revolver had been fired recently and the bullet recovered in the apartment wasn't a match. There had also been no traces of gunshot residue on John's hands or clothes.

But there was also John's backup gun missing from his apartment; he had told her he couldn't remember the last time he'd checked the old video game box at the top of his closet to see if it was there.

Taryn sat at her desk considering all this for the better part of the morning and finally traipsed into her lieutenant's office to lay out everything she had—and didn't have.

She told Desmond Harris what she was thinking, especially since they were halfway through their second day of questioning John Frankel with only seventy-two hours to hold him.

Harris listened intently, and reluctantly agreed with what Taryn was recommending.

—⁓—

"So, my client is free to go?"

Eileen Crowe was wearing another flowery blouse, providing the only bright colors to the interrogation room where Taryn felt a distinct pall hovering.

"I wouldn't quite characterize it like that," answered Desmond Harris. "Detective Frankel is being placed on temporary leave while this case is under investigation as he remains a person of interest."

"What about working to clear my name?"

The lieutenant turned his attention toward John Frankel, who was sitting beside Eileen.

"Temporary leave means you're no longer on active duty. You're not to interfere with the investigation and you're to remain within the five boroughs of New York City. Should you attempt to leave without notifying or gaining permission from this office, it will be construed as a flight attempt and it would be within our right to place you under arrest as a hostile material witness."

Frankel started to speak, but Eileen flashed him a look that silenced him. "We completely understand the guidelines, Lieutenant," she said.

Harris nodded and checked the folder in front of him. When he looked back up, it was in Frankel's direction.

"How long have we worked together, Detective?"

"Over ten years, sir," Frankel answered.

"So I'm pretty familiar with how you operate by now. I know that once you latch on to something, it's practically impossible to pull you off it. I can only imagine you have what you consider good reasons in refusing to inform us as to your exact movements in the days leading up to the murder. My guess is that you're onto one of those aforementioned 'somethings'—but with no current standing as a member of NYPD, anything you might do in a 'nonofficial' capacity is going to be viewed as willful obstruction. And you will be punished accordingly. Do I make myself clear?"

"Absolutely, sir."

"At the same time, if you feel compelled to make a further statement at this time or in the near future, Detective Meadows or I will be more than happy to take it." Harris nodded at Eileen Crowe. "In the presence of your attorney, of course."

"You better believe it," said Eileen.

"Do you have anything else to add to your statement at this time?"

"Besides the fact that I did not murder Julia Molinari?" Frankel shook his head. "No, sir. I do not."

"I hope to God you know what you're doing, John. You're one firm piece of evidence away from being hauled back here and placed in an eight-by-ten-foot room down the street until you're put on trial."

"I'm well aware of that, sir."

Harris grumbled, then glanced past Eileen and Frankel at the interrogation room door. He nodded at the uniformed cop, who could be seen on the other side of the window. The cop opened the door and addressed the lieutenant.

"Sir?"

"Please take Ms. Crowe and her client somewhere Mr. Frankel can review and sign his statement before leaving."

Taryn watched Eileen and Frankel rise in unison. She couldn't help but notice that her lieutenant no longer called John "Detective."

"Ms. Crowe?"

Eileen turned around at the door to face Harris.

"It would benefit everyone involved if you could get your client to come to his senses sooner than later."

"I'll give it the old college try, Lieutenant," replied Eileen.

"Good luck," said Harris. "I certainly haven't had much success in that department over the past decade."

Taryn gave Frankel a sad smile before he followed Eileen and the uniform out of the interrogation room.

When she turned back around to face Harris, she saw that his face was riddled with tension and disappointment.

"We could have held him for at least another day," said her lieutenant.

"And what good would that have done? You said it yourself—getting John Frankel to move off a position is a complete waste of time."

Harris shook his head. "I suppose your way is the only course we have."

"He'll have at least two cops watching his every move. We're also monitoring his cell phone—we'll know who he's in contact with."

"Let's hope you're right." Harris sighed and got to his feet. "We need some answers."

That had been Taryn's idea when she'd suggested the plan to Harris.

Hopefully, by keeping track of Frankel, they could get an idea about what he wasn't telling them and perhaps that would give them a line on who was setting him up for a fall.

Of course, there was also the chance that her partner was lying and was guilty as hell.

Chapter 7

Rachel listened to the beep, sighed, and disconnected. She'd tried Taryn Meadows right after her father had left and had gotten her very clipped, officious voice requesting a name, time, and call-back number. It seemed pointless to leave a second message—all it would do was annoy the detective. Either she'd phone Rachel back or not.

She'd figured Taryn was the most likely avenue for an update on John. She hardly knew his boss, Lieutenant Harris, and trying to bypass Taryn wouldn't do Rachel any favors; Taryn would resent it and be less willing to help her, plus Harris was under no obligation to share any information with her.

So, while waiting to hear back from Taryn, Rachel had spent the morning digging into the Hawaii of it all. Calling on her journalistic skills and instincts, she worked her laptop and cell to find out anything she could about Julia and Pablo.

They appeared to be living outside of Kona, the main city on the leeward, dry side of the Big Island. She couldn't find any record of them having gotten married, which would have surprised her, considering Julia still seemed to be John's lawfully wedded wife.

As that thought popped into her head, Rachel stopped to consider how she really felt about that. The past couple of days had been such a whirlwind, with John held at the precinct being her main concern, that she really hadn't had time to dwell on that little bombshell.

The truth was, Rachel really didn't know how she felt. On one hand, it could have been a simple oversight; these kinds of things often happen. But something about it didn't sit right—the fact that Julia had initiated the divorce papers and then refused to countersign when John returned them? Had there been some ulterior motive on her part? If so, they were going to have to learn about it from Pablo or some other Julia confidante. Otherwise, John's ex would take that answer to her grave.

At some level, Rachel could understand how John had kept it from her. She knew he wanted the wedding to be perfect, and it was just like him to be overprotective, not wanting to panic her that the ceremony might be in jeopardy unless he absolutely had to. And if that meant him rushing off to Hawaii in his slightly tarnished suit of armor, so be it.

But that clearly wasn't the end.

Julia Molinari had turned back up in New York right after that. Rachel was convinced something had happened to complicate matters the weekend John had traveled there, and for some reason he was refusing to talk about it.

Using some of the sophisticated search engines and databases at the magazine, Rachel was able to learn that Julia and Pablo had been running a small beach bar called the Papaya Seed, adjacent to the gargantuan Hilton hotel. With water slides, dolphin adventures, beach access, scuba and other water sports, multiple dining choices, dozens of shops, two championship golf courses, and a multitude of tennis courts, the hotel was able to house a couple of thousand tourists at a time, giving the Papaya Seed a good shot at a constantly changing clientele.

With the six-hour time difference, Rachel knew it was pointless trying to reach the beach bar when the sun hadn't even risen there, but she figured that someone had to be working the desk at the Hilton and could maybe give her a little intel. Within a few minutes, she'd gotten a super friendly (why not; she was *living in Hawaii*) concierge on the phone and identified herself as a journalist doing a feature for *Vanity Fair* on island life. The bubbly concierge was more than happy to tell Rachel what she knew about the Papaya Seed.

"Closed down," said Kimmie, a transplant from the Midwest who'd gotten out of the cold the minute she had turned eighteen.

"Really? For a long time?" asked Rachel.

"Just since last Monday actually. The reason I know is I usually head over there to get their daily smoothie and Mondays are, or I should say *were*, their Blue Moon Mango special. Blueberries, mango, and pineapple with yogurt, granola, and a drizzle of artisan honey."

"Sounds scrumptious," said Rachel, thinking not really. She preferred two flavors, tops, not the kitchen sink. "Maybe they decided to take a long weekend?"

"I don't think so. There was a 'Closed Until Further Notice' sign on the tarp that covered the building," explained Kimmie. "It's disappointing for the guests as well. It was a nice option for those on the beach instead of hiking all the way back into the resort to grab a drink or bite."

Rachel asked her about the couple that ran the place.

"Julia and Pablo? They worked their tails off, I can assure you," Kimmie said. "I just can't see them throwing in the towel like that. I thought they were doing well enough. Shows what I know."

Rachel's next question was interrupted by a text from Taryn.

Noon. My office.

Short. Not so sweet.

Rachel checked her watch. It was just past eleven. Not much time to pull herself together. She thanked Kimmie and asked if she could contact her again. The concierge told her any time and Rachel provided her contacts in case she should run into one of the Papaya Seed owners. Knowing that the only possibility was Pablo, Rachel found it interesting that Julia's murder hadn't made its way to the Hilton concierge desk but figured it was only a matter of time. She wondered if she'd hear again from Kimmie after that.

As she hung up, Rachel thought about the fact that the Papaya Seed, Julia and Pablo's seemingly only stake in the world, had shut down right after John's weekend trip to the Big Island. Now one of the proprietors was dead and the other had vanished.

What the hell happened that weekend?

—*m*—

Rachel was escorted by the desk sergeant to Taryn's desk and told to wait in the chair beside it. She was severely tempted to sift through the papers on the detective's desk to see where they were on the murder case but was able to resist, primarily because she was surrounded by cops working in their cubicles.

A few minutes passed, then a side door into the detective's bullpen opened and Taryn came out, followed by John and Eileen Crowe.

Rachel leapt to her feet and met them halfway across the room. She immediately threw her arms around John. She began to shake and he calmly whispered in her ear.

"I'm okay, Rachel. Don't cry."

"I'm not going to cry," Rachel whispered back. "I'm just relieved to see you."

"Me too."

"Contrary to popular belief, we got rid of the rubber hoses a while ago," Taryn said, causing both Rachel and John to turn their attention toward her.

The female detective reiterated the parameters of John's release but Rachel barely listened. All she wanted to do was leave the precinct with John before someone changed their mind.

So when John asked if she'd like to grab a bite, Rachel didn't need to be asked twice.

The Park Lane, a hotel next to the Plaza on Central Park South, might not have been one of the premier four-star New York hotels, but it did possess a restaurant with one of the best views in Manhattan. Albeit only on the third floor, the Park Room looked directly out on Central Park. They had enjoyed a number of Sunday brunches there and earlier in the year had seen a veritable winter wonderland outside—New Yorkers building snowmen, engaging in snowball fights, ice skating, and taking bundled-up strolls—while they sat inside by a cozy fire eating way too much. Now, on a warm afternoon, the vista was another postcard, summer in Central Park with all the sunshine and frivolity that came with it.

After staring at the walls of the interrogation room for the better part of two days, it had been the first place John had thought of, though it didn't matter to Rachel—she was just happy they were together. John had persuaded Eileen that he didn't need a twenty-four-hour watchdog; he just wanted a quiet lunch with his fiancée and the lawyer gracefully bowed out, saying they'd catch up later.

"Best view in the city," John murmured as he sat down across from her at the table. But he wasn't gazing out the window; his eyes were focused on Rachel. She smiled softly at the compliment, kind of a ritual whenever they came here, and for the moment, it was just a normal afternoon with the man she'd fallen in love with.

Then reality returned and Rachel suddenly felt that a Sunday wedding on the Heath across the Atlantic was an impossibility away.

"Did you get any sleep?" she asked.

"They let me crash in my office. After confiscating my cell phone and disconnecting the office lines." He gave her a slight shrug. "Not the first time I've done it, but it was usually working a case, not being under house arrest."

"They haven't eliminated you as a suspect yet."

"I wouldn't either—under the circumstances."

"Your gun came up clean, no powder burns—"

"—but there's still my backup out there somewhere," finished John. "They're probably thinking I could have worn gloves and gotten rid of it." He reached across the table to take her hand. "But I didn't."

"I believe you," Rachel told him. And she absolutely did. But there was still so much she didn't understand. "Why aren't you telling anyone where you were those days?" she asked.

"Because I'm not sure it'll prove anything," he softly said. "In fact, it could make things a whole lot worse. I just don't know yet."

"You're not going to even tell me?"

"Not even you." John gently shook his head. "In time. I definitely will."

"And when might that time be?" she asked, unable to leave it alone.

John gave her that crooked grin that drove her crazy—because it was meant to disarm and in the same moment made her desire him more than ever.

"You can't push me, Rach. I just need to find out a few things first."

The tuxedoed waiter picked that time to come over and take their order. John asked if they could still make breakfast (he hadn't had it) and the server asked what he had in mind. They agreed that French toast was a definite option and John went with that, plus a side of bacon. Rachel ordered a salad that she knew she'd just end up picking at. The moment the waiter stepped away, Rachel picked up where John had left off.

"You were expressly told to stay away from this."

"The murder investigation. They were very specific."

Rachel hesitated as her brain speeded along. "That's not what you've been doing, is it?"

"Not directly. I need to locate Pablo Suarez."

"Why? Do you think he killed Julia?"

"I've no idea. I don't even know if he came to New York when she did. She certainly didn't say as much."

Rachel stiffened. "So you did see her again."

"The day she arrived—last Saturday."

"The night you didn't come home."

John's eyes filled with concern. "Don't start thinking those things, Rachel—"

"I can't help it."

He reached for her hand again. Her first instinct was to not let him have it, but she didn't want to make a scene. But it was definitely shaking when he took it.

"Anything between me and Julia was over when she walked out the door three years ago with Pablo."

"What did she want?"

"She was going to see her family—the first time since she left. On pretty awful terms from what I understand. I don't need to tell you what that's like."

Rachel could speak to the subject, for sure. In a crazy way, if it hadn't been for that rift between Rachel and her father, she and John might never have gotten together.

"True."

"She needed somewhere to stay. I gave her the key to my place and ended up working all night."

"On what?"

"Like I said, I can't tell you."

Rachel felt a lump in her throat. Round and round, her own personal circle of hell. She realized, like it or not, she was going to have to wait on him.

But there was one question she wanted answered right that minute and she wasn't going to let him sidestep it.

"Do you still want to get married, John?"

She saw him wince. Not that it gave her a whole lot of satisfaction, but it was the kind of reaction she was praying for.

"More than anything else in the world."

"We're supposed to be a united front," Rachel told him. "You and me against everyone else."

"I feel the exact same way."

"Well, we're not off to very good start," Rachel said. "Keeping secrets like this from each other."

"I'm doing what I can to make sure we don't have to in the future."

"You're got the strangest way of doing it."

John caught a break by not having to immediately respond as their waiter appeared with their meals. Rachel had been right about the salad—she pretty much ended up shoving lettuce around her plate. Meanwhile, John devoured his like a man who hadn't eaten in a couple of days, and Rachel was fairly certain he hadn't.

"You really should eat something, Rach," John said as he soaked the bacon in a pool of syrup.

"I just don't have an appetite." She shook her head. "I pretty much haven't since I walked into your apartment the other day. It's all I keep seeing."

"No matter what, I'll regret that happening the rest of my life."

Rachel was slightly appeased by the look on her fiancé's face.

"I keep forgetting to ask, with everything that's gone on—what were you doing there?" John asked. "It's not like we had plans to meet up."

Rachel started to answer, then dug into her tote and pulled out the small Tiffany bag that had been there ever since she had left the store. She placed it in front of him.

"What's this?"

"I was going to leave it in your suitcase, so you'd find it when you packed to come join me in London."

John's eyes widened in surprise. She motioned for him to go ahead and open it. A few seconds later, the white bow lay beside the opened tiny blue box, and John held the monogrammed cuff links in his hands.

"They're absolutely stunning," he said, his breath taken away.

He read the card out loud and his eyes began to mist over.

"'I can't wait to be your wife.'"

When John looked back up, tears were running down her face.

"And I can't wait to be your husband," he told her.

"The way things are going, I'm not sure that's happening so fast."

Rachel started to dab her eyes but John beat her to it, using a gentle finger to wipe the tears away.

"Do you trust me, Rachel?"

"I want to. More than anything else in the entire world."

"Then I need you to let me see this through." He leaned in close enough that she could feel his breath. "Hard as it may seem."

Rachel found herself nodding. "I just wish there was a way I could help."

John leaned back in the booth and stared out the window at the bright New York summer day.

And just when Rachel thought he'd wandered off in his mind to somewhere far away, John turned back and gave her a nod of his own.

"There just might be."

Chapter 8

As Grant sat in his daughter's apartment, awaiting her return with her just-released fiancé, he wondered how he was going to greet Frankel. It wasn't like he knew the man that well.

Despite working side by side for the better part of a month, Frankel had remained something of a cipher for Grant. Most of their discussions had revolved around the case while doing a bit of a dance around his relationship with Rachel.

Grant knew little of his marriage to Julia Molinari except that it had gone south and he was still wearing a wedding ring a good two years after she'd left him for another man. He remembered John telling him it was purely from habit, and the ring had disappeared once the detective had fallen hard for Rachel. But Grant wondered if there were still a place in his heart for his first wife who'd somehow led John into this mess.

Thus, Grant found himself caught between being a father and a cop, and though he was no longer the latter, like he'd told Desmond Harris, old habits die hard. By the time Rachel and Frankel came back from their late lunch, Grant was feeling more conflicted than ever.

But the moment they walked in the door, Grant realized he was just pleased to see Frankel. Partly because he sensed a calmness in Rachel that he hadn't seen since he'd touched down at JFK, but also because he found it next to impossible to believe this man had murdered his ex-wife.

Grant had nothing to base this on except three decades of reading people, but he'd had enough success during his time at the Yard to trust those instincts.

The same type of gut feeling that the NYPD detective was holding back something of extreme import that would spin the case in an entirely different direction, that would only be revealed if and when Frankel deemed it proper.

But that didn't mean Austin Grant wasn't going to try to find out what that was—which was one of the reasons the former Scotland Yard man didn't completely reject the notion that Frankel had floated out to his bride-to-be at their lunch.

"Your mother and I talked about going to Hawaii every now and then, but we thought it was such a long haul from London that by the time we got there, we'd have to turn around and head home again," Grant told Rachel.

"But Julia was murdered here," Rachel pointed out.

"And whatever precipitated her coming to New York likely began over there," Grant replied. He turned toward Frankel. "I presume that's your thinking."

Frankel nodded. "Everyone's trying to trace Julia's movements once she got here. But something made her decide to come back and see her family after not talking to them for three years. I think it had to do with Pablo."

"What makes you say that?" asked Grant.

"When I saw her in the islands, she said she was worried about him. It seemed he was involved in some business arrangement that had gotten him in way over his head."

"Did she tell you what it was?"

Frankel shook his head. "She didn't know—just that Pablo was increasingly stressed out about it."

"Then how did she know that he'd taken on more than he could handle?" asked Rachel, unable to curb her curiosity.

"He told her they might have to sell the beach bar unless they came up with an infusion of cash."

Grant mulled this over. "How much money are we talking about?"

"I've no idea. But I suspect enough that she had to go looking for it somewhere she wasn't happy about."

"Her family?" asked Rachel.

"That's what I'm guessing. Julia might have gone out of her way to avoid them, but they still had something she didn't."

"Plenty of money," said Rachel.

"Exactly."

"So, let me see if I've got this straight," said Rachel. "You go to Hawaii to get Julia to sign your divorce papers, so we can get married next week, and she just opens up to you about her husband's business troubles?"

"It's not as odd as it sounds," explained Frankel. "Pablo had gone out to pick up supplies for the bar the previous evening and hadn't come back. By the time I saw Julia at the Papaya Seed, he'd been gone for two nights and she hadn't heard from him. Naturally, she was worried sick about it and told me."

"Had she told Pablo you were coming?" asked Grant.

"I presume so."

"Doesn't sound like a coincidence that he disappeared right before you got there," observed Grant. "I can't imagine he would be very happy seeing the man whose wife he stole suddenly appear on his doorstep after all this time."

"I don't know, Austin. It's not like we were going to suddenly grab dueling pistols, take ten paces, turn around, and fire. It didn't occur three years ago, so I don't expect Pablo thought that was going to happen now."

Rachel, who Grant could tell had been hanging on every word, jumped in on her father's side of the equation. "You can't ignore the timing of everything, John."

"I hear where your father's coming from. I dislike coincidences as much as the next cop," agreed John. "If Pablo took off because I was showing up, I think it would have to do with me being an officer of the law as opposed to something personal between the two of us."

"So, what you're suggesting is that Rachel and I head over there to check this all out," Grant said.

"I know it's what I'd be doing if it weren't for the restrictions they've placed on me. The missing card right now is Pablo—but NYPD is putting all its efforts on Julia's movements here and me being the primary suspect. She might have been my ex-wife, but Pablo is the man she's been living with for the past few years and he's obviously in some kind of hot water. Right now, the only way we're going to get the investigation to turn away from me is to provide a viable alternative."

What followed was a lengthy discussion as to the pros and cons of the Grants heading to the Hawaiian Islands to look into Julia's final days there, the whereabouts of Pablo Suarez and what he'd gotten himself into, and if any of it could have led to her murder on the other side of the country.

Grant pointed out that he no longer held an official status as an investigator, and he would feel even more like a fish out of water across two oceans and a huge continent from home. But as a working journalist of some repute, it would certainly be in the scope of Rachel's profession to try and pursue a Hawaiian angle to what was shaping up as a well-followed story.

"What will you be doing while we're gone?" Rachel asked her fiancé.

"I'm not exactly sure," answered Frankel. "Trying to see if Taryn or Harris will let me contribute to my own well-being."

"I'd strongly urge you to listen to the advice of your counsel if you're going to be doing that," suggested Grant.

"I'll certainly keep that in mind," Frankel told them.

After all of them admitted they would go collectively stir-crazy waiting to see if charges were going to be brought against the suspended NYPD detective, they decided that they would be better off trying find the missing Pablo Suarez and a possible connection between his disappearance and Julia's subsequent demise. And if what they discovered kept a set of handcuffs off Frankel's wrists, so much the better.

What Grant didn't tell his daughter was how they might feel if what they uncovered there made things much worse.

He didn't take any solace in the fact that the worried expression on his only child's face indicated that she was way ahead of him.

—◇—

The last time Grant had stayed at the London hotel in Midtown Manhattan, it had been the Christmas season and they had practically chucked him out after a few nights because they'd overbooked. The officious receptionist obviously remembered that visit as she greeted him with a familiar smile and salutation.

"How many nights will you be staying with us, Commander?"

"Just one, I'm afraid," answered Grant.

"That's unfortunate. I was all prepared to offer you our stay three nights, get the fourth free package. We don't actually run this particular promotion at this time of year, but it's the least I can do after your last visit got cut short."

Just his luck, thought Grant. It also occurred to him that it was easy for her to say after he had informed her of his overnight stay. He wondered if the offer would stand if he told her he'd had a sudden change of plans.

But he didn't bother. He had too much on his mind.

Since he and Rachel were going to leave the following morning, he felt he would be particularly underfoot with the three of them squeezed into her apartment. And seeing as how the other usual option was a closed-off murder scene, Grant landed on the return visit to the Whitby.

He ended up settling for the same "deluxe" category, a room that rivaled Frankel's apartment in the shoebox category. Grant considered splurging for something larger, but realized it would be a complete waste of money, since Frankel's situation clouded his mind and he wouldn't enjoy it.

The same concerns made the idea of venturing out and dining alone in Manhattan equally unappealing. He supposed he could wander over to the Astro for a hamburger and chocolate shake, but he wasn't in the mood for idle chitchat with Phyllis, as friendly and welcoming as the waitress tended to be.

He settled for room service, a club sandwich that he somehow wolfed down without realizing it because he was busy on his mobile booking flights and a hotel on the Big Island for himself and Rachel. When asked how long he was planning to stay at the hotel and for a return date by the airline, Grant said three days—negotiating rates and fares that had minimal change fees should they decide to shorten or extend their stay.

All the while, Grant kept thinking about what Frankel had told them about his time with Julia in the Aloha State, and he kept coming back to the obvious gaps in the detective's story.

By the time he settled down in front of the television to try and distract himself, he found it impossible to think of anything else. It didn't help that every other channel had a newscast with an update on the Julia Molinari murder.

After a fruitless hour of this, getting increasingly agitated, Grant got up and grabbed his cell phone off the desk.

He scrolled through his contacts and sent a brief text.

—◆—

"I actually understand you not wanting to show the cards you're holding, John. I can't say I wouldn't be doing the same thing if I found myself in a similar position."

"I appreciate you saying that, Austin." Frankel nodded as Grant kept up a steady pace beside him. "I really do."

The sun hadn't been up very long but there were already plenty of people walking through the Strawberry Fields garden in Central Park, directly across from the Dakota, where, decades before, John Lennon had been gunned down after being asked for an autograph by his killer. Grant had chosen it as a halfway point between the Whitby and Rachel's apartment to meet up with Frankel when he'd texted him the night before. The NYPD detective hadn't even asked about Rachel in his return text—he'd simply replied *I'll see you then*—sensing that the former Scotland Yard commander wanted to have a private conversation before he and Rachel got on a plane.

"But I'm not sure that my daughter feels the same way."

"You know I only want what's best for Rachel."

"I've always believed that. I still do, actually," Grant told him. "But I can't help but wonder if you've bitten off a bit more than you can chew in this instance."

"Could be."

Grant had to admit he was impressed that Frankel was willing to agree.

"If you're innocent of Julia's murder like you claim to be, what are you so worried about when it comes to Rachel?"

Frankel didn't answer right away. He kept walking and Grant couldn't tell if the man was choosing his words carefully or just hesitant to tell the truth.

Probably a little of both, thought Grant.

"I'm worried about losing her," Frankel finally said.

"Do you see her running away so fast?"

The detective shook his head. "It's one of the many things I love about your daughter. Once she commits to something, it's hard to move her off it. Even if she's wrong, she sticks to her guns."

"That pretty much describes Rachel."

Grant took a few steps forward, his mind racing back more than a few years.

"When she was a little girl, I'd say no older than six or seven, she kept pleading for me to take her to work. She wanted to see what her daddy did with his day. I was touched by the notion, but I had to agree with her mother that the Yard wasn't a place for a child."

Grant suppressed a slight grin, then continued.

"But it came up every day and pretty soon it became an obsession. It got to the point where we had trouble getting her to go to school, she was so insistent on going with me. So finally, I told her we'd go the next day, but there were things that were not appropriate for a young child to see. I said I'd give her a lay of the land, introduce her to some other policemen I worked with, and we could have lunch together at the office. I remember her saying that I didn't need to baby her; she was a big girl and was ready for anything. So, the next morning we set off for the Yard and did exactly what I said we'd do, steering clear of anything that wasn't fit for a young girl's eyes."

Grant's grin slowly faded, as they continued their morning stroll.

"Later that night, I heard some whimpering coming from her room. Allison went in, as she usually did, and calmed her down. But that wasn't the end of it—the same thing happened for a few more nights, a week at least. At one point, I told Allison that she should let me take a shot and see if I could give the poor child some peace." Grant shook his head. "That was when my lovely wife told me this was all my fault and was what I got for going against her best instincts by taking Rachel to work."

"But I thought you said she hadn't seen anything," said Frankel, who was totally caught up in this story from his fiancée's youth.

"Not while I was around, it turned out. She finally admitted to her mother that when I'd gone to fetch us lunch and left her at my desk, she'd done a little exploring. We'd been working a particularly gruesome series of killings in East London and the murder book was closed on a corner of my desk—until Rachel decided to have herself a little peek. I wasn't out of the office for more than five minutes, but it was long enough for her to get a good look at the graphic crime scene photos inside."

Frankel slowed down his pace and Grant watched him process this. "I can see how that would flip out a six-year-old girl."

"And Allison wouldn't let me discuss it with her," Grant explained. "You see, even back then, my daughter didn't want to disappoint her father—she was that intent on not letting me know that something I had done, inadvertently mind you, had caused her some sort of emotional harm."

Frankel slowly nodded.

"And you're saying she's no different now."

"She's not likely to tell you how much she's hurting until it's way too late," said Grant.

"I understand, Austin."

Grant picked that time to stop walking and face the man who was only days away from becoming his son-in-law.

"I sincerely hope so," Grant told him. "Because if things get to that point, the fallout with Rachel will be the least of your problems. Do I make myself clear?"

The detective nodded once again. "Crystal."

"And this conversation?"

"What conversation?" asked Frankel.

It was Grant's turn to nod.

He was glad to reaffirm that his daughter had chosen an intelligent man to wed.

Grant could only hope they'd get that far.

Chapter 9

"Call or text the moment you land."

"I will," said Rachel. "Promise."

Frankel kissed Rachel goodbye, then watched as Grant held open the door of the yellow cab that would take them to JFK for their noon flight to the Hawaiian Islands.

Once the door closed on Rachel, Frankel found himself face-to-face for the second time that morning with his prospective father-in-law.

He extended a hand. He was pleased to see Grant not hesitate to take it. "I really appreciate you doing this."

"I wouldn't do it if I didn't already know that," Grant said.

Frankel felt something tug deep inside as the man got in the cab and he watched it speed down Broadway. There were a whole bunch of reasons Frankel could list why he didn't deserve the trust a man like Austin Grant was putting in him.

Grant had made a sidewise accusation that Frankel was playing a dangerous game. Even though the detective would claim to be the ultimate victim here, he couldn't assure Rachel's father that she wouldn't end up being the collateral damage that Grant feared.

But it had become clear to Frankel that he couldn't do what he needed to with Grant or Rachel watching his every move.

Frankel hadn't lied to Rachel. He had vowed he never would and so far had kept that promise.

But the truth was that neither Rachel nor her father had asked the right questions yet. Frankel figured it was only a matter of time until that moment came and if he weren't going to break his promise to Rachel, he'd have to tell her everything.

That was why it was imperative he get the answers he'd been hoping to find since he'd returned from his weekend trip to the Big Island.

But he knew only so much could be accomplished on a cell phone or laptop, and either of those could easily be traced by Taryn and her colleagues.

He took a casual glance around before turning to step back into Rachel's building. Frankel thought he recognized the lanky brunette picking fruit at the corner market as someone he'd seen around the Seventeenth Precinct on occasion. He knew there was no way that Harris and Taryn weren't keeping him under watch—it would only be logical for them to also use undercover cops he didn't know.

As he headed inside, he realized he had to figure out how he was going to check out a few places without an escort. Once inside Rachel's place, he remembered that he hadn't eaten yet that morning. He started to fix himself a bowl of cereal, but his stomach was sour and he knew why.

He was taking one hell of a chance sending Rachel and Grant to Hawaii.

Rachel was a top-notch journalist; once she caught whiff of a story, she didn't let go. And he hadn't met a smarter cop than Austin Grant.

If they stumbled down the same path that Frankel had the week before, things were going to get more complicated and his life might never be the same.

Frankel had gone to Hawaii with only one purpose in mind—to get Julia's signature on a document that would free him up to marry the woman with whom he wanted to spend the rest of his life.

Surprisingly enough, Julia had agreed, having her lawyer add one codicil. At first, he'd just mistaken it for simple legalese and Frankel had been ready to sign it. But his own attorney had told him that he should take a closer look at what Julia was asking.

He had tried to get back in touch with Julia but she wasn't picking up her cell or answering a text or an email.

Frankel had been left with no choice but to dig further.

That was when Julia had showed up in New York, ostensibly to seek money from her family. But she also wanted to know what Frankel thought he was doing.

The next thing he knew, Julia Molinari was dead in his apartment.

By then, Frankel knew he had what could be construed as a reason to murder his ex-wife. Luckily for him, the cops, who had been desperately seeking a motive, didn't know what it was.

Yet.

What Austin Grant had been hinting at was right—John Frankel was definitely playing a dangerous game.

He leaned back on the sofa, stared out the window, and plotted his next move.

PART TWO

For Better, For Worse

Chapter 10

I t was the most gorgeous shade of blue that Austin Grant had ever seen. On the approach to Honolulu, given his absolute hatred of being up thirty-five thousand feet in a long metal tube, he'd been perched in his aisle seat, content to stare straight ahead, grip the armrest tight, and do his utmost to help the Airbus touch down on terra firma intact.

But on the commuter jet to the Big Island an hour later, with just two tight seats on either side of the plane, the view was unavoidable and he couldn't ignore his daughter's intake of breath, so he ventured a glance.

With the sun starting its descent, the ocean glistened like a turquoise jewel with azure highlights flickering on the tips of crashing waves. This sight, coupled with the felt-green-covered mountains and multiple volcanoes (one of which, Kilauea, was still actively spewing lava on the windward side of the island), had him staring out at this slice of paradise in wonder and realizing how very far away he was from home.

The notion of heading to the Hawaiian Islands had always been nixed by Grant when Allison suggested it. Crossing *two* oceans to get there—a total nonstarter. He had been perfectly content to spend his vacations somewhere on the European continent, and on the rare occasion they ventured offshore, like their trip to the Greek Islands, it had been by boat. When Allison had broached boarding a sea plane to check out an island off the coast of Spain, Grant had told her to have a great time and make sure to send him a postcard to let him know that she had arrived safely—they had ended up museum hopping and antique hunting in Bilbao instead.

But now that they had reached their destination, he could see the appeal and felt his blood pressure dropping with everything so lush and tranquil. This feeling was heightened the moment he stepped out the cabin door and was hit with a burst of tropical air, the warm breeze trickling through the palm trees containing just enough humidity that one could taste a sweet trace of water in their lungs.

As he came down the steps from the plane, he turned to Rachel, who had a wistful smile on her face as she took in the view.

"What do you think, Dad?"

"I see why Julia Molinari didn't want to spend another winter in Manhattan."

With that sober observation, they proceeded toward the Quonset huts that doubled as the baggage area, knowing that unlike ninety-nine percent of those exiting the plane, their visit wasn't going to be about fun in the sun, but rather fueled by unearthing a murder suspect.

—◊◊◊—

Twenty minutes later, they were in a rented Jeep, heading up the Kohala Coast on the west side of the Big Island. The landscape along the two-lane highway was breathtaking, yet schizophrenic. As this was the dry side of the island, everything east of the road heading upslope was pitch black—hardened lava from the dormant volcano, with sprays of wheat grass somehow pushing through the cracks among bleached white stones that people had arranged to spell out their names and aloha messages for those traversing the highway. Meanwhile, on the west side, heading down toward the shore, there were huge patches of bright green and plenty of palm trees. According to the travel guide Grant had perused on the flight over, this was where the resorts, golf courses, and exclusive private communities had sprung up in the past couple of decades—and for the right price, you could get your own permanent place in paradise.

A half hour north of the airport, Rachel (who was behind the wheel, as Grant wasn't used to driving on the right side of the road) turned left and made her way through the gates leading to the Mauna Kea Beach Hotel. Grant had found the resort online and not only did it offer a great summer deal (two beachside rooms for the price of one), it was ten minutes from the Papaya Seed, which would be their first stop the next morning.

A landscape of palm trees, orchids, and vibrant bougainvillea accompanied them down the winding road to the hotel, a beige building perched high above a long white beach with a tropical sunset already underway. The sky was cotton candy pink and blue, the sun looking like a fiery orange ball dangling on the edge of the horizon.

Minutes later, they were presented leis by the front desk clerk (a flowered one for Rachel, a more traditional one made of shells for Grant) and escorted down a set of paths amidst a chorus of babbling parrots and tweeting night birds. They ended up in adjacent rooms where one could step off an outdoor lanai onto a field of grass, beyond which was the west-facing beach.

Exhausted from the all-day flights, they decided on room service. Within a half hour, they were stretched out on chaise longues, nursing mai tais (because that's what one drank in the tropics, said Rachel), and picking at pupu platters.

Grant glanced over at his daughter, cast aglow by the tiki torches that lined the path beside their rooms, thinking he'd never seen her look more beautiful, and yet she was troubled. When she emitted a sigh, one that clearly wasn't one of contentment, he reached over to take her hand.

"We'll get through this, Rach."

"I keep thinking this is the sort of place that John and I should be headed to next week on our honeymoon, instead of trying to keep him out of jail."

"Consider it a dry run for next time."

"I have the feeling that when this is over, I'm going to want to shoot anyone who mentions the word Hawaii."

"Can't say that I blame you." He took a sip of the mai tai, his lips puckering at the sour but pleasant taste. "Remember, neither of us would be here if we didn't think that John was innocent."

Rachel nodded. But her subsequent silence gave Grant pause as well; he wrestled with the same thing he knew his daughter was.

What they thought about John Frankel and who he actually was could very well be two different things.

—•—

The next morning, after an outdoor buffet breakfast above a rock-enclosed bay, they got back in the Jeep and headed down to the Waikoloa resort. As they approached the complex, Grant was thankful he'd chosen their hotel as a home base. The Mauna Kea was quaint compared to the Hilton, which was the centerpiece of what could be classified as a small city—with shops, golf courses, luxury condos, trams, and jammed parking lots everywhere. Add a little neon, one would describe it as Vegas Hawaiian style.

No wonder Julia and Pablo had chosen here to capitalize on the tourist trade.

Leaving the vehicle with the Hilton valet, Rachel suggested they start at the concierge desk and see if they could find Kimmie, the helpful woman she had talked to on the phone back in Manhattan.

Only this time, Kimmie was less welcoming when Rachel introduced herself, which caught Grant a bit off guard considering the woman's job, but they quickly understood the attitude switch.

"You didn't tell me when we spoke that Julia had been murdered," the concierge told Rachel. She was a Nordic blonde, with perfect bronzed skin, which must have come from spending every available moment in the island sun.

"I realized while we were talking that you didn't know," explained Rachel. "I thought it'd be better to hear it from the authorities, instead of a perfect stranger."

"Well, that certainly happened. The sheriff and his men have been on and off the premises constantly since that afternoon."

Rachel expressed regret at having not been forthcoming, still maintaining her guise as a freelance reporter doing a story on the murder, while neglecting to add any personal connection to the case, something she and her father had agreed to trot out only when necessary. She asked if Kimmie would answer some questions.

"Not to be quoted, of course," added Rachel.

"Oh, I have no problem being quoted," said the concierge, whose requisite smile had reappeared on her face, clearly thrilled with the idea of having her name in national print. "Long as it doesn't cost me my job or anything."

"Has the Papaya Seed reopened yet?" Rachel asked.

"Not as of yesterday. I'm not sure what the story is today," said Kimmie. She glanced at a digital clock that read 9:30. "They usually get in around ten, hoping to catch the early beach-going crowd who want a snack or smoothie."

"So, you haven't seen Pablo Suarez?" asked Grant.

He suddenly found Kimmie gazing at him. "Are you a reporter as well?"

"Her associate." Grant produced his iPhone. "Take a picture where needed. Do follow-up, that sort of thing." He snapped a photo of Kimmie and she didn't shy away—actually flashing a bigger smile and putting on a bit of a pose.

"As far as I know, no one's seen Pablo. Makes perfect sense, given what happened to his girlfriend and all."

Both Grants nodded. Once it was established that Kimmie had little new information to offer, Grant asked for a resort map and directions to the Papaya Seed. A re-engaged Kimmie happily provided those and then father and daughter made their way from the open-air lobby to the beach below.

On their way, they passed a train, three cars long, built to circle the huge resort. Tourists were already out shopping and most of the beach chairs had been occupied since dawn with guests determined to get every penny's worth of sun. Swimmers were standing at a bar *in* the pool, knocking back Bloody Marys or resuming the mai tai pours they'd ended the night with—making Grant happy to see a lifeguard on duty in case one of them floated away in an alcoholic daze.

"Sounds like local law enforcement is holding up their end," said Rachel.

"At least they're asking questions," agreed Grant. Consulting the map, he said they should bear right when they reached the sand. "But it doesn't look like they're keeping up a constant vigil on the place."

He indicated a large bamboo hut that had a yellow tarp covering it, the color of a ripe papaya, naturally, so that only the pointed top of the structure peeked out the top. A logo featured a cartoonish papaya sunning itself and sipping on a smoothie beneath a beach umbrella and bright sun.

Rachel checked her watch. "I think it's safe to say that Pablo isn't coming back soon—from wherever the hell he is."

Grant walked around the shack, Rachel keeping pace beside him. She slipped out of her flip-flops as they stepped onto the beach while he shuffled slowly along, trying to keep the sand out of his shoes, feeling more and more like a beached big fish.

When they reached the ocean side, Grant found a slight gap in the tarp, enough to glance inside the place. It was fairly compact, with a bar front and center, stools folded up underneath, and a mirror surrounded by cabinets (which he presumed housed liquor) that, when open for business, would reflect the aqua-blue Pacific behind those sipping smoothies and doing shots.

"Pleasant enough," muttered Grant.

Rachel peered over his shoulder and pointed at two fridges below the double sinks. "A lot of food going to waste."

"That's unlikely," added a new voice to the mix.

Father and daughter straightened up to find a girl looking to be in her early twenties, wearing a flowered top that was somewhere between a bikini and tank that clung to her curves and accented her flowing blond hair. White short-shorts and rhinestoned sandals completed the ensemble of the fresh-faced recent arrival.

"Pablo tries to use up everything by the end of the night, figuring it's easier to say we ran out than have it rot away."

"Do you work here?" asked Grant.

"I thought I did. But it doesn't look like the place is opening up any time soon." The girl shrugged. "So much for Friday being payday."

"You think this is because of what happened to Julia?" asked Rachel.

"Well, yeah—of course. I mean, I feel sorry for Pablo and all, but you'd still think he'd let us know what was going on. I know they were a couple and everything, but it's not like this didn't affect all of us." She shook her head. "I mean, it's not like I'm not going to miss her. Julia was one of my best friends."

⸎

The Papaya Seed employee was named Aiden.

Unlike many of the workers her age at the resort, she wasn't a transplant but an honest-to-god local. It had been her mother who had come over from the mainland three decades before on spring break from UCLA; she met a native Hawaiian, fell madly in love, and never went back home. Aiden had been raised high up on the slopes of Mauna Kea, where her mother cultivated roses in the cooler temperatures and took them down to sell at the resorts, while her father secured concrete contracts and ended up paving the new roads on the Big Island made necessary by the tourist population boom.

This all came out sitting by the Hilton pool, Aiden happily taking up Grant on his offer of a late breakfast and the opportunity to talk about how she had come to be friends with Julia Molinari.

Aiden had been working at the Papaya Seed for four years, having been there during its previous incarnation as the Waikoloa Coffee Bar. Julia and Pablo had arrived two years ago to take over the place. They had previously worked at a tiny beach bar up in Hawi, on the northern tip of the island. Grant realized that must have been the place the couple had first ended up when Julia ran off with Pablo, leaving a certain NYPD detective behind.

"But Hawi is a local town and they don't take to haoles, especially when it comes to drinking," Aiden told them. "You know, trust your local bartender and all."

The place had gone belly-up in less than six months, mostly because of the local prejudice. But it didn't help that Julia couldn't work most of the time as she'd been sick with some tropical bug from the moment she'd landed on the islands.

"So how did they go from not making a local bar work to taking over this place?" asked Rachel. "Did they have some kind of backer? Hit the lottery?"

"Sort of," replied Aiden. "Pablo actually won it in a poker game."

She went on to explain. To hear Pablo tell it, he'd gotten into a situation he had no business being in—taking a huge marker for the buy-in, knowing he had no way to make good on it. But he'd had a run of better than excellent cards and pretty soon he had Petty, the owner of the Coffee Bar, back on his heels, to the point that it was just the two of them and the deed was tossed into the pot.

Between pulling an inside straight, which Petty was willing to stake his livelihood that Pablo couldn't do, and his annoyance at the man's habit of chewing papaya seeds and spitting them out into an adjacent trash can, Petty went all in when he shouldn't have with three kings, and walked away with one less beach bar after Pablo miraculously drew the card he needed.

"Naturally, renaming it was a no-brainer," said Aiden.

Grant asked how she had become such good friends with Julia.

"I could tell she was a little unsettled when they first arrived. She told me the last thing she'd thought about was owning a bar after the Hawi fiasco."

Julia was just starting to get back on her feet from the bug she'd had a hard time shaking and wasn't sure how much she was willing to take on. Knowing she needed help, she ended up being the one who asked Aiden to stay on, and the two of them had bonded quickly during the process of remodeling and rebranding the beach bar.

"She needed a friend and I needed a job. It worked out well for both of us." Suddenly, Aiden broke off. "Well—for a while at least."

"And how do you get along with Pablo?" asked Grant.

"Everyone gets along with Pablo," answered Aiden. "That's just a fact of nature."

"What do you mean?"

"You'd have to meet Pablo to understand. There are some people who, when they walk into a room, everyone just gravitates toward. That's Pablo." Aiden took a bite from her egg-white scramble. "Hell, Julia walked out on a ten-year marriage just like that for him." She snapped her fingers, punctuating her point.

"Believe me, we know," said Rachel. "I'm supposed to marry the guy she left back in Manhattan."

Aiden stopped mid-bite. "The police detective? The one who was just here?"

Rachel nodded. "That's the one."

"The man accused of killing her."

"He hasn't been accused," Grant pointed out.

"Seems like only a matter of time—"

She broke off again and turned to Rachel, giving her a sympathetic shrug.

"Sorry. At least that's what the sheriff said when I talked to him yesterday."

"Did you see John when he was here?" asked Rachel.

Aiden shook her head. "I only knew that Julia was getting together with him. Something about lawyers, she told me."

"She never signed their divorce papers," Rachel said.

"I can see how that might put a damper on your marriage plans."

"Did she tell you how their meeting went?" asked Grant.

"I never talked to her after that. Something must have happened though."

"What makes you say that?"

"Well, she ended up dead in his apartment in New York right after."

Grant knew he'd have a hard time refuting that.

"John denies having done it and says that he was set up."

"By who?" Aiden asked.

"That's what we're here to find out," Grant informed her.

Aiden seemed to chew on this and her eggs at the same time. After a moment, her eyes flickered. "You're not thinking Pablo?"

"You have to admit it's pretty odd that no one has heard a word from him since her body was found."

"That's not so strange. We hadn't seen much of him in the past month, before all this went down."

"How do you mean?" asked Rachel.

"I'm pretty sure he was working some new deal."

"Any idea what?" asked Grant.

She shook her head again. "Remember, Pablo's a poker player. He holds his cards pretty close. But Julia was asking me to work extra shifts because Pablo was spending less and less time at the Papaya Seed. I know she was worried about whatever he was doing."

"How so?" asked Grant.

For the first time, Aiden hesitated before answering. Grant had plenty of experience knowing when an interview had reached a tipping point and he sensed this was it for the young woman sitting across from them.

"You might as well tell us, Aiden. We didn't fly six thousand miles for our health. I can assure you that we won't be leaving until we find out what it was."

"I overheard them arguing—the day before your cop friend was here." She glanced back toward the shut-down beach bar. "I'd forgotten my sweater and went back to fetch it and I heard them out back, cleaning up."

"And what were they saying?"

"Pablo told Julia he was feeling pressured. And that it was a really bad time for her ex-husband to be showing up."

Grant leaned forward. "Anything more specific?"

"I heard him say they might have to shut down the Papaya Seed. That he'd gotten in over his head and they might take it all away."

"They?"

"He didn't say who. All I know is I show up here after having the weekend off and the place is locked up tight. Next thing I hear, Julia's dead in New York City and Pablo is nowhere to be found." She gave them another shrug. "I'm just saying."

Chapter 11

They spent the better part of a half hour trying to get more information out of Aiden. It wasn't that she was unwilling to help them; she insisted that she didn't know anything more about what Pablo had been up to or where the pressure was really coming from.

She finished up her breakfast, thanked them for the meal, then said she should probably spend the day looking for a new job and went on her way. Rachel couldn't help but admire Aiden's positive attitude despite the fact that she was fresh out of work.

"She's got plenty of time in her life to be further disappointed," Grant said, watching her head for the beach.

He paid the bill; they got their coffees topped off in to-go cups, then returned to the closed-up Papaya Seed. Grant said that since it was just past the time when the beach bar was supposed to open, perhaps someone else might show up who could shed light on Pablo's whereabouts.

But another hour proved fruitless. The tarped hut sat on the shore's edge like a giant wrapped yellow Christmas gift left underneath a swaying palm tree.

Rachel checked her watch, did some calculations, and realized it was already late afternoon in New York and that she hadn't checked in with John yet. It was hard to get used to the fact that they were separated by an ocean and an entire continent. She mentioned this to Grant, who said he could do some poking around at the hotel about the Papaya Seed while she called John, and suggested they meet back by the parking valet in a half hour to plot their next move.

Rachel decided to take advantage of her surroundings and moved onto the sand. She made her way down to the water and stood there with her eyes closed, letting the gentle trade winds coming off the Pacific blow through her hair and the sun beat down on her face.

She wasn't a Zen-type person, but she figured it couldn't hurt to take a deep breath to try to calm the panic that increasingly threatened to overwhelm her since she'd let herself into John's apartment days before.

The net result was her imagining John being dragged down a long jail corridor in cuffs and chains, then thrown into a windowless cell—left to rot for eternity.

So much for a Zen moment.

She had talked to him after arriving at the hotel the previous evening, but their conversation had been brief. She had obviously awakened him, as it had been long past midnight in New York. He had murmured that he loved her, which was all that mattered in the moment, and she had echoed the sentiment and told him to go back to sleep. A much more wide-awake John answered the phone this time.

"Is that the ocean I'm hearing?" he asked after they both said hello.

"I can step away or call you back if it's too loud."

"Stay right there. I can get a vicarious thrill that I'm there walking with you."

Rachel smiled. "I really wish you were."

"Rain check?"

"Absolutely," Rachel told him. "But it's only been sunny and in the high eighties, with a gentle breeze, since we got here."

"That's right. Rub it in."

They kept up the chitchat for a few more moments, even though Rachel knew it was inevitable they'd discuss why they were six thousand miles apart.

John was the one who brought it up first.

"So, tell me what you and the commander have been up to."

Rachel filled him in, ending with Aiden and their just-concluded breakfast.

"Pretty much confirms Julia came to New York looking to get bailed out," observed John. "No wonder she was struggling with how to approach her father."

"She couldn't just call him up or go see him?"

"It wouldn't have been that simple. He didn't take too well to her running off with Pablo," John explained. "The one thing Leo Molinari holds near and dear is family. It's that old Italian thing. You take a vow and you stick to it—till death do you part."

"So her father took your side in things?"

"I wouldn't go that far. But he made it quite clear he was disappointed that our marriage fell apart. He had me to the house shortly after Julia took off and begged me to try and work things out. He told me it hadn't always been good with him and his first wife—but he stuck it out and was there till the bitter end."

"I remember you telling me that she died, right?"

"Breast cancer, didn't make it to fifty. Leo grieved pretty openly for a couple of years until Sophia."

"The new wife."

"That's when things started to go south between Julia and her dad. She was always closer to her mom and dead set against a replacement, especially one that was even younger than herself. It didn't help when Leo announced at a Christmas dinner that they were getting married and hoping to start a family of their own. So things were pretty rocky by the time Pablo came into the picture."

"Lots of family issues, it seems like."

"Which would have made it hard for Julia to go to her father for money after all this time—even though Leo's actually pretty generous with it. But there are always strings attached," John told her. "One night, when he'd had a few too many, he told me about how he did business. 'The Molinari Way' he called it. He'd happily do someone a favor and then just stay in touch after that, casually checking in on them to see how they were. But he was really just biding his time and letting the pressure build."

"Until they paid him back?"

"Or returned a bigger favor. Julia and I had our share of trouble making ends meet at times, but neither of us needed that hanging over our heads. Leo would constantly ask if there was anything he could do, but Julia always refused."

"So, why the change of heart? Pablo?"

"Given his financial situation, I wouldn't be surprised if Pablo had convinced Julia to put pride aside and go to Leo with hat in hand."

"It would be nice to find him and ask," said Rachel.

John said he was doing what he could while holed up in the apartment, working his laptop and cell. All he'd gotten was a lot of *haven't seen him*s and dead ends.

When Rachel glanced at the time display on her phone, she saw that it was well past the half hour when she was supposed to rendezvous with her father, so she reluctantly began to wrap up the call.

"Make sure to give the commander my best and thank him again," John said.

"You know he no longer works at the Yard."

"It's hard to think of him as anything else."

Rachel couldn't help smiling. It was taking some adjusting on her part as well—seeing as how Grant had been a policeman her entire life. "Then I suppose calling him Dad will prove rather difficult?"

"Without question," John replied. "If we're lucky enough to get to that point."

Rachel felt a pang deep inside. In that moment, no amount of sunshine and clear skies could hide the fact that John Frankel was still in one hell of a big mess.

"We can't think that way," said Rachel.

"I'm trying not to."

"I love you, John."

"It's what's getting me through this. Love you too."

Rachel promised to call him later, then reluctantly disconnected. She took one last look at the aqua-blue sea and a sailboat past the break point.

She imagined what it would be like to be alone with John on the boat, lying on the pontoons with drinks in hand, sailing away with no particular destination in mind.

And then turning around to see police patrol boats in their wake, demanding their return to the mainland for questioning.

Rachel sighed and went to rejoin her father.

As they made their way out of the Waikoloa resort and back onto the main highway, Rachel told her father about her phone call with John.

"Makes one wonder how deep a hole Pablo had dug them into," said Grant.

"I wonder how much Julia actually knew," mused Rachel, behind the steering wheel. "Seems to me she would have told John more."

Her father agreed. They were headed south toward Kailua-Kona, the western side of the island's most populated section. According to an in-flight magazine Rachel had read, the other big city was Hilo, on the rainy side. It got more than three hundred and fifty inches a year—hard to believe when you looked out and saw nothing but blue sky, crashing waves, and the bright sun.

Grant's "poking around" in the executive suites of the Hilton had come up with two addresses. One was the realtor who had put through the deal when Pablo had secured the Papaya Seed. His office was in the main village. The other address was Pablo and Julia's home in the hills above it.

Kailua-Kona, usually referred to as simply Kona in normal speech, was a community that had been originally established in the late 1700s by King Kamehameha I, the founder and first ruler of the Kingdom of Hawaii. It was the seat of the government, and for a long time the capital, until it was moved to Lahaina on Maui and ultimately Honolulu.

A National Park now marked the settlement, highlighted by the Royal Fishponds, once trolled by the ruler himself centuries ago.

The village of Kona was a little tourist-trappy for Rachel—a one-mile stretch mostly consisting of red shacks with similar signs plastered on their sides, each offering a high percentage off local goods and souvenirs that she noticed had all been made in China. But there was a sweet pervading smell coming from flowered leis and burning incense on display in every shop. Every five buildings or so, a bar would appear, all advertising long happy hours and promising an ocean view. It was lunchtime and many were already packed, with locals perched on their usual stools, as if doing their best to get tourists to spring for their next round.

Every so often, an actual business was squeezed into the mix, and it was at one of those that her father held open the door for Rachel to enter—Macadamia Realty.

It was a small office, populated by a smiling gray-haired woman in a violet flowered mumu working the desk. A blond-haired guy in a similar patterned aloha shirt, who looked like he'd be more at home catching sets on a surfboard at dawn, was working phones in a back room.

Grant took the lead and inquired about the status of the Papaya Seed. Lexi, the happy receptionist, pointed them in Chet's direction (only a moniker like Biff would have been more appropriate, thought Rachel), and the Grants joined him once he finished his cold call.

Using his British accent to his advantage, Grant spun a story about wanting to park some money in a beachside business and how he'd heard that the Papaya Seed might be possibly up for sale.

"You handled the transition a few years back, I was told," Grant said.

"I did, but it was basically just signing documents and disclosures, and making sure that escrow went through." Chet recounted Aiden's story about the poker game, which had risen to local legend by this point. "Doesn't look like there's much to do this time either," added Chet.

"Oh, so it's come on the market, then?"

Chet shook his head. "Never did. A private transaction again, but it's still pending. Just waiting on some instructions for it to go through."

"That's a shame." Grant made a production of turning toward Rachel. "Should have headed over here last month when we first thought about it."

"Bad timing," agreed Rachel, taking her father's lead.

Grant turned back to face Chet. "I don't suppose there's any wiggle room?"

"I'm afraid we're too far along. Like I said, we're just waiting on the owner. I've got a couple of calls in to him to close things up."

"I don't suppose you can tell me who is buying the place?" asked Grant.

"Not at this point in the process," answered Chet. "It'll all be in the public record eventually. But since you're in the market for a piece of the island, perhaps I can show you some other properties."

Grant shook his head. "No, thank you. That was the one that particularly caught our fancy."

A few minutes later, they were back in the Jeep and heading up the slope of Mauna Loa, toward the neighborhoods looking down on Kailua-Kona.

"Reading between the lines, this sounds like another noncash deal," said Grant.

"Meaning Julia was probably unsuccessful in getting what they needed from her father," surmised Rachel.

She turned onto a road that headed straight up the mountain until it disappeared into a bank of clouds hovering toward the top.

"How do we go about finding out the name of the buyer?" asked Rachel.

"Maybe it's something that John can try and pursue—as my normal channels at the Yard aren't so readily available."

"I'm not sure his are very open these days."

Grant didn't disagree. It wasn't lost on Rachel how much had changed since they'd all met a few months back. Then, the data banks and resources of two of the world's most notable law enforcement agencies, Scotland Yard and the NYPD, had been at their full disposal. Now, both were basically cut off, her father by choice and John by circumstance.

"I still might have a favor or two to collect on," Grant said. "It's the middle of the night in London now, so I'll give them a try a bit later. In the meantime, let's see what we can find at the house."

The higher they got, the more lush the landscape. When rain clouds appeared on the southwest part of the island, they typically clung to the upper slopes of Mauna Loa, bringing a fair share of precipitation to the area while the sun beat down on the beaches only a few miles below. Most locals tended to live in the hills as the blazing sunshine and heat that tourists traveled from all around the world to bask in proved oppressive day in and day out. One even got a sense of the seasons the higher up they decided to settle down.

Julia and Pablo lived on one of the uppermost streets, aptly named 'Opua Road, the Hawaiian word for cloud. There were maybe a couple dozen ranch-style homes, many with porches that were on three-foot caissons as a preventative for the occasional flash floods that occurred during monsoon season. Nearly all featured well-manicured gardens with bright green lawns and myriad roses, orchids, and other tropical plants.

The house was typical of the neighborhood, except it seemed a bit more neglected. The yard looked unkempt; some weeds were starting to poke through the lawn—clearly, they hadn't employed a gardener or been tending to it themselves recently.

Rachel parked in the empty driveway and they approached the front door. A couple of doorbell rings and a few knocks later, they ascertained what they already suspected: Pablo Suarez wasn't keeping a low profile at their residence.

The Grants moved over to the closed garage, which had a thin window on the side for ventilation, clear enough to peer through and see a single parked car—a blue Honda SUV.

"Julia's?" asked Rachel.

"She more than likely got a ride to the airport to catch her plane to the States, rather than leave it in long-term parking, not knowing when she was coming back."

Rachel raised an eyebrow and could see her father process how that sounded. There was definitely an unfortunate prescience to the thought.

Grant motioned for them to continue around to the back of the house. The small yard had a half-filled wading pool, wooden furniture, and a portable grill. Like the garden in front, it hadn't been kept up. Either the residents had lost interest or lacked the ability to maintain things.

Rachel feared the latter.

She was the first to notice the back door.

"Dad."

Grant looked in the direction she was pointing.

One of the glass windows next to the back entrance was cracked open, shards of glass spread on the patio below.

A concerned look appeared on the former Scotland Yard commander's face, and he stepped in front of Rachel to approach the back door. He gently tried the knob and found it easily turned in his hand.

"You stay here," he told his daughter.

Rachel shook her head. "That is so not happening."

"Then stay behind me."

Rachel did so as her father eased open the door. He stepped inside, and before he could say anything, she was standing right beside him.

The kitchen had been turned upside down.

And it wasn't a result of bad housekeeping or neglect. Someone had been in the house and ransacked it.

Whatever the intruder had been looking for hadn't been found in the kitchen; the other rooms in the small house had been given a similar going-over. Drawers were spilled out, sofa cushions overturned, bookshelves in disarray. The two bedrooms, bathrooms, and the living and dining rooms had not been left unscathed.

As they reemerged from the bedroom area, Rachel stopped to take in the trashed living room.

"It looks like it was a cozy place before someone decided to redecorate."

"It appears to have been all for naught," observed her father.

"What makes you say that?"

"There doesn't seem to be a room or surface that hasn't been touched. Leads me to believe that whatever they were looking for, they didn't find it."

Rachel moved over to the fireplace and glanced at a couple of smashed picture frames on the floor. The photos had spilled out. One was a shot of Julia on the beach, mai tai in hand, toasting the photographer. She bent down and flipped over the other one— Julia and a handsome olive-skinned man who she presumed was Pablo, standing next to the Papaya Seed in what seemed much happier times.

"You don't think it could have been some random thief who took advantage of the fact that no one was home?" she asked.

"Seems like a coincidence, given Julia's murder and Pablo's disappearance."

Rachel nodded, seeing her father's point.

She turned to place the frame back on the mantle and screamed.

Grant instantly whirled.

A huge Hawaiian man was standing in the kitchen doorway.

He was wearing a slick suit and threatening expression.

And had his hand on his hip, where his coat had parted just enough for both of the Grants to see it was resting on the handle of a gun.

Chapter 12

The minute John Frankel hung up the phone with Rachel, he was filled with regret.

He felt bad enough that he hadn't laid all his cards on the table for her, but he still wasn't sure what sort of hand he was holding. And he'd promised himself he'd have a clear picture before he showed it to her.

He also regretted that he hadn't been able to accompany them to the Big Island to see what they could learn about Pablo Suarez. Frankel felt he was the one who should have been out there trying to clear his name.

And there was everything he hadn't asked Julia. He was beginning to worry that those answers had died with her in his apartment.

Answers that might also fuel a motive for Frankel killing her and prompt the authorities to hang a murder charge around his neck.

All the more reason to hunt down the guilty party.

There was only so much he could do from Rachel's apartment, and not being a computer expert, he'd been reluctant to do deep dives on the laptop. He knew he could erase his search history but wasn't sure some tech couldn't figure out how to recover it, so he limited his queries. The same went for using his cell phone; he knew it was basically a homing device for those who wanted to track his movements.

All of this was complicated by the certainty that he was being watched by his colleagues, confirmed the few times he'd peeked out his window to see that the lanky brunette had basically taken up permanent residence in the market across the street. Clearly, she'd come to some sort of agreement with the proprietor, informing him of her babysitting duties. Frankel was pretty sure she wasn't the only cop out there; she had just been the only one he'd spotted so far.

So he had just waited until nightfall, having ordered in some Chinese food, and watched the news. Then, around nine, he grabbed his coat and keys.

He cast one glance at the dining table and his cell phone resting on it. He left it there and as he left the apartment hoped that Rachel wouldn't try him in the next hour or two.

Once outside, he looked across the street and made sure he caught the eye of the brunette cop. Before she could look away and pretend she wasn't interested in him, Frankel pointed at the subway entrance to let her know where he was headed.

He couldn't help smiling as the expression on her face tightened, as if left with no choice but to follow him down the stairs to the trains heading downtown.

It was close to ten o'clock by the time Frankel headed up the steps of his home away from home, the Seventeenth Precinct. Before entering, he turned to notice that the brunette had parked herself right outside the building. She was obviously with him for the night.

The cop shop was pretty quiet for a Friday evening—either Manhattanites were on their best behavior or crime was getting a late start. The desk sergeant, a Puerto Rican man in his sixties named Ramirez, who'd been on the night shift as long as Frankel had worked the Seventeenth, looked up and seemed unable to hide his surprise.

"Couldn't stay away from the place, Detective?"

"It gets in your blood," replied Frankel. "But look who I'm talking to."

Ramirez let loose a little laugh as Frankel asked if either Taryn or Harris were still around—he was counting on the fact that it had been a long week for both and that they would have tried to have some semblance of a Friday night. Ramirez validated his supposition by saying Taryn had left a couple of hours earlier and that he had just missed the lieutenant.

"Too bad," said Frankel, not feeling sorry at all.

"I'll tell them you were here, though."

I'm sure you will, Frankel thought.

He told Ramirez to have a good evening and made his way to the bullpen, where a couple of detectives pulling night duty did double takes seeing their embattled colleague. Frankel exchanged pleasantries like nothing was out of the ordinary, telling them he was just picking up some papers. He moved past the duo; it was obvious that neither detective wanted to engage in any sort of conversation with a murder suspect, which was fine with John Frankel.

He rounded the corner toward his office and almost ran over Cletus Flowers, the custodian who was in the process of mopping the parquet floor. A black man built like a middle linebacker who always had a smile on his face, Cletus had been one of the first denizens of the Seventeenth Frankel had met.

"Watch your step, Detective," Cletus told him with a grin.

"I'm trying Cletus. I'm really trying."

He returned the smile and Cletus gave him the most imperceptible of nods.

A couple years into Frankel's tenure at the precinct, Cletus's teenage son Bentley had been caught with a small amount of grass in his backpack at his private high school in the Bronx. Bentley had claimed it had been planted there by a jealous classmate (it seems they liked the same girl) who had subsequently ratted him out. Cletus believed his son, and had poured his heart out to Frankel one night when the detective noticed that the custodian wasn't his usual gregarious self. Frankel had met the kid a few times and found him to be personable and sympathized with him, knowing the impending charges would keep Bentley from playing varsity basketball that year.

Frankel had taken a leap of faith and got the whole thing kicked. It wasn't that big a deal; misdemeanor high school drug cases didn't rate very high on the NYPD docket. But it meant the world to Cletus, who had worked two jobs to get his son the best education possible. Over the next few years, Frankel took pride in seeing Bentley buckle down with a grade point average in the high threes and lead the league in scoring his senior year. He'd gotten a basketball scholarship at a Division II college and Cletus was eternally grateful, always telling Frankel that he owed him one. The detective would say that it was more than enough seeing Bentley on the straight path he'd traveled ever since.

And it was, until John Frankel spent a couple of days being grilled by his colleagues over the circumstances that had led to a dead body being found on his living room carpet.

Upon his release, Frankel had sought out Cletus on his way to the restroom before joining Rachel to head back uptown. He'd told the custodian that if his offer still held, Frankel might want to finally take him up on it.

That led to Frankel giving Cletus a slight, but very thankful, nod back as he entered his office.

He sat down at his desk and made an exaggerated deal of shuffling around various folders and papers while ascertaining that no one was in sight. Then he reached down the side of his desk and opened the lower-most drawer.

It was cluttered with more papers.

Frankel lifted them aside and saw the disposable cell phone that had been left there for him by Cletus. It had definitely been less of a risk than trying to buy one out on the streets with someone watching his every move.

The packaging advertised a few hours of talk time and internet usage. Frankel reached for his wallet and dug inside for a couple of twenties, then traded them for the cell phone, which he put in his jacket pocket. He shut the drawer and spent a few moments moving things around his desk.

He kept one eye peeled on the door until Cletus passed by once more with his mop and another slight nod. Frankel waited until the custodian disappeared from sight, got up, and walked out.

He turned down a hallway in the opposite direction from which he had approached his office. He entered the bathroom at the end of the hall.

Once inside, he bypassed the urinals and stalls—and reached down to move the industrial trash can beside the sink. He placed it beneath the levered glass window on the back wall, then climbed up on top of it.

He wasn't surprised to find the latch unlocked. He counted on the fact that Cletus would make sure to lock it back up a few minutes later.

Frankel managed the eight-foot drop into the alley without breaking any bones.

He wondered how long it would take for the lanky brunette to realize that he wouldn't be walking out the front door of the precinct anytime soon.

It didn't really matter.

Frankel knew he had taken the first steps on a treacherous path from which there was now no turning back until he had the answers he was looking for.

He moved down the alley, turned the corner, and disappeared into the Manhattan night.

Chapter 13

Grant stepped in front of his daughter, putting himself between Rachel and the man in the doorway.

"What are you doing here?" asked the imposing figure.

"I could ask you the same thing," retorted Grant.

"You could. But you're not the one with any sort of official status here. I'm presuming, of course."

Grant felt his shoulders relax as he eliminated this man as a candidate for having done the demolition job on the Suarez-Molinari house.

"Police?" guessed Grant.

"Sheriff's office," answered the man. "*The* sheriff, actually. Guy Lam."

"Austin Grant. Formerly of Scotland Yard." Grant wasn't in the habit of tossing his pedigree around, but figured it couldn't hurt given the current situation. "This is my daughter, Rachel."

A quizzical expression appeared on Lam's deeply bronzed, chiseled face. "Did you take a wrong turn at Newfoundland or something?"

Grant realized transparency was the best way to go here. A check by Lam's colleagues would quickly result in the truth and Grant figured holding nothing back was the best chance at cooperation and gathering information.

"We're looking for Pablo Suarez."

"You and half the people on the island, it seems," said Lam.

Information was exchanged. Lam revealed that his office was working in conjunction with the NYPD and DA investigating Julia Molinari's death. Grant told Lam their search for Pablo was predicated on trying to find a more "logical" person to have committed the crime than Detective John Frankel, who up until recently hadn't seen his ex-wife in three years.

"Who also happens to be your fiancé, you say?" Lam asked Rachel.

"I won't deny I'm naturally biased with a distinct rooting interest."

"I know the detective pretty well myself, Sheriff. He didn't murder Julia," said Grant, looking around the trashed house. "And he certainly didn't do this—unless he's somehow managed to perfect the art of teleportation or telekinesis since we left him back in New York."

Lam nodded. "I'll grant you that, seeing as how I came by here yesterday morning and the place was locked up tighter than a drum."

"So, this is just another run-by check?"

"No, I got a courtesy call from Mrs. Liu, an elderly neighbor who spends most of her day tending roses or sitting in her window staring out at them. She saw the two of you show up about a half hour ago and got in touch."

"Did she happen to mention anyone else popping by? Say in the middle of the night with glass cutters and carving knives?" wondered Grant.

Lam shook his head. "Unfortunately, she doesn't suffer from insomnia. And she's pretty much deaf as the proverbial doornail. Give me a couple of minutes?"

Both Grants nodded.

Lam took in the carnage. "I'd tell you not to touch anything, but at this point, it wouldn't seem to matter much. Be right back."

The sheriff stepped out the front door. Rachel turned toward her father. "What do you think he's doing?"

"Calling in the break-in and checking the two of us out, I imagine. At least, that's what I'd be doing."

That turned out to be exactly what Lam was up to. He returned five minutes later. The sheriff said that a tech crew would be up shortly to go over the place. "I think I also woke up Lieutenant Harris," he added.

Grant checked his watch. "It's not even ten o'clock back in New York. I'm sorry the man has nothing better to do on a Friday night."

"Despite the grumpiness, he did have some nice things to say about you. Even if he was surprised to learn that you were here in the islands."

"I'm sure he was."

"He also said your insight might prove helpful, despite a prejudice towards Ms. Grant's fiancé."

"As fond as I am of Detective Frankel, I'd like to think I can still be objective." Grant nodded at Rachel. "And I think I raised my daughter to behave the same way."

"Then perhaps I could suggest lunch," said Lam. "And we'll compare notes."

<hr />

The Coffee Shack was deceptive, to say the least. From the outside, situated on the main highway in Captain Cook, the district just south of Kona, it gave credence to its name, a wooden, almost dilapidated structure with a carved sign and placards in the plate-glass window hawking sandwiches, bakery items, and coffee.

Once inside, customers were welcomed by a glassed-in case featuring puffy croissants, *malasadas* (Portuguese donuts), and slices of pie. A colored chalk menu on a blackboard listed Hawaiian-inspired sandwiches and various drinks made from the coffee crops of local growers.

But the best part was the covered patio outside the side door overlooking the abundant vegetation stretching down fifteen hundred feet with the Pacific a couple of miles away. The view was spectacular and one could smell the coffee plants that climbed up and down the hillsides and stretched toward the coast.

Lam, Rachel, and Grant occupied a corner table and with the lunch rush over, they had the place and its tropical vista pretty much to themselves, with only a couple of staff members eating a late meal in the opposite corner.

Having finished their sandwiches, the Grants were sharing a piece of macadamia nut pie and what they had learned since arriving on the Big Island.

"You've done quite a lot in one day," Lam said. "Seems to line up with what we know about Suarez—namely that he isn't very handy when it comes to money."

"Any idea whom he owes?" asked Grant.

"We haven't been able to dig up any specific documentation," answered the sheriff. "But he's been spending time with a fellow named Sam Erickson, a real estate developer out of Chicago. Pablo seems to be putting together a deal of some sort with the man."

"What kind of deal?" asked Rachel.

"A golf course development upslope on Mauna Kea, at about three thousand feet with jetliner views. Maybe fifty home sites, club house, championship golf course—there's even been talk about putting a hotel up there as well, but that will never fly because tourists aren't going to come over here to be five miles above the ocean, no matter how incredible the view is."

Grant considered all this—it explained why Pablo would have spent less time around the Papaya Seed, but for a guy who'd gone broke on the north shore not so long ago, it seemed like Julia's boyfriend was overreaching. "How did someone like Pablo get hooked up with a guy like Erickson?"

"The way a lot of business gets done in the islands." Lam motioned toward the ocean and golden sun beating down on it. "A few mai tais by the beach and a tropical sunset. Couple that with Pablo's supposed ability to sell ice to Eskimos, or in this case, a tract of unused land to a rich haole who wants a piece of the paradise rock for himself away from the tourist traps, and a deal is born."

"And how was that working out?" asked Rachel.

"According to Mr. Erickson? Not very well. He told me it had been a one-way cash flow so far—out of his pocket, directly into Pablo's."

Grant chewed on a piece of pie, then motioned with an empty fork. "The land belonged to Suarez?"

"I talked to the original owner," said the sheriff. "Seems like Pablo paid cash for it. Rumor is that followed a pretty good run betting on the NBA playoffs."

Grant nodded. The picture being painted of Pablo Suarez was becoming clearer—smooth-talking scammer, con artist, gambler, take your pick. At the end of the day, it was all bad news. "What was the actual arrangement with Erickson?"

"Suarez offered up the land at what he considered a discount, if Erickson put him in charge of sales, giving tours, and showing models. Erickson agreed and floated out more cash for start-up costs, building a show model unit, rental of construction equipment, etc."

"Totaling more than the purchase price, I presume," Rachel asked.

"At least triple. Maybe more," said Lam.

"And let me guess," offered Grant. "Pablo hasn't delivered a single buyer—in how long?"

"Two months. Going on three." Lam sipped his coffee. "It's not even a hole in the ground. Just a big piece of ancient lava. Go check it out."

"We plan to," said Grant. "Perhaps you can point us in the exact direction?"

Lam said he was happy to do so, even though he told them they were probably wasting their time. No one had seen Pablo Suarez in the vicinity of the development for the better part of a month. He was supposedly out selling plots.

"More than likely running off with his newfound stake," said Grant. "Any idea of how much we're talking about?"

"From what I can gather, around two hundred grand."

Rachel and Grant exchanged glances. "I wonder how much money Julia planned to ask her father for," she said.

Grant nodded, thinking the same thing. Given Pablo's penchant for gambling, he wouldn't have been surprised if it were in the neighborhood of, or exceeded, that amount. He turned toward the Hawaiian sheriff. "How does any of this connect to the break-in at the house?"

"Just was wondering that myself," said Lam. "Sam Erickson doesn't strike me as the type of fellow who works that way."

"And what were they looking for?" asked Rachel. "If it's money, you'd think that Pablo took that with him wherever he disappeared to."

"One would think," agreed the sheriff. "That's if he has any of it left."

"And how does any of this relate to Julia ending up in John's apartment in New York City?" asked Rachel.

That, of course, is the big question, thought Grant.

He sipped from his cup and stared out over the porch balcony. Despite the picturesque view and smooth Kona coffee, he was left with a bad taste in his mouth.

Grant had insisted on paying for lunch in exchange for directions to the Erickson/Suarez development site and a direct cell number for the sheriff so that they could stay in touch.

They all shook hands outside the Coffee Shack.

"How long are you planning to stay on the islands?" asked Lam.

"For as long as the information keeps accumulating or we find Pablo Suarez," answered Grant. "Not that we're even close to understanding the former or finding the latter."

The sheriff wished them luck. They got in their respective vehicles and headed back north on the state highway.

As Rachel drove, Grant checked out a map. Unless you were a sun worshipper (and given Grant's dual disqualification as a native Brit with pale skin that practically glowed in the dark, that certainly did not apply) or a water enthusiast (again—scuba, surfing, and snorkeling were all foreign to a man who had been cooped up at the Yard for decades), tourists spent a good deal of their day traveling back and forth on the road in search of a seaside bar, golf course, or family attraction.

As they traveled through three different climates along a thirty-mile stretch of coast—a sudden downpour just south of Kona that threatened for a moment to wash them off the road, a subsequent heavy windstorm near the airport, and then bright sunshine in a suddenly cloudless sky—Grant felt something building inside that he hadn't experienced in quite a while.

A puzzle to reckon with.

It wasn't so much the lure of the hunt or pursuit of a criminal. He'd never been the sort of policeman who'd relished the excitement of running down a fugitive, slapping a pair of cuffs on their wrists, and putting them away.

Grant had joined Scotland Yard for two reasons.

The first was a compunction to set things right, maintaining a sense of order, okay, justice, if one insisted on putting a label on it.

The other was the conundrum itself, the actual enigma presented him.

Grant wasn't totally sure where it had come from. Perhaps it was reading tons of mystery novels as a child or having always been a crossword addict. He just loved the process of solving things, keeping his brain at work.

That need to complete the puzzle, to make sure every part of the jigsaw fit, was what had driven him his entire life. And for the past six months, he had not been faced with anything to solve.

Until now.

Not that he was thrilled that the man who was slated to be his son-in-law was at the center of it.

But he couldn't deny that the activation of what Agatha Christie's Hercule Poirot used to call the "little gray cells" had been missing in recent days.

He'd have to remember that when this whole sordid business was over.

"I think that's it up ahead on the right," said Rachel, snapping him out of his reverie.

She was pointing at a sign that read *Hala Kahiki*—the name of the development that the sheriff had provided them. There was a tiny arrow at the bottom of the sign and a notation beside it read two miles.

Rachel turned the Jeep onto a dirt road and they began heading up the side of another dormant volcano, the snow-capped Mauna Kea, where you could actually ski right below the observatories and their massive telescopes in the morning and still hit the surf to catch a few waves the very same afternoon.

As they moved up the road, Grant recalled that Lam had told them that *Hala Kahiki* meant pineapple in Hawaiian, so he looked for a field of the distinctive fruit.

But when they arrived at their destination, it turned out to be a tiny guard shack with a signal gate arm lowered, indicating it was the end of the road. Rachel placed the vehicle in park as a perfectly round Hawaiian man in his twenties, who looked like he should be enrolled in sumo-wrestling school, struggled to extricate himself from the small booth.

"Take a wrong turn?" asked the guard, his English clipped by a native accent that probably went back a few centuries.

"Not if this is Hala Kahiki," said Rachel.

"It is," said the guard. "Or I should say, it hopefully will be someday."

"Where are all the pineapples?" Grant couldn't help asking as he looked out over a sheet of black lava rock, stretching seemingly forever.

"It was an off year for crops," replied the guard, flashing a smile.

A bit of a comedian, thought Grant.

Couldn't say he blamed the man for trying—he had to do something to keep himself occupied up here all day long.

Grant let himself out and crossed in front of the Jeep to join the guard. Rachel did likewise.

"I don't suppose Sam Erickson is around?" asked Grant.

"If he was, you'd more than likely see him, don't you think?"

The guard indicated the bleak expanse of land.

"So, he doesn't come up here much?"

"Once a month, maybe? But he calls most days." The guard nodded toward the booth. "Want to leave a message?"

Grant glanced at Rachel. She gave him an *it couldn't hurt, right?* nod. He provided his name and the hotel they were staying at.

"Were you interested in purchasing a lot?"

"We were really interested in talking to Pablo Suarez," said Grant.

The guard's expression went from happy-go-lucky to grim.

"Him." The response was more a grunt than an actual word. "He hasn't been round here since about the time I came on."

"When was that?" asked Rachel.

"Three months. Give or take a week," replied the guard.

"I thought he was up here giving tours."

The guard let out a big belly laugh. "Tours? I can give you a tour." He pointed at the lava rock. "Clubhouse in the center. Golf course around it. Homes surround the course."

Grant started to respond, but the guard raised his hand.

"Or houses spiraling out from the center. The golf course surrounding the homes. The clubhouse at the far end over there."

He pointed north for a moment. Then east.

"Or maybe there."

Then to the west. "Possibly there."

Grant frowned. "Meaning there isn't a tour."

"That's the point, man. There isn't *anything*."

"But you have a job," Grant pointed out.

"Exactly."

Twenty minutes later they were driving back through the gates of the Mauna Kea, Grant staring out the window at the resort's swaying palm trees and vibrant bougainvillea.

He wondered if this type of landscaping was what Erickson had in mind when he'd signed on to back Hala Kahiki.

And if Pablo Suarez had any intention of doing anything except separating the Chicago businessman from as much of his money as possible before vanishing.

They drove past a golf hole at the bottom of the road where one teed off across an ocean cove to reach the green atop a rocky cliff. Grant wished he was one of the golfers currently on the tee, sipping cocktails while freely swinging clubs against the setting tropical sun with no worries but making a par.

Instead, his head felt like one of the balls being whacked into oblivion, with so little of what was going on inside it making any kind of sense.

Rachel's cell rang, interrupting his musings. "Some five-one-six area code I've never seen," said his daughter. "Spam no doubt." Grant nodded as she ignored it and pulled up in front of the hotel to leave the Jeep with the valet.

As they exited the vehicle, Rachel's phone sounded again. This time it was a text; she stopped short. She read it and glanced over at her father.

"It's John. He's saying the five-one-six number is his and that I should call him back."

"Go ahead," said Grant. He motioned to the lobby in front of them. "Fill him in and I'll wait here for you. Then we can figure out what to do next."

Rachel smiled and moved off, already punching the missed call number on her cell.

Grant crossed the lobby to stand at a railing that looked down on the magnificent beach below. It was going to be quite a sunset, the sky already turning a multitude of pastel colors.

"Mr. Grant?"

He turned to find that the concierge had gotten up from her desk and was approaching him.

"Yes?"

"I was just going to send this message to your room, but now that I see you're here—"

"Certainly. Save yourself the trip," said Grant.

"It's from Mr. Sam Erickson. He was wondering if you and your daughter would like to join him for dinner this evening?"

That was fast, thought Grant.

"That would be lovely," replied Grant. "Did he say where?"

"He's reserved a table at our luau for 7:30 p.m."

Grant's face slightly pinched. "Luau?"

"Every Friday night, directly below the pavilion. Aloha wear is strongly recommended."

She gave him a cursory glance, taking in his oxford shirt and slacks.

"I see," said Grant.

"Our plaza shops are open for another hour, if that's convenient."

"Of course they are."

Grant wanted to say that he had rolled up his sleeves, but figured that wasn't aloha enough.

He sighed and thanked her, then waited for Rachel to finish her call, so that she could take him shopping.

Chapter 14

"A burner phone?" asked an incredulous Rachel. "What the hell are you thinking?"

On the other end of the line, John quickly explained the situation, saying how the police and DA's office were monitoring his every move, cell usage, and browsing history.

"I needed some wiggle room," he told her.

"Wiggling your way back into a jail cell seems more like it."

"Going off the grid gives me a chance to check out a few things."

"And I don't suppose you're going to tell me what those things are?"

"Soon, Rach," John assured her.

She became aware of a steady clattering sound. "Are you on a train?"

"I am now. A few buses before that—zigzagging my way north."

"North? Where north?"

"Maine, actually."

"What's in Maine?"

"I'll tell you when I know. Promise."

"You realize you're acting like a guilty person."

"I know that's the way it looks—"

"I really don't understand." Rachel shook her head, frustrated. "Does this have something to do with what Julia told you?"

"It started there," said John. "I just need to play this out; then we can see how it lines up with what you're finding out about Pablo. Tell me how it's going over there."

Rachel filled him in, starting with their finding the Papaya Seed closed down and ending with their trip up the slopes of Mauna Kea to the abandoned lava field.

"Sounds like if you find Pablo, we'll get the answers to a lot of questions," he said.

"But how does this end up with Julia dead in your apartment?"

"Maybe someone's trying to teach Pablo a lesson. You don't get rid of the person who owes the money—but you can definitely increase the pressure on him to get it back."

Despite the humidity, that caused a chill to run through Rachel. John said that she could always text or call him on this number. The only ones who would have it would be her and, of course, her father.

He told her he was going to try to grab a couple hours of sleep on the train while he could and that he loved her.

Flustered, literally almost half a world apart, Rachel could only say that she loved him too; she then begged him to be careful.

After promising to be in touch the next morning, he was gone.

Rachel sighed and crossed the lobby to join her father, who had just finished a conversation with the concierge.

"How's John?" he asked.

"Infuriating. It's like he's auditioning for the lead in *The Fugitive* sequel."

She relayed the substance of their frustrating conversation. Rachel noticed that Grant didn't seem that surprised and asked him why.

"I'd probably be doing the same thing if I were in his situation," Grant explained. "Better than sitting on idle hands. Seems to me that John is running towards something, rather than away from it."

"I hope to God you're right."

Her father gave her a supportive hug, then motioned toward the collection of stores on the floor below the lobby.

"Time for a little shopping trip," he explained. "It seems we suddenly have dinner plans."

———

The walk from their rooms to the grounds where the luau was to take place was so enchanting that it almost made Rachel forget John's predicament and the reason they had traveled to the Big Island.

The sound of a conch shell being blown echoed through the resort, informing one and all that the festivities were about to begin. Rachel and her father emerged from their rooms, a half hour removed from a quick shopping trip where Grant had bought the most muted aloha shirt (cream-colored with yellow orchids) he could find and a beautiful print dress for Rachel. They'd almost been run down by a bare-chested and barefoot handsome Hawaiian with a tiki torch in hand. He'd paused just long enough to light a few lanterns, then continued to move down the path. The Grants fell into step behind the runner, along with other guests, heading past flora that glistened in the pink and turquoise remnants of the setting sun. With the waves crashing down onto the crescent-shaped white sand beach off to one side, and the hotel hanging over the cliff on the other with the fading light reflecting in hundreds of glass window panes, Rachel let herself get lost for a few moments in paradise.

Arriving at the outdoor pavilion where the luau was to take place, they were escorted by a hostess to one of the long picnic tables that had been set up in front of a raised stage made of stone. Blazing tiki torches illuminated the luau grounds with no electric lights in sight, providing a magical aura to the whole proceedings.

Waiting for them at their table was a man in his fifties, who introduced himself as Sam Erickson. He looked quite elegant in a form-fitting aloha shirt and khaki slacks, like he'd just stepped out of a Tommy Bahama catalogue. His brown hair was just starting to fleck with gray, as was a neatly trimmed mustache—he looked exactly like the successful Midwestern businessman that Rachel's Google search had said he was.

"Thank you for getting together on such short notice," said Erickson.

"We were happy to do so," replied Grant. "Considering we were trying to get in touch with you."

"The gatekeeper passed along the message. Your name came up with Guy Lam as well."

"You talk to the sheriff often?" asked Rachel.

"We have a mutual interest in finding Mr. Suarez."

"As do we all," concurred Grant.

"Do you live here in Hawaii?" asked Rachel.

"I go back and forth from Chicago," Erickson answered. "But I try to spend as much time over here as possible. Both kids are in college, so it's just me and my wife, and she loves the Big Island. She'd be happy to move here permanently, but I still need to keep some sort of business presence back home."

"But you're investing in the islands?" asked Grant.

"We built a couple of shopping centers over in Hilo the past few years."

"What about developments like Hala Kahiki?"

"Why don't we eat before getting into all that?" suggested the developer. "Then we can talk before the show starts."

Rachel's father looked perplexed. "Show?" he asked.

"Wouldn't be a luau without hula dancers and fire-eaters."

"Fire-eaters?" Grant repeated.

"Just wait and see," Erickson told them.

He stood up and motioned for the Grants to follow him toward the back of the luau grounds where massive buffet tables were set up with a feast fit for King Kamehameha. Displays piled high with papaya, mango, pineapple, strawberries, and such were surrounded by sashimi, shrimp, sushi, lobster tails, and crab legs with rich-looking sauces. Another table had a dozen different salads with a massive carving station beside it where a quartet of chefs cut up prime rib, turkey, chicken, and the centerpiece of the entire feast, the pig that had been imu-roasting in the fire pit for hours until it was cooked perfectly.

Erickson recommended various items and told them to save room for dessert, indicating a table off to the side stacked with Hawaiian pastries, pies, cakes, and anything that could be made with a macadamia nut.

As Grant filled his plate, he murmured, "If we stay here much longer, I'm going to get so fat I'll be the one they're roasting on that spit next time around."

Rachel and Erickson both chuckled; they all headed back to their picnic bench where everyone ate for a while and didn't talk about what had brought them together. Grant finally shoved his plate away and asked Erickson point blank about Pablo Suarez.

"I can honestly say that I'm sorry I ever made the man's acquaintance," Erickson responded.

"From what the sheriff said, it sounds like Pablo was out of his league a bit?"

"I'd say so." Erickson took another bite, then continued. "Not that I was intent on taking advantage of him, but it sort of goes with the territory. What he was offering seemed like a chance to do something different than just plunking down another resort on a beach—the last thing the islands need right now."

Rachel jumped in, intrigued. "You must have done some background-checking?"

"Enough to know he was a man who took risks. But in truth, real estate speculation is just another form of gambling."

"How did the two of you meet?" asked Grant.

"At his beach bar. I'd gone there with a couple of buddies after a golf round. Pablo had turned the Papaya Seed into a success and seemed to be the enterprising sort who wanted to spread his financial wings. As I mentioned, the deal was pretty enticing—a relatively small purchase price for the exclusive right to collect sales commissions. I figured he was in it for the long haul."

Erickson pushed his plate aside; he shrugged his shoulders.

"I have to admit, I didn't see him being a short-timer, just skipping off with all the start-up costs. At first, I figured it was just a hard sell—high up off the coast, no model home or even a blade of grass to show. I have to say that he hid his desperation really well."

"Owing money elsewhere?" guessed Grant.

"Gambling debts, which according to local gossip have yet to be paid. I know this fellow Daswick is not pleased."

"Daswick?" asked Rachel. "That's a new name."

"Andy Daswick," Erickson told them. "He doesn't bandy his name around unless necessary, seeing how he controls the majority of the bookmaking interests on the Big Island."

Rachel's father leaned forward—she could practically see his curiosity raised. "What else do you know about him?"

"He comes from the West Coast, headed over here in his teens to qualify for the Asian golf tour. When that didn't pan out, he stuck around and gave lessons at one of the clubs up in Waimea to locals. What he was really good at was setting up matches and taking a piece of the action. That branched out into him taking other bets, and you know how that goes—if you're good enough to even up the money on both sides, you'll make yourself a handy living on the vigorish. He's had a pretty good run from what I've heard."

"That seems to be more than a passing interest in the man," Grant observed.

"I like to know where my money has gone, but it appears that Mr. Daswick hasn't been able to recoup what's owed him either."

"How much are we talking about?" asked Rachel.

"You'd have to ask him," replied Erickson. "Maybe you should go to Merriman's at lunch tomorrow and see if you can find out."

"Merriman's?" questioned Grant. "What's that and why there?"

"Best restaurant on the island—up in Waimea. Daswick holds court there most days after the morning high-stakes golf matches he still runs."

"Have you done that?"

"I got together with the man recently, yes. But it's not like I expected him to pay me what he hadn't gotten from Pablo yet." Erickson shook his head. "Like you, like Mr. Daswick, like our friendly sheriff—I just want to know where Pablo has gotten himself off to."

The developer leaned forward, making sure he had their full attention. "It's not so much the money. I can afford the loss. The project was still in its infant stages and I've had much bigger ones fall apart. It's my reputation that is at stake. Once word gets round that I can be fleeced by a nobody like Pablo Suarez, it opens up a floodgate of doubt and con men popping up left and right that becomes impossible to shut down. "

"What do you think I can get out of Daswick that you can't?" asked Grant. "It's not like we have any sort of official authority."

"But you have the appearance of it," Erickson informed them.

"I don't suppose you had a reason to have Pablo's place torn apart?"

"Sheriff Lam mentioned that when he called. I'll tell you what I told him. The man took over two hundred thousand dollars of my money. If he's taken off like everyone supposes, it's unlikely he left that just sitting around."

Rachel looked over to see her father nodding. She turned to Erickson. "Do you think it's something this man Daswick might do?"

"Again, you'd have to ask him," replied Erickson.

Suddenly, a loud gong sounded.

Both Grants, especially Rachel's father, visibly reacted. "What's that? Not more food, I hope. I couldn't eat another blessed thing."

"The show is about to start," explained Erickson. "I realize you're not here on vacation, but there are certain things worth experiencing that you won't find in New York City or jolly old England."

Rachel, after a week that had been more exhausting than any she could remember, welcomed the respite. She hoped her father felt the same way and was happy to see that he seemed engrossed in the performance once it was underway.

After a few torches were extinguished, an older Hawaiian woman in a multicolored mumu took center stage and began to emcee a show that encompassed the history of Hawaiian dance and tradition—replete with gorgeous hula dancers and shirtless fire-eaters with physiques that belonged on any NFL squad.

Rachel found herself caught up in the music and stories, happy to forget about dead bodies and missing suspects, not to mention wondering why her fiancé was heading up to Maine.

At one point in the show, the emcee called upon audience members to join the hula girls in the hukilau, the most recognizable of Hawaiian dances. Naturally, sitting in the front row of tables with an expression on his face that said *they'd better not pick me*, Grant was the first chosen to go up on stage. He immediately protested, saying he wasn't a dancer, but was chided and shamed enough by both Erickson and his daughter that he had no choice but to join half a dozen other tourists in learning how to swing his hip, cast his "net out into the sea" and get the "'ama'ama" to come "a-swimming."

Rachel and Erickson both laughed watching the former Scotland Yard commander clumsily work his way through the moves. But he eventually got the hang of it—and though she knew her father would never admit it, Rachel was convinced that he'd actually enjoyed himself.

"I'll never forgive you for dragging me to this thing," Grant told Erickson when he rejoined them, not fully succeeding in hiding the trace of a grin.

"I only wish Mom could have seen that," said Rachel.

Her father nodded. "She would have loved it. That's for sure."

Once the show ended, people started to get up from the tables and head back to their rooms. Grant told the waitress to put the meals on his bill, but Erickson wouldn't have it, saying dinner had been his idea and that Grant's performance had well been worth the price.

As Erickson signed the credit card receipt, he told them he hoped he had been helpful.

"There is one thing we haven't really discussed," said Grant.

"And what would that be?"

"Julia Molinari."

"The poor girl." Erickson handed the receipt to the waitress and turned back toward Rachel and her father. "I only met her a couple of times.

Early on. She seemed totally dedicated to Pablo—definitely caught up in his dreams. That's about all I can say."

"Any reason to believe that Pablo might have killed her?" asked Grant.

"That seems to be more your department than mine," answered Erickson. He thought about it for a moment. "I think it's safe to say Suarez is nothing more than your common con man or hustler. He obviously isn't the type to let a business arrangement or sense of morals stand in the way of getting what he wants, but I think he'd stop short of murder."

He shook his head.

"So, I'd have to say no—but, of course, that's just *my* opinion. Look at the ride that Pablo's taken me on—he certainly fooled me."

———

As they left the luau area, Erickson told them to make sure they checked out Manta Ray Cove. After giving Grant his direct cell number and asking to keep him updated on what they found out about Pablo, he bid them both goodnight and headed up to the lobby.

Rachel and Grant went in the other direction, following the insignias of a manta ray painted on lava totem poles with arrows directing them to a steep set of rocky steps descending to the ocean. At the bottom of the stairs, a number of guests were leaning against a curved stone wall illuminated by tiki torches, peering at the swirling water below.

A pair of bright floodlights illuminated a cove of rocks and surging tides, where two of the huge fish that gave the spot its name circled back and forth in a steady, graceful rhythm. They stared at the manta rays that could have been twins in a synchronized swimming competition, mesmerized by their massive wingspan, long pointed tails, and ability to glide along with ease.

"Pretty majestic," Rachel said softly, as if she were afraid to disturb them.

Grant nodded and continued to watch them swim along, never varying from their path. "I know how they feel," he finally said.

"How so?"

"We've spent the entire day asking questions about Pablo, going around in circles like these fellows down below, and keep ending up back in the same place. Pablo is still missing and owes everyone money."

"You have a different suggestion?"

"I realized talking to Erickson just now about Julia that we'd almost forgotten the reason we're here—trying to find out why someone would do what they did to her."

"You're saying we should refocus?"

"We should absolutely go see this bookmaker at lunchtime tomorrow," said her father. "But we should also start backtracking what Julia Molinari was doing right up to the time she ended up in New York."

Rachel felt her stomach tightening. "You're talking about the weekend that John was here."

She turned toward him and could see the fatherly concern in his eyes. "I could pursue that myself if it's difficult for you," he told her.

"I'm here, right?" She shook her head. "We've come too far to avoid the truth."

The next morning, Rachel was sitting on the chaise outside her room, sipping a cup of coffee as the sun rose over the white-capped Mauna Kea, the light reflecting off the domes of the observatories atop it. She was just starting to search her contacts for Aiden, the girl who worked at the Papaya Seed, wondering how early she could call and set up a time for her and Grant to get together for a follow-up chat about Julia, when her cell buzzed.

Rachel studied the caller ID and after noticing a number of missed calls from the same number, paused, seriously thinking about not answering it, but in the same moment realized that the caller would just persist and that talking to her was unavoidable.

"Taryn?"

"What the hell are you doing in Hawaii?" The NYPD detective's voice came through loud and clear from six thousand miles away. She didn't sound pleased.

Rachel's mind raced, remembering that the sheriff had woken Lieutenant Harris on Friday night.

"I'm sure the lieutenant has already told you what's going on, Taryn. You really can't expect us to just sit around and do nothing to help John."

"Speaking of your fiancé, have you talked to him recently?"

Ah, thought Rachel. *The true purpose of the call.*

Rachel knew she was suddenly in a position where she had to think quickly—especially with the stakes at hand.

"What do you consider recently?" Rachel asked, trying to buy a few seconds.

"The last time you talked to him. It's not a difficult question." The detective was clearly losing patience.

Rachel sighed inwardly and made what she hoped was the right decision.

"Early this morning, first thing," Rachel responded, neglecting to mention the call from the burner phone shortly before they headed to dinner. "Why?"

Rachel listened with growing concern as Taryn relayed the circumstances of John sneaking out of the precinct the previous evening and not being seen or heard from since. Even though she knew that John had ditched whoever was watching him, Rachel had no idea he had gone to such extraordinary lengths to shake them.

"Care to reconsider your answer?" asked the detective.

Realizing she had to stick with what she'd already told Taryn or get caught in a half-truth which could only lead to more trouble for John, Rachel decided to double down.

"I told you, Taryn. Early this morning, this afternoon your time."

There was a definite pause on the other end of the line. Rachel could imagine John's partner seething at her desk.

"You'll let me know when you hear from him next?" Taryn finally asked.

"It depends on what he has to say."

At least there's a ring of truth in that statement.

"He's my partner, Rachel. I feel just as bad about all this as you do."

"I sincerely doubt that, Taryn."

And knowing there was nowhere for the conversation to go after that, Rachel said goodbye and hung up.

She stared out at the breaking waves on the beach, watching the tide recede along with any hope that this whole mess would end up being something besides John, Rachel, and her father against everyone else.

Not for the first time since they'd arrived in paradise did Rachel Grant find herself praying that her fiancé knew what the hell he was doing.

Chapter 15

Taryn Meadows couldn't believe it.

Rachel had actually hung up on her. Taryn thought she'd squeezed a quick goodbye in, but a hang up was a hang up.

Part of her couldn't blame the woman. Probably had been thinking of her wedding day since she was five and now here it was, a week away, and suddenly her fiancé is one step from a murder one charge. And instead of preparing for the big day, she was on a tropical island, not with her husband-to-be, but her father, playing amateur sleuth, trying to put another suspect in front of Taryn and her colleagues.

The other part of Taryn couldn't look past John Frankel. Despite her loyalty to her partner, she was still a cop and couldn't deny that current circumstances looked very bleak for Rachel making that trip down the aisle.

It was more than just the fact that Frankel's *ex-wife* had been found dead in *his* apartment. There was his refusal to narrow his movements and provide any alibi for the time frame of the murder. And now he was acting like a guilty man—most recently slipping his surveillance.

Dunham, the plainclothes cop who'd been on Frankel watch, had sat outside the precinct for over an hour before deciding to venture in and check on what John was doing. When she didn't spot him in his office and asked the few cops on duty if they'd seen the detective head out, Dunham had intensified her search of the building until it became clear that Frankel had slipped out the back.

This had resulted in Taryn being awakened in the middle of the night by Dunham with the bad news.

Taryn wasn't sure if she was more disappointed that she hadn't seen this coming or that it actually meant her partner might have murdered his ex.

Either way, it had meant coming into the precinct on a Saturday, probably to get reamed by Lieutenant Harris.

She had called Rachel, and when she'd finally reached her after numerous tries, she told Taryn she hadn't heard from Frankel since he had ditched Dunham. Taryn didn't believe Rachel Grant for a single second. She also knew she'd have a hard time proving it. With over a decade as an NYPD detective, Frankel knew his way around phone traces and credit card checks well enough to not let Taryn, Dunham, Harris, or any of the techs keep up with him.

So she'd trudged back down the hall to her superior's office to tell him as much and was actually surprised when Harris didn't lay into her.

Instead, he asked Taryn if she'd talked to Carla Esposito yet.

Taryn shook her head.

She'd never heard the name before it came out of her lieutenant's mouth.

Carla Esposito had been wrestling with her conscience for three days.

That was how long it had been since she'd first caught the news story about the murder in the cop's apartment and seen the dead woman's picture.

She probably would have made a phone call that first night but she had been worried about Benito.

The two of them had been going out for a year and were talking about getting married. Benito treated her like a princess, which no other man in her twenty-eight years on planet Earth had ever done. He was kind, worked hard for his money in a garage up on 107th Street, and split all the bills with Carla for the tiny studio apartment they shared in Queens.

The problem was that Benito was in the country illegally, and both of them were constantly waiting for ICE to bang down their door and haul him a couple thousand miles south to Mexico with no hope of his getting back across the border.

So getting in touch with the cops had been the last thing on Carla's mind—not wanting to bring them anywhere in Benito's vicinity, where they might figure out he was a nonresident of the United States of America.

But she couldn't stop thinking about what she'd seen in Broadway Union, the small diner where she was a waitress. It was a steady job; she'd gone from dishwasher to being in charge of closing up three nights a week in just two years, and there was talk of a promotion to manager in the near future.

If only she hadn't been working *that* particular night.

Benito had noticed something weighing on her and she'd finally told him what she'd witnessed. When she said she was worried speaking up might jeopardize their being together, Benito told her she had to come forward.

First of all, Benito had nothing to do with the situation and there was no reason for his name to come up.

And secondly, it was her civic duty to go—he longed for the day they would be wed and he could get his green card (Carla being a second-generation American) and he could exercise his rights as a responsible citizen in the same way.

It was just one more reason she loved him so much.

And that's how she found herself in an interview room at the Seventeenth Precinct on a Saturday afternoon in late June, speaking with Lieutenant Desmond Harris and Detective Taryn Meadows.

"How come you waited till now to come see us, Ms. Esposito?" asked Harris.

"I only caught the news report yesterday," Carla responded. "I've been working the late shift and I'm pretty much dead on my feet when I get home."

Okay, a little white lie. But there's no way for them to know I saw it earlier.
Carla watched as both cops nodded.

"That's understandable," said the other cop. "Tell us a little more about what happened last week. It was near closing time, you said?"

"Yeah, around nine thirty. We stay open till ten but when business is slow, we sometimes shut down a bit early. It was just me and Vince there when she came in."

"Vince?" asked the female detective.

"The cook—and he didn't see anything because he was back in the kitchen," Carla explained. "So, she wanders in and asks if it's too late to get a cup of coffee. I couldn't very well say no, not with the sign saying closing time's ten on the door."

"And by 'she,' we're talking about Julia Molinari?" asked Harris, sliding a photograph across the table.

Carla took it reluctantly, worried she was going to be looking at some photo of a corpse, but was relieved to see it was the headshot she'd seen on the newscast.

She nodded. "Yep. Definitely her."

Harris held up a second shot. "And this man came in soon after that?"

Carla nodded again. "That's him. Showed up when I was serving her a cup of coffee. He's a cop, right? Does he work here?"

"Usually," said Taryn. "But Detective Frankel's on temporary leave right now while we further investigate the matter. What happened once he came in?"

"He asked if we had chocolate milkshakes. I said we did and he said he'd have one if it wasn't too much trouble. Very polite, he was. I said sure and went into the kitchen to whip one up."

"Leaving just the two of them in the restaurant?" asked Taryn.

"Like I said, I was getting ready to close. We're pretty much a breakfast and lunch place—it's quiet at night. Especially on the weekends."

"And what did you see when you brought the milkshake?" asked Harris.

"The two of them were obviously arguing—"

"Obviously?" prodded the lieutenant.

"Well, she was actually crying and he was doing most of the talking."

"Was he yelling?" asked Taryn.

"Not so much. But he did slap his hand on the table a couple of times. I heard him say—'Why won't you tell me?' or 'What aren't you telling me?'"

"Which one was it?"

"I really don't recall. But they stopped the moment they both saw me, and that's when she got up."

"Got up and left?" asked Taryn.

"Went running out. Definitely in tears."

"And then?"

"He—Detective Frankel—threw some money on the table and went chasing after her."

"Anything after that?"

Carla shook her head one more time. "They disappeared around the corner and that was the end of it. Me and Vince closed up and knocked off for the night."

Both cops scribbled furiously on notepads. The lieutenant was the first to look back up at Carla, who was just relieved that Benito was nowhere on their radar. She couldn't wait to tell him that he'd been absolutely right.

"And this was last Sunday night?" asked Harris.

"Absolutely," answered Carla. "The night before her body was found, right?"

Eileen Crowe knew that she should have accepted the invitation out to the Hamptons, but she had too much damn work and the last thing she wanted to do was sit on the Jitney for three hours on a Friday night just to turn around and take what would probably be a longer return trip on Sunday.

So she was unfortunately home in her Chelsea apartment on Saturday afternoon when the doorman rang to tell her that a police detective was in the lobby asking to see her.

Five minutes later, Eileen opened the door to let Taryn Meadows inside. The detective took in the modern décor and bright western exposure that made the vibrant colors of her Hockney and Lichtenstein lithographs really pop.

"The lawyering business seems to be awfully lucrative," observed Taryn.

"I'd be happy to give you an art tour if you'd like, but I suspect this isn't a social visit on a Saturday afternoon."

Eileen imagined it took a lot of effort for Taryn to fashion what had to be a forced smile.

"I need to talk to your client."

"Isn't he your partner? I'd think you'd know how to find him."

"Well, that's where you're wrong, counselor."

Eileen had no choice but to listen as Taryn told her how John Frankel had evaded the surveillance put on him and had apparently dropped out of sight.

"When's the last time you saw or talked to him?" asked the detective.

"Two days ago, when we left your precinct. I was going to check with him after the weekend unless something came up before that."

"Something has—which is why we need to talk to him again."

"Well, if and when I hear from him, I most certainly will pass that along."

The smile had long disappeared from Taryn Meadows' face. Eileen watched the detective glance around the room.

"Would it be okay if I used your restroom?" Taryn asked suddenly.

"By all means," Eileen said, indicating a corridor off the dining room. "Feel free to check out the bedrooms and office as well. I don't think you'll find Detective Frankel hiding away in any of them, but you never know."

Despite the glowering look, Eileen was impressed that Taryn didn't miss a step and headed toward the other rooms in the apartment.

She returned five minutes later and Eileen noticed that the smile had returned to her face and she didn't like it one bit.

"Here's the deal," said Taryn. "I want John Frankel in my office between now and Monday morning at ten o'clock. If he isn't, we will immediately issue a BOLO and arrest warrant for your client and I guarantee you won't be able to put him back on the streets as easily this time. He will be classified as a flight risk and charged with violating the restrictions placed on him at the time of his release. Understood?"

"Perfectly," replied Eileen. "And what exactly has come up that you want to talk to him about?"

"Find your client, Ms. Crowe. Then, come on down and we'll chat."

At which point Taryn said she would find her way out, leaving Eileen wondering if it weren't too late to take her friends up on the Hamptons offer and join them for the rest of the summer.

Chapter 16

Heading up the hill to the inland town of Waimea, Grant sat in the passenger seat, once again considering the perilous path that Frankel was on. There was no question that his "escape" from the Seventeenth Precinct looked like the act of a guilty man and Grant had to imagine that Lieutenant Harris and Detective Meadows were finding it increasingly difficult to believe their colleague had nothing to do with the death of his ex-wife.

So, it wasn't surprising when Rachel voiced similar doubts from behind the steering wheel.

"Why won't John tell us what he's up to?" asked his daughter as they continued to climb the road.

"Perhaps because you can't share what you don't know with the authorities," replied Grant.

"But we're already guilty of lying to them—saying that we haven't heard from him since he went on the run." Rachel flicked on the windshield wipers, as raindrops started to splash the windshield from a bank of storm clouds that had gathered above Mauna Kea. "Well, at least I am."

"I would've done the same thing."

"That's nice of you to say."

"It's true. You haven't done anything illegal. So far, it's just an inquiry by the police wanting to know John's whereabouts. And you've got no idea."

"I know he's headed to Maine."

"Not one of your larger states, but it doesn't exactly narrow things down. Especially if John hadn't told you the truth."

"You don't believe him?"

Grant gave her a slight shrug before answering. "Let's just say I want to."

"Me too," said Rachel with a sigh.

They had arrived at Merriman's in the middle of the lunch hour, figuring they could get back to the hotel by three o'clock to meet Aiden, who had agreed to see them again.

The restaurant was in a cottage on the main road into Waimea. It seemed to be doing a brisk business, with most of the parking spaces occupied.

The Grants ducked through the now-constant drizzle and made their way inside, where they were greeted by a smiling hostess. When asked if they had a reservation, Grant shook his head and asked if Andy Daswick was dining with them that afternoon.

"He is," acknowledged the hostess. "Is he expecting you?"

Grant said no, but turned on his British charm and wondered if she might tell him they just needed a few moments to discuss Pablo Suarez. The pleasant accent seemed to do the trick and the hostess told them to wait while she went and checked.

A few minutes later, Grant and his daughter were being escorted through the restaurant. It was a brightly lit space with different sections separated by moveable planter boxes housing miniature palm trees. They arrived at a corner table adjacent to the kitchen, allowing its occupant easy access to a constant stream of Hawaiian delicacies and a view of the entire room, so that no one could show up at his table unexpected.

Andy Daswick was an extremely large man. There was really no other way to put it. His garish aloha shirt draped a rock-solid upper body, which Grant figured must have come from endless hours spent in a weight room, transforming the huge amounts of food he had piled in front of him into bulging muscles. Grant wondered how far the man could have crushed a golf ball when he was trying to become a professional. One thing he knew—he wouldn't have wanted to be on the receiving end of a swing by him.

"Sorry to interrupt your lunch, Mr. Daswick," said Grant.

"I should think so," agreed the man. His voice was gravelly, only adding to an imposing presence. "Especially when it concerns my least favorite subject."

"Pablo Suarez," suggested Rachel.

"My own personal Voldemort."

Grant looked confused and glanced at Rachel. "A Harry Potter reference," she told him. "The name that shall not be mentioned."

"Ah," said Grant, not fully understanding but letting it pass.

"I'd be correct presuming you're not here to make good on his debt?" asked Daswick.

"You would be," answered Grant.

He could feel the bookmaker sizing him up. "Let me guess. He owes you money as well."

"The only thing he owes us is an explanation for where he was around the time his girlfriend was murdered in New York City."

Grant further explained the situation, starting with their connection to the victim, then their journey to the islands and conversations with the sheriff and the developer Erickson.

"You've been busy. But I don't see how any of this connects me to the dead girl."

"Pablo Suarez owes you a substantial amount of money. It's not beyond the realm of possibilities that you're exerting pressure to get it paid back."

"By killing a woman half a world away from here? You're giving me credit for a much longer reach than I have. I've got my hands full dealing with eight islands here, never mind the mainland," explained Daswick.

"How much money does Pablo owe you?"

"One hundred and forty thousand dollars. By the end of today, it's one hundred and fifty."

Grant might have whistled out loud if he'd been able to do so. "Quite the interest rate."

"I'm a bookmaker, not a money lender."

"How does someone lose that much gambling?" asked Rachel.

Daswick's chuckle rippled the orchids and palm trees on his shirt. "By picking lousy teams."

"No, I meant, how do you allow him to get in the hole that much without collecting?"

"Suarez had won and lost similar amounts over the past few months—and always paid up before this. He had a hot streak early on, but if you play long enough, you're going to give it back. And owe dough you don't have."

"Meaning he went through the money that Sam Erickson had advanced him?" asked Grant.

"I don't really care where it came from. The check cleared my bank account. That's all that mattered."

"When did he lose the money he owes you now?"

Daswick was quiet for a moment, then mentioned a date.

Grant wasn't surprised to hear that it corresponded with the week prior to Julia's murder— around the time Frankel had come to the Hawaiian Islands.

"What happens if he refuses to pay?" asked the Scotland Yard man.

"You don't need to worry about me," Daswick told him. "The interest hits a certain number, my money becomes guaranteed."

Grant's eyes widened with the realization. "The Papaya Seed."

"You've done your homework."

"You'll be happy to know the realtor didn't identify you by name," Grant informed him. "Just that a transaction was in the works."

Daswick nodded. "When Pablo's picks began to hit the skids, I told him he had to put the place up as collateral if he kept insisting on trying to get whole. Of course, this was when I'd hear from him on a daily basis. But it's been over a week since he last placed a bet."

"But people aren't under any legal obligation to pay you," Rachel pointed out. "How do you make sure you always collect?"

"You need not worry about me, Ms. Grant. I *always* get paid."

"Any chance you dropped by his place to make your point?" asked Grant.

"Me personally?" Daswick shook his head. "It's not the way I roll."

"But someone you know?"

Daswick let out another little chuckle—one that Grant felt a touch unnerving.

"You don't really expect me to answer that, do you?"

Neither Grant nor his daughter pushed the issue, but at least one mystery had been solved. Not that anyone would be able to pin the break-in on the man.

The bookmaker pointed to the half-dozen plates on the table that would be a feast for a quartet of diners but that in Daswick's case just qualified as lunch.

"Can I interest you in something to eat? They are known throughout the islands for their charred ahi."

Grant shook his head. He was pretty certain he didn't want to owe this man anything—even a meal. He thanked Daswick for the offer and his time.

The Grants took their leave. Moments later, they were back in the Jeep. During the brief time in the restaurant, the rain clouds had dissipated and the sun was back to baking the upper reaches of the island as well as the beaches down below.

"It's hard to believe that there isn't some correlation between Julia's death and Pablo's debts," Rachel said, as they began their descent down the hill.

"She supposedly was in New York to see her father about money. Perhaps it was to bail out Pablo?"

"Certainly a question worth asking," agreed Rachel.

—⁓—

Half an hour later, Rachel posed it to Aiden.

"Julia didn't mention money specifically, but I knew she was worried about getting in touch with her father."

The three were walking along the white-sand crescent beach stretched out below the hotel. The former Papaya Seed employee was wearing shorts and a tank top while Rachel had slipped on a skirt and T-shirt. Grant, who had definitely not packed for the tropics, was back in his newly purchased shirt and had his khakis rolled up to his knees, exposing way too much pale white British skin, as the edge of the gentle tide trickled against their feet.

Grant had told her about Pablo's debt to Andy Daswick, and this had all been news to the girl.

"I had no idea he owed that kind of money. But it certainly explains the Papaya Seed shutting down," said Aiden.

"What about Julia?" asked Grant. "What was she like right before she left? Was she anxious? Depressed?"

"Maybe a bit pressured. But it goes with the territory, right? Running a beach bar's kinda treacherous—keeping up with the trends and next hot spot." She turned toward Rachel. "But things seemed to get more intense after she heard from your fiancé."

"How so?" asked Rachel.

"She told me she was pretty blown away, not having spoken to him in three years. She also seemed to be kicking herself, saying she should have seen it coming."

"Seen what coming? Being called out for not signing the divorce papers?"

"She wasn't specific. Just told me she regretted the way she'd left things with her husband. That she'd acted stupidly and now it was all catching up with her."

"Acted stupidly?" repeated Rachel, who Grant could tell was having trouble with where this was heading. "Do you mean she wished she'd never left John?"

"No, she was in love with Pablo. There was no denying that." Aiden shook her head. "I think it had something to do with those first few months she was here—back when they had tried to make a go of that place up in Hawi. I remember Julia telling me it turned out to be a lot harder than she ever thought—like it wasn't what her and Pablo had signed on for. But I didn't know her back then; we only met once before they took over the Papaya Seed."

"So you mentioned," said Grant.

"But I know some folks up there who work the beach. I could ask around, see if there's someone worth talking to who could tell you more."

"That would be really helpful."

"It's the least I can do. Julia was a good friend. But I always felt she was holding a part of herself back. It didn't make me care for her any less, just a little sorry that she'd been dealt more than her share of bad cards in life."

"But she had a few lucky ones with friends like you," said Grant, giving her a genuine warm smile.

"Thank you for saying that." Aiden turned to face the ocean, her expression darkening despite the afternoon sun. "A lot of good it did her in the end."

Grant walked Aiden up to the lobby and told her not to hesitate to get in touch with anything else she remembered. He was surprised when she gave him a big hug and wished him luck in finding out what had happened to Julia.

"We won't stop till we get to the truth," vowed Grant.

"She deserves at least that," said Aiden. She wiped her moist eyes, hopped in her car, and drove away from the hotel.

When Grant returned to the beach, he found Rachel sitting atop one of the rocks, seemingly having inherited Aiden's glum mood. Grant climbed up and sat down beside his daughter, who was staring out at the turquoise sea.

"Thinking about John?"

"It's hard not to." She turned to face him. "What if things weren't done between him and Julia? Maybe John's been yearning for her ever since she left him and things suddenly heated back up once they saw each other again. For all I know he was just working up the nerve to call off the wedding when—"

Rachel suddenly broke off, as her father smiled.

"I'm starting to spin a bit, aren't I?"

"A little, perhaps."

Grant's cell buzzed. He looked at the number.

"Aren't you going to answer?" Rachel asked.

"It's no one I know."

"Maybe it's John, using a different burner phone."

Grant nodded and took the call. "Austin Grant."

"Exactly who I'm looking for."

The voice had the slightest trace of an accent. Spanish, if Grant weren't mistaken. He asked who was calling, even though he had a fairly good idea.

"Pablo Suarez."

"Pablo," said Grant, watching Rachel visibly react to the name. "We've been wanting to talk to you. We're over here on the Big Island. Any chance of us getting together later?"

"That might be difficult," said Pablo. "I'm on the mainland."

"New York?" asked Grant.

"No. I'm actually up in Maine."

Chapter 17

"I'm putting you on speaker phone," said Grant.

"I'm not talking to the cops," blurted Pablo on the other end of the call.

"The only person with me is my daughter Rachel. The two of us came to Hawaii looking for you."

Rachel watched her father tap the speaker button on his cell.

"Well, that seems to have been a waste of time, wasn't it?"

Pablo's slight laugh echoed in the ocean air.

"It's Rachel Grant, Pablo. What are you doing in Maine?"

"Getting the answers to my troubles."

"Seems like you've had more than just a few," Grant pointed out.

There was a pause on the other end of the line.

"I didn't kill Julia," Pablo finally said.

"Perhaps you should tell that to the New York Police Department," said Grant.

"I figure you can do that for me."

"I'm not in the habit of being a conduit," Grant told him. "Is that why you're calling?"

"I'm just telling you that I couldn't have done it."

"I don't think your word carries much weight these days."

"I understand why you'd say that," said Pablo. "But I was on a plane to meet up with Julia when she was killed."

"There's no record of you taking a flight that day," Rachel pointed out.

"I caught a ride on a private plane with a buddy. Feel free to check it out."

Pablo provided a name and a phone number. Rachel quickly entered it on her cell phone.

"Instead of looking for me, you should tell Erickson and Daswick that I'll have their money shortly. Probably by the end of the week."

"How's that going to happen?" asked Grant.

"I'm not prepared to say just yet."

"For a man who got in touch with me to talk, you haven't been very forthcoming, Mr. Suarez."

"Just let Erickson and Daswick know."

"How did you even know we were over here looking for you?" asked Grant.

Instead of an answer, the Grants got a click as Pablo hung up.

A clearly puzzled Rachel turned toward her father. "John's on his way to Maine too."

"That fact wasn't lost on me."

Rachel tried her fiancé's burner phone number, but all it did was ring. There hadn't been any voice mail set up, so there wasn't even the expected beep and she was unable to leave a message. John said she could text, so she sent one, urging him to get in touch as soon as possible.

As Rachel looked up at her father in frustration, one thing was clear.

Whatever was happening right now in the Julia Molinari investigation was playing out in the northernmost state of Maine, while the two of them seemed to be wasting their time in the Hawaiian Islands.

It was time to head back home.

More phone calls.

While Rachel made a few checking them out of the hotel and securing reservations on a pair of connecting flights back to New York, Grant dialed the number given them by the elusive Pablo Suarez.

He'd ended up reaching a wealthy playboy-type named Manulis, who had a bit of the gambling bug himself. It turned out that Pablo had hooked him up with the very same high-stakes poker crowd that a few years back had netted Julia's boyfriend the rights to the Papaya Seed. A grateful Manulis, who had cleaned up in the game, had been happy to let Pablo hop aboard his private jet back to the mainland on the previous Sunday evening, the night before Julia Molinari's body had been discovered in John's apartment.

They had landed in Pittsburgh midday on Monday and Pablo had rented a car to drive to Manhattan from there, making it seemingly impossible to be in town in time to murder his girlfriend.

Grant figured this was something easily enough checked on by NYPD and was much more concerned with what was happening up in Maine, where both Pablo and John were apparently heading. Certain that this was no coincidence, he was anxious for his daughter to get some sort of reply from her text message to John.

But by the time they had packed their luggage and left the hotel, they still hadn't heard from him.

They were halfway to the airport when the next call came.

On Rachel's phone. She glanced at the phone display.

"It's Eileen Crowe."

Grant asked if she could put it on the Jeep's Bluetooth system. As a total Luddite, he certainly wouldn't have been able to pull off that small miracle. Rachel punched a few buttons and the attorney's voice came over the speaker.

"Hi, Rachel. It's Eileen."

"Hi, Eileen. I've got you on the speaker with my dad. We're on our way to the airport."

"Headed back, are you?"

"Yes," said Grant. "Our plane leaves in about an hour. We've got a short layover in Honolulu, then should get into New York tomorrow morning."

"Not a moment too soon," said Eileen.

Grant didn't like the sound of that.

And a few minutes later, after Eileen had filled them in, he liked it even less.

The lawyer explained how she'd been paid a visit by Taryn Meadows, who'd demanded that John appear in the precinct by Monday morning or there would be a warrant out for his arrest. The detective had been reluctant to tell her anything more, but Eileen had done some digging and discovered that a waitress at a downtown diner had placed Frankel and Julia there the night before the murder, having an argument that had ended with Julia leaving in tears.

He watched Rachel throughout the tale and was glad she kept the car on the road, knowing she must have the same sick feeling that he did.

"Have you heard from John recently?" asked Eileen.

Grant exchanged glances with Rachel. She started to open her mouth—and seemed to think better of it, as if waiting for a cue from her father. Grant raised a solitary finger, indicating that he could take the lead.

"What's the old adage? Lawyers should think long and hard before asking a question they don't know or don't want to know the answer to?"

"Ah, that old adage." He could hear Eileen repress a sigh. "I seem to recall hearing that on my first day in law school."

"So, you were asking?"

There was a pause. Grant imagined Eileen's brain whirring.

"What I *meant* to say was that on the off chance you should hear from Detective Frankel, it might be a good idea for him to know where things stand."

"*If* we hear from him, you can be certain that we will do so."

"Absolutely," echoed Rachel. "We hear you loud and clear."

Grant told Eileen that they would be in touch once they got back to New York and the lawyer ended the call. He turned toward Rachel. "I'm sure that John has some sort of explanation."

"He keeps having to come up with more and more of them." Her eyes strayed to her cell in the Jeep's cup holder. "That's if we ever hear from him again."

Grant wished he could offer up more words of comfort for his daughter. But given the information just provided by Eileen and Frankel's recent actions, he feared anything he'd say would be futile.

It was a half hour later when another call came.

By that time, Grant and Rachel were sitting in the bright sunshine under makeshift bamboo hutches, the structures that constituted the waiting area at the Kailua-Kona airport.

Grant noticed Rachel reach for her cell and then the look of disappointment that crossed her face when she realized the ringtone had come from her father's phone. He glanced at the number. He didn't recognize it but answered anyway.

"Hello. This is Austin Grant."

"Oh good—I got the right number."

It wasn't Frankel—unless he was suddenly in the mood to do his impression of a young woman's voice.

"Who's this?"

"Heidi. Heidi Spangler—I'm a friend of Aiden's? She gave me your number just now."

"You must live in that town at the north of the island? Hawi, is it?"

"I did," answered Heidi. "But I moved over to Hilo on the other side of the island about a year ago. The weather sucks, rains night and day, but I got a steady job on an orchid farm. It beats going from day job to day job on the beaches. I definitely spent more time looking for work than actually doing any when I was in Hawi."

Heidi, like so many other young people on the Big Island, was originally from the mainland, having come over straight out of high school with the hope of owning a restaurant of her own. But she could never get past a waitressing gig and finally shucked it to tend orchids for a year or two, long enough to save up enough cash to head back to the mainland.

It was definitely more information than Grant needed to hear, especially with a plane to catch. He finally managed to steer the conversation in the direction he wanted by asking if she was calling about Julia Molinari.

"I can't believe what happened to her," she said, after confirming that Aiden had called her because she had worked the Hawi beach bar with Julia.

A plane landed in the background and began taxiing toward their gate—the increasingly loud noise making it hard for him to hear Heidi on the other end of the phone. Grant stepped away and headed for the side of the souvenir shop, where it was quieter, protected from the activity on the tarmac.

"How long did you work together?" asked Grant.

"On and off for a few months," answered Heidi. "She took a whole lot of sick days, poor girl."

"What was wrong with her?"

"She thought she'd caught some sort of parasite. Not too long after they got to the islands. She'd show up at work, feeling like crap—and then have to go home sick to her stomach and sleep for a few days. I ended up working a whole bunch of double shifts, but was happy to do so as I could really use the money. After about three or four months, she just stopped showing up altogether. That's when Pablo threw in the towel and they closed the place down."

"Did you continue to see her after that?"

"No, she and Pablo basically disappeared. It wasn't until, what, maybe almost a year later, I'm running on the beach down near Waikoloa and I see the two of them working the Papaya Seed. I couldn't believe it—I was convinced she'd packed it in and headed back to the East Coast."

"And how'd she seem?"

"Pretty great, actually," Heidi told him. "Much like the girl I met those first days up in Hawi—before she got sick."

"Did they ever find out what was wrong with her?"

"It turned out to be some kind of tropical virus with this long Latin name I can't pronounce, let alone remember. She said she was just happy to be past it all."

Grant started to ask another question, but noticed Rachel waving at him. She was pointing at her watch, then the plane, and Grant realized they were due to depart for Honolulu.

He thanked Heidi for phoning and asked if he could call again should more questions arise. Heidi said he was more than welcome to do so—just try her cell.

Grant rushed back to join Rachel, just in time to board the interisland flight, all the while trying to figure out what was bothering him about Julia Molinari's timeline in Hawaii.

Something.

When he couldn't come up with it, he did what he'd done for years at the Yard—tried to ignore the feeling, knowing the answer would reveal itself at some unexpected time in the future.

Hopefully sooner than later.

As they waited in the terminal at the Honolulu airport for their overnight flight to New York, Rachel still hadn't heard back from Frankel.

Her cell rang right after they boarded the American Airlines jumbo jet and were getting ready to taxi down the runway.

Rachel recognized the burner cell's number right away and picked up after one ring.

"John—are you still in Maine?"

"Yes, in a town called Lowell. I just got here an hour or so ago. Sorry I didn't get back to you sooner, but it's been a little nuts."

"We heard from Pablo Suarez. It turns out he's in Maine as well."

"That actually makes sense," said John.

"What?" Rachel was confused. It didn't make sense to *her*. "I don't understand—"

"Ma'am?"

Rachel looked up. A stern-looking flight attendant who'd likely been flying the Pacific route way, way too long was standing over her.

"Yes?"

"We're taking off now. You need to turn off your phone."

"Okay. I'll wrap it up," Rachel told her.

She cursed silently to herself as the woman moved past her down the center aisle. Rachel turned her attention back to the phone and John.

"Sorry. I'm back."

"What was that?"

"Dad and I are on a plane headed home. We're just about to take off."

"What's that—a ten-hour flight or so?" asked John. "That should get you into the city around lunch tomorrow. I should be back by then."

"You'd better be," Rachel said, with a lot more emphasis than she meant. But she was way past frustrated, and more than a bit scared.

"Don't worry, Rach—"

"I can't help it! The police want to talk to you again, John. If you're not in their office by Monday morning, they're issuing an arrest warrant!"

"It's okay. I think I've finally got a handle on this," John assured her. "I got thrown a curve or two—"

Rachel interrupted him. "But what's Pablo doing there?"

"Ma'am."

This time the tone was even more severe.

Rachel looked up to see the flight attendant pointing at the phone, her hand outstretched like she might grab it right out of Rachel's fingers.

"Phone off. Now."

Rachel nodded. "I've got to go," she whispered to John.

"I'll see you at home," he promised.

Rachel ended the call, offered up the woman a chilly smile, and watched her head down the aisle.

Rachel took a deep breath, then snuck her hand down to open the text feature on the cell. She quickly typed out a familiar message.

ILY XO

She waited for what seemed like an interminable time, but it was maybe less than fifteen seconds.

A return message showed up. *ILY XO*

The inscription on their wedding bands.

Rachel could only sigh.

Five minutes later, they were in the air, heading across the Pacific.

Shortly after takeoff, Rachel tried a follow-up text, but it didn't go through.

She settled back in her seat—knowing it was at least five hours over the water before they would get to the west coast of the United States where the flight's spotty Wi-Fi could be counted on again.

With no cell service or text messaging—there wasn't a single lifeline or way to communicate with John Frankel.

The way things were going, she didn't even want to think about what else could transpire up in Maine during that time.

Chapter 18

When Rachel didn't respond to the subsequent text (*CU TOMORROW XO*) with a red heart emoji beside it, Frankel realized she must be up thirty-five thousand feet in the air, way past cell range.

It was just as well.

He would feel much better when this was all over, with his suspicions confirmed and the ability to tell her everything.

Including how he'd ended up in the Pine Tree State.

After a week of working every angle and contact, he'd finally managed to get two names and an address—Margaret and Joseph Talbot of Lowell, Maine.

With no ability to take a plane there because there was no direct flight from the tristate area to Lowell, nor any desire to run the risk of using his ID to secure a ticket, it had been three train rides, four bus lines, and a half-hour cab ride that had deposited him at the house on Preble Road late that afternoon.

Only to find that the place was abandoned—a small ranch house with a weed-infested garden that looked like no one had tended it in the last year.

Doing his best to curb his disappointment, Frankel took to learning what had happened to the mother and son who had once resided there.

Counting on the fact that there was always an elderly man or woman in small towns like this who made it their business to know what everyone was up to, he had finally made the acquaintance of Mildred Snow, an octogenarian who had lived in the same house her entire life, having inherited it from her parents when they had died nearly a half century before.

When he had patiently finished listening to her recitation of the family tree, he'd managed to get her to concentrate on the Talbots, who had once occupied the ramshackle house down the street.

"Oh, that place has been empty for a couple of years now," said Mildred.

"Do you happen to know where the two of them went?" asked Frankel.

Sadly, Mildred's nosiness only pertained to the immediate area.

"I don't know exactly," she had told Frankel. "But it was only Margaret who left."

Frankel felt a tug in his chest.

"Just Margaret?"

Mildred gave him a sad nod. "Can't say I blame her for wanting to get away from here. Given what happened and all—such a tragedy."

The tug turned into a bigger pull, the hurting kind.

He got Mildred to tell him the rest.

It had led him to where he stood now in the darkness, the only light coming courtesy of a nearly full moon and the starry sky above.

Bright enough for him to read the sign above the closed iron gates.

West End Cemetery. Lowell, Maine.

With the graveyard gates closed since sunset and a locked chain around them, Frankel was left with no choice but to scale the adjacent rock wall.

As he dropped down onto the grass, he tried to pinpoint the last time he'd broken into a cemetery. He really couldn't remember, but vaguely recalled it had involved too much beer and a high school dare.

Mildred had told him where to head—a back corner of the graveyard underneath a stand of oak trees, their overgrown branches throwing the headstones into almost complete darkness.

When he reached the oaks, he pulled out the burner phone and used the light from the display to illuminate a small group of graves. He quickly found the one that Mildred had described, a solitary slab of white stone off to one side ("no one wants to be near it—let the pour soul rest in peace" had been Mildred's exact words).

He dropped down to his knees and trained the light on the grave.

He took one look and made the sign of the cross.

The inscription was simple.

JOSEPH DARREN TALBOT. IN OUR HEARTS FOREVER. BORN FEBRUARY 16, 2019. DIED JUNE 22, 2019.

Sudden crib death according to Mildred.

Not that Margaret Talbot had discussed it. She just wanted to privately grieve and get the hell out of town.

Frankel reached into his pocket for a small notepad. He trained the cell light on it and flipped to a page with a name and date he'd jotted down.

JOSEPH D. TALBOT 2/16/19

It matched.

The second date was something he hadn't been aware of.

Frankel shook his head and sat down beside the grave.

All that work, everything he'd not told Rachel the past weeks. To end up here.

He felt something sticky on his hand.

Sticky and oozing.

He flipped the cell phone back on and moved the beam down toward his palm.

Blood.

Fresh blood.

He shifted the light, so it took in the space right behind the grave.

The last time John Frankel had seen Pablo Suarez had been in the apartment building he'd lived in with Julia. Pablo had come upstairs to check a clogged sink. A week later, Pablo ran off with his wife.

That had been three years ago and Pablo had been very much alive at the time.

As opposed to the state he was in now.

Dead. Bleeding from a gunshot wound in his head.

Frankel's mind began to race. Then his heart did as well when he heard the sound of an approaching siren.

Less than a minute later, he could see the lights of a police car pull up to the gates, along with another car.

It was too far away to make out the faces of the two men who emerged from the cars but quiet enough to make out a few words.

"Gunshots fired—"

"I've got a key—"

Frankel didn't need much imagination to deduce that one was probably the caretaker. The other was unquestionably a cop.

And he knew exactly how this was going to look.

He did the only thing he could think of doing.

He got up, crossed to the back wall of the cemetery, and climbed to the top.

Then he jumped down onto the sidewalk behind it and raced off into the deep, dark Maine night.

PART THREE

For Richer,

For Poorer

Chapter 19

Grant got his first indication that things had gotten worse once the American Airlines 767 reached the California coastline. It came courtesy of his daughter's sigh, as she'd finally been able to connect to the in-flight Wi-Fi.

"Word from John?" he asked.

"Not exactly," replied Rachel, showing him her iPad screen that featured a headline reading MANHUNT FOR MURDERER IN MAINE.

Later, as they flew over the Grand Canyon, they learned that the state police were pursuing a man who had killed someone in a small Maine town. No naming the victim or suspect—but the fact that the town was Lowell was enough to make both Grants' stomachs churn.

More details emerged above the Midwest plains; the killing had taken place in a cemetery the previous evening.

Grant handed Rachel back the tablet. "John didn't mention that he was headed to a graveyard by any chance?"

Rachel shook her head. "Just that he had a handle on things after being thrown a few curves."

Grant indicated the iPad. "This would qualify as another one."

Shortly upon reaching the Eastern Seaboard and beginning their final approach to JFK, there were a couple of more. The victim was identified as Pablo Suarez from Kona, Hawaii, and the man police were searching for was an NYPD detective named John Frankel, who'd been held and questioned a few days earlier about the murder of Pablo's girlfriend, Julia Molinari.

Grant tried to come up with words to reassure his daughter, but for the life of him, couldn't think of a thing to say.

Rachel tightly gripped her father's hand.

Under normal circumstances, it might have been Austin Grant reaching out for support to quell his flying phobia, but he was so distracted in the air that the fear of a crash landing was the furthest thing from his mind.

So, Grant just held his daughter's hand and wondered what was waiting for them once they touched down.

It turned out to be a woman outside baggage claim holding a sign that read "Grant."

"I didn't know you hired a car," said Rachel.

"I didn't."

The sign holder wasn't a limo driver, but one of the Seventeenth Precinct detectives sent by Lieutenant Harris, a one-woman welcoming committee to escort them back to his office.

She also happened to be the detective that Frankel had ditched a few nights earlier by climbing out the precinct's bathroom window, and consequently made it clear that she wasn't going to let his fiancée and soon-to-be father-in-law out of her sight until she'd delivered them to the Seventeenth.

Unfortunately, that was the only information the Grants were able to extract from Detective Dunham. So they sat silently in the back seat of the unmarked sedan as it worked its way on the LIE back to the city.

It was shortly before noon when Dunham deposited them in Desmond Harris's office. She told them that the lieutenant and Detective Meadows would be with them shortly. Dunham pointed out that the windows were double locked and didn't possess any sort of ledge—just in case they were thinking of replicating Detective Frankel's exit.

Grant thanked her for the intel and watched her walk out the door.

He realized it had already been half a day since John Frankel had disappeared in the Maine night, and that as each hour passed without anyone hearing from him, he looked increasingly guilty and was solidifying himself as NYPD's prime suspect.

"Did you try texting that number again?" Grant asked.

"Once an hour, like you suggested. Nothing."

"He must figure that the police are monitoring your mobile. I'd imagine that burner phone currently resides somewhere deep in the Maine forest by now."

"Then how are we supposed to get in touch with him?"

"John's an enterprising young man. I'm sure when he wants to reach out to you, he'll find a way."

Grant noticed this didn't placate his daughter, but he didn't have a chance to say more as the office door opened. Lieutenant Desmond Harris and Detective Taryn Meadows walked in. Neither looked happy nor appeared to have slept much.

"How was Hawaii?" asked the lieutenant as he settled behind his desk.

"Under normal circumstances, it would have been quite lovely," quipped Grant. "I did enjoy the luau I attended."

"You'll forgive me if I don't ask what you had for dinner or if you managed to get in any swimming. I'm much more interested if you've been in touch with Detective Frankel recently."

"Since he told us yesterday that he was in Maine?" Grant shook his head. "Not since then, no."

Taryn, who'd settled on the desk's edge, leaned forward. "So, you *have* been in touch."

"Sporadically," answered Grant. He sensed Rachel's eyes on him and gave her the slightest nod, hopefully indicating that she should fall into step alongside him. "My daughter even relayed the message you left with Ms. Crowe."

"I told John that you wanted to talk to him again; otherwise, you were going to issue a warrant for his arrest," confirmed Rachel.

"Obviously, circumstances have changed in the past few hours," said Harris. "We put one out late last night."

The lieutenant filled in the details.

The Lowell police had received a couple of calls about shots being fired in the West End cemetery just after nine o'clock. An officer had been dispatched to the scene where the caretaker led him inside the gates and they'd subsequently found the dead Pablo Suarez lying graveside. A canvass of the neighborhood yielded two witnesses who, having been alerted by the approaching sirens, had seen a man matching Frankel's description running down the street.

"Did they say how long after the gunshots this was?" asked Grant.

Taryn referred to her ever-present notepad. "Maybe twenty minutes or so."

"That timing seems a bit odd, doesn't it?" said Grant. "Why would one stick around that long after shooting Pablo?"

"How am I supposed to know that?" countered Harris, clearly frustrated. "Whatever Frankel was up to, he must have hung around until the sirens scared him off."

"Or maybe the real killer fled immediately after the murder, then phoned in the gunshots to set up Detective Frankel once he'd arrived on the scene."

"Sounds overly complicated to me," said Harris.

"Or like you're going out of the way to protect your future son-in-law," added Taryn. "You can't deny that Pablo Suarez was the man his ex-wife left him for."

"Three years ago," Rachel pointed out. "That's a long time to hold a murderous grudge and suddenly go on a killing spree."

"Until someone comes up with a better theory or suspect, we're focused on Detective Frankel." Desmond Harris squeezed the bridge of his nose, obviously not enjoying any of this. "I've had nothing but absolute respect for John Frankel over the years. No one's more surprised by this turn of events than me. But I have to follow the path this investigation is taking us on—and right now, that's headed toward him."

"And you're unwilling to entertain the notion that someone is directing you to look that way?" asked Grant.

"Nothing would thrill me more. But I need something to go on," said Harris. "What did you find out in the islands?"

Grant proceeded to lay out what he and Rachel had uncovered. He told them about the Papaya Seed closing up because of Pablo's gambling debts and how he'd been desperately trying to pay back the bookie Daswick and offer the developer Erickson some sort of return on his investment on the upslope of Mauna Kea. There'd also been the ransacking of Pablo and Julia's place—something Frankel could not have done, as he was under police surveillance in Manhattan and subsequently en route to Maine at the time.

"None of this precludes him from committing either murder," said Harris.

"But it gives you two other people that Pablo had upset recently."

"Even so," said Harris. "Were either of them in New York City when Julia was killed? And why murder Pablo's girlfriend when their beef was with him?"

"It's your investigation," Grant told them. "We're just trying to be of assistance."

Harris nodded. "We've been in touch with Sheriff Lam. He's made us aware of some of Pablo's escapades."

"I have a question, if you don't mind," said Rachel.

All eyes turned toward Grant's daughter, who had spent most of the session watching her father and the two cops serve and volley murder theories.

"Do you have any idea what John or Pablo Suarez were doing in a Maine graveyard in the first place?"

"We were about to ask you the same thing," Harris said. "We got a list of those buried in West End cemetery and at first glance, there aren't any Suarezes or Molinaris there, so it's not like this involves an immediate family member."

"That doesn't eliminate friends, acquaintances, or business associates," Grant pointed out.

"We're just getting started," claimed a defensive Taryn.

"And it's not like the grave we found Suarez next to has any apparent connection to either of them." The lieutenant picked up a piece of paper and handed it across the desk to the Grants.

"Joseph Darren Talbot," read Grant. He looked back up at the two cops. "A four-month-old child who died nearly two years ago?"

Harris nodded. "It's hard to get a lot of information on a Sunday morning in a small town like Lowell. From what we've gathered so far, it appears the boy succumbed to SIDS and the grieving mother moved away. We're trying to get a line on her." The lieutenant shrugged. "What this has to do with a boyfriend and girlfriend being murdered in two different states six thousand miles from their home is beyond me."

"Maybe John arranged to meet Pablo Suarez there and things went off the rails," suggested Taryn.

Grant had remained silent during this go-round. Something was gnawing at his brain again but before he could grasp it, Desmond Harris was addressing him.

"Commander?"

Grant looked up. "Yes?"

"You've gone awfully quiet all of a sudden. Anything to offer here?"

"Not immediately," answered Grant. "Except it seems you have a lot of dots to connect here. I think you'd want to do that before you slam the jail door on my daughter's fiancé."

Grant turned to glance at Rachel, whose eyes were locked on him. The gratefulness there was easy enough to spot—along with a dose of curiosity as to what was up the former Scotland Yard man's sleeve.

———

The rest of the meeting devolved into what had become familiar warnings and admonishments, only now they were more serious than ever. Frankel was the prime suspect in *two* seemingly connected murders. Preliminary findings showed that the same weapon had been used, with the bullet in both cases identical to the caliber of Frankel's missing backup gun. Harris said that if either of the Grants failed to report *any* contact with the detective, they could have aiding and abetting charges leveled against them.

It was fairly simple. The longer Frankel remained on the run, the worse it would get for him and the more it would be seen as an admission of guilt. Grant assured Harris that they would stay in touch, a vague-enough assertion that he thought would give him the room needed to ascertain how deeply in trouble John was, should they actually hear from him.

More importantly, Grant was eager to leave the precinct and follow up on what they'd just learned from the lieutenant and Detective Meadows.

It wasn't until they were in a cab heading to Rachel's apartment that Grant checked his contacts (away from the eyes and ears of the law) to get a number for Heidi, the girl who'd worked the Hawi beach bar with Julia. He did a little calculating in his head.

"Eight o'clock on a Sunday morning isn't too early, is it?" he asked.

Rachel told him that it depended on what sort of Saturday night the person in question had.

The answer seemed to be a late one with a few imbibed spirits, judging from Heidi's groggy tone when she picked up.

Grant apologized profusely for calling so early, explaining that something had come up in the investigation and he needed a little clarity about Julia's first few months on the island, back when the two girls had worked together.

He took Heidi through Julia's tenure there—getting specific dates (or at least as close to what a likely hungover Heidi could recall) and confirming what she had told him on the phone just before they'd departed the Big Island the day before.

As soon as Grant hung up, Rachel started to ask what that was all about but her father quieted her with a look that took in their cab driver.

"In due time, Rach. Let me think—maths was never my strong suit."

Twenty minutes later, they were seated at the tiny table in Rachel's apartment. Grant had drawn a little chart on a piece of paper, crossing out a few things. Then he leaned back in his chair, satisfied with the result of his scribbling.

"So?" asked Rachel.

"Julia's tropical disease," said Grant.

"The one she kept missing work for."

"Exactly. Heidi said that Julia started work a couple of weeks after she and Pablo arrived on the Big Island, in June, three years ago. She worked on and off for about three months, then stopped showing up completely that fall in, what did Heidi say—" Grant checked his makeshift chart. "October, or thereabouts. That was when Julia and Pablo both disappeared, not to resurface until the following summer when Heidi came across them at the newly christened Papaya Seed. And Julia had made a complete recovery from her 'mystery tropical disease.'"

He eyed the chart once more and pointed at a number next to the second month of the year.

"But let's go back to February—that would have been *nine* months after Julia first got sick."

Rachel's eyes widened; Grant could see that she had caught up.

Grant continued. "According to Lieutenant Harris, that's the exact same month that—"

"—the child in the grave up in Maine was born," finished Rachel.

"Like I mentioned, you probably should check my math."

Rachel shook her head. "No, Dad. It lines up perfectly. Julia could absolutely have been pregnant. All the time she took off, it could have been from nasty bouts of morning sickness. And disappearing in October like that—it would have been the time she started to show, right?"

"That's pretty much how I'm figuring it."

"So, you're thinking that Julia came back to the mainland, Maine in particular, and had a child there?"

"The numbers don't rule it out," concurred Grant.

"Unbelievable."

"What they don't explain is how that child came to be known as Joseph Darren Talbot."

Chapter 20

John Frankel hadn't known about the existence of a baby.

He'd not even seen it as a possibility, given that during their marriage, Julia had seemed dead set against bringing a child into the world. When pressed for reasons, she seemed to have plenty. She was still trying for some kind of career in the fashion business, even though she'd drifted from job to job. She didn't think she had the capacity to put forth the devotion needed to raise one, let alone have any desire to do so. And there was her family—she hadn't loved growing up under the watchful and judgmental eye of Leo Molinari and she had no interest in subjecting an innocent to any sort of replay.

Frankel had always figured that someday he'd be a father, and he'd been thrown when Julia had voiced her objections shortly after they'd gotten married. At first, he had thought it was just a phase—she was young, with her whole life in front of her, and would eventually come around. But as the years passed and the pressure built, everyone wondering when they were going to start a family (especially Leo at Sunday night dinners, asking if there was "anything happening in the making-me-a-grandpa department"), Julia had dug her heels in and said she wasn't ready. And when she and Frankel finally had it out about the subject, Julia confessed she didn't think she'd ever be.

And then came Pablo.

He never quite knew what had driven Julia into the arms of their former building supervisor. Frankel always thought it had been his own dedication to the job—long hours and an inability to leave his caseload at the precinct when he'd come home at night. But now he wondered if he'd put too much pressure on Julia to have a child and the result was her seeking comfort elsewhere.

As he sat staring out the window of the southbound train, his face shielded by a low-slung Yankee cap and dark sunglasses, he realized that with both Julia and Pablo gone, he would probably never know the reason.

But that wasn't going to stop him from trying, perhaps by uncovering the secrets behind Julia's death and how it had led to the shocking discoveries up in the Lowell graveyard.

Once again, Frankel couldn't help thinking that if he hadn't met Rachel and fallen in love, none of this would have happened. Who would have thought that seeking something as simple as a wedding license would lead to such a series of tragedies?

It had all begun three years earlier when he'd returned home one night to find Julia's closet and dresser cleared out, and a short note saying she needed a fresh start.

He had been truly stunned.

It wasn't like he'd been unaware that he and Julia had been drifting apart, but he never would have thought she would just pick up and leave.

He hadn't even suspected something was going on between her and Pablo.

He hardly knew the man—only coming into contact with him when there was a problem in their apartment.

Obviously, that hadn't been the case with Julia.

It wasn't until Pablo's name was mentioned in the note that Frankel realized what Julia had been doing with her days, and some nights, while he had been working round-the-clock investigations.

Suddenly his world completely changed, and for a couple of weeks he'd had no idea where the two of them had disappeared to.

That was when a package had arrived at the precinct with a return address on Hawaii's Big Island. Inside were divorce papers claiming irreconcilable differences and a lawyer contact in Waimea. After a few back-and-forth communiques with the attorney, a phone call was arranged between Frankel and Julia where she told him there was no going back. She said he should just sign the papers and get on with his life—as she was doing already.

After that, Frankel had spent the better part of a month taking on extra shifts, trying not to mope around their apartment and stare forlornly at the documents that would dissolve the decade they'd spent together.

When he was contacted by a creditor inquiring about an unpaid balance on one of Julia's accounts, he noticed she'd gone back to her maiden name.

He'd signed the divorce papers the next day and sent them back to the lawyer in Waimea, assuming that was the end of things.

Until the notice came from the wedding license bureau.

Upon learning that she had never signed the papers, and hadn't ever walked down the aisle with Pablo (and was still his own lawfully wedded wife), Frankel had reached out to Julia. But his efforts were ignored—no returned phone calls or responses to emails. The latter had been bounced back as undeliverable, Frankel correctly theorizing that she had changed her email address.

That should have been his first clue this wasn't going to be resolved as easily as he'd hoped.

He'd actually had to use some NYPD resources and search engines to run down a current contact for Julia, finally locating her just outside of Kona. When he reached her at last, she'd been reserved and clipped, not really willing to talk about or concede that she hadn't signed the papers.

When she'd hung up midway through the conversation, Frankel realized he was going to have to deal with this in person. That led to his "bachelor weekend" with Tim Francis, a lifelong friend, one to whom he'd confided the truth of his predicament and who swore to go along with "the trip to Wisconsin" story.

For the duration of the ten-hour flight to the islands, Frankel had wrestled with his decision not to tell Rachel what he was doing.

Now, looking back, he wondered if something had been tickling that instinctive cop sense where he knew there was more here that he wanted to get to the bottom of before revealing all to his fiancée.

He ended up meeting Julia at the Papaya Seed and the two of them walked the beach together. She had been shocked that Frankel had flown all the way to the Big Island, not realizing how important it was that their divorce was finalized. She'd apologized for the misunderstanding—hearing from her ex-husband had clearly caught her totally off guard.

Frankel could tell she was deeply troubled. Even though it had been three years since they'd seen one another, he knew her stress signals. The lower tone of her voice, the welled-up eyes; he'd quickly ascertained that things were tense with Julia and Pablo, and that was the reason she had not responded to Frankel when he'd reached out.

Though she hadn't provided specifics, Julia had told him that Pablo was in debt to a host of characters he refused to talk about, but who were becoming an increasing threat—definitely financially, and quite possibly physically. Frankel, despite the messy way things had ended with Julia, couldn't help but offer a sympathetic ear and said if there were something he could specifically do, Julia should let him know.

She had appreciated that and said she might take him up on the offer, sooner than later. She promised to contact her attorney and sign the divorce papers in a few days. She even wished him well in his upcoming marriage, seemingly happy that he'd found someone he wanted to spend the rest of his life with.

Frankel had flown back to New York, figuring the matter had been put to rest. Crisis averted. The wedding plans could proceed on schedule.

That was until he got a call from *his* attorney a couple of days after his return from the Hawaiian Islands.

Julia had sent back the divorce papers.

She had signed them after making a few changes that updated the document. But there was an addendum that the attorney thought she should bring up with Frankel.

The wording was rather vague—it said that by countersigning the papers to make them final, Frankel revoked all rights to any issue from the marriage.

"You mean a child?" Frankel had asked.

"That's the normal interpretation," responded the lawyer. "I guess it could apply to a pet of some sort, but that would be a stretch."

"We didn't have any children."

"That's what I remember. I can only presume it was added at the suggestion of Julia's lawyer as a pro forma, all-encompassing addendum. I wouldn't worry about it."

But over the next couple of days, that was all Frankel did.

Worry. A lot.

He'd tried to think of the last time that he'd actually been with Julia and was pretty sure it had been the week before she'd run off with Pablo. At the time, it had been one more thing about the situation that had bothered him—the fact that Julia must have been sleeping with Pablo and Frankel at the same time. He had tried to put all of that on her, as something she had to live with, but it hadn't made him feel any better about himself, unable to come to grips with what he'd done to cause her eye and heart to wander.

Issue.

The word nagged at him.

Because there suddenly might be a very good reason that Julia had never signed the papers.

An added complication.

A complication she would have to reveal before signing off on the divorce because there might be repercussions for the rest of their lives.

Finally, Frankel had called Julia from his office one night and asked her the question flat out.

"Did you have a child?"

She didn't answer, but the intake of breath thousands of miles away told Frankel everything he wanted to know.

"Don't lie to me, Julia," Frankel had said. "Not about this."

The only sound had been the crashing waves in the background, and Frankel realized he must have reached her on the beach by the Papaya Seed.

"You know I won't stop digging until I get the truth."

He would never forget the hesitation in her voice and what amounted to a tortured whisper.

"I did."

Frankel had felt his heart tighten.

"Who's the father?"

"John—"

"Who's the father, Julia?"

Once again, all he could hear was the pounding surf.

When Julia answered, Frankel could hear the sob caught in her throat. "I don't know."

"What do you mean you don't know?" Frankel had asked, incredulously. "There *are* such things as blood tests—"

"It's more complicated than that."

Boy, had that been an understatement.

"Next stop, Englewood. Englewood, next stop."

The automated voice came through the speaker above his head.

Frankel looked back out the window as the train pulled into the New Jersey station.

He couldn't believe what had transpired in the week since that phone call.

Both Julia and Pablo were dead.

Police up and down the Eastern Seaboard were searching for him, considering him armed and dangerous.

Again he wondered what would have happened if he'd told Rachel the truth in the first place.

Now he was going to have to.

Because like Julia had said—it had gotten *really* complicated.

Rachel was the only one he could trust. And possibly her father.

But did they still trust him?

Chapter 21

There had been very little information about the life and death of Joseph Darren Talbot.

He had only lived a scant four months, but Rachel thought his death would merit more than a slight mention in the *Lincoln News*, the local paper in Lowell, Maine, but that had basically been it.

Joseph Darren Talbot, age four months, the only son of Margaret (Maggie) Talbot, succumbed to an undetermined disease on June 22nd. In lieu of flowers, donations can be made to the local chapter of the March of Dimes.

"You'd think the death of a child would cause more of a stir in a small community like that," said Grant. He had just peered over Rachel's shoulder and quickly scanned the news item on her laptop.

"How did John know to head to Maine in the first place?" asked Rachel.

"Well, seeing as how Pablo wound up there as well, I'd say the common denominator must have been Julia."

"You think she told them to go there?"

"Possibly. The only other thing I can think of is he went to see this woman Margaret Talbot to establish what kind of connection she had to Julia."

"And ended up in a graveyard."

"No stranger than you and me prowling through a lava field on an island in the middle of the Pacific Ocean."

"Sad but true," lamented Rachel.

Her cell phone dinged with an incoming text.

Rachel glanced at it and felt her stomach tighten.

"John?" asked her father hopefully.

"I think so," answered Rachel.

She showed him the cell phone display. *Sheila Rice. 9pm.*

"Who's Sheila Rice?"

"Long story," said Rachel.

Frankel lowered the cell phone and considered the message he'd just sent Rachel. He was fairly certain she'd know what it meant; they'd joked about it on more than one occasion. He was sure that his fellow cops would try and monitor Rachel's cell usage, so he had no choice but to be as obscure as possible.

As the train pulled into the Elizabeth station in New Jersey, he considered how he would lay out the story to Rachel, should they be lucky enough to meet up.

There was so much he still didn't know—especially having run into a literal dead end in the cemetery up in Lowell.

The phone conversation with Julia had almost ended a couple of times. Looking back, he figured it had been his insistence upon learning the truth—and that Julia had lived a decade with Frankel and knew the detective wouldn't let go—that resulted in her painstakingly telling him about her pregnancy.

It had come as a complete surprise and was the last thing that Julia wanted at the time. She hadn't even been sure she could conceive a child, so when she was a couple of weeks late shortly after arriving in Hawaii, she chalked it up to the change in climate or the tropical bug she was certain she'd caught.

She'd taken the pregnancy test at the behest of a local doctor and gone through a few kits because she couldn't believe the positive result. Worse yet, she'd really had no idea who the father was as she'd been with both

Pablo and Frankel before running off to the islands—and the conception date fell into that window.

At first, she hadn't told Pablo, knowing a baby would derail the plans the two of them had to build a business that would require them working 24/7, let alone having to tell him the child she was carrying might not be his.

One small piece of good news was that three months in, when she was just starting to show and had to break the news to Pablo, he took it better than she thought he would.

It turned out he was even less inclined to be a father than she was committed to the concept of motherhood.

But having been raised in a good Catholic family, terminating the pregnancy had never entered her mind. And speaking of family, having already frayed the relationship with her father over her disapproval of his marrying a girl half his age and later running out on her own marriage, Julia had no intention of letting Leo Molinari know that a grandchild was on the way. She didn't need to remind Frankel how overbearing and controlling the Molinari patriarch was—he'd gotten a good dose of it in the years they'd been married.

"And during all of this, you never thought to get in touch with me?" Frankel had asked. "Didn't you think I had a right to know what was going on?"

Julia had admitted the thought had weighed heavily on her mind. But she had no idea what to tell him—especially with the birth still months away. It had been the reason she hadn't signed the divorce papers; she hadn't known what to do.

That was when she remembered Caitlan Hill.

She'd gone to high school with Caitlan in Little Falls, New Jersey, and for a time they'd been best friends. Members of the same cheerleader squad, double-dating the football team's backfield, cribbing each other's essays. But they'd drifted apart around graduation, with Caitlan having gone to Penn intent on pursuing a career in the medical field while Julia skipped college altogether, trying to break into the fashion business without much success.

Their communication had dwindled down to the yearly Christmas card from Caitlan and an occasional response from Julia. But Julia recalled the one she'd received the previous year when she was still living with Frankel, and how Caitlan had mentioned she was working for an adoption agency up in Maine, using her nurse practitioner skills to look after the infants who had been put in their care while looking for good homes to place them in.

Julia had gotten in touch with her high school friend and explained her plight, resulting in an offer for her and Pablo to go stay with Caitlan for the duration of her pregnancy, during which time Caitlan could begin the process of arranging for Julia's baby to be adopted by a suitable family.

It hadn't taken much convincing for Pablo to move east for those months—he'd hated working the beach bar in Hawi because there was absolutely no growth potential in the tiny town and he was looking for a change. He'd commuted back and forth, while Julia remained in Portland as her pregnancy came to term.

Then, shortly after Valentine's Day, two things had come to fruition. On the sunny shores of the Big Island, Pablo had emerged from a poker game with the deed to the Papaya Seed, while in the middle of a Maine blizzard, Julia gave birth ten days early to a baby boy.

Pablo had rushed back to Portland just in time to see Julia with the child who might or might not be his son, right before Caitlan swaddled up the newborn and delivered him to his new home.

As Frankel disembarked the train in Elizabeth, dipping the Yankee cap even closer to shield his eyes (sunglasses at night would raise more suspicions than they would keep people from recognizing him), he remembered asking Julia whom the child had ended up with.

Julia had told Frankel that she didn't know. She had just wanted to move on with her life with no regrets and had never asked Caitlan.

Sheila Rice had been a girl that Frankel had gone out with in high school.

"Odd time for him to be bringing up that blast from his past," said Grant.

Rachel repressed a chuckle. She could see how her father might have been perturbed at John working his way through his dating history—first Julia, now the aforementioned Sheila.

She quickly elaborated. "There's this place on a hill, just outside Elizabeth, with the most breathtaking view across the Hudson of the Statue of Liberty and lower Manhattan spread out behind it. John took me there one morning when we first got together and said it was his favorite view in the world. I said that he probably brought all the girls there and he told me the only other one had been his high school flame, Sheila Rice."

Grant nodded, getting it. "And he wants to meet you there at nine o'clock."

"Unless, like you say, he's just taking a random stroll down memory lane."

"And what do you suggest we tell Lieutenant Harris and Detective Meadows?"

"Nothing yet," answered Rachel quickly. "You're retired now, remember? You're no longer under compunction to follow every letter of the law."

"Old habits die hard, my dear." Grant indicated the text message on Rachel's cell. "And that right there is what Harris meant when he was going on about aiding and abetting a fugitive."

"You know as well as I do that John didn't kill Julia or Pablo."

"I don't *know* that for a fact, but yes, I find it hard to *believe*."

"And the best chance we have of finding out exactly what's going on with John and convincing him to turn himself in is if I go and meet him."

"You know Lieutenant Harris has someone, possibly multiple some-ones, watching our every move—fully expecting John to get in touch with one of us, most likely you."

"And expects me to lead them right to him."

"Precisely," said Grant.

"About that—"

—⁓—

The walk to what Rachel had chidingly referred to as Rice's Ridge would have taken Frankel a few hours from the Elizabeth train station, so he ran the risk of jumping into a cab. Luckily, the Persian driver seemed more intent on the WhatsApp chat he was having than paying attention to his passenger. Frankel gave him a location near the bottom of the hill, then leaned back to ruminate on what else he was going to have to tell Rachel.

Caitlan Hill.

Julia had been less than thrilled when Frankel said he was going to get in touch with her. She'd been hesitant to give him Caitlan's number, but had finally done so when Frankel reminded her he had NYPD resources and other ways of chasing her down.

But Caitlan had proved to be less forthcoming than Julia. Hearing her voice on the phone, Frankel was reminded of the few times he'd met her, early in his marriage to Julia. He recalled her being tall, blond, and slightly hardened, an overall attitude that seemed on a perfect track for med school, and that had somehow gotten switched to adoptive services and infant care.

Caitlan did express surprise at hearing from Frankel, having figured Julia had no intentions of telling him about the child. But when it came to revealing where Julia's baby had been placed, she told him that she was under no obligation to do so. That would be something left up to Julia, who had chosen not to be in any contact whatsoever with the child once she'd resumed her life in Hawaii.

Not being the sort to drop a pursuit, especially when it was something so personal to him, Frankel was ready to continue pushing the ball uphill when something even more surprising happened.

Julia had appeared on his doorstep in Murray Hill.

She'd seemed even more exasperated and desperate than she'd been a few days earlier in Hawaii, and they went to a diner near Union Square where she told him there were two reasons for her arrival in New York.

The first problem was the increasing financial pressure being brought to bear on Pablo. Unwilling to discuss the particulars, all Julia had told Frankel was that she was starting to fear for the physical safety of Pablo and herself. She'd decided to do what she'd swore she would never do: see her father and ask him to bail them out.

When Frankel asked if there were anything he could do, Julia brought up the second reason.

Couldn't he just let this thing about the baby go, sign the divorce papers, marry Rachel, and live happily ever after?

For some reason that Frankel still couldn't comprehend—whether it was the impending wedding, what he was already keeping from Rachel, or more likely the possibility of him having a child he had never known about, he'd snapped.

Right there, fortunately in an empty diner on a Sunday night, Frankel had lashed out at Julia. It wasn't bad enough that she'd run out on their marriage without warning, but she'd gone and had a child that very easily could have been his and totally neglected to tell him—and now that he finally knew about it, she was saying he should just simply forget about it? After trying to sneak it past him by having her lawyer slip an addendum into the divorce papers?

Julia had begun sobbing, then ran out of the diner. Frankel had to chase her three blocks before he'd caught up with her.

By that time, he had sufficiently calmed down and said all he wanted to know was the truth. Once they got all the facts, he and Julia could make an informed decision about how to move forward with their lives.

And he could finally tell Rachel everything.

Julia had said she would call Caitlan and get her to provide them with a name.

When he'd asked where she was staying, Julia said she had no idea. She'd used practically her last dime to pay for the plane ticket. And given the fact that she hadn't seen or talked to her father in close to three years and was about to ask him for money, she was dubious about spending the night in the house she grew up in.

Frankel had made a spur of the moment offer he had no idea would come back to haunt him.

He'd given Julia the key to his apartment and told her she could camp out there, seeing as how he spent most nights at Rachel's.

Frankel apologized for his blowup in the diner and wished Julia good luck in dealing with Leo.

An hour later, he got a text from Julia.

She'd gotten in touch with Caitlan and she'd provided a name and a city. Joseph Darren Talbot. Lowell, Maine.

That had been the last he'd ever heard from Julia Molinari.

Less than a day later, she was dead in his apartment.

And by the time Frankel had crawled into bed beside Rachel late that evening, he didn't know what the hell to tell her.

Rachel and her father had gone round and round about the merits of her meeting John. She insisted he was innocent and deserved to be heard. Grant said he was acting like a guilty man and should turn himself in before things reached a violent end. Rachel repeated her claim: that it was the former Scotland Yard commander talking, not John's prospective father-in-law in the real world.

Grant couldn't remember when he'd won an argument with his daughter. This time wasn't any different.

"So how do you expect to get to this New Jersey hill without the cops following you there?" asked her father.

"I figured you could help me with that."

"I was afraid that would be your answer."

Shortly after the sun set, Grant and Rachel headed out of her apartment and got into an Uber.

Earlier in the day, Grant had mentioned to Rachel that he was long overdue in paying a visit to Leo Molinari at his New Jersey home, having intended to do so ever since he'd been dismissed by Julia's brother in the electronics store before they'd headed to Hawaii.

Rachel pointed out that since she was already headed across the river to the Garden State, it might be a good time for Grant to unexpectedly drop in on Julia's father, armed with everything they'd learned in the islands, especially now with the possibility that there was a grandchild in the picture.

Rachel began conversing with the driver and asked if he'd be interested in tripling his fare across the GW Bridge. The man was gung ho about the chance to turn a slow night into a payday and asked what she had in mind.

Twenty minutes later, on a turnout leading to the West Side Highway, their Uber driver pulled up directly beside a Toyota driven by a colleague of his.

Grant, who had ducked down in the back seat, creaked open the door on his side, then slid out of the car and stayed low to the ground as he stepped through the already open door of the Toyota.

Within seconds, both cars hopped onto the highway, spreading lanes apart.

Rachel peered over her shoulder to see a car swerve across the highway to follow the Toyota. She smiled, knowing that not only had her father been correct in their movements being watched, *her* instinct was right—that when they pulled off the switch, the cops would end up tailing the one that her father made a break for.

Half an hour later, the Uber driver deposited Rachel in front of an all-night Hertz outlet. She paid the driver the agreed-upon charge and went inside. Moments later, she drove off in the most nondescript Ford Taurus she could find.

Three turns later, she was back on the Turnpike headed for Exit 13, which would land her in Elizabeth.

———

Frankel didn't remember such a vertical climb to the hill in Elizabeth. But he'd never navigated it on foot before—he was usually in his unmarked car with Rachel.

He tried to ignore the strain on his lungs by concentrating on the rest of what he needed to confess.

He'd known he was in deep trouble the moment he'd heard the story break about Julia's body being found in his apartment.

The secret trip to Hawaii to see her. The argument they'd had in the diner the night before she was killed. And it was only a matter of time until the cops learned about the child that Julia had given up without telling Frankel anything about it, suddenly giving him one hell of a motive to kill her.

Even though Frankel knew he was innocent, someone else was aware of those facts as well and clearly using them to frame him.

It was why he'd spent the time since his release trying to locate either Caitlan Hill or Margaret Talbot.

He'd failed on both counts.

Frankel had tracked down the adoption agency that Caitlan worked for, the Bradford Clinic in Portland, Maine, only to find out she was on a sabbatical with no firm timetable marking her return.

Efforts to reach Margaret Talbot had proved even more fruitless. Zigzagging his way undetected up to Maine, he'd learned that Margaret had fled Lowell in grief upon the passing of the young boy she'd adopted, all of four months old.

Frankel had been devastated standing over the grave of the child that very well could have been his. And what Pablo Suarez was doing dead in the same cemetery was a complete mystery.

Frankel knew the frame around him was tightening. The cops already had him on the hook for Julia. Now, he had the blood of the man that she'd left him for on his hands.

By the time he reached the top of the hill, he was hyperventilating.

Was it the climb or panic taking over? He suspected it was a bit of both.

He was still trying to catch his breath a few minutes later when a car pulled up beside him.

The window rolled down and Rachel looked out at him.

Frankel drummed up his best smile.

"You could have at least gotten here a little earlier to save me the walk up the hill," he told her.

"You could've told me that you and Julia had a child together."

Frankel started to say the baby might not be his.

But he wasn't an idiot.

He did the smart thing and let her decide what happened next.

Chapter 22

"It's like Hollywood, East Coast style."

Grant listened as the Uber driver pointed out where stars like Chris Rock, P. Diddy and Mary J. Blige lived. Apparently, Stevie Wonder used to have a place around one corner, as had Wesley Snipes before he ran afoul of the taxman.

Not that you could see much—partly because it was dark, but mostly because each of the places were spread out in the distance behind massive gates.

Leo Molinari wasn't a household name. But he'd made a fortune peddling small electronics. Enough so he could reside in a compound of his own beside the elite in the small town of Alpine, New Jersey.

The Uber driver pulled up in front of stone gates and Grant dug into his wallet and gave the man a sizable cash tip, and then asked if he'd wait to take him back to the city.

"Fine by me, man," the driver said. "That way I don't have to deadhead back into Manhattan."

Grant got out of the car. As he approached a post with a bell and speaker, he glanced behind him. The road was empty, but he was fairly certain that someone was back there watching him with their lights off, having followed him from the city.

He rang the bell and waited a half minute before a young woman's voice came over the speaker. "Yes?"

He used his former title, figuring the words commander and Scotland Yard would get him through the door, and said he wished to speak to Leo Molinari. There was a bit of a hesitation, as he could tell he was being checked out by whatever cameras were hidden nearby. He must have passed the eye test; a sixty-something man in a suit didn't pose much of a threat, as consequently there was a buzz. The gates opened and Grant proceeded up the long driveway.

Strategic lighting illuminated impressive landscaping and the Tudor mansion in the middle of it. Grant thought about his tea garden in Maida Vale, realizing a couple dozen would have fit on the property—and that was just in the front yard.

It took a couple of minutes to reach the front door. By the time he got there, it had swung open and the woman who'd answered the bell was waiting for him.

"Mrs. Molinari?"

"Sophia. Please, Commander."

"Austin. I'm not here in any official capacity," Grant said with a smile, making sure to get that clarification out of the way as soon as possible.

Sophia nodded, and despite the toddler clinging to her hip and the bulging belly of a woman fairly far along in her pregnancy, she managed to gracefully usher Grant inside the front door.

"Leo should be home any minute." She gave the youngster, a tow-haired handsome boy with a dimpled smile, a squeeze. "Bedtime's always a little crazy around here. This one refuses to go down until he says good night to his daddy."

"I understand."

He also understood why Julia hadn't welcomed Sophia into the Molinari family with open arms. A striking brunette who probably hadn't hit the north side of thirty yet, it didn't matter that Sophia seemed pleasant and friendly enough—Julia must have felt betrayed by her father replacing her beloved mother with what amounted to a girl in her mind. Grant could only imagine how Rachel would have reacted if the first woman he took up with after Allison were someone half his age.

"I don't even want to think what it'll be like to juggle a newborn and a three-year-old who's going two hundred miles an hour, twenty-four-seven," added Sophia, indicating her protruding stomach.

"I'm sure you'll manage just fine."

"Can I get you something to drink while we wait for Leo to get back?"

Grant said he was fine and followed her into a living room that looked big enough to host a Premier League match. He had a choice of at least three separate seating areas—an oversized sectional couch, a table with half a dozen designer chairs, or a grandiose bar at the far end of the room. Sophia indicated Grant should take the sofa while she put the toddler on the ground.

"Teddy, why don't you go finish your puzzle, so you can show it to Daddy when he gets home?"

Either the word "puzzle" or "daddy" seemed to do the trick, as the boy eagerly toddled off toward a corner where jigsaw pieces were strewn all over the floor like the fall-out from a storm called Hurricane Teddy.

"When are you due?" Grant asked, as Sophia settled onto the opposite end of the sectional.

"The end of August. But I'll be lucky if I make it till then," she answered, patting her stomach. "Teddy came earlier than expected, so I figure his sister won't want to be outdone."

"A girl. That's wonderful. I've got a daughter, my only child, somewhere around your age I expect. She's been the delight of my life."

"I'll look you up in sixteen years or so," said Sophia. "I remember what a terror I was as a teenager."

Grant made a point of looking around the room, taking in the trappings and the young boy on the floor trying to put together puzzle pieces that didn't match up. "It looks like things worked out."

"I'm definitely blessed." Grant could see her heart swell as she watched her son. But Sophia's smile quickly vanished when she turned back to face him. "As opposed to poor Julia, which I presume is the reason you're here."

"Unfortunately, yes." Grant went on to explain his connection—how his daughter was about to marry Julia's ex-husband in just over a week.

"I have a hard time believing John's done what they're accusing him of," Sophia told him. "It doesn't seem like the man I've met, that's for sure."

"Obviously, I feel the same way, or I wouldn't be here."

"Granted, I haven't seen him in a few years. We just met a few times—mostly around the time Julia's mother took ill."

Sophia proceeded to tell Grant about how she had come into Julia's life, and more specifically, Leo's.

She'd been working as an assistant manager in the flagship store when Leo's first wife, Joyce, had been diagnosed with breast cancer. It had been a losing battle from the start and more than Leo could handle. Both of his grown kids, Julia and her brother, had been so caught up in their jobs, Julia trying to get a design business off the ground and Tony managing the flagship store, that they couldn't provide the round-the-clock attention their mother needed. This didn't upset Leo, who, seeing where things were headed, didn't want his children to watch Joyce waste away right before their eyes, so he'd turned to Sophia. She had incredible organizational skills and a gentle touch, and she was the perfect solution to manage the Alpine mansion with Joyce no longer able to do so.

As Joyce's health declined, Sophia became an integral part of the Molinari household and Leo found himself increasingly leaning on her. When Joyce passed away, it had been Sophia who had taken on the funeral arrangements, because Leo was overwhelmed. In the months that followed, at Leo's insistence, Sophia had remained in place at the house, and there were many nights where she would sit and keep her employer company, lending an ear to his reminiscences of happier times and trying to encourage him that there were brighter days ahead, even though he was having trouble seeing them.

When things eventually changed, Sophia had been caught completely unaware, since Leo was her boss and old enough to be her father. But love arose in the most unexpected times and places—and here she was a few years later, with a husband she adored, a caring, loving man (despite his reputation as a despot in business, a title that he claimed was a necessity on the road to success), and a child she loved more than life itself, with another on the way.

"How would you say things were with you and Julia?" asked Grant.

"Strained?" Sophia shrugged, as she picked up on Grant's look. "I guess that would be a way of putting it mildly."

"She didn't take kindly to you marrying her father."

Sophia shook her head. "Being the same age, it was easy to put myself in her position. I wouldn't have been crazy about the idea either. I kept trying to tell her that it didn't mean Leo felt any different about her. But I guess the whole situation just blew things out of proportion."

"What do you mean by that?"

"That everything became a much bigger deal than it should have. When Leo told her that we were thinking about starting a family, Julia lost it—asking him why Tony and she weren't enough. Leo tried to explain that he was doing it for me, that I shouldn't be deprived of my own chance at happiness. I thought it was sweet and genuine, but she didn't see it that way. She and John split up soon after that, and though it wasn't like Leo and him were really close, he certainly preferred John to someone like Pablo."

"Your husband knew Pablo?"

Sophia shook her head again. "Not only had they never met, he'd never heard of him. Julia running off like that shocked the hell out of everyone. And despite what you might've heard about Leo, he takes family very seriously. It all added up to an even bigger rift with Julia, and no matter how much I told him to be the bigger person, it couldn't be mended. And now it never will be."

"So, he hadn't seen Julia in what—close to three years?"

"None of us had," answered Sophia. "When I saw her last week, it was the first time since she took off for Hawaii."

"That's right. She came to the house?"

"She suddenly appeared, asking to see Leo. He was at one of the stores, but I immediately called him and said that Julia was here. Once he got over the shock, he told me he was headed straight home." She lowered her head. "Unfortunately, they never got to see each other."

"What happened?"

"I'm not really sure," Sophia told him. "Obviously, there was a bit of tension between us, but I tried to make her feel at home. I mean, it's the house she grew up in, right?" She nodded toward the young boy who had managed to put most of the puzzle together. "She met Teddy, we talked a little about the baby coming—then suddenly she had this change of heart and said she had to go. I guess she got cold feet about finally seeing her father."

"Do you have any idea why she showed up after all this time?"

"She didn't say. I suspect it had something to do with money—only because I asked the same thing and she mentioned there being a matter she needed to discuss with Leo. 'Matter' sounds like money, but I could be wrong."

"I think you're probably right," Grant told her. He gave Sophia a little insight into his and Rachel's trip to Hawaii and what they'd learned about Pablo's finances, or lack thereof. But before Sophia could respond, there was the sound of the front door opening and the little boy squealing.

"Dada!"

As Leo Molinari entered the house, he offered up a sweet smile for his young wife and a conciliatory nod toward Grant—but he only had eyes for one person, his young son. The toddler rushed across the room and Leo gathered him up in his arms. He immediately nuzzled the child and gently buried his face into the side of his son's neck, blowing air on his soft skin and the reddish birthmark there.

"R-r-raspberry—" gurgled Leo, as his son squiggled happily in his arms.

"St-strawberry!" corrected a giggling Teddy, in what Grant realized must be a nightly ritual greeting. It brought back memories of Rachel as a child, waiting up for him to come home from the Yard—and how it had made up for all the horrors and bureaucracy that Grant had to deal with each day.

"What'd you do today, sport?" asked Leo.

"Song!" the boy cried out. Teddy shifted around in his father's arms and looked across the room at Sophia. "Song, Mommy!"

Seconds later, Grant got to witness Teddy's rendition of "I Want to Hold Your Hand"—though his version was "I Want to Wash Your Hands" and he screamed instead of singing the chorus accompanied by Sophia playing the piano.

Leo sidled up to Grant and indicated his son.

"I've been showing him videos of the Beatles on *Ed Sullivan*," Leo explained. "He thinks the song was meant to be screamed at the top of your lungs."

"I actually grew up in Liverpool," Grant told him. "And remember watching it live on television."

"Me too," said Leo, confirming Grant and Julia's father were close in age, definitely from the same era.

After appropriate applause from one and all, Sophia told the child it was time for bed and to say goodnight to everyone. There were more hugs for his father, a "bye-bye" to Grant, and Sophia telling the former Scotland Yard man that it was very nice meeting him. Mother and son headed upstairs, leaving Grant alone with Leo Molinari.

Getting his first good look at the man, Grant was impressed by the way he carried himself. Not particularly tall, actually slightly less than average height, he was solid and compact, like an extra in a Scorsese film. His hair was tinged with gray, his handsome face a map of worry lines that had probably come with amassing his fortune, and he held a strong grip that made sure when you were in his presence, he and only he held your attention.

The first point of discussion turned out to be the one they had in common—John Frankel, a former son-in-law, and now a son-in-law to be.

"I never had anything against John," Leo told him. "For a while there, when Joyce was alive, we'd have Sunday dinner together as a family. He was usually quiet and very polite, quite deferential to both my wife and daughter, and being old-fashioned, I have to say I liked that."

"But once Sophia came into the picture—"

"It was my daughter who pulled back, not me," finished Leo. "John fell into line taking Julia's lead, and I can't fault him for that."

"And the two of them splitting up?"

"It upset me greatly. Like I said, I was a fan of John's—especially compared to that home-wrecker Suarez. I never met the man, but that's a good thing. I certainly would have given him a good piece of my mind, and then some." Leo shook his head. "Breaking up her marriage was bad enough; putting her into a hole of debt she couldn't crawl out of? That's a different matter altogether."

"You knew about that?"

"Just because I hadn't seen my daughter in three years doesn't mean I hadn't kept tabs on her the best I could." Leo explained how he knew all about Pablo winning the Papaya Seed in a poker game and overextending himself with Erickson. "It was only a matter of time before things got so bad that either Julia would finally leave him or come back looking for a way to bail the loser out. When Sophia called me that day to say Julia was at the house, I knew it was one or the other."

Leo looked off toward the front of the house. Grant guessed he was imagining his long-lost daughter finally making her way back through his doorway.

"When she didn't stick around, I figured it was the money she wanted and lost her nerve." Leo sighed and turned back toward Grant. "Even so, to my dying day, I'll regret that I didn't get back quick enough."

"Yet you didn't want to go identify her," pointed out Grant.

"Even if I'd been able to put the hurt between us aside, I preferred to remember her like I'd last seen her, instead of on a gurney in some ice-cold morgue."

Grant gave him a solemn nod.

"Does any of this help you with clearing John's name?" asked Leo. "I presume that's why you're here."

"I'm trying to learn what really happened. It's something that plagues men like me, even after they've left their profession," said Grant. "Come to think of it, men like John Frankel as well."

"Is that what he was doing in Maine?" asked Leo. "You can't turn on a television or radio without hearing about it."

"I don't really know. We haven't been in touch very much lately," Grant answered, which was pretty much the truth. "I can't be sure, but I think he might have been up there looking into the possibility that Julia had a child."

"A child?" Grant watched as Leo went visibly pale. "What are you talking about?"

Grant told the clearly shaken man about what he and Rachel had learned in Hawaii, and how that lined up with the grave in the Lowell cemetery. The more Grant told him, the farther Molinari shrank back in his chair.

"You had no idea?" Grant asked him.

"None," murmured Leo. He remained silent for a moment and Grant let him ruminate on this news that had to alter the way he saw the world. "There was a time, the months you're talking about, that I did lose track of Julia. I knew she'd quit the job she was working, but those days were pretty sketchy. Plus, Sophia and I were out of touch ourselves, being overseas most of that time."

"Overseas?"

"Italy," Leo told him. They'd gone there shortly after Julia had fled to Hawaii with Pablo, with Sophia suggesting a big trip might distract him and they could visit relatives of Leo's. Shortly after landing in Rome, they'd realized Sophia was pregnant, but there had been complications and she was put on immediate bed rest. Leo insisted they stay overseas at that point out of concern for Sophia and the child she was carrying. When they finally returned to the States, they'd been blessed with Teddy and now, a few years later, awaited the arrival of his baby sister.

Leo shook his head, obviously still trying to wrap his head around what Grant had told him. "He died when he was four months old, you said?"

Grant nodded. "We don't have all the details yet."

"And the father?"

"I'm presuming it was Pablo. But I suppose it could have been John. No way of knowing, short of exhuming the grave and getting DNA tests from John and a dead man." As he spoke the words, Grant felt himself cringe at the thought.

At the same time, tears had actually started to form in Leo Molinari's eyes, enough so that Grant asked if he were going to be all right.

"I just can't help thinking that if things were different, my child and Julia's boy could have grown up together," Leo told him. "Might have been a second chance for all of us—for me and Julia to get back on track again."

Grant could only nod in agreement.

"And how did this child end up in Maine?" asked Leo.

"There are a lot of people still trying to figure that out."

"I'd appreciate you keeping me up to speed with anything you find out."

"I will. And if anything else occurs to you—"

"I will be certain to let you know."

Leo got to his feet. Grant did as well, knowing that he was on the verge of overstaying his welcome.

"If what you say is true, you realize this makes things worse for John," Leo pointed out. "Julia not only leaves him, but doesn't tell him about giving birth to what could have been his child?"

"That hasn't escaped my attention," acknowledged Grant. "Along with the fact that Pablo Suarez was the man who ran off with his ex-wife in the first place."

"I hope there's another answer to all this."

"You're not the only one."

A few minutes later, Grant stepped outside and was about to start making his way across the football field–sized garden when Tony Molinari emerged from the garage. He had just parked a nifty sportscar in one of the stalls. Julia's brother stared at Grant, clearly recognizing him from his drop-by at the Molinari flagship store.

"What the hell are you doing here?" demanded Tony.

"Talking to your father about the baby that your sister had."

Grant got the expected response from the blunt declaration—the younger Molinari's jaw dropped a foot.

"What the fuck are you talking about?"

"Maybe you should talk to him about it."

"Maybe you should go back to wherever you came from."

"The country is called England," Grant informed him, matter-of-factly. "And nothing would please me more at this particular point."

That seemed to render Tony Molinari speechless. Grant gave him a tiny wave before he could recover and moved on down the driveway.

When he emerged through the stone gate, Grant wasn't surprised to see that the Uber driver was no longer in sight.

But he was caught a bit off guard to find Taryn Meadows leaning against her nondescript police sedan.

"I took the liberty of telling your driver that you were going to be a while," Taryn said.

"You did, did you?"

"Need a ride back to the city?"

Grant couldn't tell if that were a question or a demand.

He figured he didn't have much choice in the matter.

Taryn opened the passenger door; he moved to step inside the car. Then he stopped short.

"I don't suppose the driver gave you back the twenty dollars I'd given him to wait for me?"

Taryn laughed. "You're in America now, Commander. No one gives anything back here."

Grant got inside the car.

Chapter 23

Two conversations.

The first was pretty one-sided—at least for starters.

Rachel sat in the front seat of the rented Ford Taurus and listened as John told her everything he'd been up to since his "bachelor party weekend in Wisconsin."

She had been surprised at how he suddenly held nothing back, especially after keeping so much from her. It hadn't taken any prodding either; his immediate response to her query about having a child with Julia had been a guilt-ridden "I so wanted to tell you"—and the rest proceeded to gush forth in a half-hour burst that sounded to Rachel like an unburdening of the soul.

When he finished up with his torturous venture into the Lowell graveyard and subsequent train trip south like an escapee in a B movie, she tried to take it all in.

Why hadn't she fallen in love with someone normal? Like a stockbroker, doctor, or teacher, instead of a man who seemed to live his life on a tightrope over a pit of crocodiles. She presumed it had something to do with growing up around her father, but that would take endless shrink sessions to unravel and, in the end, wouldn't change the fact that she didn't want to be with anyone else.

She just prayed it wasn't going to be one of those jailhouse romances where she spent the next couple of decades separated by thick prison glass from the man she loved, destined to a life of pen pal love letters and bringing a fruitcake with her each time she visited during the holidays.

When she finally did speak, it was to ask the one question that had been preying on her since all this madness had started.

"Why didn't you think you could tell me any of this?"

John hung his head, unable to look her in the eye. "Me having a child wasn't part of the deal. I needed to find out if it was true or not."

"Because—?"

When he finally looked at her, she saw that his eyes had welled up.

"Because if it were true, I'd understand why you might not want to marry me."

The second conversation was one-sided as well.

But instead of a confession, it was more like a lecture.

Taryn Meadows just couldn't help herself.

She'd spent most of the drive back to the city admonishing Austin Grant for everything that he and his daughter had been holding back from her.

It wasn't like she had anything against the man. She actually admired the former Scotland Yard commander. His career had been nothing short of extraordinary, culminating in the case the previous year that he had worked with John Frankel. If she could accomplish half of what Grant had done during his time at the Yard, she would settle for that right now.

It also didn't make her feel great that the subject of said lecture was John Frankel.

Taryn didn't want to believe her suspended partner was guilty of anything he was suspected of doing. Up until Julia Molinari's body had been discovered on his living room floor, Taryn had held John in the same esteem as she did his father-in-law-to-be. But as each day passed with John seemingly on the run, it had been harder for Taryn to cling to that opinion.

She said as much to Grant and waited for a response as she swung off the GW Bridge.

But he just stared straight ahead.

A few minutes later on the West Side Highway, Taryn couldn't take it.

"Aren't you going to say anything?"

When Grant still didn't respond, she thought she might scream.

"I'm hungry," he finally told her. "How about you?"

———

Rachel stared at him.

"Why would you even say that?"

"It wasn't like we ever talked about kids," John told her.

"It's been such a whirlwind that there are a lot of things we haven't gotten around to discussing. I just figured we would at the appropriate time."

John nodded. "So?"

"What? You want to talk about this? Now?"

"Seems as good a time as any."

"You do know half the cops on the Eastern Seaboard are looking for you."

"So we'd better get to it before they catch up with us."

Rachel couldn't help smiling. Part of her was still furious with John for keeping her in the dark, but the other part (which was winning for those keeping score) was completely touched, realizing his actions had been totally governed by how strongly he felt about her.

"Three."

"Excuse me?"

"Two girls, oldest and youngest," said Rachel. "A boy in the middle."

"You've obviously thought about this."

"That way each has their own identity. One's girl's the oldest, the other's the youngest. And then there's the only boy," explained Rachel. "Meanwhile, the estrogen count still outnumbers the testosterone in the family."

"Of course."

Rachel leaned across the front seat and took his hand.

"Listen carefully to me, John Frankel. Like I told you at lunch the other day, if this is going to work, we have to be a united front. That means no secrets—"

"I couldn't tell you what I didn't know—"

"I realize that," Rachel said. "But we're *both* on this journey. Things are going to come up when we least expect it and we're going to make mistakes. I'd just prefer we make them together."

"I'm not sure what I did to deserve someone like you."

"Just make sure you keep telling yourself that."

John laughed out loud. But it didn't hide how exhausted he looked.

"When's the last time you got some sleep?" she asked.

"I can't even remember."

"Well, it's not like we can go to your place or mine."

He gave her one of those grins that made her go all mushy inside.

"You're not going to turn me in?"

Her response was a slight but not so innocent shrug.

"They're not offering a big enough reward."

John raised an eyebrow. "And I am?"

"That remains to be seen."

"Wow. Look at you going all Bonnie Parker on me."

"Shut up and come over here, Clyde."

He didn't need to be asked twice.

—⁓—

"Well, this is a new one," said Phyllis.

The seventy-something Astro Diner mainstay placed two menus on the table shortly after Taryn and Grant had settled into the booth.

"Pardon?" asked Grant.

She looked directly at Taryn. "I'm used to seeing you with the detective a couple times a week." She turned her attention to Grant. "And I've waited on him and you more than once or twice. But I haven't seen this combination before."

She waggled a finger back and forth between the two of them.

"Just keeping you on your toes, Phyllis," Taryn told her.

"You'd better be keeping that good man out of a jail cell he doesn't belong in."

Her definitive tone made it impossible for Taryn or her dinner companion to argue. Phyllis asked what she could get them.

Both decided on sandwiches, and in honor of the missing detective that had brought them here in the first place, each ordered John Frankel's favorite—a chocolate milkshake.

Once Phyllis retreated to the kitchen, Taryn turned back toward Grant. "So, you've done this before?"

"By 'before,' I presume we're not talking about Phyllis's shakes, which are delicious, by the way."

"It makes me crazy that John doesn't put on a pound having at least three or four a week." Taryn shook her head. "No, I meant be involved in a case that hits so close to home. With a fellow officer, investigator, or whatever the hell you folks call each other over there?"

Taryn watched as Grant considered the question.

"There was a colleague who we suspected was tipping off a ring of drug dealers on impending raids," Grant recalled. "It was maddening. We couldn't figure out how we just kept missing them, always getting there just a little too late. That's when we realized they were getting fair warning from inside the Yard and someone I worked hand in hand with was the one all the fingers pointed at."

"Did you end up recusing yourself?"

"I certainly thought about it. But then my direct superior pointed out that I knew the accused better than anyone and I would hopefully notice when he varied from his routine or if there were a distinctive change in his behavior."

"Did it turn out to be him?"

Grant shook his head. "His wife, actually. She had a brother who was an addict. My colleague would bring his work home and casually mention what he was up to. The brother would pass the information to his supplier and got to maintain his habit."

"And you figured this out?"

"Shortly after it dawned on my colleague. The guilt was practically dripping off his face. I'm not sure I needed to be the one who got him to fess up to our superior, but it might have taken a bit longer had we not been so close."

"It's a bit different between me and John," Taryn admitted. "Not that I've been able to talk to him the past few days. But I think I've gotten to know him pretty well and none of this fits the detective I've been riding with all over Manhattan the past six months."

"I presume you've told Lieutenant Harris this?"

Taryn nodded. "He's torn as well. He has nothing but the utmost respect for John but he's getting pressure to make an arrest. And right now, John's the only suspect."

"Then you must understand how Detective Frankel is feeling," said Grant. "I'd imagine he's worried that unless he provides a suitable replacement, he's going to be locked up in a cell on his way to a jury trial with his head on the chopping block."

"He can't run forever, Commander."

"I'm sure he knows that. And it's Austin—I left the title back in England six months ago."

"And how have you been dealing with that?"

She watched Grant start to answer, then seem to think twice about it. Suddenly, Taryn felt bad about prying.

"Sorry. I can't help being nosy. Comes with the territory."

"No, that's alright," Grant reassured her. "It's actually something I've tried to avoid thinking about these past few months. At first, especially how that last case ended with Detective Frankel, I was happy for the break. I got to work in my neglected garden, read some books I had stacked up, and catch up with films I missed."

"But—"

"The novelty wore off quickly. The more time I had on my hands, the more I realized I missed what I'd spent the better part of my life doing. And even though this situation concerns John and that means it affects my daughter, trying to unearth the truth has gotten the old blood stirring again."

Taryn found herself nodding in agreement. "As frustrating as I find the job sometimes, I can't imagine doing anything else."

"So you understand."

"Totally."

She also understood this was a good honest man sitting across from her.

And consequently, that didn't make what she was going to have to do to him any easier.

Rachel buttoned up her blouse and let loose a giggle. John turned toward her while straightening his own clothes and caught the grin on her face.

"What?"

"I can't help thinking about Sheila Rice," Rachel told him.

"*You're* thinking about Sheila Rice?"

"I certainly hope you weren't just now," Rachel countered, motioning toward the back seat they'd just climbed out from.

"Well, I wasn't," insisted John. "And even if I were, I'd certainly know better than to tell you."

Rachel laughed again. "*That* I wouldn't want you to."

"Thank God," said John. "I'm having a hard time keeping the rules straight."

She gave him a playful punch in the arm.

"You still didn't tell me why *you* were thinking of Sheila Rice," prodded John.

"I kind of feel sorry for her. She missed out."

John started to react and Rachel raised her hand.

"And don't tell me she didn't," she added.

"Wouldn't dream of it."

That resulted in another playful swat. Followed by Rachel realizing they could no longer avoid the inevitable—dealing with what happened next. John took the first step by asking his favorite simple question.

"So?"

"You're wondering if that was just one for the road before I turn you in?"

"The thought might have crossed my mind."

Rachel started to glower and John quickly shook his head.

"Kidding."

"You know every minute Taryn or Harris don't hear from you, that ring around your neck only gets tighter."

"And everything I just told you gets ignored. Caitlan Hill disappearing, as well as the woman who adopted the boy—"

"Margaret Talbot."

John nodded. "Not to mention Pablo showing up at that grave right before me. That has to be connected, but the DA's office doesn't care because they have a prime suspect with ironclad motives for killing Pablo and Julia."

"He stole your wife and she gave away your child."

"Rolls right off the tongue, doesn't it?

Rachel nodded. Suddenly it was her turn to ask the question of the hour.

"So?"

"I just take off to keep looking for answers and you pretend you never saw me—"

"How come I feel there's an *or* coming?"

"*Or*—you come with me and help."

"I was afraid you were going to say that."

Rachel didn't say no right away. She hesitated long enough that it was suddenly John's turn again.

"So?"

"I guess if I stuck with you, I wouldn't have to answer those annoying 'when's the last time I spoke to John Frankel' questions."

There was that grin again. Damn it.

"That's my Bonnie."

"You do know how that ended for the two of them, don't you?"

"That's why we have your father. He won't let them harm a hair on your head." He gently kissed her lips. "And neither will I. I'll turn myself in first."

"I can't believe we're even discussing this."

Rachel closed her eyes, wishing it was just a nightmare. But when she opened them back up, there they were—no better off than a pair of teenage runaways in a rental car every cop in the tristate area would be hunting for.

She told him as much.

"I have an idea what to do about that," said John.

Rachel already didn't like the way this sounded.

"You do, do you?"

"Remember my Uncle Joe?"

"The one who died last winter right before we met? That Uncle Joe?"

"That one."

"Your dead uncle is going to help us."

"Absolutely."

Now Rachel knew she really didn't like the sound of this.

The opportunity availed itself sooner than Taryn planned on.

She thought she was going to have to do some sleight of hand when they returned to the car, perhaps drop something on the ground exiting the sedan, counting on Grant's chivalrous nature to give her the distraction she needed.

It actually did turn out to be his good manners that gave her the small window she needed—just not the one she'd expected.

After dinner, Grant had insisted on paying the check. At first she'd protested, but looking at the tabletop she suddenly relented; sitting right there was what she'd been looking for—Grant's cell phone.

Taryn's luck held when he took the bill to the register and left the phone.

Taking advantage of his back being turned as he settled up with Phyllis and engaged in what Taryn knew wouldn't be a short conversation with the chatty waitress, the detective quickly slid the phone across the table.

In a matter of seconds, she pulled out a mini-transmitter and swapped it with a SIM card out of Grant's phone that was exactly the same size.

Taryn had the phone back in place by the time Grant returned.

She promptly thanked him for dinner and when he said he'd catch an Uber back to Rachel's now that they were back in the city, Taryn shook her head.

"It's barely out of my way."

Grant graciously accepted and a few minutes later, Taryn was driving him back up the West Side.

It was the least she could do.

She couldn't help but feel bad about resorting to the duplicitous action.

But as she had told Grant over dinner, she was a cop—and didn't know how to be anything else.

Chapter 24

Frankel sat on a wooden dock's edge and stared out across Greenwood Lake.

He had gotten up with the first glimmer of the rising sun over the trees in New York State, where he presumed every cop was looking for him (and probably Rachel). He wondered how long he could keep this up.

Long enough to get a few answers, he hoped.

His uncle's small cabin rested on the southwest shore that was actually in Jersey, with the seven-mile lake diagonally crossing the border between the two states about an hour out of Manhattan. When his father's older brother died the previous fall, Frankel had been named the executor of the estate—basically the cabin, a beater Volvo parked in an adjacent toolshed that doubled as a garage, and enough books to think he had stumbled into the Garden State adjunct of the Strand, the massive bookstore back in the city.

He couldn't remember his uncle without a book in his hand. For most of his childhood, he'd had no idea what Joseph Frankel did for a living. Pushed for an answer, he would have said Uncle Joe was a professional reader. It wasn't until he was in his teens that he learned that he translated Nordic crime novels into English. His specialties were Icelandic and Norwegian authors, stemming from a year as a foreign exchange student in both Reykjavík and Oslo. So, the young Frankel's assessment would have been right—the man did make money reading and spent most of it on buying more books to fill the cabin's shelves, tables, and any other exposed surface with volumes piled high.

It had been the books that kept Frankel from selling the property. He wasn't quite sure what to do with them. The skitter-scattered nature of his uncle's collection made finding one buyer to take it off his hands impossible. Breaking it up into separate lots was something he didn't have the time to do. And he wasn't emotionally prepared to give away what amounted to the only legacy of Joseph Owen Frankel to 1-800-GOT-JUNK.

It was this hesitancy that had given him and Rachel a place to operate where Frankel was fairly sure nobody would come looking for them.

"I don't think I've seen that many books in one place in my entire life."

Frankel turned to see Rachel approaching along the dock. She was wrapped in a sweater and the clothes she'd worn the previous evening.

"I told you when we walked in last night that Uncle Joe was a bit of a bookworm."

"A bit? I didn't get the full effect until it got light." She settled down beside him. "I even found stacks inside the kitchen cabinets. I went looking for a coffee cup and came up with a bunch of Swedish serial killer books."

It had been late and quite dark by the time they had arrived the previous evening. They'd dropped the Ford Taurus at the rental car lot at Newark airport, then ridden three different buses through northeast Jersey (not wanting to test the memory of a nosy Uber driver when the cops came a-calling) until they reached West Milford, the town just to the south of Greenwood Lake and east of the Hewitt forest, places that Frankel had spent plenty of adolescent summers in.

It had taken an hour to hike up to the lake and the cabin. It was there that Frankel pointed out they'd have an untraceable set of wheels in the Volvo that Uncle Joe had nursed since acquiring it during the Clinton administration.

He had gathered sheets and blankets to make up the bed in the main bedroom. Then, with Frankel having last slept on the train up to Maine and Rachel emotionally drained from the whole ordeal and her fiancé's revelations on Rice's Ridge, the two had fallen asleep almost instantly, in each other's arms, completely clothed.

Now, with day breaking, Frankel set his mind to what they needed. Knowing that his face was plastered all over the media, they agreed it was best that he stick close to Uncle Joe's while Rachel drove off in the Volvo to the central Jersey suburbs, far enough away from the cabin, to stock up on essentials. The previous evening, Rachel had the foresight to withdraw a couple of thousand dollars from the ATM near the airport right before returning the car, allowing them to use cash. The plan was for her to pick up a few changes of clothes from a thrift shop or discount store and to get enough food and drink to get them through a few days.

"A few days?" Rachel asked, reacting to that last statement.

"Could be. There's a lot to unravel. Look at the way this thing has already twisted," Frankel pointed out. "You and your dad fly to Hawaii searching for Pablo and instead I find him dead in a cemetery in Maine; I wasn't even looking for him."

"How did he even know to go there?" asked Rachel.

Frankel shrugged. "I certainly didn't tell him."

"Yet when Pablo called my dad, he was already on his way to Maine. Which means—"

"—someone gave him the info he needed to get there," said Frankel. "Julia?"

"Possibly. She'd been given the adopted mother's name and the town she was living in."

"A lot of good that will do us," said Rachel. "Seeing as how both Julia and Pablo are no longer available to ask about it."

"But there *is* the woman who gave her the name in the first place."

"Julia's old friend. The one you were telling me about."

"Caitlan Hill."

"Who has also vanished," pointed out Rachel.

"Which is what I'll be looking into while you're out shopping."

Rachel gave him a slight smile. "Is that my cue to go?"

"It is if you want something to eat." Frankel motioned toward the calm waters stretched out in front of them. "Uncle Joe used to say the lake was filled with tons of bass, but I never caught one. Still, if you're willing to take your chances, I could scrounge up a boat and some bait—"

Rachel cut him off by leaning in and giving him a peck on the cheek. "I'll try to get back as soon as I can."

———

Rachel used the Maps app on her iPhone to navigate her way into the small town of Haskell, New Jersey. The village seemed a safe distance from the lake and a good place to look for food and clothing outlets.

The first thing she did was to stop at an out-of-the-way service station to gas up the Volvo; she added a baseball cap and cheap pair of sunglasses to the fuel purchase. She threw on the shades and wore the Mets cap low as she made her way into a small market to gather up simple staples—eggs, milk, cereal, bread, lunch meats, and frozen pizzas. She found a shop calling itself a general store that was nothing more than a glorified thrift shop, but perfect for her needs.

The last thing she did was change a five-dollar bill for some quarters and then spent a good half hour prowling the town looking for that artifact from a previous century—a pay phone. Even out here in the sticks, it was a cellular world. But she and John had agreed to stick to burner phones or preferably go old-school if they were lucky enough to find a phone booth, which Rachel finally located outside a laundromat.

She had tried her father the previous evening from a pay phone near Newark airport and gotten no answer, and by the time they'd arrived at the lake, it was too late to call. This time, Grant picked up, but the call lasted all of one minute.

"Dad—"

"Hi."

Rachel could tell she had caught him off guard. Perhaps it was not recognizing whatever number the pay phone brought up on his cellular display.

"I tried you last night but—"

"Are you okay?"

His interruption confirmed what she suspected. She asked, "You're not alone?"

"Not right now. No."

The answer was distinctly clipped.

Rachel paused a few seconds and considered what information she needed to give him before hanging up.

"We're both okay. But you'll definitely hear from us later."

"That's good to know."

"I love you, Dad."

It was all she could offer at that point, having no idea what the rest of the day—hell, make that the next few hours or minutes—held for her and John.

"Talk then," Grant said.

Her father disconnected and Rachel wondered who he was with that he couldn't return the form of endearment.

She realized there could have been any number of people interested in talking to the woman who had run off with the man who was number one on New York's Most Wanted list.

Rachel sighed. Being a fugitive wasn't all it was cracked up to be; the movies made it seem a whole lot more glamorous than it really was.

Frankel hadn't realized how hungry he was until he'd whipped up a second order of eggs and toast for both him and Rachel. Rachel told him about the aborted phone call with her father.

"Who do you think he was talking to?"

"I've no idea. More than likely one of your colleagues," suggested Rachel. "I hate lying to him."

"It's not lying exactly," said Frankel with a smile. "Call it omission."

Her response was an eyeroll.

"Besides, he'll be caught up soon enough," added Frankel.

That seemed to appease her as she pointed at a pad of paper with lots of numbers and scribbles lying next to a laptop that had belonged to Uncle Joe.

"So, what are we doing that we're not telling him about?" she asked.

"Funny you should ask."

He had been busy while Rachel had been gone.

He had decided to double down on trying to locate Caitlan Hill; he got back in contact with the Bradford Clinic, where she had worked. Masquerading as her brother, he had inquired to her whereabouts and kept getting the same answer—Caitlan had taken a long overdue sabbatical.

On the day before Julia had ended up dead in his apartment.

Frankel had tried to press for more information, but that was all he could get.

Until he got under the skin of one last officious assistant, who'd snidely remarked that she didn't know why he was wasting her time.

"Since you're her brother, I think you'd know, since Caitlan said she needed to head back home," the woman said before hanging up on him.

Knowing that Julia had gone to high school in Little Falls, he was able to match up a Caitlan Hill who had lived in nearby Totowa two decades before with her single mother, Loretta.

It turned out that a Loretta Hill still lived at that same address all these years later.

"And you're thinking of paying this woman an unexpected visit?" asked Rachel, now that she had caught up.

Frankel shook his head. "Not me. You."

⸺

Rachel had to admit that John's logic made sense.

Having no idea if Loretta Hill was a news junkie or even aware of the all-out search for John, they didn't want to run the risk of exposing him to anyone unless absolutely necessary.

And with Rachel being a freelance reporter, it was certainly simple enough to say she was working a story for a national magazine and was interested in talking to Caitlan as an expert in the adoption field on whatever scandal that Rachel thought the woman would buy into.

While Rachel drove and considered her exact pitch, John filled her in on Totowa, a suburb of the much larger Paterson. It had been said that Newark was the armpit of the great state of New Jersey. If that were true, the other armpit could be found in the heart of Paterson.

John had been to Totowa with Julia, who had given him the nickel tour of the town that she'd grown up in. Though it wasn't as downtrodden as Paterson, it was the kind of place the Molinaris sought to escape the moment they were able to financially manage it. Leo's electronics stores didn't become moneymakers until after Julia had graduated from high school, so that was when her father, mother, and brother Tony had ventured east—first to the bedroom community of Englewood and eventually the posh streets of Alpine. As a result, Julia didn't have any reason to head back to Totowa except for nostalgia's sake, and it had been one more reason she'd fallen out of touch with her high-school classmates like Caitlan.

The Hill family, consisting of Caitlan and her mother, hadn't been as fortunate, as evidenced by the house that Rachel pulled up to in the Volvo. The records that John had dug up showed that she'd lived there for close to thirty years in a small two-story in need of a paint job over a decade ago.

John lowered himself in his seat and wished Rachel good luck as she stepped out of the car. She moved up a stone path with cracks that looked older than Uncle Joe's Volvo. She climbed the steps to the porch where a screen door with numerous holes in it covered a paneled door.

Rachel rang the bell and waited.

She was just about to punch it a second time when the door opened, revealing a woman who Rachel could see the years had not been kind to. Her once-blond hair had shades of gray poking through and there were enough fret lines on her face to form a maze of their own. She was probably in her sixties, though looked like she was in her seventies, and given what John had said about overstaying one's welcome in Totowa, she might have actually been fifty-something and the victim of really hard times.

"Loretta Hill?"

"Who's asking?" responded the woman. There was a rattle deep in her throat, the sort Rachel thought went along with tobacco and alcohol abuse.

"My name's Rachel Grant and I was wondering if your daughter, Caitlan, was around—"

Rachel was about to jump into her feature article pitch when Loretta threw that entirely out the window.

"What is it about you women?"

"Excuse me?"

"My girl blesses me with her presence—for the first time in a couple of years, mind you—and suddenly you gals come crawling out of the woodwork thinking she's planted herself down here permanently."

"I don't understand," said Rachel, barely getting a word in; Loretta Hill was on a roll.

"I'll tell you what I told the other one," Loretta continued. "Caty was here for maybe an hour, barely said hello, and then took off again."

A whole lot of thoughts ran through Rachel's head. But three words in particular rang out.

The other one.

"Other one?" repeated Rachel.

"Yep. She and Caty went to high school together." Loretta looked at Rachel, as if sizing her up for the first time. "I doubt you and them were in the same class—what with that fancy English accent you got goin' there—"

"No, we weren't. But this girl—"

"You know the one I mean," Loretta interrupted. "The one that got herself killed and was all over the news the next day."

"Julia Molinari?"

"That's who I'm talking about," said Loretta.

Rachel pointed at the house.

"Julia Molinari came here?"

"Yup. And missed seeing Caty by maybe a half hour—an hour at the most." Loretta pointed directly at Rachel. "You're more than a week late."

Chapter 25

Grant dug into his pocket and came up with the key that had been given to him by John Frankel on his last trip to visit them.

At least the yellow tape has been removed, thought Grant.

He wondered who had gotten rid of it. Had the cops taken it with them because it was no longer a working crime scene? Or had one of the neighbors or a building manager taken it down because it was a blatant eyesore and vivid reminder of the tragedy that occurred within?

As he entered Frankel's apartment and flipped on the light, his eyes were immediately drawn to the dark stain on the carpet where the life had literally drained out of Julia Molinari's body.

When it had been suggested earlier that morning to meet here, it'd dawned on him that he hadn't seen the place where the nightmare began for John and Rachel.

The twelve-thousand-mile round trip to the Hawaiian Islands had left him with such a bad case of jet lag that he'd barely slept upon returning to Rachel's place the previous night after his late-night meal with Detective Meadows.

Worrying about Rachel hadn't helped matters either; he'd gone to bed with no word from her since they went their separate ways in the Great Uber Switch on the West Side Highway.

He'd tried her cell a few times but it had gone to voice mail, making Grant realize that Rachel had more than likely shut it off. It made it hard for the NYPD to draw a bead on her, but also frustrated Grant that he had no way to get in touch.

And, of course, when she finally did call, he'd been tied up with an unexpected visitor.

He felt like he'd only been asleep for twenty minutes when his mobile awakened him, though in truth he'd collapsed from exhaustion around three a.m. on the sofa bed he hadn't even bothered to unfurl.

It had been Sam Erickson, who had flown in on his private plane from the Big Island, having landed just after dawn at Teterboro.

"Free for breakfast, Commander?" Erickson had asked, once the dazed Grant had gotten his bearings.

Consequently, Grant had ended up back at the Astro Diner, just a few hours after having had dinner there.

He wasn't surprised to see Phyllis on her usual perch, the stool behind the register. Grant thought she probably never went home and just camped out in one of the Naugahyde booths, as he'd never been in the diner without her being there.

Phyllis pointed toward the back where Erickson was nursing a cup of coffee. The real estate developer waved Grant over, tapped the menu, and smiled.

"My kind of joint," said Erickson. "Give me a place that serves a good burger and Mom's apple pie anytime over some foo-foo restaurant with who cares how many stars. Those sauces play havoc with my insides."

"They make a good milkshake," Grant told him, wondering why the man from Chicago had dragged him off the sofa bed.

"Maybe I'll get one for the road."

They ordered breakfast, then Erickson got down to the business of telling Grant why they were breaking bread. It was pretty simple—it came down to Pablo Suarez and the money that he owed Sam Erickson.

"He called me and told me he was about to get it," Erickson told him.

"Really. When was this?"

"The afternoon he was killed." Erickson sipped his coffee. "He told me he had just gotten off the phone with you."

"He said pretty much the same thing to me."

"What else did he tell you?"

"That he hadn't killed Julia and was on his way to Maine to figure out things."

Just as Erickson started to respond, Phyllis arrived with their orders. The real estate developer waited for her to leave before continuing.

"Unless someone's keeping it quiet, and believe me, I've asked around, I haven't heard anything about cash being found by his body in that graveyard."

"Perhaps he never got it," Grant said.

"Or maybe whoever killed him took it."

Grant hadn't needed Erickson's pointed glare to see where the man's thought process was headed.

"John Frankel doesn't have your money, Mr. Erickson."

"You don't know that for sure."

"Despite what the media and police will have you believe, John didn't kill Julia or Pablo. And I'm fairly certain he didn't take your money."

"What makes you so sure?"

"Him swearing on the life of my daughter that he's innocent. And three decades of an instinct about this sort of thing that I've come to rely on."

"Then why is he on the run?"

"Knowing John? He's trying to find the person who did it and more than likely set him up."

That was when Grant's cell rang and he glanced to see a number flashing that he didn't recognize. His suspicions had been validated when he excused himself to step away from the booth to answer it and finally hear his daughter's voice.

Perfectly bad timing.

With Sam Erickson watching his every move, Grant had kept the call cryptically brief—simultaneously frustrated that he couldn't get more out of Rachel but feeling relief that she and Frankel were together and, for the moment, safe.

When Grant returned to the booth, Erickson asked if that had been John Frankel on the phone, having overheard enough of the conversation on Grant's side to incorrectly surmise it had been the missing detective calling.

Grant was happy he didn't have to lie, saying it wasn't his prospective son-in-law and was a matter he could deal with later.

Just wanting breakfast to end without having to promise something he couldn't deliver, Grant told Erickson that if he heard the authorities had stumbled upon a sizable amount of cash, he'd suggest they get in touch with him, which seemed to satisfy the developer.

A half hour later, Grant had just made it back up to the door to his daughter's apartment when he got a third call—from Eileen Crowe.

She had been the one who'd suggested they get together at John Frankel's studio apartment.

When Grant had asked what was going on, Eileen had said she'd rather not discuss it on the phone, so when she appeared in the doorway of Frankel's place, Grant was still in the dark.

The minute Eileen stepped inside, he noticed her eyes stray toward the same spot on the carpet.

"Gives you an eerie feeling, doesn't it?" asked Eileen.

"Taryn Meadows shared some of the photos a few days ago, but it doesn't compare to seeing it for yourself." Grant turned away from the bloodstains and faced the attorney. "I was surprised to hear that you wanted to meet up here."

"It wasn't exactly my idea."

She reached into her bag, pulled out a computer flash drive, and waggled it in front of him. "This arrived in my office first thing this morning. It was placed in a FedEx box at the Newark airport last night."

Newark. That got Grant's attention.

Meanwhile, Ellen was digging out her cell phone from the seemingly bottomless oversized bag. "Once I listened to it, I realized I needed to call you and downloaded it to my phone. I figured it'd be easier for you to hear it that way."

She negotiated the display on her cell and within seconds, John Frankel's voice poured out of the phone's speaker.

And suddenly Grant understood what his daughter had meant when she'd told him that he'd be hearing from them.

"Hello, Ms. Crowe. Sorry to get in touch with you all *Mission Impossible*–style but given the circumstances, I figured it was a good idea. I'm not totally up to speed on the latest technological advances and spyware, but I'm pretty certain it's getting easier to have unexpected guests on private phone calls. So this will have to suffice for now."

Grant gave Eileen a nod and they continued to listen.

"I'm recording this on a train heading south from Maine where I plan to meet Rachel and share what I'm about to tell you. As my attorney, I think it's important that you hear my side of the story without it having to go on the record, unless you and I agree it would be beneficial to do so. At the same time, I'd ask you to share it with Austin Grant and, when I'm done, I have a suggestion for how to do that."

At that point, Frankel paused long enough for them to hear the rumble of the southbound train in the background.

Then, after once again maintaining his innocence, the suspended NYPD detective laid out everything he'd been doing, from going to Hawaii to meet up with Julia to discuss his unsigned divorce papers to discovering Pablo's bloody body in a graveyard in Maine.

What followed confirmed that Julia had given birth to a baby boy and arranged for an adoption. Four months later came the death of that child, who John Frankel thought could very well be his own. Along the way, Caitlan Hill and Margaret Talbot, the two women who might have the answers he was seeking, had gone missing, and John was no closer to finding out the child's true parentage than he was to shedding the label of prime suspect.

Grant listened intently with a sense that a whole set of mismatched pieces were being floated around him looking for some kind of connection.

Toward the end, Frankel suggested that Eileen get together with Grant and play this for him in his Murray Hill apartment, using the key that

Rachel and Frankel had given him so he'd have a place to stay when he came to visit.

"And speaking of keys, you now understand why I don't have one of my own," said Frankel. "I gave it to Julia the last time I saw her—the day before she died. Unless I'm mistaken, I didn't hear that it was found on her by Taryn or any of the other detectives."

Grant motioned for Eileen to hit pause on her phone. He looked at her questioningly. "Was it?"

"Not on any of the police reports I was shown."

Grant told her to resume the recording and Frankel's voice continued.

"If that's true, there's a chance it could be lying around the apartment somewhere and perhaps the two of you want to give the place a good going-over to see if you can find it."

That made perfect sense to Grant. He and Eileen spent the better part of an hour searching for any place a key might have been put or slipped into. The studio apartment was small enough that they were able to check most everywhere at least twice.

They didn't find it.

That led them to replay the final thing that John Frankel had said on his call.

"If you can't find it, then there seems to be only one logical explanation. Whoever killed Julia must have taken it off her body and used it to lock the door when they left."

Chapter 26

Rachel stared at Loretta Hill incredulously.

"Did Julia say why she wanted to see Caitlan?"

The older woman shook her head. "She was pretty upset though. She'd obviously been crying and seemed ready to start sobbing again. When I said she'd just missed Caitlan and that I didn't think she was coming back, Julia went running for her car and sped off."

"Did you tell the police this?"

"Why would I do that?" asked Loretta, suddenly tensing up.

"Julia was murdered less than twenty-four hours later. You'd think the authorities would find that information pertinent to an investigation."

Loretta looked off in the distance. Rachel could tell that this must have crossed her mind in the past week, but she seemed to be struggling with it.

"Me and the police aren't on the best of terms," she finally told Rachel. "Why not?"

"It's all in the past—the wilder days of my youth. But I still try to have as little contact between me and them as possible." The older woman took a harder look at Rachel. "Who are you and why are you asking all these questions?"

Rachel had thought she'd been prepared for this, having readied the "journalist working on a feature" story suggested by John. But the Julia revelation had thrown her; it was enough to make her reconsider her approach. Rachel wondered if Loretta's reluctance to talk to the police might give her and John Frankel some common ground—enough that she risked turning toward the Volvo and giving it a slight wave.

Loretta watched curiously, then visibly reacted as John emerged from the passenger side of the car.

"Isn't that—"

"He didn't do what the police are accusing him of," explained Rachel. "We're trying to clear his name."

"You still haven't told me who you are."

"My name is Rachel Grant." She reached out and took John's arm as he cautiously joined her on the front step. "And this is my fiancé, John Frankel. We're supposed to get married this Sunday and I'm hoping by you talking to us, we might still do that."

—∗∗∗—

A few minutes later, they were in Loretta Hill's living room.

The interior matched the exterior—not so much having gone to seed but as if it were still mired in yesteryear, like nothing had changed since Loretta had settled there over three decades before. All that was missing were those plastic slipcovers that people placed over their furniture when they went out of town on a prolonged trip. It simply looked forgotten, pretty much like the woman who resided there.

Loretta hadn't threatened or attempted to call the authorities upon seeing John, giving credence to Rachel's theory that whatever Loretta's past transgression with the law had been, it was enough to not want the police in her house. She seemed much more interested in why they were so interested in her daughter.

John talked about the four-month-old boy buried in the Lowell cemetery, a child that apparently Caitlan Hill had arranged the adoption for as a favor to Julia.

"Well, I really don't know anything about that," Loretta told them. She turned toward Rachel. "Like I told you, I have barely seen my daughter since high school. I remember Julia—she was a fiery sort of girl—and for a long while, her and Caitlan were best friends. But they had some sort of falling out right around the time they graduated."

"Over what?" asked Rachel.

"Teenage girl stuff, the result of too much partying. Caitlan never told me exactly what happened." Loretta's eyes strayed past them, as if remembering. "I was so wrapped up feeling sorry for myself and trying to crawl into the bottom of whatever bottle I could get my hands on that I had no idea what my girl was up to. She made it through college on a scholarship, which was lucky for her because I didn't have a pot to piss in and could barely keep a roof over our heads. Could've knocked me over with a feather when I found out she'd gone into the business of arranging adoptions. I didn't even think she was interested in having anything to do with kids."

When Loretta turned back to face them, there was a wistful sadness in her eyes. "I don't know. Maybe she was making up for all my shortcomings in raising her."

"I'm sure that's not true," said Rachel.

"Look around you, sweetheart. This ain't exactly Buckingham Palace. Caitlan couldn't get out of here fast enough." Loretta laughed. "Of course, that makes it ironic now that she owns the place—which for the life of me, I don't know why she wanted to."

"She bought your house?" asked John.

Loretta nodded. "Couple of years back. Went and paid up the mortgage when the bank talked about foreclosing on me, because I couldn't come up with the monthly. She said it was better than playing the stock market, figuring the real estate market was always going up, even in a shithole like Totowa."

"And when was the last time you saw her before she showed up here?"

"Not since we did the paperwork two years ago. Like I told your girl here, no one would mistake us for being close."

"Why do you think she dropped in all of a sudden?" asked Rachel.

"It wasn't so she could catch up with her dear old mom, I'll tell you that. She barely had time to say hello—just made a beeline for her room and was out the door five minutes later."

Rachel shook her head. "Five minutes?"

"If that. However long it took for her to find her high school yearbook. She's just lucky I never throw anything out," said Loretta. "Well, except her father thirty years ago, but that's a whole other story that's definitely not worth revisiting."

Loretta had let them take a peek at Caitlan's room. While not quite a shrine, it appeared to be unchanged since her daughter had occupied it as a teenager, as if Loretta were waiting for her to return for some sort of do-over. There were posters of teen heartthrobs from the early aughts, a few stuffed animals tucked on shelves, and a flowered bedspread that looked handed down from a distant generation.

Their main focus had been the bulletin board on the wall above a pink desk. Yellowed high school announcements and papers adorned it, along with a few pictures, again mostly teen idols and a few forgotten rock bands. But one photo was a formal one of a cheerleading squad. John had immediately recognized a teenaged Julia standing front and center.

Loretta pointed to the tall lanky blonde who had her arm entwined with John's ex. "That's Caty—back when they said they'd be best friends forever."

"Those things never quite work out the way we hope," observed Rachel.

John asked Loretta if they could borrow the photograph, promising to get it back to her.

"Don't see why not. It's only been sitting there for close to twenty years."

A few minutes later, they were headed toward the door. Loretta asked John what she should tell the cops if they asked.

"That I didn't string you up by your toes and skin you alive?"

That caused Loretta to smile, and she said that John didn't seem like much of a killer.

"Tell them that, then."

As Rachel started up the Volvo, she glanced over at John in the passenger seat to see he was staring at the photograph.

"Odd, isn't it?" she asked.

"Oh, I don't know. It looks like every other high school cheerleading squad photo I've seen."

Rachel shook her head and pulled out into the street. "Not that. I'm talking about Caitlan showing up out of nowhere to suddenly pick up her high-school yearbook on the same day her best friend from back then is murdered."

"Oh. That." John nodded. "*That* is definitely odd."

Twenty minutes later, Rachel Grant pulled up next to the library at Passaic Valley Regional High School in Little Falls.

The school, which also served Woodland Park and Totowa, was currently in summer session, so the library was indeed open but barely occupied, as the last place any high-school student wants to find themselves on a sunny day in June.

Rachel pressed a silent button at the front desk where she waited until a woman in her fifties, whose red hair was definitely helped along by some beauty supply store's concoction, appeared. She wore a name tag that said Mrs. Winston and a friendly-as-long-as-you-keep-quiet smile that was a prerequisite for anyone who chooses small-town librarian as a profession.

"Can I help you?" asked Mrs. Winston.

"I was wondering where I'd find the class yearbooks?"

The librarian's smile never faded but Rachel could see the curiosity in her eyes, obviously stemming from such an inquiry by a visitor with a British accent. She motioned to a series of bookshelves on the wall behind her.

"We keep them back here. May I ask what year you're interested in?"

Rachel had anticipated this question, and having calculated that Julia had graduated in either 2003 or 2004, she asked to see both, throwing in the explanation that she was planning a surprise birthday party for a close friend who had graduated from Passaic Valley.

Mrs. Winston retrieved both maroon volumes and handed them across the counter to Rachel. "I hope you find what you're looking for."

"I do too," Rachel responded, knowing she had no idea what that would be.

She crossed the room, weaving through study tables and carrels, passing only one student, a teenage boy who couldn't have looked more miserable if he'd been shackled to the desk. Rachel was sorely tempted to tell him things could be worse—he could be a murder suspect on the run—but thought better of it. She headed to the rear of the room where the man that actually *was* one had situated himself.

"Quite the nostalgia tour you have us on," Rachel said as she pulled out the chair beside John. "Lovers' lanes, summer fishing cabins, now your ex's high school. What's next? The malt shop you had your first chocolate shake in?"

"Very funny," he said, taking one of the yearbooks from her. "That was Baumgart's in Englewood, a few towns over. Excellent food, by the way."

It took John only a minute to ascertain that Julia and Caitlan had been in PVRH's 2004 graduating class. Not only were both girls' senior pages in the volume, they had appeared in other photos, often together. They came across the same cheerleading squad photo that John currently had in his pocket, as well as another one at some awards ceremony where a few student honorees and their proud parents had been photographed. Both Julia and Caitlan had been there, along with Loretta Hill and Leo Molinari with his first wife, Joyce.

"She was a lovely woman," said John. "She didn't say much at those Sunday dinners as it was hard to get a word in edgewise with that clan. But you knew Joyce was probably the only person in the world that Leo Molinari ever listened to."

"Any idea why Caitlan Hill wanted to suddenly get her hands on this?" asked Rachel after both of them had taken a turn flipping through the yearbook.

"It must have something to do with Julia, right? But I can't see it." John shook his head. "I don't suppose we can take this with us."

John's supposition had been right. When Rachel asked Mrs. Winston if it were possible to do so, the librarian said the yearbooks had to stay in the reference section, not to mention library privileges were only for the students and faculty. With the possibility of aiding and abetting a fugitive hanging over her head, Rachel didn't think surreptitiously removing the volume from the library was worth the try, especially with Mrs. Winston sitting right there, so she asked if there was a copy machine available. Rachel spent a good half hour feeding coins into a machine and made copies of any picture or notation that featured either Julia or Caitlan.

After returning the book and thanking the librarian, Rachel walked toward the exit to join John. Along the way, she passed the forlorn-looking student and couldn't resist giving him a piece of friendly advice.

"It's a beautiful day outside," she told him. "If you took an hour off, maybe you'd find whatever you're working on easier to deal with."

"Tell that to my mom," said the student, motioning toward Mrs. Winston, who was watching them from her stool behind the front desk.

Rachel suppressed a gulp and took that as her cue to exit, grateful indeed that she hadn't tried to swipe the yearbook.

⁓

On the way out of Little Falls, looking for the highway that would take them back north toward Greenwood Lake and Uncle Joe's cabin, something suddenly occurred to Rachel.

It had been spurred by the small store they had just passed on the main street, a bridal shop that advertised, "We Have Everything For Your Blessed Day."

Not for this girl, thought Rachel.

"It's Monday, isn't it?" she asked John.

"I think so. But I've sort of lost track with all the comings and goings," admitted John. "Why? What's up?"

"Dad and I were supposed to meet with the florist in London today."
She checked the time on the instrument display, did some quick figuring,
and sighed out loud. "About six hours ago."

"Maybe your father canceled it."

"Have you met Austin Grant? If it didn't have something to do with
the Yard, my mother would have to remind him half a dozen times what
to do or where to be—and it was still fifty-fifty it would get done or he'd
show up there."

"Perhaps he'll surprise you."

Rachel shook her head. "What are we thinking? There's no way we're
getting married this Sunday."

"We could just elope to Atlantic City."

"That is not happening for sooooo many reasons."

Rachel turned to look at him.

"The least of which is that you'd probably be arrested or shot on sight.
Not to mention that we still don't have a proper wedding license, which
is how this whole bloody mess started!"

John reached over and placed a gentle hand on her knee. She responded
by turning away from him and keeping her attention on the road.

"I was just kidding, Rach—"

"Maybe we should just call the whole thing off."

"No. Don't do that. Please."

The earnest tone in his voice made her turn again. There was an
imploring look in his eyes, the first real hint of desperation she'd seen
there since they'd reunited on the hill in Elizabeth.

"Seriously, John—"

"Rachel, I know it seems like the most far-fetched thing in the world
right now. But becoming your husband, even the outside hope that
it might still happen this Sunday, is the *only* thing that is getting me
through this. So, please—please don't take that away from me right now."

Rachel realized she'd been holding her breath during this entire
outburst. When she was finally able to inhale and exhale at something
resembling normality, she spoke.

"I don't know what to say, John."

"Say that you're in this with me to the bitter end. Till death do us part."

"I was sort of planning to say that on Sunday."

"You still should."

There was *that* grin again.

Damn him. Love him.

"You're crazy, you know that, don't you?" Rachel asked.

"Crazy about you."

"Now you're piling it on."

"Maybe a little."

Rachel swatted his hand away—but now she was smiling too.

"So, how do you suggest we go about getting to the church on time?" she asked.

"Keep looking for Caitlan. We might also try and find where the mother, Margaret Talbot, disappeared to. She could probably fill in a bunch of these missing pieces, especially if we can't find Caitlan."

Rachel nodded. "I know you're convinced this all revolves around Caitlan and what happened up in Maine, but what about Julia's actual murder? That was back in New York—"

"—which is why we sent that drive to Eileen to play for your father." He glanced at his watch. "They should have gotten together and checked out my apartment by now. I wonder if they found the key."

"Guess we can stop and find out," said Rachel. "You have any coins?"

⁓

Fifteen minutes later, Rachel pulled back up in Haskell, a block away from the laundromat.

She got out of the Volvo while John remained ducked down in the passenger seat. She crossed the street and headed for the pay phone she'd used earlier that morning to call her father.

She dug into her purse and came up with enough coins and started to pump them into the slot.

But she hadn't even gotten a chance to finish, let alone dial a number, when someone called out behind her.

"Hands where we can see them!"

Rachel immediately let go of the receiver and did as she was told. She slowly turned to see that two uniformed officers had exited the laundromat, one from the front door, one coming out the back.

Both had drawn their guns.

"Where is John Frankel?" demanded the one who had stepped out the front. Tall and muscular, he would have been formidable even if he hadn't been pointing the revolver directly at her.

Rachel thought about screaming for John to run for it, but worried the cops would start shooting.

She looked past them toward the Volvo across the street and saw John get out the passenger side with his hands in the air.

"Let her go!" he called out. "I'm the one you want!"

The cops whirled around and quickly advanced toward him.

Rachel couldn't believe that John was actually grinning at her.

"I've always wanted to say something like that," he told her.

Seconds later, she was openly sobbing and he was in handcuffs.

Chapter 27

Find the key.

Find the killer.

Was it really that simple?

It was the question that Grant had been asking himself ever since they'd left Frankel's apartment and the same one posed by Eileen Crowe as they sat down at the table in the Starbucks just down the street. He handed her the mocha latte she had ordered and poured a little sugar into his cup of English breakfast tea.

"It certainly would solve our little locked-room murder mystery. Not to mention get our friend the detective off the hook."

"But who are we looking for?" asked Eileen after taking a sip of the latte and wiping a trace of foam from her mouth.

"Now, that's the question, isn't it?" He tested the tea and put it down, wondering why so many American coffee shops served beverages at luke-warm temperatures. He presumed it was a litigious society that made corporations leery of burnt mouths and scorched body parts. It made him yearn for the tea shop around the corner from his house across the Atlantic.

They discussed the revelations on the flash drive that Frankel had sent his attorney. Clearly, he seemed to be concentrating on the events surrounding the birth, adoption, and early death of Julia's baby. Her high-school friend Caitlan Hill seemed to be in the middle of it. Grant figured her disappearance wasn't a coincidence but didn't have a clue about how to go searching for her.

"There is one question I hesitate to ask because I probably don't want to know the response," said the attorney.

"What would that be?"

"One that you probably don't want to answer."

Grant figured he might as well beat Eileen to the punch. "Have either Rachel or I been in touch with Detective Frankel?"

"No wonder you had such a successful career at Scotland Yard."

"I can tell you that I haven't seen or talked to John since we returned from the islands," Grant answered truthfully.

"And what about your daughter?"

Grant hesitated, wondering how he wanted to respond. Eileen didn't press him, her eyes having drifted past him toward the coffee bar.

"You mean Rachel?"

Eileen's expression tightened, then she turned back to Grant and gently patted his hand. "That's all right, Austin. I think I already know."

She pointed at the television set on the wall above the register. A silent newscast played, but the picture and chyron told Grant everything that he needed to know and all he had been dreading ever since he and Rachel had gone their separate ways on the West Side Highway the previous evening.

Rachel and John were being escorted into the Seventeenth Precinct by a phalanx of policemen who also held off the gathered reporters and photographers.

The headline blared.

FUGITIVE AND FIANCÉE CAPTURED.

The two calls came almost simultaneously on their cab trip to the Seventeenth Precinct. Eileen's was first—John Frankel's allotted one—and she assured him she was on her way to see him, and not to utter a word until she was in the interrogation room. Rachel phoned Grant shortly after that and he told his daughter that he and Eileen would be there soon. Their conversation was brief, but long enough for Grant to know she was safe and actually calm, expressing more concern about what was going to happen to John than herself.

Upon arriving at the station, Eileen and Grant had to navigate the chaos of the press gauntlet. Questions were hurled but unanswered, as more than a few recognized Grant from the serial-killer case the last Christmas. Eileen went into full client-protective mode, even though Grant didn't qualify as such.

They immediately headed for Desmond Harris's office, where Eileen threatened to raise hell unless she was taken to see her client that very minute. One of Harris's detectives finally appeared to escort her to the holding area, where she would meet Frankel. Eileen told Grant to hang in there, saying she'd be back to fill him in as soon as possible, particularly about what was up with Rachel.

After Eileen left, Grant tried to find either Lieutenant Harris or Detective Meadows but was informed by Harris's assistant that both were in a meeting. A half hour later, after flipping through magazines that didn't hold his concentration, Grant understood what had been occupying the lieutenant and Taryn's time, as Tony Molinari emerged through a door that led to the back offices. Grant wasn't sure who looked more surprised. It probably would have been a draw, as neither man had expected to see the other again, certainly not this soon.

"What did I ever do to you?" sputtered Tony, seeing the former Scotland Yard man.

"What do you mean?"

"Are you tailing me or what?"

"Should I be?"

This seemed to confuse Tony even further. "I've got nothing more to say to you."

"I didn't ask you anything. But now that you mention it, why are you here?"

"You've got some balls askin'," exclaimed the younger Molinari. "Why do you think? After you go telling my pop all that stuff about Julia having a baby and not letting Frankel know it might be his? You think I'm not going to tell the cops?"

"As you say, I told your father. Not you," Grant pointed out. "How come you're here instead of him?"

"The old man's been all broken up ever since you left last night. After he told me, I said the cops should know this, so it fell to me because he certainly wasn't up to it. Someone has to stick up for my sis."

"I didn't think you and Julia were that close."

"She was still my fuckin' sister." Tony waved a hand toward the depths of the police precinct. "I don't give two shits about what happened to this Pablo prick—but if Frankel did what they're sayin' to Julia, I hope they fry the bastard."

Grant didn't have an immediate response, but it didn't matter as Tony used that as his exit line and walked out of the room. Grant settled back down in one of the chairs, wondering what this sudden display of brotherly love meant.

Probably nothing good for John Frankel.

That theory was proved correct about an hour later.

A number of people had crammed into Desmond Harris's office. Its primary occupant sat behind the desk with his lead detective on the Molinari case, Taryn Meadows, standing beside him. Three chairs had been pulled up in front of the desk, with Rachel sitting between her father and Eileen, the latter acting as her attorney.

"We've decided not to bring any charges against Ms. Grant," Harris said.

Grant breathed an inner sigh of relief, but suspected there was more to come.

"Detective Frankel insisted she had done her best to try and convince him to turn himself in, but he refused to do so," continued Harris. "Though I suspect there is some wiggle room in the validity of that statement, it's the deal that was negotiated by Ms. Crowe just now—Rachel Grant is allowed to walk and the detective has agreed to cooperate fully with us."

Harris turned to Rachel.

"Your fiancé spins an elaborate story about what he's been up to since all this started. I don't know what's fact or fiction, but none of it obfuscates him having the means, opportunity, and, most importantly, motive for killing Julia Molinari and Pablo Suarez. Given these motives, the evidence, and Detective Frankel's flight from justice, we are left with no choice but to bring two charges of murder in the first degree against him."

Rachel audibly sighed. Grant reached over to take her hand. He leaned over and softly spoke, but it was loud enough for everyone in the room to hear.

"This isn't over, Rach."

He saw her attempt a grateful smile, but it just wasn't happening.

Grant thought of his late wife. Allison had always told him the one thing he shouldn't ever do was promise their daughter something he couldn't deliver.

He had every intention of following through on the one he'd just made. He just didn't have any idea how.

⁓

It was dinnertime when Rachel and Grant arrived back at her apartment, but neither had much of an appetite. They went through the motions of ordering up some Chinese food but a half hour after it arrived, it remained untouched.

"Maybe we should just start drinking," suggested Rachel.

"I won't deny that the same thought crossed my mind."

His daughter gave him a hapless shrug; Grant could see Rachel trying her best to keep her tears in check. "Oh well. Always a bridesmaid—"

"Don't say that, Rach."

"You have to admit, this puts a crimp in the old wedding plans."

"Temporarily. I'm not ready to give up and I certainly won't let you. There's still too much we don't know." Grant realized they hadn't had a chance to catch up since they'd gone their separate ways the night before. "Why don't you tell me what you two have been up to since I saw you last—maybe something will click."

Rachel proceeded to relay the events of the past twenty-four hours, starting with the trek from Elizabeth to the Greenwood Lake cabin, the visit to Caitlan Hill's mother and subsequent trip to the high school library. When she got to the aborted second call at the pay phone, she shook her head.

"I can't believe they were waiting for us there," she lamented. "I'm sure no one saw or recognized me when I'd been there earlier that morning. It was a practical ghost town and I was on the phone barely more than a minute."

Grant started to respond, but stopped short.

"It wasn't even that, right? I was with Sam Erickson when you called." He told her about the real estate developer's unexpected visit. "Did you call anyone else after that?

"Of course not. Like I said we were trying to be as careful as possible—"

Rachel broke off as Grant raised a finger and brought it to his lips. She looked at him curiously, but stopped talking. Grant dug in his pocket and pulled out his mobile, thinking when he might have left it unattended.

And remembered the late-night dinner with Taryn at the Astro Diner.

He made idle talk as he fiddled with the side of the phone, the miniscule SIM card tray in particular. He slid it out and revealed the peculiar looking chip that was in the slot, definitely not the type that came with the phone, especially as it had a micro-sized blinking red light on it.

Rachel's eyes widened in shock as Grant placed the phone on the table between the kung pao chicken and peanut noodles. He motioned for Rachel to move with him toward the front door.

Minutes later, they emerged from the building and Grant indicated it was safe for his daughter to speak.

"How the hell did that get there?"

"Taryn Meadows."

He took the opportunity to fill in Rachel on what he'd been up to recently. His conversation with Leo Molinari. Taryn waiting outside afterward. Their subsequent ride back into the city and what Grant had thought was a semi-friendly dinner. "She must have made the switch when I went to pay the check."

Rachel offered up a sad smile. "I always knew that gallant nature of yours would end up getting you in trouble."

"Remind me next time."

"What are you going to do about your phone? Are you going to say anything or just get rid of it?"

"I'm not sure just yet. I'll need to discuss it with Eileen." Grant considered it for a second or two. "Right now, I think we set it aside and get ourselves a couple of those disposable ones."

"Good idea."

Grant checked his watch. It was already past eight. "Any idea where we might get them this time of night?"

Rachel laughed. "It's New York, Dad. The town that never sleeps, remember? There isn't anything you can't get when you need it, no matter what time it is."

She linked her arm in his and off they went to search. It didn't take long to find—less than four blocks—at a newsstand kiosk that sold newspapers, magazines, and small electronic devices including disposable phones.

After loading plenty of minutes on each, they headed back toward Rachel's apartment and discussed what to do next.

Grant considered Rachel's visit to Loretta Hill in Totowa. "This all seems to start with Julia and Caitlan. It can't be a coincidence that Caitlan comes home for the first time in years and Julia suddenly comes looking for her there."

"Speaking of coincidences, what about Pablo ending up where Julia's baby was buried at the same time as John?"

Grant nodded. "That child seems to be at the center of all this."

"Which is why it would be great to find Caitlan and get her to tell us exactly what happened back then."

"Except she clearly doesn't want to be found," observed Grant.

"Unfortunately."

Grant mulled it over, convinced there must be an explanation why all roads kept leading back to the small graveyard in Lowell, Maine.

He suddenly found himself refocusing.

Rachel looked his way. "I know that look. What's going on in that Scotland Yard brain of yours?"

"There *is* someone who knows better than anybody what happened to the baby that we haven't even talked about."

Rachel's eyes brightened. "The adoptive mother. What's her name?"

"Margaret Talbot."

"And how are we supposed to find her?"

"Good question," answered Grant. "But I think I know where to start."

———

A few minutes later, with his cell turned off and tucked away in a suitcase in the closet, Grant placed a call on one of the disposable phones to Mildred Snow, the eighty-year-old woman that Frankel had talked to in Lowell.

Being of an older generation, Mildred was still listed in whatever passed for a telephone white page directory these days, so the only question was whether she was home or if Grant would wake her up.

Luckily, she was indeed home and still awake, admitting to being an insomniac who spent most of her late evenings watching reruns of *Everybody Loves Raymond*.

After identifying himself and his connection to John Frankel, Grant asked if he could put her on speaker, so that his daughter, John's fiancée, could hear as well. Mildred was happy to oblige, saying it was a nice distraction from watching Ray wriggle his way out of whatever trouble he happened to be in with Debra.

But when it came to any information about Margaret Talbot and her late child, she wasn't able to provide much more insight than she'd told John.

"I barely ever saw the woman," said Mildred. "Maybe three times the entire time she was here with the baby. It makes me think the child was ill from the start; it's not like she ever took him out for a walk in the pram. She brought the baby home one day, next thing we hear she's burying the poor thing in the West End graveyard."

"And how long after the funeral did Mildred leave town?" asked Rachel.

"Almost immediately. I think the house was put back on the market two days later and she was already gone."

Grant asked about Julia and Caitlan. Did Mildred ever see either of them up in Lowell? He did his best to describe them (never his strong suit) and as a result, Mildred said that she'd really need a picture to tell anything.

Rachel jumped in at that point and said they had one—back when they were seniors in high school, but a pretty fair representation. She asked if Mildred had access to a computer. If so, she could send the photo along.

"I don't have one," said Mildred. "But I do have an iPad that my grandson Jack has been giving me lessons on. It was all Greek to me at the start, but I'm finally getting the hang of it. I can probably open an email with a picture in it, fingers crossed."

Rachel quickly found the cheerleading picture she'd copied in the high school library, scanned it, then sent it along to the email address that Mildred provided.

Their luck held as Mildred was able to open the message and download the picture attachment.

"We're talking about the two girls in the center, front row," Grant told her. "The brunette is Julia. The taller blonde is Caitlan Hill."

There was a sudden intake of breath on the other end of the phone.

"Mildred?" Grant asked. "Are you still there?"

"Yes, I am," she finally responded. "I certainly don't remember seeing the dark-haired girl. Julia, you said?"

"That's right. She's the one who died last week. The blond girl is her friend Caitlan," Grant said. "Why—have you seen her before?"

"Absolutely," replied Mildred. "But I don't know why you're telling me her name's Caitlan."

"I don't understand," said Grant.

But somewhere deep down inside, he already did.

"That's Margaret Talbot," Mildred told him. "The mother whose child is buried in that graveyard."

PART FOUR

In Sickness and In Health

Chapter 28

Caitlan Hill stared out the window, and not for the first time wondered how things had ended up going so wrong.

For the longest time she'd been waiting for things to catch up with her and had only recently relaxed, thinking the whole matter had been put behind her; the secrets she desperately had clung to buried six feet underground in a tiny patch of dirt in northern Maine.

She should have known better.

Caitlan knew someone would eventually come looking for Margaret Talbot, the identity she'd taken on for a few short months and just as quickly abandoned after the private ceremony in the West End graveyard, with just a priest to administer a few prayers and condolences to the grieving mother.

She'd left Lowell the very next day, wanting to put the Margaret persona behind her, trying to reclaim her life as Caitlan Hill and pretend that she'd never worked the system that had allowed her to take Julia's newborn as her own.

She'd actually gotten away with it too—until John Frankel had showed up nearly three years after she thought she'd put Maggie Talbot and her poor son Joseph to rest for good.

As she waited, Caitlan wondered what life might have been like if Julia hadn't gotten in touch from Hawaii in a desperate panic about her pregnancy.

A whole lot simpler; that was for damned sure.

It had been years since the two women had really talked. It hadn't been Caitlan's choice to lose touch—Julia had begun to pull back. Caitlan had found it increasingly hard to maintain any relationship with the girl who had been her best friend since grade school because of what had transpired over the holidays during their senior year at Passaic Valley.

They had grown even more distant with their choices upon graduation. Caitlan had gone to an Ivy League school, while Julia stayed home, forgoing college to conquer the working world. Even so, Caitlan always blamed herself for the dissolution of their friendship—she knew that she should have handled things differently back in the day but could never bring herself to come out and apologize for what had happened.

So when Julia had told her she was pregnant with no idea who had fathered the child, and that all she wanted was for the whole thing to go away, Caitlan had felt she couldn't turn her back on her former friend.

At the time, Caitlan hadn't even considered adopting Julia's baby.

That had come later—a few months into the pregnancy, when Julia wondered what kind of home her child would be placed in.

A chance encounter had woken Caitlan to how her life would change for the better should she arrange to adopt the child herself.

It had been surprisingly simple to fashion the application and credentials of one Margaret Talbot and make sure that Julia's baby boy was placed in her hands after the birth—a process that Caitlan oversaw from start to finish. It was one of the advantages of working in a small facility like the Bradford Clinic; unwed mothers were entrusted into the capable hands of a midwife who guided them through the pregnancy and made sure the future needs of the child were properly tended to, working hand in hand with a sister agency to place the newborn into a good home.

Caitlan had just circumvented the outside agency altogether, unbeknownst to Julia, who just wanted the whole process done as soon as possible.

All that was left for Caitlan to do was to take a long-deserved sabbatical from the Bradford Clinic and head off with the child to a new life up in Lowell.

Julia had barely even seen her son, holding the baby for less than five minutes after the birth, which Caitlan had documented with a Polaroid, something she'd done on a whim while caught up in the emotional moment of seeing Julia with the baby she was about to part with forever.

A photograph that Caitlan was now very happy that she'd taken and kept for herself.

If there was one thing Caitlan did know, it was that Julia Molinari should never have started the affair that had ended her marriage to John Frankel.

She had met the detective a couple of times over the years, at the rare event where Julia and Caitlan had run into each other because they shared mutual high-school friends. Caitlan had found him to be personable; she thought of him as a good but odd fit for Julia—considering the Molinaris spent much of their life doing everything they could to tippy-toe around cops and their like.

Frankel certainly didn't deserve the years in a federal prison he was looking at now that he'd been charged with Julia and Pablo's murders, as reported on the morning news.

Still.

Better him than me, thought Caitlan.

Because Caitlan Hill was a survivor and opportunist.

She'd moved past that disastrous situation in high school and pursued a career that she hadn't planned on that got her the hell out of Totowa.

And when years later Julia had unexpectedly come back into her life, Caitlan had been able to seize another opportunity to improve her situation—even if it meant pretending to be someone else for a while.

Unfortunately, it had led to John Frankel trying to unearth what Caitlan had been certain was dead and buried in that Maine graveyard.

And consequently, Julia Molinari and Pablo Suarez had to pay the ultimate price.

So, when the opportunity came to tighten the noose around the detective's neck, Caitlan made sure to do what was necessary to pull it taut by not revealing her part in things.

Now Caitlan just needed for it to stay that way.

As she heard the car approaching outside, she knew she'd find out in the next few minutes if she were going to be able to pull that off.

Or be left with an alternative she had never wanted to consider.

Before heading for the door, she picked up her handbag and reached inside, making sure the gun was easily within reach.

Chapter 29

Grant had double- and triple-checked with Mildred Snow, but the octogenarian refused to back off her claim, insisting that Caitlan Hill and Margaret Talbot were one and the same.

When pressed for more information, Mildred apologized. She'd had very little contact with mother or child, so there wasn't much more to tell. She'd heard a rumor that the infant was sickly, thus accounting for the woman who was calling herself Maggie staying inside their home for the four months of the child's life. Still, its subsequent passing had come as a shock to the small community, but as the single mom had chosen to grieve alone, the people of Lowell had given her space.

Grant thanked Mildred and said they might be in touch again later.

"Later?" asked Rachel after Grant ended the call.

"I've heard Maine is lovely this time of year," answered her father.

Grant's first instinct had been to drive, but since it was an eight-hour trip just to reach Portland and the Bradford Clinic, and Rachel pointed out that it was impossible to navigate the I-95 corridor through New England without running into at least a few closures, accidents, and roadwork that threatened to double the estimate, the self-confessed aviophobe had begrudgingly agreed to fly.

The next morning the Grants battled traffic to get across the Triborough Bridge to catch an eight a.m. plane out of LaGuardia to Portland.

Even though the last sighting of Caitlan Hill had been a brief stop at her childhood home in Totowa, Grant realized he had no idea where she had gone from there. More than likely, the answers lay in Maine, at the clinic where Caitlan worked and Julia had her child two and a half years before, and in the small town two hours north of Portland.

Rachel hadn't hesitated when Grant suggested they head there.

"I'd totally understand if you'd rather stay here because of John," he'd told his daughter.

She said there wasn't much she could do with him locked up and agreed that finding Caitlan (or Maggie, or whatever she was calling herself) was the best way to get to the bottom of the mess that her fiancé found himself in.

Grant had never been to LaGuardia and was tempted to rethink his travel itinerary once he saw it. Constantly ranked as one of the world's worst airports, its runways were so tight and short that it was often referred to by pilots as the USS LaGuardia because it was like landing on an aircraft carrier. He found himself longing for the jumbo jets at nearby JFK and Newark, especially when the commuter plane had taken off and made a sharp banking turn that Grant was certain would end up spiraling them into the churning Atlantic just below.

Rachel, knowing her father's fear of heights, reached over and took Grant's hand. "You all right, Dad?"

"Would you believe me if I said yes?"

"Probably not."

For the first time that morning, the two shared a smile.

"I'd been looking forward to spending some time together the last week before the wedding," Grant told her. "But this isn't exactly what I had in mind."

"That makes two of us."

Grant had spent the early morning hours on the phone with various vendors (caterers and florists), telling them nothing had changed despite the news they'd heard coming from overseas about the groom's arrest, which had prompted the flurry of calls in the first place. Rachel had said he was crazy—the wedding was less than a week away and here they were on what could amount to a fruitless trek up into New England instead of doing a final dress fitting or meeting up with old friends at the bachelorette party that she'd instead just scrapped.

"Cancel now and maybe you'll just lose the deposits," Rachel had told him.

But Grant refused.

"Why?" she asked. "Are you really that anxious to give me away?"

"Hardly. I just want you to be happy, Rach. And I've never seen you more so than when you're with John. I won't give up on that."

But now, with each mile the jet sped north, that happiness seemed further away as evidenced by Rachel growing quieter and quieter. By the time they landed at Portland International an hour later, she was barely speaking, making Grant more determined than ever to get answers to the whereabouts of Caitlan Hill.

All they got at the Bradford Clinic were more questions.

The facility wasn't large, housing a small staff consisting of two doctors and a couple nurse practitioners, with only three examining rooms. Its clientele was exclusively women; they had access to medical and psychiatric services along with a birthing center set up with rotating resident midwives. That clearly jibed with what John had told them about Julia's pregnancy. Everything she would have needed to bring the baby to term was on hand—regular checkups, sonograms, and a safe and private place to deliver the child, which was the whole idea for unwed single mothers who found themselves with nowhere else to go.

Conveniently, the agency Adoptive Placement Services was located in the adjacent building and they worked hand in hand with the clinic's clients from the moment they declared that they were unable to raise a child. With that synchronicity in place, APS had usually located a home for the infant by the time they entered the world.

Such had obviously been the case for Julia Molinari and her baby boy.

Less obvious was that Caitlan Hill had managed to take the child herself, having manufactured a completely false profile for Margaret Talbot, a single mother of sufficient means who on paper was a perfect candidate to adopt the newborn.

Audrey Wilson, the director of the Bradford Clinic, told the Grants that she knew nothing about it. She hadn't worked there when Julia had delivered the child, having arrived only recently when the former director had relocated to the Australian outback to work with underprivileged young women.

Grant didn't need a world map to know that getting in touch with Audrey's predecessor would be complicated. He also knew that he was on unsteady ground even asking the new director questions about Caitlan as neither he nor Rachel had any official standing.

He carefully laid out what had brought them to Maine.

The clinic director listened to every word. When Grant was done, she just shook her head.

"That's quite a tragic story. But I don't see how I can help you. This all happened before my tenure, and with both the mother and child dead, there's not much to offer. And I can't open the files without a court order." She looked directly at Rachel. "Perhaps it's something your fiancé's attorney might make a motion for, but regardless of that—"

"There's still Caitlan Hill," observed Rachel.

"True," said Audrey. "But she no longer works here."

Grant and his daughter exchanged looks. "Since when?" he asked.

—⁓—

It turned out that two days after Caitlan had told her colleagues she was taking a long weekend to go home to Totowa, her resignation had shown up on Audrey Wilson's desk. The director had tried to get in touch with her but failed to connect; as a result, she had been left with no choice but to accept the resignation and was already in the process of interviewing prospective replacements.

The resignation date was the same day that Julia's body had been discovered in John Frankel's apartment.

"That can't be a coincidence," said Rachel.

She had just steered the rental car they'd gotten at the Portland airport onto Route 295, which would link up with I-95 to take them north to their next destination.

"Absolutely not," agreed Grant.

The original plan had been to stay overnight in Portland. But after running into the dead end at the clinic, Grant figured they could reach Lowell by midafternoon and see what they could unearth in the small town where Joseph Talbot and Pablo Suarez had perished, Margaret Talbot had once resided, and things had gone so drastically wrong for John Frankel.

"Something definitely happened around that time," continued Grant. "Remember, Julia suddenly showed up at the Totowa house looking for Caitlan then as well."

"Do you think she found out that Caitlan had been the one who adopted her baby?"

"Possibly. She'd only gotten the Margaret Talbot name from Caitlan a day or two earlier." Grant thought about it for a second. "Once she had it, Julia might have done a little digging on her own and put two and two together like we did."

"And went to confront her?"

"The only one who can tell us at this point is Caitlan. And she's making herself unavailable."

Rachel swung over into the fast lane of the highway.

"They could have gotten together in John's apartment, since that's where Julia ended up staying," said Rachel.

Grant nodded. "The conversation goes sideways and Caitlan ends up killing Julia. She suddenly looks around, realizes what she's done and that it would be simple for John to take the blame. All she has to do is take the key off Julia's body and lock her inside."

Grant noticed that his daughter was actually smiling.

"What's going on?" asked Grant. "What did I do?"

"You're enjoying this, aren't you?"

"Pardon?"

"The whole exploring *this* theory, *that* theory, figuring out *who* did *what* and *how* it was done sort of thing," explained Rachel. "It's what you do."

"It's what I *did*," corrected Grant. "I'm retired, remember?"

"I was there. We almost all got killed before you got to hang it up, in case you've forgotten."

"Oh, I haven't forgotten."

He'd almost lost everything that had ever mattered to him in a split second that night.

"You're not denying it," prodded Rachel.

"I just said I didn't forget."

"Not *that*, Dad. I'm talking about *this*." She motioned all around them. "The investigation, the thrill of the hunt. Whatever you want to call it."

Grant hesitated, suddenly caught. "Well—"

"See!" Rachel laughed out loud. "I knew it. You miss this."

Caught, because he actually did miss it.

"Okay. But before you go and pat yourself on the back and send us hurtling into a ditch doing so, let me say I'm not enjoying *this*—looking to clear the name of a man who we've both come to grow very fond of."

"And you should know that I appreciate that," said Rachel.

"But as to the other part—"

"Yes?"

"I admit there are only so many books, crosswords, and garden plantings one can fill the day with."

"You didn't have to retire from the Yard."

"No, the time had come. Three decades of doing the same thing was enough. Plus, once your mother was gone, it didn't feel right coming home at day's end to an empty house. All it made me do was wonder what I'd been working so hard for."

"She wouldn't have wanted you boring yourself to death either."

It was Grant's turn to smile. "She would have certainly kicked me in the rear end before letting me do so; that's for certain."

"So, what are we going to do about that?"

"Let's see about getting you married off first," Grant quipped. "Otherwise, I'll have to spend all my time worrying about you."

Rachel gave him a playful poke in the shoulder. "Very funny."

—⁓—

A couple hours later they pulled into Lowell and went directly to the house where Caitlan Hill had lived as Margaret Talbot.

It was a gray wooden tinderbox that looked ready to go up in flames at the first sight of a match. It had an address—15 Preble Road—but it was the only residence in sight. It was at least a quarter mile in any direction to find a neighbor.

"Talk about living in the middle of nowhere," exclaimed Rachel as she climbed out the driver side.

Grant got out to join her and walked over to peer at a real estate sign, mostly hidden by high weeds that looked to have been growing ever since Caitlan/Margaret had occupied the house more than two years before.

This was confirmed a half hour later when the Grants sat across from Archibald "Call me Arch" Sanders, the seventy-, possibly eighty-year-old realtor who had been ready to call it a day when they arrived. Arch got all excited when they inquired about the Preble Road house. It had been on the market since that "poor woman and child" lived there a few years back.

"This woman?" asked Grant, showing him the picture of the teen-aged Caitlan with her arms wrapped around her fellow Passaic Valley cheerleader, Julia.

"Yes, but older when she lived here," replied Arch. "In her midthirties, I'd say."

Grant saw the gleam go out of Arch's eyes, along with the possibility of a sale, as he realized he was going to still be stuck with the eyesore on Preble Road. But, much like his Lowell neighbor Mildred, Arch Sanders loved to gossip more than anything else; frankly, that was all he really did these days, since many residents had passed and were unable to join the Lawn Bowling Society that Arch chaired.

"Tragic, just tragic, what happened to that little boy of hers," Arch lamented.

"What exactly did he die from?" asked Rachel.

"We never did find out. SIDS, we were told," answered Arch. "But she got out of town so doggone fast, none of us got to really hear the details."

"How fast was fast? Do you happen to recall?" wondered Grant.

"The day after the funeral. I know that for a fact."

"How so?"

"The reason I remember is that I'd been trying to get ahold of Margaret for a couple of weeks prior to that. She'd only leased the place for four months and it was coming time to renew. The lease actually ran out the day after the funeral."

Something pulled at Grant, deep inside. "Really."

"Naturally, I cut her a little slack, figuring I'd give her a little time to decide what to do, but it ended up proving unnecessary. She was gone the next morning, completely cleared out."

Arch lowered his voice, as if someone might hear what he said next.

"It's a horrible thing to say but what ran through my head at the time was that she had leased the place knowing she only needed it for a certain amount of time and that was that." The old man shook his head. "But that's way too macabre, isn't it?"

Maybe, thought Austin Grant. *But then again, maybe not.*

Chapter 30

Night.

At least that's what John Frankel thought it was.

With no windows in the tiny cell, it was impossible to tell the time of day. But the activity outside the heavy door seemed to have quieted down considerably, indicating that most of the jail's denizens were asleep and that it had been hours since he'd appeared before a judge for the arraignment.

He had stood by Eileen Crowe and listened to the charges brought against him for the murders of Julia Molinari and Pablo Suarez, then was asked to offer a plea. Frankel declared himself not guilty, and was promptly refused bail on the basis that he was a flight risk, which was hard for him to argue with seeing as how he'd ditched his police tail, fled the murder scene in a Maine cemetery, and then shacked up with Rachel like she was his gun moll while half the cops on the Eastern Seaboard hunted him down.

Rachel.

This was supposed to be the happiest week of her life and she'd almost been thrown in jail herself.

He wondered what she was doing now.

Rachel and her father sat across the table from Mildred Snow. It was Lowell's nicest restaurant, at least according to the woman who had been talking nonstop since the moment they'd arrived.

Mildred couldn't have been sweeter or more desirous of their company.

She also tended to go on and on—resulting in Rachel's mind drifting off to how they'd ended up as three for dinner in the first place.

After talking to the realtor, Arch Sanders, the Grants had secured two rooms at a motel that put a capital Q in Quaint. She imagined it did a booming business when autumn rolled around and the leaf peepers made their way north, but Rachel thought they might have been the only customers on a warm summer night when tourists had more active and glamorous destinations in mind than Lowell, Maine.

Grant had suggested they drop by to see Mildred in case she remembered anything else about the few months Caitlan Hill had spent in town as Margaret Talbot. Mildred had been overjoyed to see them, starved for company, but had very little to add about Caitlan.

"She made me look like a social butterfly, and I never go anywhere."

There had been more than a touch of loneliness in that declaration, enough so that when Grant asked if Mildred could suggest a place where Rachel and he might grab some dinner, he politely asked if she would like to join them. Mildred had fetched her coat and purse practically before the invitation had left his lips.

With little to share about the woman she'd known as Maggie Talbot, Mildred treated the Grants to a nostalgic look at her years in Lowell. Many had been spent with her husband, Tom, and their two children, who had grown up and gone; Tom was laid to rest a decade ago not too many plots away from the Talbot child.

As Rachel listened to the recital of what had been a happy marriage and blessed family, she wondered if the chances for her to experience either of those were slipping through her fingers.

Adding to this sudden wave of self-pity was the realization that she should have just been getting back from her bachelorette party in

London—dinner at one of her favorite Soho haunts and the requisite pub crawl with a dozen old girlfriends.

Lovely as Mildred Snow might be, dinner at the Whitehall Inn was a far cry from celebrating a union that now might never take place.

But she supposed it was better than where her fiancé was spending the evening, and quite possibly many more to come.

———

John Frankel shifted around on a cast-iron cot that was as uncomfortable as anything he'd ever tried to sleep on. No wonder everyone in prison was in such a foul mood. It was bad enough being cooped up in a six-by-ten cell for months upon years; a sore back just added to an overall miserable experience.

But the bed wasn't the only thing keeping Frankel awake.

He sensed that he'd forgotten something.

Something important that might lead to putting behind bars the person who was really responsible for the crimes Frankel was on the hook for.

He just couldn't think of what it was.

———

Taryn Meadows was worried as well. She was wondering if they'd rushed to judgement on her suspended partner. There was no question that Frankel had motives to kill both his ex-wife and Pablo Suarez. He fit the role of guilty party like he was out of central casting—and that was what bothered her. John wasn't a stupid man. Neither was he careless. As a result, Taryn spent a good part of the night staring at the ceiling.

———

Desmond Harris, on the other hand, was fast asleep. It wasn't so much that he'd been able to relax; rather, it was the slumber of the exhausted.

But even that respite had been short-lived. At three in the morning, the NYPD lieutenant made the mistake of checking his email on the way to the bathroom. His inbox was flooded with more queries from reporters about John Frankel—charges, a trial date, a possible plea bargain. He spent the next few hours pacing in the hallway outside the bedroom where his wife still slept, responding to emails while stuck in a waking nightmare, which Harris realized wasn't going away any time soon.

—⁓—

The C ward's newest resident wasn't sleeping either.

Frankel was too busy recounting the events after his incarceration, wondering if what he couldn't get a grip on had occurred during that time.

But everything after the arraignment had been straightforward and by the book.

Go Directly to Jail. Do Not Pass Go. Do Not Talk to Anyone but Your Lawyer.

Even that conversation had been brief and one-sided. Frankel had nothing left to tell his attorney that he hadn't already put on the flash drive he'd popped into the FedEx bin in Newark the night before last.

The only thing he was getting was a massive headache.

—⁓—

Eileen Crowe was at her desk in her home office at two in the morning.

It was when she got her best work done.

Being an insomniac helped.

She'd been drafting an appeal for John Frankel's bail but had abandoned it halfway through. No one knew their way around legalese and case examples better than Eileen. She therefore knew she was facing quite a battle going forward.

She had listened numerous times to the converted flash-drive file given to her by the detective, which had left her with a lot of questions.

Questions that defied the number-one adage she had discussed with Austin Grant.

Don't ask questions you don't know the answers to.

Eileen thought about where that left her client.

Forget Shit Creek. The stores weren't just out of paddles, the factories had stopped making them.

Along with the canoes.

John Frankel lay in the darkness. Sleep at this point was only a concept.

He retraced his steps further back.

Hawaii. It had all started there.

Had he missed something right from the beginning?

Or had it been something that Rachel and Grant had encountered on their trip to the islands and told him about?

He patiently took himself through it.

Paradise.

Yeah. Right.

It was six hours earlier in the Hawaiian Islands.

The horizon was a marmalade of pink, turquoise, and lavender pastels as the sun dipped below it, bidding farewell to another day in the tropics.

For most it was mai tais and piña coladas coming right up. Drink, call it a night, resume, and repeat the next day.

But for a select few on the Big Island, the events that had recently unfolded on the east coast of the mainland had broken that rhythm.

On the hill leading up to Mauna Kea, the security guard at Hala Kahiki locked up for the evening. It had been one more day of doing nothing at the resort-to-be; he wondered how many of plots he had left, having spent the afternoon surfing the net about the death of the man who was supposed to be selling it to the public.

In a real-estate office down in Kona, a realtor named Chet handed the Papaya Seed deed to a multimillionaire named Erickson, who had bought it off a bookie named Daswick for twenty cents on the dollar because he couldn't pass up a deal. Which had left one man feeling like he'd gotten shortchanged on his commission and the other wondering what the hell he was going to do with a beach bar.

Up in the town of Waimea, that same bookie Andy Daswick was knocking back pineapple daquiris, trying to think how he was going to get his hands on the hundred and twenty grand owed to him by a dead man with no heirs to lean on. He supposed he could try and make it back on a hefty wager, but only baseball was in season and it was impossible to pick a winner in a sport where any given team could beat another on any given night. So he ordered up more daquiris.

Back in Kona, Sheriff Guy Lam continued to stare at the police report for the break-in at the Suarez-Molinari home, as he had for the past week. He decided to stash it in the unsolved file, since both residents were dead. At least that way he knew where it was should someone come around asking about it.

And then there was Aiden.

She'd moved down the sand to work at the Beach Tree at the Four Seasons. Sure, the clientele was richer and tips more substantial. But she knew, now more than ever, it was only a temporary gig.

Pablo hadn't been the world's greatest boss, but he'd never hit on her or treated her badly. More than that, Julia had been a good friend. Now they were dead, and it was increasingly difficult to take an order or deliver another froufrou drink without thinking about them both.

She wondered if someone were trying to tell her something.

Aiden walked into her tiny apartment that night, kicked off her flip-flops, checked her bank balance, then picked up her phone and made a call.

She was about to hang up when someone finally answered.

"Hey, Mom. It's me. I think I need to get away from here for a while," Aiden said as she wiped the tears from her eyes.

Frankel continued to toss and turn.

Thinking about Hawaii wasn't helping. Probably because it wasn't really the beginning.

It went back much further than that. The same place it had ended the day before.

New Jersey.

Back before he'd even met Julia.

Leo Molinari was reading *Amazing Airplanes* to Teddy for the third time that evening. The boy giggled throughout. Leo loved hearing him finish the ends of sentences he'd obviously memorized. He tucked his son in bed, kissed him goodnight, then stood in the doorway to watch Sophia come in for her series of hugs and cooing. He turned on the nightlight and waited for her to join him by the door, and they left the room together.

In the hallway, Leo leaned over and planted a soft kiss on his wife's protruding stomach. "I can't wait to read that to her," he said.

"We'll need to get a whole new set of books," Sophia responded with a smile. "She's not likely to be as airplane obsessed."

"You never know."

They shared a laugh, then Leo told her he was going out on the balcony for his nightly cigar. Sophia gave him a gentle hug and told him not to inhale.

Minutes later, he was in his favorite position, sitting on a deck chair, his feet up on the balcony, a lit Cuban in hand. He leaned back and thought, as he did most nights, how lucky he'd been to find love again with Sophia. Most men weren't blessed once, and here he had been shown grace twice.

He was still there a half hour later when his son Tony pulled up in a sports car you could hear a couple of miles away. He waved to his father, then slipped inside the house.

Leo took a deep breath as he did most every night. His nearest and dearest were back safe and sound.

Except for Julia.

But he'd lost her long ago. Headstrong and determined to make a life with John Frankel.

What he wouldn't give to have her under the same roof. The entire family all together.

It had always been his biggest regret. And now it would be for the rest of his days.

He felt his eyes well up and reminded himself again to count his blessings.

And started to consider what they were going to call their little girl.

—◆—

John Frankel's mind wouldn't stop drifting in the darkness.

Julia and Caitlan.

Best friends who had drifted apart. Then thrown together again when Julia needed Caitlan most.

It couldn't have been a coincidence. Could it?

———

Meanwhile, not so many miles from the Molinari mansion, in a house one-fifth the size, Loretta Hill wondered when she'd see her only daughter again. Like Leo Molinari, with whom she'd attended a few PTA meetings, Loretta had hardly been in touch with her child the past decade.

When Caitlan had suddenly appeared the week before, Loretta's hopes for a reconciliation had been raised. But the visit had been so short that, as each day passed, she began to wonder if it had even happened and lost faith they could ever be part of each other's lives again.

But that didn't stop her from sitting up late at night.

Waiting for the phone to ring.

Or a knock at the door.

———

Julia and Caitlan were front and center of the cheerleading squad, leading the other girls in a complicated choreographed dance set to Free's "All Right Now."

When it was done, Frankel stood up in the stands and applauded loudly. But he was the only one there.

He bolted up inside his jail cell.

He had finally fallen asleep.

It had taken a dream to let him know what had been bothering him.

Julia and Caitlan.

He still couldn't quite put his finger on it.

But it was there somewhere.

Somewhere back in the beginning.

Chapter 31

"Something bothering you?"

Rachel turned back to look at her father across the tiny table and realized that he had caught her glancing around the coffee shop.

"I keep waiting for Mildred to join us," she told him.

"Why would you think that?"

"She recommended this place for breakfast. I'm surprised she didn't pop by to bend our ears more about life in Lowell. I don't know about you, but all those stories started to sound the same after a while."

"She's lonely, Rach. You have to imagine what it's like to live alone like that."

"Given where my fiancé's at? I'm starting to."

"We can't give up hope just yet." He poured syrup onto a stack of blueberry pancakes.

Rachel indicated his food. "I don't know how you can eat. My stomach's churning."

"A healthy appetite fuels the working brain."

"I don't see what there's to work with. We came up here looking for two women who happen to be one and the same, and can't find a trace of either one."

"That's exactly the point. For starters, Caitlan's duplicity in masquerading as Margaret is a crime. The fact that Margaret existed for only a four-month period and the house rental expiring at the exact time as her child? It's hard to believe that's not connected."

"You're thinking there's something suspicious about how Joseph Talbot died?" asked Rachel. "You don't believe it was SIDS?"

"The fate of that child seems to be the key to all this. If Caitlan were the one responsible and Julia found out? It certainly gives Caitlan a motive for killing her."

"And Pablo?"

"If Julia learned the truth, she easily enough could have told him."

If Rachel weren't hungry before, thinking about the death of a four-month-old curbed any hint of an appetite. She pushed the plate of cinnamon swirl French toast away from her, untouched.

"So, with both dead, and the person who might have done it nowhere to be found, how do you suggest we find out what really happened?"

"I know where we can start," said her father. "Not that I expect anyone there to tell us very much."

<hr>

Rachel couldn't imagine a more quiet place than West End Cemetery at nine-thirty on a weekday morning. Besides its silent permanent residents, the only other person in the graveyard was a gardener sitting atop his lawnmower, earbuds firmly in place; he methodically made his routine crisscross over the grass plots, circumventing the bronze plaques like they were exposed land mines in a pattern he knew so well he could emerge from it unscathed, even if blindfolded.

The Grants approached the grave site that a few nights earlier had doubled as a crime scene. Rachel was surprised not to find any remnants, no yellow police tape, chalk marks, or bloodstains. She stared at the inscription on the gravestone, an indelible record of Joseph Darren Talbot's short existence. The longer she looked, the more merit she gave her father's supposition—the key to everything seemed to lie with Joseph.

Four-month-old children were not supposed to die. She said it out loud.

"It had to be why Pablo came here," observed Grant. "Same reason that John did, trying to find out what happened to the little boy that could have been theirs."

Rachel laid a hand on the grave marker. The granite looked freshly polished, keeping in line with the neatly trimmed grass and not a stray leaf in sight. "It's certainly peaceful here. And well kept up."

Grant started to reply, then stopped.

"Of course," he murmured.

"That's not always the case, Dad. You should see some of the grave-yards on the way to the Rockaways—"

"That's not what I meant." He shook his head and pointed at the headstone. "Someone has to pay to maintain this."

Rachel's eyes widened. "And there's only one person who'd do that, right?"

A few minutes later, they were knocking on the door of a small brick house near the entrance to the cemetery.

It was opened by the man they'd previously seen atop the lawnmower—Harold Winslow, a sixty-something-looking specimen who turned out to be West End's jack-of-all-trades. Harold told the Grants that not only did he run the mortuary, which had maybe a dozen intakes in a busy year, but he was also the graveyard's caretaker and had been the first person on the scene the night of Pablo's murder.

Harold said he had been fast asleep when he was awakened by what he thought might have been a gunshot and had called the local police. He admitted to not being a brave man by nature and, despite his job description, said he'd never gotten used to roaming around a graveyard in the middle of the night, so he'd waited until he'd heard the responding sirens to step outside and lead the first cop to the Talbot grave.

He'd also been one of the people who had caught a glimpse of John Frankel scooting over the cemetery's back fence, a fact that hadn't scored any points with Rachel.

Grant casually made mention of his former profession while neglecting to say he'd left his post at the start of the year. Rachel watched him smoothly steer Harold back to the days surrounding Joseph Talbot's funeral and couldn't help but admire how easily the former Scotland Yard man got strangers to open up to him. Rachel thought she could pick up some interview pointers for future investigative pieces.

"It was pretty straightforward," said Harold. "We didn't even do the intake as the child had been cremated and Ms. Talbot showed up with a death certificate and box of ashes."

"She didn't do the cremation here?" asked Grant.

"We're a tiny operation and don't even have a wall or building to house cremations per se, so we don't provide those services. But she wanted her son's final resting place to be close by, so loved ones could come and visit."

"And have there been many? Visitors, that is?"

Harold's brow furrowed, his face squinching up. "Now that you mention it, I can't remember anyone specifically stopping by. But that doesn't mean someone hasn't—it's not like I see everyone who passes through. The gates are open from dawn till dusk every day and visitors are free to come and go as they choose."

"What about maintenance and upkeep? I presume Margaret Talbot has been paying for that?"

"She's billed every six months like anyone else and has paid within the grace period, I believe," answered Harold. "I'm not sure why you're asking all these questions though."

Perhaps it was the aforementioned enmity Rachel felt for him because he'd been the one who'd put the police onto John. Or maybe she'd just grown tired of tiptoeing around what they were really there for.

Either way she'd had enough.

"Because Margaret Talbot isn't her real name. She actually might have murdered the child whose remains you placed in that grave a couple of years ago."

Rachel noticed two things.

Her father's tacit nod of approval with the trace of a smile on his lips.

And that Harold Winslow started stuttering.

"How was I s-supposed to know that?"

Rachel was more than happy when Grant took over.

"By possibly asking a few more questions at the time instead of taking what the woman told you at face value?"

Grant's no-nonsense tone had an immediate effect. Harold was already swiveling in his desk chair to face the file cabinet behind him.

"I should have the information right here. Just tell me what you want to know."

It turned out that all roads led back to New Jersey.

Englewood, in particular.

And in the case of a billing address for the upkeep of a cemetery plot in northern Maine, it was a P.O. box located in the post office on the main shopping street of the affluent bedroom community.

Upon investigating further, Harold told the Grants that Margaret Talbot had paid with a money order, making it next to untraceable. Clearly, once Caitlan Hill had abandoned the Margaret persona and left Lowell, she wanted to make it as difficult as possible to find her.

As Rachel sped down I-95 toward the Portland airport, Grant brought up the fact that despite all Caitlan's time spent in Maine, she seemed inexorably pulled back to where she had come from.

"She takes a leave of absence from the Bradford Clinic right after Julia gives birth and poses as Margaret until the baby died," reminded Grant. "And even though she returned to the clinic afterwards, she's been having bills from West End, and I presume other correspondence, sent back to New Jersey."

"So?"

"One usually gets a postal box close to where they reside, so they can check it every once in a while."

"You're thinking she has a place in Englewood?"

"She gave up her apartment near the clinic when she left Portland a couple of weeks ago—"

"—and she was *definitely* in New Jersey right after that because she dropped by her mother's house," finished Rachel, excitedly.

"Precisely."

Rachel thought about it. "But how are we supposed to find out where Caitlan's staying if she's gone to such lengths to keep herself hidden? No forwarding address, money orders, and such?"

"Something we did back in the day at the Yard before everyone became so dependent on computers, iPhones, and all the other electronic crutches."

"And that would be?"

"Good old-fashioned footwork."

He elaborated on what he was thinking as they continued to travel toward the airport.

An hour later, they were back up in the summer clouds, heading for Newark. Rachel spent a good part of the trip watching her father fashion a time line on a piece of paper, tracking Caitlan Hill's movements over the past few years, and found herself resisting the urge to grin.

She'd been right saying he was most at home working a case. When he walked off the plane there was a bounce in his step that had been missing the past six months.

But was any of this going to make a difference when it came to John spending more time in his six-by-ten cell?

It was late afternoon by the time the Grants landed at Newark International, secured another rental car, fought rush-hour traffic on the New Jersey Turnpike, and finally arrived in Englewood. They made their way to the main street in town and stopped in front of the post office to get their bearings.

Grant had told Rachel it would be pointless to try to ascertain information regarding the box that Caitlan had rented, as they'd already pushed their luck squeezing Harold Winslow; they didn't have a legal leg to stand on when dealing with an establishment that prided itself on the anonymity of its clientele and had the power of the federal government behind it.

On the plane, Rachel had used her iPad and a graphic program to map out the various businesses surrounding the building they were now standing next to. The two of them started to canvass the shops in opposite directions. Each was armed with an updated photo of Caitlan that Rachel had found on a website for the Bradford Clinic; they'd agreed to meet every half hour to report whether any of the locals recognized her as someone who might have frequented their businesses. Or better yet, in the case of those who made deliveries in the immediate area—take-out food places, florists, drugstores, and cleaners—perhaps one of them had actually brought something directly to her residence.

But as the sun set, they'd had no success. Most people refused to even engage with them, and those who did had never run across Caitlan. By the time eight o'clock rolled around, they'd circled back to the main street, with only sore feet and grumbling stomachs to show for their trouble.

It was at that precise moment that Rachel realized she hadn't eaten anything that day, including the French toast she now regretted leaving on her plate in the Lowell coffee shop; she stopped and pointed at a restaurant across the street.

"Baumgart's!"

"Baum what?" asked her father, who was rubbing the small of his back.

"That place over there. John told me they make great chocolate milkshakes."

Grant peered at the neon signs flashing in the window. "It says *Chinese* and *Deli*."

"Beggars can't be choosers at this point." Rachel took her father by the arm and led him across the street.

Describing Baumgart's menu as eclectic would have been an understatement. The restaurant looked like a cross between a diner and ice cream parlor with a menu boasting combos of a pastrami sandwich and orange chicken, and for dessert numerous homemade gelatos and sorbets.

The Grants sat at the counter, Rachel going for the pastrami and her father trying the chicken. Both were scrumptious full portions and quickly finished off, but that didn't stop Grant from ordering a chocolate shake for dessert while Rachel opted for two scoops of wild blueberry gelato. While they waited, Rachel pulled the iPad out of her oversized bag and placed it beside the updated pictures of Caitlan. She had just finished rerouting the map to plan their next steps when their server, a freckled, red-headed girl in her twenties, arrived with the shake and gelato.

Grant no sooner took one sip of the shake, proclaiming it to be one of the best he'd ever tasted, when the waitress pointed at Caitlan's picture.

"You guys are friends with Becky?" she asked.

Rachel didn't miss a beat and, without giving her father a glance, gave the waitress a vigorous nod. "She's the one who told us about this place!"

All it took after that was a couple of quick questions and a sizeable tip to get what they needed. It turned out that the server had delivered food to Becky's building a couple of times in the past few weeks and didn't think twice about providing an address.

As they left the restaurant, it occurred to Rachel that maybe she and John had finally been dealt a dose of good karma. They were certainly due some. If John hadn't mentioned Baumgart's to her, Rachel and her father might have walked the streets of Englewood for the entire night and then some.

It also didn't escape Rachel's notice that Caitlan Hill was going by yet another name.

———

Becky Michaelson, as Caitlan was apparently calling herself to those who knew her in Englewood, lived in a town house about six blocks east of Baumgart's, in a development that had gone up in the past decade or so. The place was a considerable upgrade from the dilapidated house where she had grown up and that her mother was still living in, just twenty miles due west in Totowa. Two of the abandoned homes that Caitlan had occupied in Lowell would have fit inside her current residence with room to spare.

The front porch lamp was on, along with a number of lights in the house, indicating that someone was home or didn't care much about their electric bill. Grant motioned for Rachel to stay behind him as they walked up a neatly laid stone path toward the front door.

Rachel tugged at her father's coat. "What are you going to ask her? She might have killed two people for all we know."

"Well, first off, we don't know that it's definitely her," replied Grant. "Besides, I don't think she's going to come out the door with guns a-blazing and cause all her well-to-do neighbors to rush out of their houses."

"You'd hope not," murmured Rachel.

Grant pressed the doorbell and they heard it ring inside. When there was no response, her father tried again and got the same result.

Nothing but summer crickets chirping all around them.

Grant knocked a few times. There were no footsteps. No one calling out that they would be right there.

Her father tried the doorknob and it opened in his hand.

"Dad—"

He turned around to face Rachel. "Stay here," he commanded.

"But—"

"Just wait here, Rach."

His stern tone was all she needed to hear.

She stayed put on the front step while he went inside. She waited for what felt like a couple of minutes, but it really wasn't more than twenty seconds. Then her father quietly called out.

"Come inside and shut the door, Rachel."

She did so with trepidation, as the tone in his voice had her enter the house with the expectation of finding something very bad there.

It was worse.

They had finally located Caitlan Hill after all this time.

She was lying on the living room couch.

Rachel didn't need to see her father shaking his head to know that the woman who once called herself Margaret and was now going by Becky was dead.

The blue tinge to her once-white skin told her as much.

"Oh my God, Dad. Is that—"

She broke off, pointing at the gun lying on the sofa beside the body.

"The gun that killed Julia and Pablo?" asked Grant. "I can't say for sure. But it's a .45. Just like the backup missing from John's apartment."

Grant crossed the room to put an arm around her. "Are you going to be all right?"

Rachel managed a nod.

"There's something else you need to see," he told her.

Grant indicated the table in front of the sofa the dead woman was lying on.

There was a white piece of paper there. A discarded blue pen rested beside it, likely used to scrawl the three shaky words there.

Forgive me Julia.

Chapter 32

It was like a pageant of the law's greatest hits.

Grant noticed that as each entity arrived on the doorstep of the Englewood town house, they grew in importance, starting off unimpressive, then finishing off with the heavy hitters.

First on the scene was a uniformed officer who responded to the 911 call Grant made shortly after they'd discovered Caitlan Hill's body. Officer Tanner entered alongside Rachel, who had gone out to await someone's arrival. Grant noticed that when she returned with the young man, she was no longer carrying her oversized bag, having decided to leave it in the boot of the rental.

The officer looked like he should have been in high school instead of a police uniform, fresh-faced and blond haired. It was clear to Grant that Tanner hadn't been around too many dead bodies, as he stayed clear of Caitlan and the couch, busying himself by calling for backup and asking how the Grants had come to be there in the first place.

Grant gave a brief recitation about coming to see Becky Michaelson, whom they knew to actually be Caitlan Hill, a woman they had sought in conjunction with the recent murders of Julia Molinari and her boyfriend, Pablo Suarez.

This news seemed to unnerve young Tanner even more and he immediately asked if the Grants had touched or disturbed anything.

"If you're referring to the body, absolutely not," Grant told him. "But we've been here close to an hour, so it's impossible not to touch anything."

Grant had spent most of that time hovering over the dead Caitlan and the immediate vicinity, trying to ascertain what happened. From what he could tell, everything lined up with Caitlan taking her own life: an empty pill bottle on the table, a drained water glass, the note beside it, and her blue-tinged body; from Grant's years of experience, it indicated she'd died at least a few hours ago.

Rachel had understandably tried to distance and distract herself from the dead woman. She'd busied herself over by the bookshelves, scanning titles and absently flipping through a number of them. After they'd been asked by Tanner about it, Grant realized she'd shifted some books around, but didn't think it worth mentioning, seeing as how the officer's concern properly rested with what had transpired on the living-room sofa.

The next people through the door, much to Tanner's relief, were a pair of Bergen County detectives. Both in their fifties, they were practical carbon copies, so much so that Grant never quite landed on which one was named Connelly or Jackson, or more senior than the other, thus putting them in charge. They alternated asking questions and spent equal time with the crime scene techs and medical examiner who arrived a short time afterward.

The Grants repeated their reasons for being there and it was the apparent connection to the murders in Murray Hill and Lowell that resulted in the eventual appearance of two cops who were much more familiar—Detective Taryn Meadows and Lieutenant Desmond Harris.

Neither seemed thrilled to have crossed the Hudson to the Garden State, or to encounter the Grants.

"This stumbling across dead bodies is becoming a nasty habit," said Taryn when she first saw Rachel.

"I don't derive any pleasure from it, I can assure you," insisted Rachel.

Harris just looked exasperated.

The New York cops led them into the adjacent dining room, where they sat around a rectangular oak table, and the Grants took them step-by-step through the journey that had started with a phone call two nights before to Mildred Snow.

When Grant was done, the lieutenant's exasperation gave way to a pounding headache and Harris told them so.

"I'd think this would make everything easier, Lieutenant," said Grant, motioning over his shoulder toward the living room.

"Shows how little you know," grumbled Harris. "We don't know how long she's been dead, if she wrote that note, or if that's the gun we're looking for. Not to mention that we're now dealing with *three* jurisdictions—here, New York, and Maine."

That was when Oliver Freeman, the Manhattan District Attorney himself, arrived. He'd been pulled away from a fundraiser down in Tribeca, which accounted for the tuxedo he was wearing and the foul mood he was in because he'd gotten the call from Harris right before the thousand-dollar-a-plate dinner had been served.

The Grants had to repeat their story for the fourth time about how they'd ended up in Englewood.

At which point they were dismissed by Freeman, told to go home, and that someone would be in touch.

A half hour later, the Grants were back in the rental crossing over the GW Bridge to New York City and discussing where things exactly stood.

"They should let John out now, right?" asked Rachel as she steered them onto the ramp leading down to the West Side Highway.

"One would like to think," responded Grant.

But unfortunately, jurisprudence didn't always run so smoothly.

That's when Eileen Crowe stepped in.

Grant had contacted the defense attorney upon returning to Rachel's apartment, and Eileen told him she was on it.

She had immediately started applying pressure, particularly on Oliver Freeman, whom Eileen had known since they were in law school together. Grant wasn't privy to their conversations but knew some progress had to have been made when he got a phone call the next day requesting his and Rachel's presence in Freeman's office at three o'clock that afternoon.

When Rachel and Grant stepped into a conference room in the DA's office downtown, they found the same trio from the Englewood town house the previous evening waiting for them—Taryn, Harris, and Oliver Freeman.

Along with a smiling Eileen.

Once everyone was seated, Eileen looked across the table at the district attorney. "Oliver, do you want to do the honors?"

Freeman shook his head. "I wouldn't want to spoil your party, Eileen."

She turned to face the Grants. "The district attorney is dropping the charges against John," Eileen told them. "He's being processed now and should be released within the hour."

Grant felt his heart swell and a grip on his wrist. He looked to his left to see it had come courtesy of Rachel, who seemed barely able to contain her happiness.

"That's wonderful news," said Grant. He turned to face the NYPD detective and her lieutenant. "The gun checked out?"

Taryn nodded. "Preliminary ballistics appear to be an exact match. We don't expect the final to prove anything different. It's definitely Detective Frankel's gun but the only fingerprints on it belong to Caitlan Hill."

"And the note?"

"Same story," Harris chimed in. "We found some correspondence in the desk drawer and our calligraphy experts say there's no question that Caitlan wrote it."

"That didn't stop them from considering that John forced her to do so under duress at gun point, made her swallow the pills, and planted the gun," added Eileen.

Grant nodded, thinking it would have been the first thing to go through his head as well. "But that was abandoned because—"

"The ME's initial report," answered Taryn. "According to her stomach contents, it looks like the last meal that Caitlan ingested was around lunch on Tuesday, the day before the two of you found her."

"Which happens to be almost twenty-four hours after you placed John in custody," Grant said.

Desmond Harris nodded, solemn. "So there you have it."

Grant could tell that the lieutenant would rather be anywhere else than sitting there having to admit they'd arrested and charged the wrong man, a fellow officer no less.

"We appreciate you telling us all this. But you could just as easily have released Detective Frankel without calling us all in here," said Grant. "I can't help but think there's another reason."

"Very perceptive, Commander," said the district attorney. "We're just having a hard time understanding Caitlan Hill's motives in all this. Perhaps you could shed some light—since you and your daughter, and Detective Frankel for that matter, had set your sights on her way before we did."

"Well, let's just say we had a bit more interest in finding an alternative suspect," said Grant. "As for why Caitlan did what she did, we might never know exactly, but it seems it has to do with Julia Molinari's baby."

He went on to carefully explain the events that led Julia to trusting her high-school friend to help with the birth of her child and finding a proper home for the newborn.

"Why Caitlan suddenly wanted a baby will probably remain a mystery as well. Perhaps because it was Julia's and she couldn't bear seeing the child of a lifelong friend go to just anyone. What we do know is that Caitlan took a leave of absence from the clinic and went to Lowell with the boy under an assumed identity: Margaret Talbot. Whether she planned to remain there for years or had a different plan altogether, possibly moving into the Englewood town house, we'll never know."

"Because the child suddenly died," finished Freeman.

"Precisely. Supposedly due to SIDS, but I suspect that's not the truth," said Grant.

"What makes you say that?" asked Taryn.

Grant relayed the circumstances of the burial. A quick cremation, a funeral that had taken place with no one save a priest, and "Margaret" disappearing from Lowell the next day, never to be heard from again.

"Shortly after that, Caitlan returns to the Bradford Clinic like she'd just taken an extended leave of absence," Grant told them. "Whatever happened to the baby very much sounds like something Caitlan Hill wanted to put behind her, and managed to, until Frankel got Julia to start digging around again."

"And what do you think Julia found out?" asked the district attorney.

Grant considered before answering. "We know Caitlan gave her Margaret Talbot's name. She probably thought she'd covered her tracks as well as she could. Julia would learn the child had died and that should have been it. But she might have also figured out, like we did, that Caitlan and Margaret were one and the same."

"And that would have flipped her out," observed Taryn.

"Certainly enough to try and get back in touch with Caitlan," agreed Grant. "Remember, Julia showed up at Caitlan's mother's house looking for her after that."

"They could have finally caught up with each other at John's apartment," added Rachel.

"What do you suppose happened?" asked Freeman.

"This is all supposition, mind you," prefaced Grant. "But I'd think Julia would have confronted Caitlan with what she'd found out. She would have felt betrayed by her illegally adopting her child and held Caitlan personally responsible for its death, whatever the cause. More than likely, Julia was the one who fetched Detective Frankel's gun."

Rachel leaned in, as if to take up the tale. "She would have absolutely known where John kept it—they'd been married for ten years and it's still in the same place it's always been, an old video game box he hung on to. I know this because he's shown it to me."

Lieutenant Harris asked how Caitlan had gotten the weapon. Grant told him he could only make another educated guess.

"There was probably a struggle for it and Caitlan must have gained control. Whether she shot Julia by accident or intentionally, she needed to figure out what to do next. She must have realized she could frame Detective Frankel by taking the gun with her and the keys off Julia's body to lock her body inside the apartment—"

Grant suddenly broke off as a thought occurred to him.

"Speaking of which, did you find the keys when you searched the town house?"

Taryn shook her head. "Not so far."

"You might not find them at all," Grant said. "She could simply have gotten rid of them. It's not like they'd prove useful for anything else."

There were nods and grumbles of agreement all around.

Then the district attorney moved on to Pablo Suarez, wondering how he had fallen prey to Caitlan as well.

"If Julia had figured out the truth about the child's adoption, it makes perfect sense the first person she would tell would be her boyfriend," said Grant. "After Julia died, I think there's an excellent chance that Pablo got in contact with Caitlan and demanded they get together in the Maine cemetery."

"What makes you say that?" asked Taryn.

Grant told them about the phone call he'd gotten from Pablo on his way to the airport on the Big Island. "He told me he was about to settle a huge gambling debt with his bookmaker. He must have thought he could get the money from Caitlan by threatening her with what he knew."

"But how does a woman like that have that kind of dough?" asked the lieutenant.

"How did she have the money to buy a town house like that?" countered Grant. "Did you check to see if she owned it?"

Taryn flipped through a file in front of her. "Free and clear. Turns out, she paid for it in cash about two and a half years ago. The name on the deed is Rebecca Michaelson."

"I suppose we'll have to dig further into Caitlan's life," Harris said, nodding. "Not that it would do much of anything at this point but clarify a few things."

Freeman shook his head. Grant felt a bit sorry for the man—there was so much they would probably never get the answers to, what with Julia, Pablo, and now Caitlan silenced forever.

In the end, Grant thought that perhaps Caitlan Hill had made all their lives simpler by taking the easy way out.

An hour later, Grant sat beside his daughter in a drab room, their eyes fixed on a drabber door situated on a barely beige wall that was probably the drabbest thing of all.

"I can't believe it's really over, Dad."

"Just know we might never have gotten this far if you hadn't stuck by your belief in John all this time."

Rachel looked at him through glassy eyes. "And you didn't?"

"I wanted to."

"But—"

"—there was a mountain of evidence against him," continued Grant. "It was hard for the cop in me to deny all that."

He took her hand and held it tight.

"But it was harder for the father in me to do nothing and watch his daughter's heart breaking. I had no choice but to take the same leap of faith as you."

The buzz of the industrial door opening made them both straighten up.

Eileen Crowe stepped into the room. Grant felt his heart drop when it seemed that the attorney was by herself.

John Frankel appeared right behind her.

"John!"

Rachel rushed across the room and threw her arms around him. Eileen flashed a grin at Grant, who couldn't help but return the smile.

"I love you so much," Rachel murmured, her face buried in John's chest.

"I love you too," John murmured back.

He looked over Rachel's shoulder to catch Grant's gaze.

"Thank you, Austin. For everything."

"Never a dull moment with you, Detective."

"I promise to be more boring going forward."

"Oh, I sincerely doubt that," said Grant.

Rachel actually laughed, then disentangled long enough from her betrothed to open her arms and invite them all in for a group hug.

"You too, Eileen."

Grant and the attorney exchanged brief glances. He suspected that like himself, Eileen Crowe wasn't one for spontaneous outbursts of public emotion.

But there were definite exceptions.

As Grant let himself be swallowed up by his daughter and Frankel, the former Scotland Yard man forgot about all the questions he still had.

He was just happy to see joy in the eyes of his only child for the first time since he'd touched down again in America.

Chapter 33

Rachel turned over and saw that John was wide awake, staring at her from the other side of the bed in the predawn gloom.

"Again?" he asked.

"Seriously?"

He raised an eyebrow. "Well, I was locked up in jail—"

"For two days."

"Still, you know that's a long time to go without it."

There was *that* grin again. Rachel sighed. "I suppose."

John shifted his body so that he nudged a little closer to her, then reached out with one arm—

"But can we listen to something besides *The River*?" she asked.

—for his iPhone lying on the nightstand right behind her.

"It's just a little early for 'Crush on You' again."

John fiddled with the phone display. "*Devils and Dust*?"

"Is that one of the quiet ones?"

"We've been through this. *Nebraska*, *The Ghost of Tom Joad*, *Devils and Dust*, and *Western Stars*. Those are the acoustic albums."

John swiped through a few screens on the iPhone as Rachel rolled her eyes.

"Forgive me if I don't possess your encyclopedic knowledge of the Springsteen catalogue."

"Everyone can't be perfect."

As the first gentle strums of the Boss's guitar sounded, John placed the phone back on the nightstand and planted a sweet kiss on Rachel's lips.

"But you are in every other possible way."

"Flattery will get you anywhere—"

She nuzzled closer into the crook of his strong arms and returned the kiss.

"—except we're not putting on the *Live* album after this."

"It was worth a try."

They both laughed. The next half hour was taken up by exploring hands, sighs, and what naturally follows.

Afterward they lay spent in each other's arms as the first hints of sunrise came through the cracks of the blinds from the bedroom's window.

"What's today's date?" asked John.

"You weren't keeping track on the wall with a piece of chalk while you were locked up in there?"

"Funny."

"Friday. The third of July."

"We can still make it."

"What?" Rachel, still a little light-headed from the previous exertions, suddenly focused on what he was suggesting. "The wedding? Seriously?"

He propped himself up on one arm and looked at her in earnest.

"Why not? We spend today packing up, hop on a plane first thing tomorrow morning, end up in London for a celebratory dinner, and then on Sunday you can make an honest man out of me by walking down the aisle on the Heath."

"I told my father to cancel everything after you were charged with double homicide."

"Well, if he did, we just tell them things are back on."

"I'm not sure it's that simple."

"Of course it is. That's what credit cards are for."

He wrapped his arms around her and stared directly into her eyes. "C'mon, Rach. I don't want to spend another day not being married to you."

The grin that followed was almost overkill.

Almost.

"Well, when you put it that way."

—◊—

Rachel spent a few hours after breakfast sitting at the dining table on her cell, contacting various vendors to get the nuptials back on track. She had earlier risked awakening her father at his nearby hotel, where he'd spent the night to allow the reunited couple some privacy, to tell him what she was doing, and it turned out that he'd been up since dawn on the phone with some of the very same wedding contractors himself. Grant had been telling them that he needed to check with his daughter to see if the wedding was still on before canceling it completely.

So, with her father's full support and his saying he'd drop by in a bit to see what he could help with, Rachel had undertaken the task of pulling together their nuptials an ocean away.

John had been on the phone most of the time as well, seeing what was needed to get reinstated on the Seventeenth Precinct detective squad. He was on his third cup of coffee when he disconnected and came up behind Rachel to give her neck and shoulders a tender squeeze.

"What did they say?" she asked.

"Looks like everything's set. Just have to sign some paperwork later, get my gun and shield back, and I'm good to go when we get back from England."

"And what about Taryn?"

"I told the lieutenant that I was fine with the two of us being partners if she still wanted to be."

Rachel looked up at him, her eyes filled with concern. "She arrested you for murder, John. Not to mention resorting to whatever it took to do so, including bugging my father's cell phone."

"She was just doing her job. Same thing I would have done if the situation had been reversed."

She reached back and squeezed his hand that was still kneading her shoulders. "You're a much more forgiving person that I am," she told him. "I'd still be bearing a grudge—for maybe the next decade or so."

"And I'd have to break in another partner, a hassle worth avoiding."

"Meaning she lets you listen to Bruce whenever you want?"

"I wouldn't go that far."

Rachel laughed. "Maybe I'm giving her less credit than she deserves."

John kissed the top of her head. "How's it going here?"

"Amazingly enough, everyone seems to be able to pull it together so far," Rachel told him. "I just need to double-check the guest list. I'm sure everyone on it has been watching the news and wondering what the bloody hell is going on."

"Anything I can do to help?"

"You can fetch me my tote from the closet by the door," Rachel said. "That's where the most current version of the list is, I think."

John crossed the room while Rachel turned her attention back to the pad she'd been scribbling notes on.

"What have you got in here?" asked John a few seconds later, as he came back holding Rachel's oversized bag. "Barbells?"

She took the bag from him, opened it up, and dug inside. Her eyes immediately widened. "Oh my God, I totally forgot."

She pulled out a hefty maroon hardbound book.

"Is that what I think it is?" asked John.

Rachel nodded. "Caitlan's copy of her high-school yearbook."

Sure enough, emblazoned on the front were the words *Hornets 2004*.

"Do I even want to hear how you got it?"

"I found it in her town house while we were waiting for the cops to arrive."

Rachel went on to explain how she'd been trying to avoid looking at the dead body on the sofa by flipping through books in the living room. The annual had been sitting atop a stack on the middle shelf.

"And I know I'm going to hate this answer, but what's it doing here?"

"I couldn't help but wonder why she'd gone to the trouble of showing up at her mother's house looking for it all of a sudden. I had started glancing through it when the first round of cops showed up," Rachel said. "I figured it wasn't going to do Caitlan much good anymore, so I thought I'd go through it later and we could always return it to her mother. I just never got around to it because I was preoccupied with things—like whether they were going to spring you from jail or not."

"Unbelievable." John shook his head. "You just can't go and remove evidence from a crime scene."

"The woman committed suicide and confessed to both murders, John." Rachel tapped the cover of the yearbook. "How can this have any bearing on that?"

"Does your father know you took it?"

Rachel looked at her fiancé like he'd just accused her of being from outer space. "Are you kidding? The by-the-book Scotland Yard commander?"

"My point exactly."

"Stand there and tell me you're not curious why it was so important to Caitlan after all this time."

"Of course I am. But I'm a cop as well—"

"Not right now you're not. You just said you haven't been reinstated yet."

Rachel could tell from his sigh that she was getting to the curiosity part of him that temporarily shoved law and order to the side.

"Is this what I have to look forward to the rest of my life?" asked John.

"You better believe it."

He let out another sigh and sat down beside her. "Okay, let's hear what's going on in that crazy head of yours."

Rachel let loose a smile and placed the yearbook between them.

"It suddenly occurred to me when I was flipping through this that it wasn't the yearbook *itself* but the fact that it was *Caitlan's* copy," explained Rachel. She opened the book and indicated a few pages. "And not so much what was *in* it, but—"

"—what was *written* in it," finished John, looking at the scribbled words in different colored ink from classmates, faculty, and friends.

"Exactly," said Rachel. "Though I haven't been able to make heads or tails of any of it. Maybe you'll have more luck than me."

They spent the better part of an hour going through the annual, concentrating mostly on the pictures or pages where Caitlan was featured or mentioned. Most of the notes were from classmates with the expected salutations and well-wishes—*will miss you, love you, congrats, Hornets forever.*

But the page they kept coming back to was the one in the middle of the book, with the picture of a teenaged Caitlan and Julia at an awards ceremony, the one they'd noticed back in the Passaic High library with the girls flanked by their parents—Loretta Hill, Leo Molinari, and his wife Joyce. It wasn't the picture so much that drew their attention, but the fact that it had been marked by a loose Polaroid photograph.

A snapshot that neither Rachel nor John had ever seen before.

It featured Julia in a bed, holding her newborn baby boy in her arms.

"I thought that might grab your attention," Rachel softly said.

She could see the immediate effect it had on John as he was suddenly getting his first look at the child that could have been his. She reached over and gently took his hand.

"He was perfect," he murmured.

"A beautiful boy," agreed Rachel.

They sat in silence as John gathered himself.

"You think it's in this particular spot for a reason?" Rachel finally asked. "Or did she plop it randomly in the book for safekeeping?"

"No way to know for sure. But there is that picture of the girls with their families, so maybe it's there on purpose. Who knows?"

They studied the picture more closely. Everyone had inscribed a note in proximity to themselves. Julia had written *BBF!* Loretta had scribbled *So Proud!* Joyce's note was a simple *Congrats* while her husband Leo had penned *Stay in touch* with the numbers *12-12* beside it.

Rachel pointed at the numerals. "What do you suppose that means?"

"A date?" suggested John. "Maybe the day the picture was taken?"

"I guess that makes sense."

John continued to stare, then shook his head.

"What is it?" asked Rachel.

"Something regarding the girls that happened back then. I've been trying to put my finger on it the past couple of days but just can't remember."

"It'll come to you when you least expect it," said Rachel. "Always does, right?"

They were still going through the yearbook a few minutes later when Grant let himself into the apartment with his key.

"Hope I'm not interrupting anything," her father said, making a production of covering his eyes with one hand.

"You told me you were coming over, Dad. So we decided to keep our clothes on," Rachel told him with a grin.

"Thank goodness." Grant placed the bag he was carrying on the table. "I brought bagels in case anyone was interested."

"Zabar's," said John, inspecting the bag. "Best in New York."

Grant pointed to the yearbook. "What's happening here?"

John glanced at Rachel. "I think this is where I let you explain."

"Chicken," Rachel said, giving him a slight dig in the ribs.

She took a deep breath and proceeded. And was surprised when he didn't overreact or even admonish her.

"I was wondering when you were going to tell me," Grant simply said.

"Excuse me?"

"I thought something looked different on the bookshelves when you stepped out to the car with your bag. But with everything going on, I figured you'd let me know when you got around to it."

"Nothing gets by you, Dad."

"A frequent complaint of your mother's as well," mused Grant. "Are you going to tell me what you found?"

Rachel and Grant showed him the yearbook and Grant simply followed along.

But when they got to the page with the awards photo and Polaroid snap, Grant slid the yearbook toward him and peered more closely at it. He picked up the picture of Julia and her newborn.

He stared at it, then audibly sighed and shook his head.

"What is it, Dad?" Rachel finally asked.

Her father lowered the Polaroid and looked at the two of them. Rachel thought that he actually looked flustered.

"I'm afraid we've been looking at this all wrong," said Austin Grant.

Chapter 34

The Boss was singing about sometimes feeling like a rider on a downbound train.

As Frankel swung onto the George Washington Bridge, he felt like he could relate. It never ceased to amaze him how whatever song showed up on E Street Radio, the satellite radio station that played Springsteen music 24/7, seemed to fit the particular mood he was in. And despite the fact that he was no longer a double homicide suspect, had regained his freedom, and had his nuptials with Rachel on the horizon, in this moment Frankel felt like he'd bought a ticket on that train and couldn't get off.

That was because he couldn't stop thinking about Julia Molinari.

He wasn't having second thoughts about marrying Rachel—he just kept wondering if Julia would still be alive if he had handled things differently.

In retrospect, he realized that when he had found out about her affair with Pablo, Frankel hadn't lifted a finger to fight to keep his wife. He had stepped aside gracefully, choosing to let Julia flee to the islands without protest ("If that's what you feel like you have to do") and he'd just worked his cases even harder and spent a lot of lonely evenings feeling sorry for himself.

What if he had decided to win her back and succeeded? What if he had learned she was pregnant and told her he didn't care whose child it was, his or Pablo's? Would they be living in some Jersey suburb spending their weekends chasing a toddler around a small backyard or taking countless walks to the park? And even if he had to grapple the rest of his life with the fact that his wife had rushed into the arms of another man and Frankel had to wrestle her back, wouldn't it be enough to know Julia was still alive?

A lot of ifs, ands, or buts.

Even if he'd done all the above, Frankel knew life had a way of getting things back on track despite your attempts to reroute it. There could always have been a Pablo the Second, or so much resentment built up between him and Julia that they split anyway. Suddenly they would be looking at a custody battle; for that matter Julia might not have looked both ways when crossing the street and things would be back to the way they were right now, like the twist in some *Twilight Zone* episode.

Looks like I'm not getting off that train so fast, thought Frankel.

He moved beneath the road sign pointing the way to Jersey on the upper roadway of the bridge and continued to consider alternative scenarios.

Such as what would have happened if he'd never contacted Julia about the divorce papers?

A nonstarter because he wouldn't be able to marry Rachel.

But what if he had paid no attention to the addendum that Julia's lawyer had slipped in, the one that asked Frankel to revoke any "issue" from the marriage? What if he'd just signed the papers instead of giving in to the cop inside him that never stopped until he got to the bottom of things? Would there have been any reason for Julia to poke around and revisit the circumstances of putting her son up for adoption and placed into the hands of Caitlan Hill?

It might not have changed the child's fate, but wouldn't Julia be alive?

Frankel kept trying to tell himself that Julia would have found out the truth eventually. But would that have led to the same series of tragic events that had unfolded the past couple of weeks?

He wasn't sure.

So when "Glory Days" came on the radio, the upbeat song actually didn't change his mood or get him to revel in the "years gone by."

He was still trying to get off that goddamned train.

Which was the reason he exited the GWB and headed north on the Palisades Parkway toward the town of Alpine.

———

Rachel had suggested going with him, and though Frankel appreciated the support, he thought this was something better done himself. He presumed there was a curiosity factor on Rachel's part as well and couldn't blame her; he imagined he'd feel the same way with the situation reversed. But still, his relationship with Julia's family had predated Rachel by more than a decade.

His ring of the bell was met by an eager "I'll get it, I'll get it" on the other side of the door, followed by what sounded like frustrated exertions trying to open it. It ended up being Sophia Molinari who ushered him inside, simultaneously scooping up the young boy who had tried to navigate the doorknob high above his tow-colored head.

"Hi, John."

Sophia flashed him a smile and Frankel was struck once again by how young she was. No wonder Julia had felt uncomfortable around her. Not that there was anything threatening or onerous about Leo Molinari's second wife. Quite the contrary; she'd been nothing but sweetness and light whenever they'd met. But as far as Julia was concerned, Sophia should have been a girl she went to high school with, not a substitute for her departed mother.

"Hi, Sophia. It's been a long time."

His look took in the toddler squiggling in her arms and Sophia nodded. "A lot has happened since I last saw you, that's for sure." Her smile took in her son as she patted her bulging belly for emphasis.

"When are you due?"

"End of next month. Maybe sooner, if this one's any indication." She gave the baby boy a squeeze.

"I do hear the second ones come even earlier, but what do I know?"

"Whatever the case, I'm sure I won't be ready," she said with a sigh. She leaned in and spoke softly in the young boy's ear. "You going to say hello, Teddy?"

"Who are you?" asked the child.

That caught Frankel by surprise. Not exactly sure how to explain that to a toddler, he offered up a smile of his own. "I'm John," he said. "I'm a friend of your daddy's."

"Daddy's having his night juice," Teddy happily informed him.

Frankel could see Sophia noting the confused expression on his face. She laughed and translated Teddy-speak.

"An after-dinner glass of wine. Something I definitely miss these days."

"Ahhh."

"Leo's expecting you. He's in his study. I presume you remember the way."

"I do." Frankel nodded. He started to take a step, then stopped. "I'm so sorry about Julia."

"The whole thing's just horrible. I'm still trying to wrap my head around it," Sophia said. "But I'm glad to see they came to their senses about you and dropped the charges. I found it hard to believe any of the things they were saying about you."

"I really appreciate that, Sophia."

"I hear you're getting married."

"This weekend, actually. In London. We're leaving first thing in the morning."

"Some good news for a change. Congratulations." She leaned forward and gave him a hug. "Don't be a stranger. Bring her around some time."

"I'd like that."

Sophia gave Teddy another playful nudge. "Say bye-bye to John?"

"Bye-bye," said Teddy, giving Frankel a toothy smile that would warm anyone with a beating heart.

Frankel raised a hand up in the air. "High five?"

The boy slapped it and giggled. "High five."

Frankel lowered his hand for a low five and got one back. He took Teddy's tiny hand and shook it gently. "Pleased to make your acquaintance."

When the boy mimicked the words back in a high-pitched giggly lisp, Frankel thought he could die right there.

But he said goodbye again to Sophia and headed toward the study instead.

———

A few minutes later, he sat across from Leo Molinari, having declined the offer of wine and delivered his condolences for Julia.

The study was definitely a retreat for Leo; bookcases were lined with commendations and awards earned in business over the years and a ton of books that Frankel, knowing his former father-in-law, would wager he'd never opened.

Leo finished off his glass, placed it on a small table, and shook his head.

"I've gone over it countless times in my head since I heard what happened to her, wondering if there was anything I could have done to make things turn out differently," he told Frankel. "She'd actually come here to see me the day she died."

"That's what I heard."

"I keep telling myself that if only I hadn't gone to work that day, or if I could have gotten home sooner, if I'd just been able to talk to her—maybe that would have changed things. But I suppose that woman would have caught up with her at some point, regardless."

"Do you remember Caitlan?" asked Frankel.

"Of course. The girls were best friends for the longest time growing up and back in high school. But not so close after that."

"Do you recall why?"

"I don't really know." Leo shrugged. "I'm sure it was the type of falling out that happens all the time with teenage girls. Someone says something that the other takes the wrong way, things get all blown out of proportion. Next thing you know, they're no longer talking."

"Does the date December 12th mean anything to you?"

Leo shook his head. "Not offhand. Why?"

Frankel explained the circumstances regarding Caitlan's copy of her high-school yearbook. How she'd fetched it from her mother's house on the same day that Julia had been murdered, how it had come into their possession, and what they'd found written inside it.

"I'm lucky if I remember my wife's birthday, and you're talking about something that happened almost twenty years ago," Leo told him. "You think it holds some sort of significance?"

"Enough so that she marked it with a Polaroid picture of Julia and her newborn baby boy."

Leo visibly reacted. "Really?"

Frankel nodded. "I presume Caitlan was the one who took it. Probably right after the baby was born. It's the first proof I've seen that Julia actually had a child."

"My grandson."

Leo brought his hand up to his face and squeezed his eyes. Frankel could tell that his fingers were moist when he brought them away.

"I'm sorry," Frankel said. "I didn't mean to upset you."

"It's all right. I'm still trying to come to grips with the idea that I had a grandchild that I didn't know about, even if he only lived a few months. Ever since Commander Grant told me, I keep kicking myself for not being there when the boy took ill. There must have been something I could have done."

"You're not the only one who has been beating himself up about it. Even though I don't know if he was actually mine, I can't help but feel that I lost something I didn't even know I had."

Leo reached over and gave Frankel a consoling pat on the shoulder.

"It would have been wonderful for Julia's boy to grow up with Teddy, who would have been his uncle, right?" Leo stared off in the distance, as if musing on the possibilities of what would never come to pass. "I'd love to see that picture some time."

"I thought of bringing it along, but didn't want to be insensitive. Maybe when I get back from London—"

"That's right. When's the wedding?"

"Day after tomorrow. We're taking the first flight out to Heathrow in the morning."

"It would mean a lot seeing it." Leo exhaled and shook his head once again. "Of course, I don't even know if Julia would have let me back into her life. I was sort of hoping she'd come around after Teddy was born, but I think the whole concept of me starting a second family drove an even bigger wedge into our already fragile relationship."

"I totally understand."

"That's why I was so happy she wanted to finally talk. Even though I suspect all she really wanted was for me to bail out her scumbag boyfriend from his gambling debts. But maybe that would have started some sort of reconciliation. I guess I'll never know."

"Did you ever meet Pablo?"

Leo shook his head, vehemently. "I made it quite clear that he wasn't welcome in this house." He nodded toward Frankel. "I know that you and I were never really close, but you always treated my daughter with respect and put her first, and that wasn't lost on me."

"I certainly tried to, sir."

"Though maybe to your own detriment, if you don't mind me saying so. I wouldn't have been upset if you'd gone over there and laid Pablo out on his ass and won her back."

"The thought has crossed my mind more than once recently."

Leo poured more wine and asked once again if Frankel cared for any. When he declined, Leo raised his glass in a solitary toast.

"Well, I wish you and your bride nothing but the best."

"Thank you, sir."

Leo sipped the wine and placed the glass back on the table.

"After all these years, you should at least call me Leo."

"I appreciate that, Leo. And again, I'm sorry for your losses."

"Both of our losses, John. You have my condolences as well."

302

"He might not even have been mine," said Frankel.

"It doesn't really matter, does it?"

"Pardon?"

"In your mind, and I can tell you've already made it up, he was. It's understandable that you're grieving."

The only thing John Frankel could do was nod.

"I hope that Rachel brings you the same happiness that I've found with Sophia. Not many people get a second chance. Make sure you remember that."

Frankel told him he would.

A half hour later he was back on the GW Bridge replaying the conversation in his head. With all that had transpired the past couple of weeks and the regrets that Frankel would forever have about his relationship with Julia Molinari, he was just thankful that he'd been offered another opportunity at bliss.

He gave the accelerator an extra push, hoping it would get him back that much quicker to Manhattan and into the loving arms of his salvation.

Chapter 35

Teddy had happily prattled away the entire time, from the moment they left the Alpine house until they reached the FDR Drive on the east side of Manhattan.

Leo Molinari could understand the boy's excitement.

It was the Fourth of July and the child was going to witness his first fireworks show. And not just any show. The biggest one in America, put on by Macy's and this year occurring up and down the East River for everyone in New York City to see.

It had been all that Teddy had talked about for the past month, since seeing a commercial on television advertising the celebration; he'd stared incredulously at the massive bursts of color in the sky and told his parents, "I want to see *that!*"

And when it came to Teddy, Leo couldn't deny him anything, even if it meant wading into the midst of a million New Yorkers crowding sidewalks to find a good place to watch the festivities. Leo had known better than to try and drive his family from Jersey into the city. Finding a place to park the car would have resulted in at least a half-hour walk to the East River and a massive headache in the process. So he'd hired a town car to pick them up after an early dinner and the driver dropped them on First Avenue in the upper forties, just north of the United Nations.

After helping the pregnant Sophia and hyped-up Teddy out of the back seat, Leo turned toward his son Tony, who had climbed out of the front seat on the passenger side.

"See if you can find us a good spot, huh?" Leo asked. He pointed toward the expansive green lawn on the north side of the United Nations complex.

"I'm on it, Pops," said Tony. His son swung around to the back of the town car, popped the trunk, and pulled out three portable deck chairs. Seconds later, he had them tucked under his arm and was headed across the street.

Leo approached the driver, dug in his wallet, pulled out a couple of hundred-dollar bills, and handed them to the man. "You'll pick us up in the same place afterwards?"

"Absolutely." The two C-notes disappeared into his pocket in a smooth move that would do a magician proud. "Thank you, sir."

Leo moved back to join his wife and Teddy.

"Up you go," he said as he reached down and lifted the tow-haired toddler into his arms. "Ready Freddy?"

"Ready Teddy," giggled the little boy.

Leo laughed, as did Sophia. Carrying the boy in his right arm, Leo swung his left around his wife, and the happy family crossed First Avenue together.

A few minutes later, they caught up with Tony, who had secured a prime spot on the river side of the park. Leo suspected some sort of cash transaction had taken place, as most of the crowd had been there a few hours already.

His son had learned well. What was the point of making a lot of money if you didn't use it on things that made you happy?

And his brood definitely looked happy.

A nice change from the cloud that had hovered over all of them recently.

The quartet settled down on the lawn chairs, with Teddy sitting in his mother's lap, babbling away about everything he expected to soon see shooting through the sky.

A half hour later, an anticipatory buzz was building through the crowd, as the sun had set and the darkness promised that the show was about to start.

Suddenly Leo reached into his pocket for his cell phone. He punched a button and the digital display lit up. He stared at it for a moment, then sighed.

"Something wrong?" asked Sophia.

"Problem at the flagship, it looks like."

"But it's a holiday—"

"And one of our busiest weekends," explained Leo. "Give me a minute."

He got up and moved off with the phone in hand.

He returned a few minutes later with a grim look on his face.

"I've got to go in there."

"Now?" protested Sophia. "But the show's about to begin."

"Something's wrong with the server and we can't have the website down, not with the holiday sales and everything." Leo motioned behind him. "The driver will take you home after the show—"

"But you—"

"—will never get back in time before it's complete madness on the streets. I'll Uber or Lyft back to Jersey later."

He leaned over and gave her a kiss and nuzzled Teddy.

"You'll tell me what I missed when I see you later?"

"Fireworks!" cried Teddy.

"Yup. You'll see plenty!" Leo told him.

Tony sidled over to his father. "You sure this isn't something I can handle?"

"You just look after Sophia and your brother. Okay?"

"Will do, Pop."

Leo started to apologize but it was lost in the first fireworks blast going off in the sky high above the river.

Teddy squealed with delight, pointing upward.

Leo flashed a smile at the family he would do anything for, then turned around and headed for the street.

Knowing that trying to hail a cab would be futile, Leo decided to walk to his destination. It would take him less than twenty minutes to get there and it was a warm summer evening.

Framed by the technicolor extravaganza taking place in the night sky, he turned and headed west.

The deeper he moved into Midtown, the celebratory mood he had felt with his loved ones slipped further away. He was increasingly overcome with the melancholia that had practically suffocated him for the past couple weeks.

As he walked along, he thought about his conversation with Frankel the previous evening. He found himself envying the man, knowing he and his new family had landed in England by now, probably fast asleep on the eve of the day he would begin a new life with his hopes and dreams intact.

As opposed to Leo, who knew that no matter how much money he made or even the any-minute-now addition of a baby girl to the family, he would never be able to replace what he had lost.

Julia.

He had meant every word he'd said to his former son in law. The regret they shared in Julia's loss was more than palpable for Leo; it was all-encompassing. It had taken everything in his being to carry on and be strong for Sophia while remaining ever present for Teddy. Leo didn't worry so much about Tony—he knew his eldest would never come close to filling his shoes, but the good news was that he didn't aspire or need to. Tony would be just fine, with an already healthy salary and what he would inherit once Leo was gone. The Molinari store franchises were cash cows that even his high-school dropout of a son couldn't fuck up.

As he reached the intersection of East Forty-Eighth and Lexington, he checked his coat pockets.

Everything seemed to be accounted for.

He pulled out the cell phone he'd just pretended to receive a text and make a fake call on and checked the time.

Just past nine thirty p.m.

Most of Manhattan was still wrapped up in the Fourth festivities and the streets were nearly empty.

He returned the phone to his pocket and kept walking.

But instead of moving straight ahead toward Midtown and the Molinari's flagship store, he turned left and headed south on Lexington Avenue.

Down toward Murray Hill.

The last time he'd been at the apartment building, Leo had arrived in a blind panic—having finally reached Julia on the phone and gotten her to tell him where she was staying. But she'd refused to let him enter after he had persistently rung the bell, so he had resorted to punching other buttons, mumbling "delivery" to the one that finally answered and subsequently buzzed him in.

This time, he just waited until there was no one in the vicinity of the building, crossed the street, and dug into his pocket for the set of keys he now possessed.

The ones that had belonged to John Frankel.

Leo quickly unlocked the front door and moved inside the lobby.

He crossed to the opposite wall and moved into the building's stairwell. He climbed one flight of steps, then slowly creaked open the door to the second floor and peered out into the hallway.

Empty.

This figured, seeing how it was still too early for people to return from wherever they were spending the Fourth, or they were inside their apartments, having decided to stay in and avoid the insanity outside.

He moved out of the stairwell and approached Frankel's apartment, still holding the set of keys.

He quickly slipped one inside the lock, turned it, and heard the tumbler click.

Leo opened the door and stepped inside the studio apartment.

And found John Frankel, Austin Grant, and his daughter, Rachel, waiting there for him.

The embattled detective gave Leo a casual shrug.

"Change in wedding plans," Frankel said. He held out his palm, indicating the keys still dangling from Leo's fingers. "I believe those are mine."

Leo didn't resist as Frankel delicately took hold of them by the ring and slipped them into a clear plastic baggie he'd pulled from his pocket.

Grant stepped forward. "Fingerprint evidence," said the former Scotland Yard man. "Since no one else has probably touched them since you took them off your daughter's body."

Leo shook his head and was finally able to mutter a protest, albeit a mild one.

"That isn't proof—"

"Coupled with this it will be," said Grant.

He pulled a maroon book off the desk that was lying beside his cell phone. He showed it to Leo, who looked like he was going into shock.

"I presume this is what you came here looking for," said Grant.

He pulled something that was sticking out of Caitlan Hill's Passaic Valley yearbook.

And showed Leo the picture of Julia and her newborn baby boy.

"I noticed it the moment I saw the picture," said Grant.

"I-it?" questioned Leo. "W-what are you talking about?"

"The baby's birthmark," replied Grant, pointing to the tiny reddish spot on the side of the child's throat. "What did you call it? A raspberry?"

Leo could only stand there.

"Your son has the exact same one," explained Grant. "Only Teddy isn't your son. He's your *grandson*. Julia's baby boy, who you paid Caitlan Hill to give to you. And when your daughter finally found out about it—you killed her."

Chapter 36

"It was an accident."

Grant noticed Leo Molinari glance at the carpet and imagined he was remembering what had transpired the last time he'd been in this apartment.

"I know you have no reason to believe me," said Leo. "But I swear to God that it was an accident."

Grant actually didn't find the notion that far-fetched. He'd proposed a similar theory the day before in the DA's office when it was thought that Caitlan Hill had been the one who murdered Julia.

"Why don't you tell us what happened?" Grant gently prodded.

"W-what happened?" Leo repeated, his eyes beginning to well up. "I killed my little girl."

Leo choked off a sob. When he finally continued, Grant felt like he could see the terrible burden that Leo Molinari must have been carrying the past two weeks slowly lift off his weighted shoulders.

Leo banged his fist on the apartment door.

"Open up, Julia! I'm not leaving until you do!"

He made good on that promise by continuing to pound away on the door and call her name until he finally heard footsteps approaching from the other side and the knob begin to turn.

The door opened and Leo saw his daughter for the first time in more than three years.

She was shaking—and pointing a handgun at him.

"Go away."

Leo stiffened, but stood his ground. He pointed a finger at the weapon.

"Put that down, Julia. We need to talk—"

"I've got nothing to say to you."

"Just give me a chance to explain—"

"Explain? What's there to explain?!"

Julia backed away from him into the apartment. Leo used the opportunity to enter the room and close the door behind him.

"You've been raising my son for over two years and I'm just finding out about it now?"

"You gave him away, Julia. You were willing to have him brought up by perfect strangers!"

"That was my choice. Not yours!" *She began to cry.* "Can you imagine how I felt when I walked in there today and saw that woman holding him in her arms?"

"I'm surprised you even recognized him!"

"A mother always knows her son!"

"Don't give me that!" *shouted Leo.* "How long did you even have him before you cast him aside—"

"I remember every inch of him like it was yesterday." *She wiped the tears from her eyes.* "Including the birthmark on his throat."

"His raspberry," *murmured Leo.*

"What?"

"His raspberry. That's what Sophia started calling it and it stuck," *explained Leo.* "She's so good with him, Julia. And he loves her so much."

"Does she know?"

"Know?"

"Does she know she's raising your grandchild?"

Leo shook his head. "I thought it was more than she could handle at the time."

"You think?!!"

"You don't understand. We were in Italy. She was pregnant and lost the baby when she was three months along. She was devastated, we both were. When the opportunity came—"

"Caitlan."

Julia spit out the name. Leo could see the distaste in the air.

"Yes, Caitlan. I jumped at the chance and told Sophia we could rush the process but we needed to raise the child as our own, like she'd actually had the baby herself—"

"—because what you did was fucking criminal!"

She waved the gun in front of her father for emphasis.

"We gave your son a home, Julia." He took a step toward her. "It's more than you ever thought of doing."

"I'm going to tell her."

Leo shook his head vehemently. "No, you can't—"

"Don't tell me what to do!" she cried out. "She needs to know—"

She continued to wave the gun, the look in her eye even more crazed.

"You can go to jail for this!"

"Then what? Are you going to reclaim your long-lost child who doesn't even know who you are and take him back to Hawaii with that loser you ran off with?"

"I don't know what I'm going to do!"

She shook her head in dismay and lowered the gun for a split second.

Long enough for Leo to lunge and try to grab it from her hand.

But Julia immediately clamped down on it. Suddenly father and daughter were wrestling for control of the handgun.

"Give it to me, Julia! Before someone—"

The gun went off.

They were so entangled, Leo couldn't say for sure whose finger had actually pulled the trigger. But he didn't feel any pain, so he knew the fired bullet had somehow missed him.

That was when his only daughter crumpled in his arms, her hands grasping her chest that was already starting to spurt blood.

"Julia!"

He looked into her eyes that were staring at him in disbelief. All the life disappeared from them; she exhaled her last breath and died in his arms.

When Leo finished his tale, he was openly sobbing, much like he had for the longest time in the same apartment nearly two weeks earlier.

As he calmed, he told the Grants and Frankel what had happened after that.

After deciding to forgo the police because he didn't want to abandon Sophia, Teddy, and his soon-to-be-born baby girl, Leo had framed John Frankel, taking the detective's set of keys and the gun with him when he'd locked his daughter's dead body inside the apartment.

"Did Caitlan know what you'd done?" asked Frankel.

"Not at first," Leo answered. "We really haven't talked since she came to Italy with the baby a couple of years ago."

"How did that arrangement come to happen in the first place?" asked Rachel.

"Caitlan called me, shortly after Sophia had her miscarriage."

"To tell you Julia was about to have a baby?"

"It wasn't like that," recalled Leo. "We talked around the holidays every year—ever since the girls were in high school."

"Around December 12th specifically?" asked Frankel.

Leo's eyes narrowed. "I suppose."

"We Googled the date, Leo," Frankel told him. "You were charged with reckless driving that night in 2003, a few months before Caitlan and Julia graduated from Passaic. The same date in Caitlan's yearbook with a message from you saying to stay in touch. That can't be a coincidence."

Leo hung his head.

"The girls were at a Christmas party," he said. "The usual teenage stuff. Too much to drink, getting behind the wheel of a car when they shouldn't. Caitlan plowed through the window of a convenience store.

Luckily, the place was closed, so when they called, I got down there before the cops showed up. Caitlan would have lost her college scholarship with an underage DUI. So, I told them it was me who skidded on the ice and lost control."

"Caitlan must have been extremely grateful," said Rachel.

"She asked me what she could do. I just told her to stay in touch."

"The Molinari Way," said Frankel.

Leo stared at the detective.

"Don't forget, I was your son-in-law for a decade, Leo. I know how you do business. I'll scratch your back and one day, sooner or later, you'll scratch mine."

"It doesn't always work out that way."

"This time it did."

Leo didn't deny it. "Whenever she checked in, I always asked if she'd been in touch with Julia. For the longest time, the girls didn't talk, because of the 'incident.'"

"Julia once told me something happened between them back then, but wasn't specific," said Frankel. "I've been going crazy trying to remember."

"She didn't appreciate how easily Caitlan let me take the blame. Those were the days when I still had some kind of relationship with my little girl."

Leo wiped his eyes, remembering.

"This time when I asked about Julia, Caitlan hesitated. She eventually told me how she had gotten back in touch and what was happening with the pregnancy."

"Because she owed you," Frankel said.

"Because she wanted her friend's baby raised in the best home possible."

Out came the rest—starting with the arrangement.

Caitlan had jumped through the proper (and some improper) hoops to facilitate Julia's baby being adopted by Margaret Talbot, a single mother newly residing in Lowell, Maine. Caitlan had rooted down in Lowell, posing as Margaret, showing her face just enough to establish a presence there and then took a side trip to Italy, where she handed over the baby boy to Leo. Caitlan returned to Lowell just long enough to announce the "sudden death" of her darling Joseph, had an urn of dirt placed in a grave in West End cemetery, and left town the next day. Leo had rewarded Caitlan by paying for the Englewood town house in cash and giving Caitlan the deed in the name of Becky Michaelson, thus bonding the two of them with a secret should someone look into the whereabouts of a little boy who'd been on this earth for a blessed little while.

And it had all held up until John Frankel had decided to get married in England and needed a wedding license to do so.

It had led to Julia coming back to the mainland to ask her father for money to bail out Pablo. She'd ended up at the mansion in Alpine and saw Sophia holding the boy she recognized unmistakably as the child she'd given up for adoption a few years earlier.

Julia couldn't handle it and left the house without saying a word. Leo, hearing what had happened, rushed into Manhattan and tragically caught up with his daughter.

Pablo, to whom Julia had told everything she'd learned, got in touch with Leo after the murder, and demanded that the electronics king show up in the Maine cemetery with his checkbook handy.

Leo knew he didn't have a choice in the matter.

"As much as Julia didn't deserve to die, that blackmailing son of a bitch got what was coming to him."

"And you didn't think twice about setting me up for that as well," Frankel added.

"I didn't plan it that way. You didn't help yourself by showing up there at the same time." Leo shook his head. "I wasn't lying last night when I said I never had a bone to pick with you, John. I often think of how things might have worked out differently if you and Julia had stayed with each other. You might be raising that child together."

Grant watched Frankel's expression darken.

"Don't go trying to put this on me, Leo."

"I'm not. I did what I felt I had to do to protect what was left of my family. Having you be put away for my crimes was the last thing I ever wanted. Which is why I seized the opportunity to change that when I could."

"You're talking about Caitlan now?" asked Grant.

Leo slowly nodded. "You asked before if Caitlan knew what I'd done? I don't know when she actually figured it out. Probably after Pablo died. She called up in a panic, insisting I meet her at the town house, saying everything was coming apart."

"And that's when you decided to fake her suicide and place all the blame on her?" wondered Rachel.

"I didn't really know what I was going to do at that point."

As Leo answered Rachel, Grant saw the toll everything had taken on him. He looked infinitely frailer than the man he'd encountered less than a week ago.

"She said that she was ready to come clean with the cops about everything we'd done. I told her not to be ridiculous, she was just as guilty as me—"

"She hadn't killed anyone," Frankel pointed out.

"She said the same thing. I told her she was still looking at a long time in jail. She said she didn't care. She even tried to pull a gun out of her bag to force me to make the call, but her hand was shaking so much, I just grabbed it from her and said she should calm the hell down. We needed to be patient and things would soon return to normal."

Leo stared out the window. Grant could tell he was replaying the whole thing in his head.

"But I knew I couldn't trust Caitlan anymore." Leo turned back toward the trio. "I told her to have a drink and went into the bathroom to throw some water on my face and figure out what to do next. That's when I saw the sleeping pills in the medicine cabinet."

Leo gave a helpless shrug.

"You can figure out the rest."

Grant looked at the high-school yearbook on the table beside his cell phone. He thought about picking up the latter, but saw Frankel out of the corner of his eye. The detective was shaking his head.

"I think we need to hear it," said Frankel.

Leo nodded, grimly.

He had sat down across from Caitlan and pulled a gun on her.

But not the one he'd taken from her. He kept that in his coat pocket. Leo pointed John Frankel's backup at her, the one that had killed Julia and Pablo, which he'd brought on the off chance he would have to use it once again.

It was easy enough to get Caitlan to take the first few sleeping pills. Two drinks certainly helped. It had only been a matter of getting her to scribble a message to Julia and make sure he got enough pills down her throat to do the trick. As she lapsed into unconsciousness, Leo had wiped Frankel's gun completely clean, then, using a handkerchief, wrapped Caitlan's hand around it.

Once he knew she would never wake up again, Leo had slipped out of the town house, knowing it was only a matter of time until someone came across her.

Completely spent, Leo Molinari hung his head once again.

"Thank you, Leo," Grant finally said.

The former Scotland Yard commander reached over, picked up his cell, and spoke into it.

"I think you have all you need, Detective."

A clearly confused Leo looked up just in time to see the apartment door open and NYPD Detective Taryn Meadows step inside.

Leo shook his head in disbelief. "I don't understand—"

Grant indicated the cell phone. "Detective Meadows took the liberty of placing a listening device in my phone a few nights ago. I only told her this morning that I knew about it but suggested we might as well put it to good use. I'm not sure how much will hold up in court, but you've got a number of witnesses who've heard your story. Official and not."

Leo shook his head again. "I'm not denying any of it."

"Then you understand I need to place you under arrest?" asked Taryn.

Leo grimly nodded. "But before you do? One more thing?"

"What's that, Mr. Molinari?"

Julia's father turned toward the Grants and Frankel. "Whatever happens, don't let them take Teddy away from his mother." He started to openly sob again. "Because that's what Sophia is. His mother. The only one he's ever known. And she loves that child with every ounce of her being." Leo fixed his bleary eyes on Grant. "You saw them together. You know what I mean."

Grant could only nod.

Because something was still not right.

Leo turned to face Frankel.

"And you saw them too, right? Just last night—"

"I did," Frankel softly responded. "They were incredible together."

"Then promise me you'll let her keep him," pleaded Leo. "Even if he turns out to be yours—promise me that Teddy will stay with his mother."

"I hear you, Leo. But it's not just up to me. Or any of us here."

Leo wiped his eyes.

"Okay. I've said my piece."

He nodded one last time.

"I'm ready."

And with that nod, Grant suddenly remembered what he was trying to wrap his head around.

Caitlan's gun.

The one that Leo had switched out with Frankel's backup.

Leo Molinari pulled it from his coat.

No one in the room had a chance to stop him.

Leo brought the gun up to his own head and pulled the trigger.

To Love and To Cherish

When her father helped her down onto the bench, the first thing that ran through Rachel's head was that she was so glad she hadn't gotten a dress with any sort of train.

She could only imagine him trying to navigate the excess material.

Austin Grant was many things.

He'd been one of the greatest commanders in the history of Scotland Yard. He'd been a devoted husband and turned out to be one hell of a good dad.

But hardly a fashion expert, thought the bride.

The second thing that occurred to Rachel was that she had never imagined she would have started her wedding day out in a graveyard.

But then again, she and Frankel had chosen to get married on the Heath, just steps from where her mother was buried.

Her father settled beside her on the bench that he had donated to the cemetery upon her passing. He tried to come visit every Sunday, and Rachel had accompanied him a number of times since they'd come back into each other's lives.

Grant looked resplendent in his morning suit. Rachel had tried to convince her father to choose something less formal but he'd insisted on giving away his daughter in nothing less. John, therefore, not to be outdone, had purchased one as well. Rachel had caught a peek of him trying it on that morning before they'd left the Covent Garden Hotel (where they'd begun their relationship the previous winter) and more than approved. Both of her men looked quite dashing.

Her father nodded toward the well-kept tombstone that each of them had just laid a pink rose on.

ALLISON REBECCA GRANT

BELOVED DAUGHTER, WIFE, AND MOTHER.

"It would have meant so much to her that you chose to get married in the same place we did," Grant said.

"John and I only wish she could have been here today."

"She is, in her own way." Grant reached over and took her hand. "I hope the two of you will be as happy as we were for all those years."

"I've never been more so, Daddy."

She leaned over and gave him a warm kiss on the cheek.

"That is all a father needs to hear."

Rachel thought she detected a catch in his throat.

"You're not going all mushy on me, are you?"

"When was the last time you saw me cry?" asked her father.

Rachel thought about it and laughed.

"There's always a first time," she said.

After Leo Molinari's suicide, John Frankel's first instinct had been for the two of them to take the red-eye to London with her father, get married, and move on with their lives as quickly as possible.

But it had been Rachel who had urged John that he get some kind of closure, or at least some answers, when it came to Julia Molinari's baby. She told him whatever happened, she would be there for him. If John were indeed the father of the little boy now known as Teddy, Rachel would help him figure out how the child fit into their lives going forward.

"Whatever you want to do," she had told him over and over.

Sophia Molinari had been flabbergasted to learn that she had been raising her stepdaughter's son. Neither the Grants nor Frankel doubted her sincerity for a moment, nor questioned her desire to hold on to the child she loved so dearly.

But everyone agreed that knowing Julia's son was very much alive, it was in everyone's interest to determine the child's proper parentage and what was to be done as a result.

John willingly submitted to a blood test and samples were quickly taken from Pablo's remains up in Maine.

"What are you hoping they find out?" Rachel had asked one night as they lay in bed, their arms wrapped around each other.

John had thought about it long and hard and said he really didn't know.

"There's part of me that wants us to start fresh—so we can be there for our family right from the beginning," he finally answered. "But then again, if someone has a different plan in mind for us, I'd consider ourselves blessed, and like you say, we'll figure it out."

It didn't take long to get an answer.

John's blood type turned out to be an impossible match to produce the child and Pablo was confirmed to be the father by subsequent DNA tests.

"You seem disappointed," Rachel said, after they found out.

"Maybe a little," John admitted.

"I think you fell in love with that boy."

"I only saw him the one time."

"You know what they say about love at first sight." She put her arm around him and held him tight.

"It's kind of hard to believe we went through all of that to get to this point," John said. "And now the poor thing doesn't have a mother *or* a father."

"He has Sophia, who wants him desperately," Rachel pointed out. "And if that's not a case of nurture winning out over nature, then I don't know what is."

John didn't disagree.

And when, a couple of weeks later, the widow Sophia Molinari was granted a temporary conservatorship of the young boy, there wasn't a happier person than either John or Rachel.

Well, except maybe the only mother that Teddy had ever known, who nuzzled his "raspberry" night after night and sung him his favorite lullabies.

And when soon after that Sophia delivered a beautiful baby girl, who had the same gorgeous blue eyes as her late husband (who had left them well-off), both John and Rachel realized that someone, somewhere, might have had a blessed plan after all.

—﹏—

Rachel was greeted at the top of the flower-laden aisle up on the Heath by a harpist playing a rendition of "If I Should Fall Behind."

A wedding ballad written by none other than Bruce Springsteen.

Yes, it was supposed to be the bride's day, but she figured she could at least grant her husband-to-be that one concession.

As her father walked her toward the makeshift altar at the front of the garden, Rachel took in the wedding guests. She was touched that so many had actually made it, many traveling from faraway places and rejuggling their busy schedules to attend the ceremony that had been pushed back a month.

She wasn't surprised to see her London girlfriends, living close by and fulfilling their promise to be there when Rachel "got around to doing the bloody deed."

But she hadn't expected some of the other guests.

Phyllis, the waitress from John's favorite haunt, the Astro Diner, had declared that she was taking off the month of August like the great chefs of Europe and "closing the joint down," with the wedding giving her the perfect excuse. Rachel beamed when the septuagenarian actually blew her a kiss.

Eileen Crowe had made it as well. The attorney had said she wouldn't miss it for the world, feeling somewhat responsible for the event even taking place, having helped John secure his freedom. Eileen had promised him that she was coming on her own dime and he wasn't going to be charged by the hour for her time, which was a relief as that alone would have broken the wedding bank.

Rachel had expected a few of John's longtime colleagues on the force would have made the journey across the pond to take part in the festivities, but she hadn't thought that both Taryn Meadows and Desmond

Harris would make the trip as well. As she walked by them, Rachel gave them a gracious smile, realizing more than ever that NYPD blood was blue and would continue to run through John Frankel's veins for a long time to come.

Eileen had overseen John's reinstatement in a seemingly effortless manner, though Rachel suspected there had been threats of wrongful arrest charges thrown about every corner of the Seventeenth Precinct by the hotshot lawyer. And the icing on the legal cake was that Eileen had waived all her fees, saying she had done it pro bono.

It certainly didn't hurt Eileen's future business to have her name spread all over the Manhattan tabloids, networks, and Twitter feeds for the better part of a week. She told John she wouldn't have blamed him if he'd claimed a commission from future law enforcement clients that sought her services, but in the same breath, said she would fight him should he decide to do so. Neither Rachel nor John doubted that for a minute.

Meanwhile, things continued on the Big Island at the usual pace—not much quicker than the sea turtles that crawled out of the ocean to bask in the heat, one sun-drenched perfect day in paradise after the next.

Sam Erickson abandoned the project on the slopes of Mauna Kea and took a tax loss he could always use. He gave the loyal guard a job behind the bar at the reopened Papaya Seed that Erickson now owned outright and began looking into the feasibility of turning it into a nightclub in the evenings.

Andy Daswick had a run of good luck betting exhibition football and recouped the money that Pablo Suarez would never pay him—until the Dallas Cowboy threw four pick-sixes in one half and put him back in the red. But that didn't dissuade him from trying to win it all back. For gamblers like Andy, there was always the *next* game.

Chet, the perennial surfer and sometimes real estate agent, showed a lot of houses and got a few bites. One of them oddly enough had come from Sheriff Guy Lam, who liked the house that Pablo and Julia had lived in, high above Kona. Enough so to buy it at a low price from the bank that was ready to foreclose on it as the former occupants were both deceased.

And as for Aiden, the former waitress at the Papaya Seed and the one true friend that Julia Molinari had in the Islands, she had fled for the mainland.

And as it turned out, beyond that.

She took her savings and fulfilled a dream to backpack through Europe.

Aiden had also gotten in touch with the Grants to inquire about what had finally happened with Julia and Pablo. When she'd told Rachel she would be on the continent around the same time that she and John were going to wed, Rachel had told the girl that if she felt like spending a weekend in England, they would love to have her come to the wedding.

—※—

Which is how Aiden turned up in the second row of invited guests and got a big smile from the bride.

Her father gave the transplant from the islands a friendly wave that Rachel realized was an attempt at a Hawaiian aloha, and she had to suppress a giggle.

Then Rachel allowed Grant to lead her up the two steps to the flowered altar where John and Father Gill, the Grants' resident priest at St. Matthews, their neighborhood church in Maida Vale, awaited their arrival.

The song ended, the crowd settled, and Father Gill stepped forward.

"Who gives this bride away?" he asked.

All eyes turned toward Grant, who Rachel realized was so overwhelmed by everything that she had to give him a tiny nudge and whisper.

"Dad, that's your cue."

Her father did what practically amounted to a double take and grinned.

"One thing to do and I basically blew it."

That produced a huge laugh from the gathered celebrants as Austin Grant managed to pull himself together.

"I do," he answered. "Along with her mother, who we all dearly wish was here."

He kissed his daughter.

And Rachel realized in that moment she had never loved her father more.

It had been quite a twenty-four hours for the former Scotland Yard Commander.

The previous evening, he had hosted a dinner for the out-of-town guests and extended family—which turned out to be practically everybody—at one of his favorite London restaurants, the Wolseley in Piccadilly Circus.

Grant had taken over the back room and spent most of the night making sure that everyone had plenty to eat and drink. Rachel and John were toasted by more than a few well-wishers and a wonderful time was had by all.

At the end of the night, Grant had taken center stage to make a speech.

He started out by saying that he couldn't be happier for the two of them, but as they were beginning married life together, he was going to have less reason to fly across the Atlantic and just barge in on them.

As a result, he was going to have even more time on his hands, something that Rachel, and others who knew him well, had recently voiced their concern to him about.

Which was why he had decided to take over the lease on John Frankel's apartment in Murray Hill and open a small investigative agency two blocks south at Lexington and Thirty-Sixth Street.

This was met by much applause and happy grins from the wedding couple.

"Let's hear it for my father-in-law, the private eye," called out John.

"I prefer to think of it as discreet enquiries," said Grant.

"Whatever you call it, I'm sure my colleagues and I will have plenty of business to toss your way," John told him.

"I like the sound of that," Grant responded. "I think."

This was met by more laughs and then her father introduced Aiden, who it turned out hadn't needed much convincing from Grant that manning the agency day to day would be a good way to broaden her horizons.

Grant gave an emotional toast that he somehow managed to get through before saying if the happy couple would indulge him, he wanted to bestow their wedding present on them.

He handed Rachel an envelope, which she quickly opened. She took one look and glanced up at her father.

"Plane tickets?"

"For your honeymoon—all expenses paid by yours truly."

"These say they're for Hawaii." She pointed at the tickets. "I don't mean to sound ungrateful, but Hawaii? Really, Dad? After everything we just went through?"

"Oh, I'm sorry." Her father smiled. "The other tickets aren't there?"

"Other tickets?" asked John.

Grant made a production of patting his pockets and produced a second envelope. "Here they are. I meant to say that the flight *lands* in Hawaii and then you *change* planes to head to Bali."

He ended up handing that envelope to John, because Rachel was too busy crying and wrapping her arms around her father, who she should have known always had one more trick up his sleeve.

Grant returned to his seat in the front row and Father Gill continued with the ceremony.

He gave a few chosen Bible readings and the couple his blessing, then told them it was time to say their vows.

John went first and got a healthy laugh from the guests when he promised to try and lead a "little bit less exciting life" than they'd had in their time together so far.

Rachel got an even bigger one when she told him there was pretty much no chance of that happening.

When it came her turn, Rachel took out the slip of paper she had spent a couple of nights composing her vows on, then suddenly ripped it in half.

"Can't I just say that I love you more than anything else in the whole wide world and can't stand the idea of waiting one more minute to be your wife?"

John gave her *that* grin.

"It's okay by me if Father Gill's down with it," he said.

All eyes shifted to the priest, who laughed and said if no one objected, he saw no reason that he couldn't pronounce the two of them man and wife.

Father Gill did just that and told John Frankel he should kiss the bride.

He took Rachel into his arms, happy to comply.

The guests cheered in unison.

After they finally broke apart, the priest introduced them as "Mr. and Mrs. John Frankel," and the newlyweds made their way down the steps and up the flowered aisle toward their joyous guests.

The first person they saw was Rachel's father.

John whispered in his new wife's ear. "Check out the commander."

Sure enough, there were tears streaming down his cheeks.

As she reached her father, Rachel flashed a smile.

"Guess there's a first time for everything."

Austin Grant didn't even bother to answer. He just threw his arms around his daughter and hugged her tight.

And as she wiped the tears from his face, Rachel Grant Frankel couldn't help but think that spontaneous outburst of joy from the father she absolutely adored was the best wedding present of all.

Acknowledgments

I am forever grateful to Otto Penzler for his guiding hand, the opportunity to bring these characters to life and his belief in this being a continuing series. Many thanks go out to Charles Perry, Jacob Shapiro, Mike Durell, and the rest of the Mysterious Press gang for making the books a reality.

I am lucky to have a team of Tinseltown reps in Robb Rothman, Vanessa Livingston, and Amy Schiffman, who have encouraged me to continue on the novel track. Equal kudos to Gretchen Koss and Meg Walker of Tandem Literary and Carol Fitzgerald from Bookreporter for continuing to get the good word out.

Benee Knauer's contributions are invaluable as always, and her friendship is something I never take for granted.

I've been blessed to make the acquaintance of a number of mystery and thriller writers who have been so collaborative and supportive in this process, some old friends, many others new. Thanks to Julie Clark, May Cobb, Brian Freeman, Michael Koryta, Hank Phillippi Ryan, Karin Slaughter, Lisa Unger, Wendy Walker, Tessa Wegert, and F. Paul Wilson for sharing their experiences and offering up such great advice over the past year.

Seth Gelber, Sibyl Jackson, David Reinfeld, and Connie Tavel are early readers whose feedback was extremely helpful. Special shout-outs go to Cindy McCreery and Dan Pyne for the dual role of being partners on projects in TV-land and constant readers, along with Rodney Perlman for listening to me kick around countless plot and character arcs during numerous golf rounds.

This book was written during the pandemic and I spent a good part of it with just my wife Holly and this computer screen. Anything good about the finished product is a result of her keeping me safe and sane.